# *Black God — White Goddess*

Saladin was growing huge, immensely huge. His shape was filling the entire hall. Then, abruptly, there was a clap of thunder and he was standing on High Table level, his normal, mostly non-glowing self again. A woman appeared beside him. At least it looked to be a woman. Her clothing made it difficult to tell.

She was cloaked from head to foot in a boxy, snow-white burqa, a deliberately all-concealing costume usually only seen in the most fundamentalist areas of the Muslim world beyond the Cathonic Dome. Even her eyes were veiled. Murray squirmed nervously. Sundown tightened his grip.

The chanting began: "HAIL, SALADIN! HAIL, MASTER! ALL HAIL!"

Saladin reached his arm upwards. The sword, the shield, the chain of crimson stones, with its triangular medallion so reminiscent of the pyramidal eye on the back of the American dollar bill, lifted off him. As they vanished as if into the night's sky, which could be seen through the hall's glass dome, Star Sedon looking down, he embraced his escort.

In one motion she tore off her unappealing garment and kissed him on the lips. The cheering immediately quelled. Were the people sucking in their collective breath, were they shocked by what they had just seen her do to their reclusive, witch-hating Master, or were they simply stunned by the woman herself? Probably the last.

She was undeniably as statuesque as any female pureblood in the Weirdom.

Broad at the shoulder, tight in the bosom, waist and hips, she was wearing a diaphanous outfit as white as her skin and so clinging it was difficult to tell where the outfit stopped and the skin began. A white skull-cap covered all of her hair. Two rabbit ears of cloth stretched out of her just-below-knee-length skirt, hid her breasts, and were tied around the back of her neck. That was it, no shoes, leggings, jewellery, makeup, nor any other ornamentation.

She was the perfect compliment to the Master. If he was the black god, she was the white goddess.

"Finally figured out why I'm holding onto you so tightly, Jerry?" Sundown queried sardonically. Due to contact with Murray's arm, the Cheyenne Creature of the Cosmos could see as well as Jervis could. Put better, since they were using the same set of eyeballs, he could see exactly what Jervis saw.

Murray grunted in understanding. "Didn't think it had anything to do with love, Johnny."

"Not on my part it doesn't."

**The black god's white goddess was Wilderwitch**

This is a work of fiction. All the characters portrayed in this book are either fictitious or used fictitiously.

# DECIMATION DAMNATION

## THUS BEGINS THE OPEN-ENDED SAGA OF '*WILDERWITCH'S BABIES*'



## A *PHANTACEA* MYTHOS MINI-NOVEL

Conceived, written and produced by Jim McPherson
Front and Back Cover Collages by Jim McPherson

**Phantacea Publications**

(James H McPherson, Publisher)

74689 Kitsilano RPO

2768 West Broadway

Vancouver BC

V6K 4P4 Canada

**Library and Archives Canada Cataloguing in Publication**

**McPherson, Jim, 1951-, author**
**Decimation damnation / Jim McPherson.**

**(Wilderwitch's babies ; 1)**
**Issued in print and electronic formats.**
**ISBN 978-1-927844-15-1 (paperback).--ISBN 978-1-927844-16-8 (pdf).--**
**ISBN 978-1-927844-17-5 (ebook)**
**I. Title.**

**PS8625.P535D44 2016 C813'.6**
**C2016-904423-8**

**C2016-904424-6**

**Phantacea Publications featuring**

## *Jim McPherson's*

## *PHANTACEA* MYTHOS

- ***PHANTACEA* One to Six**

(1977-80, a series of comic books with artwork by various artists)

- **Forever & 40 Days – The Genesis of *PHANTACEA***

(1990, a graphic novel with artwork by Ian Fry, background material and a short story featuring the Damnation Brigade, the Death Dodgers & Signal System)

- **Feeling Theocidal**

(2008, Book One of *'The Thrice-Cursed Godly Glories'* trilogy*)

- **The War of the Apocalyptics**

(2009, the first full-length entry in the *'Launch 1980'* story cycle*)

- **The 1000 Days of Disbelief**

(2010-11, Book Two of *'The Thrice Cursed Godly Glories'* trilogy, consisting of three mini-novels: 'The Death's Head Hellion'*, 'Contagion Collectors'* and 'Janna Fangfingers'*)

- **Goddess Gambit**

(2012, Book Three of *'The Thrice Cursed Godly Glories'* trilogy*)

- **Phantacea Revisited 1: The Damnation Brigade**

(2013, graphic novel featuring a complete story sequence primarily excerpted from Phantacea One to Five, various artists*)

- **Nuclear Dragons**

(2013, the second full-length entry in the *'Launch 1980'* story cycle*)

- **Phantacea Revisited 1: Cataclysm Catalyst**

(2014, graphic novel featuring a complete story sequence excerpted from Phantacea One to Seven and Phantacea Phase One #1, various artists*)

- **Helios on the Moon**

(2014, the third and final full-length entry in the *'Launch 1980'* story cycle*)

- **Wilderwitch's Babies**

(2016, tentatively consisting of the mini-novels: 'Decimation Damnation', 'Destination Damnation' and 'Tsishah's Twilight')

**E-versions also available*

JimMcPherson

# Decimation Damnation

The *PHANTACEA* Mythos continues with
'Wilderwitch's Babies, Part 1'

# DECIMATION DAMNATION

## AUCTORIAL PREAMBLE

********

***Thus begins Phantacea Phase Two.***

Only thirty-five years late, you might say. You might, I wouldn't. I'd rather say: About time!

It's something of a misnomer anyhow. After the non-appearance **Phantacea Seven** in 1981 – due to the fact pre-orders didn't warrant continuing the Phantacea Mythos in comic book form – I was left with all these characters, tons of ideas and way too many storylines to ever do justice to, in any format.

Still don't see continuing the Phantacea Mythos in comic book form. Writers may not expect to get paid, not if his name's Jim, he created it, and has no intention of giving up his IP ('Intellectual Property', not 'Internet Protocol'), but artists certainly do. Can't say I blame them, either. The characters, ideas and storylines wouldn't go away, not all of them, so I became a weekend writer.

Was a terrible typist and even worse at cursive long hand. (Remain quite good at cursing, however.) Then Smith Corona or someone like them devised the Personal Word Processor, which meant you could use an electric typewriter and an attached screen to pre-edit, albeit page by page, before printing. (Still have my PWP and, yes, it is a Smith Corona. Don't know where to get it repaired or buy a new ribbon for it, though.)

Next, IBM concocted the Personal Computer. Then someone else – some say the US military, others say CERN (The European Organization for Nuclear Research) – invented the Internet. Whereupon I came up with ***PHANTACEA*** web-serials, which got me writing and publishing again. "Decimation Damnation" (DecDam), first known as 'Month One – After Limbo', was one of the last serials to see the interior light of the computer screen worldwide.

Now it's back, howsoever expanded, in print, PDF digital and e-book formats. So, let me rephrase: *Thus begins Phantacea Phase Two … officially.*

========

So, where were we?

Not with a decision to make. Did that when I decided to carry on with the Damnation Brigade storyline rather than revisit any of the 1938 web-serials or pick up the Ringleader storyline in 1955, parts of which also became serials. Or Web Wheaties, as I used to like to say.

"Helios on the Moon" (Helmoon) ended the '*Launch 1980'* story cycle, my personal project to novelize the ***PHANTACEA*** comic book series. Perhaps unexpectedly, it also wound up the previous trilogy, *'The Thrice-Cursed Godly Glories'*, albeit with one of the titular goddesses, who struck out so badly in "Goddess Gambit" (Gambit), stuck on the moon. Guess what? She may have died there. Or at least come as close to dying as Master Devas (devils) ever do.

She, once Harmony, nowadays Nihila, had already been reincarnated. Rather, she had according to her, in "The War of the Apocalyptics" (War-Pox). That would be as Wilderwitch, half of our overall title. (The other half, 'Babies', in the plural, mostly remains for the future file. DecDam is strictly present tense.)

Here's how her part in Helmoon, um, climaxed:

*The Untouchable Diver – Yama Nergal, King Harvest, the devic Grim Reaper, beside him – led the Glorious Dead against the Weirdom of Cabalarkon. Yehudi Cohen was wearing the Crimson Corona, had the Amateramirror strapped to one arm like a shield and was brandishing the Susasword with the other.*

*Turned out it was just the Master's dream becoming something everyone could see. What Wilderwitch was experiencing that very moment, in that very bed, was real.*

***'YES. YOU'LL DO JUST FINE!'***

*She began to scream.*

========

As you'll shortly be reading, if you haven't already, that's not how DecDam begins. It does so with a different dream and, as you probably already know, most anything can happen in dreams; all the more so now that Phantast Thanatos, devic uncle of D-Brig's already 'decimated' Elemental Twins, Aires and Thalassa once thought D'Angelo, has been decathonitized.

But wait … what the heck does that mean?

Well, you see, there's this stellar eye-mouth in the sky; the sky above the Hidden Continent of Sedon's Head, that is. He's the Devil, capitalized; likes to appear that way anyhow, when he's out and about in the immortal flesh. And it – the sky, not the eye-mouth – is called Cathonia, also the Cathonic Zone, Dome and/or Sedon Sphere.

Most of its brightest stars are actual devils, small case, punished by being catasterized for egregious misbehaviour. (Read murder, wilful or accidental, of lesser beings, thus depriving their siblings, cousins, fathers and, most seriously, solitary grandfather, this Devil, the Moloch Sedon by agreed upon name, of their worship.)

Phantast the Dream Weaver was but one of the 60-plus devils that escaped the Dome moments after the launching of the Cosmic Express on the Outer Earth on the 30th of November 1980. Some ended up beneath the Dome, others beyond it, yet no one seems to know what's become of him. (Won't be finding out in DecDam either. That much I can tell you.)

We do know that, later on the same day, far to the north of its Hawaiian launch site, ramifications of that selfsame event reunited the bodies and minds of the ten members of the thereafter self-proclaimed Damnation Brigade after twenty-five years in what they'd come to call Limbo. They're the damned to be decked, as it were.

Should add ... On second thought, probably shouldn't. Not right now.

Won't leave you altogether in the lurch, though. A lot went on in Phantacea Phase One and to help you get a handle on it, at the back of the present volume, short as it is, you'll find a Character Companion, long as it is. Read it to start, read it to finish, don't read it at all or … here's my recommendation … mark and refer to it as you go along.

Better make it: ***Thus begins the open-ended saga of "Wilderwitch's Babies"***.

Jim McPherson
Creator/Writer
**The *PHANTACEA* Mythos**

********

# Chapter Titles


- **AUCTORIAL PREAMBLE ...** v
- One-Babies: **PANHARMONIUM ENDS ...** 1
- Two-Babies: **THE WEIRDOM OF CABALARKON ...** 9
- Three-Babies: **HEAD HAUNTERS ...** 23
- Four-Babies: **WITCHES DEMONIZED ...** 34
- Five-Babies: **BLUR OF THE MOMENT ...** 48
- Six-Babies: **BLACK GOD – WHITE GODDESS ...** 60
- Seven-Babies: **DAMNATION DISAPPEARING ...** 76
- Eight-Babies: **D-BRIG 4 ...** 89
- Nine-Babies: **FAY TAILS ...** 99
- Ten-Babies: **SEEING-EYE SUNDOWN ...** 109
- Eleven-Babies: **CEREBRAL INCINERATION ...** 126
- Twelve-Babies: **CYNTHIA MASTERWIFE ...** 137
- Post-Babies: **DAEMONIC DEPRAVATION ...** 150
- **CHARACTER COMPANION ...** 159

# DECIMATION DAMNATION

**— 9 Tantalar - 1 Yamana 5980 —**

Jim McPherson

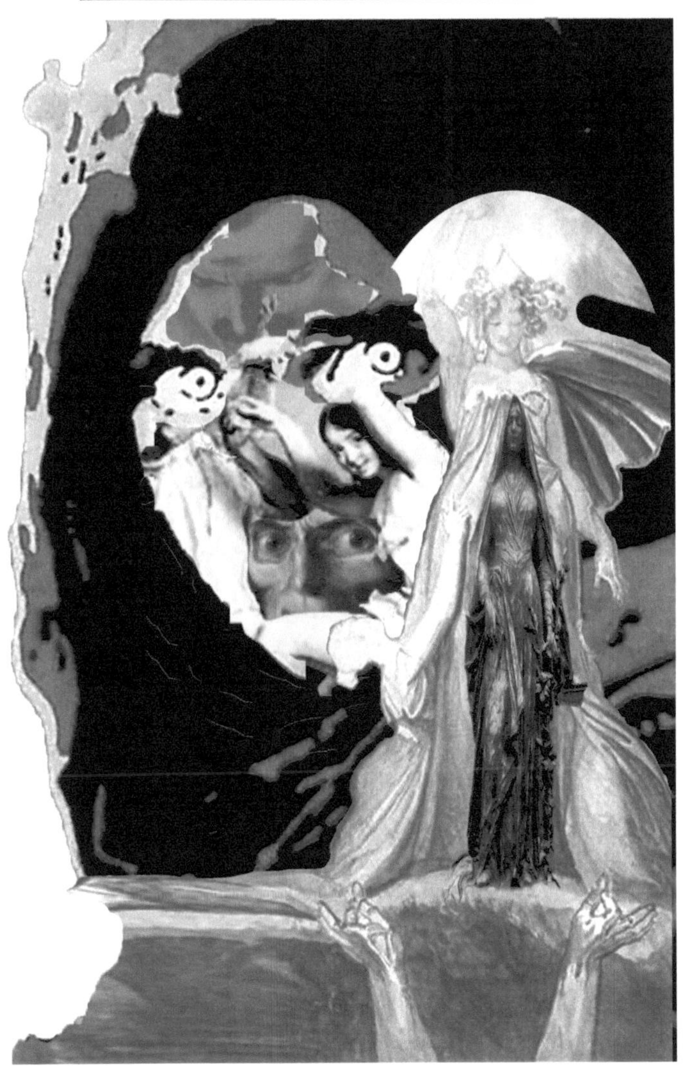

**A *PHANTACEA* Mythos Print Publication**
**James H McPherson, Publisher**

ISBN 978-1-927844-15-1
First Published 2016

# One-Babies: PANHARMONIUM ENDS

========

| **If you die in your dreams you die in your life.**<br>**She wasn't dying. She appreciated that. She was, however, dreaming.**<br>**Hoped she was anyhow.** |
|---|

**Saturday, 19 September 1981**

*Greater Vancouver had been washed out to sea in the Second Great Flood, that of late November 1980.*

========

So had much of the Fraser Valley. What was now called New Vancouver had once been a small town called Hope. The Fraser River emptied itself here, just as it had on the southern border of Old Vancouver before the Deluge. The Liberation Brigade's celebratory reunion, which was being filmed for everyone with a television on the reunited planet to see, was taking place in the gardens of old Hope's now reconverted city hall. It too was called Hope, though 'Haven' had been added to give it a better ring.

Outside it Wilderwitch, the only name she acknowledged with any regularity, was sitting on a stone bench away from the gathering crowd, of whom an ever increasingly many were uninvited. Even in the wondrous new reality of a whole-again Earth, celebrity retained its magnetic field and the surviving members of the supranormal Liberation Brigade, the Witch being one of the most comparatively ordinary, were well up there in the pantheon of Panharmonium.

Looking like the fit, albeit very baby-belly-heavy, off-white, gypsy-type she was, she had been counting down the days, weeks and months ever since she became pregnant. Was now counting down the hours. Figured it'd take a few more before she could start kicking back. Fifty-three might seem a bit old to be pregnant. It helped when you were a witch; helped even more when you were a supranormal witch. Besides, kicking back was one of the things she did best.

Spotting her sitting alone, Athena Zeross, age 7, decked out in her finest frills, blues and yellows for the most part, detached herself from a group of similarly attired children, and came rushing up to her. Blonde, though not quite as much so as her mother, whose hair was akin to Christmas tree tinsel, Tina was the youngest of three hybrid daughters of the new Master of Weir, Melina born Sarpedon, 60,

Mel-Illuminatus as the Witch still sometimes thought of her. Before Mel's promotion, as it were – mostly due to a dearth of challengers in the wake of an anything except a dearth of death amongst her potential rivals for the title – she was the High Illuminary of the Weirdom of Cabalarkon.

She was also, even before that, a one-time Althean witch-healer and a degree-granted, medically certified physician; had only reluctantly traded in her caduceus for the Master's Mace. Her howsoever heroic, indubitably tragic and definitely late husband Harry, Aristotle, Ringleader, Tina's Greco-Cretan father, also a Dr Zeross, was one of the main reasons there was a Panharmonium. Not to mention the remnants of a Liberation Brigade left to publish their memoirs and reap concomitant rewards.

Not far behind Tina was her middle sister, Helen, whose thirteenth birthday was coming up on the approaching Autumnal Equinox, which was once celebrated as Harmony's feast day on the no longer hidden Headworld. Although some of Mel's apprentice Illuminaries were in the vicinity, Helen and their eldest sister, Persephone, 16, who was probably indoors, attending their mother, were Tina's designated shadows for the day.

Were most days, but today was special. Once the ceremonies started, their mother, a full-blooded, white-as-light Utopian woman – in contrast to full-blooded Utopian men, who were black as midnight on a starless night – would be in Mastery mode. And before that there were all the announcements and formal greetings to be made and endured.

Obadiah Melvin Power, the patriarch of the formerly strictly Outer Earth based, Illuminated Faith of Xuthros Hor, was the nominal host for Hope Haven's dedication and the festivities to follow. Since he was the father of her unborn child, as well as the father of her first and to date only other child, albeit thirty-five years earlier, the Witch would have to be on her feet for most of the formal fluff as well.

Too bad she didn't have a designated baby-belly supporter the same as Tina had sisterly shadows. Maybe what Tina had in that shoebox she was carrying would jumpstart the smile muscles.

"Look what slimy Auntie Fish caught for us, fat Auntie Wildie," enthused the youngster, all but thrusting the box in her face.

While not much of a supra compared to some of the others, whose abilities approached godlike, Wilderwitch did have an affinity for animals; could communicate with them on an empathetic level, as she sometimes described that aspect of her abilities, and indeed, should she be sufficiently persuasive, even get them to do what she wanted them to do. Consequently, she already knew what was in the box.

"My hair look that bad, Tina?"

"What's your hair got to do with anything?"

"When I forget to comb it out people call it a rat's nest. And you've brought me a rat to nest in it."

The Witch was right about that last. Her dark hair was so thick and long a lot more than a rat could hang out in it. She'd gone to the sweathouse this morning, and in addition to having herself scrubbed nearly raw, made sure it was thoroughly washed and brushed down as straight as it ever got. As a result she was fairly confident nothing besides herself and her unborn baby were living in or about her body.

"It isn't a rat," Tina protested, opening the shoebox. Inside it was a rat-like creature but, Tina was correct, strictly speaking it wasn't a rat. "It's a tee-tee."

Wilderwitch deigned to peer into the box. The rodent was no more native to the former Outer Earth than mermen and mermaids, Simian Sapiens, sentient Saurs, Lemurian frogwomen or anthropomorphic ant-men, though Myrmidons did figure in ancient mythologies, as of course did mermen and mermaids. Like all of the above it could talk, if you pulled its tail, and what it talked about was usually some story or another it traded for its life; hence the term tee-tee tales.

"So it is. Did you pull its tail?"

"Sure we did and it told us some stupid story about you getting almost killed by one of the Mother Murder Medusa's Quadrang Nucleoids – Flying Doltaur, it called her – in Subcranial Temporis. But that isn't what happened at all. Daddy killed Mother Murder on the moon, right?"

"Sometimes tee-tees just make things up, Tina. But every tee-tee's got two tales to tell, so maybe its other one's better."

"Read it for me then."

Virtually every creature on both sides of the Cathonic Zone, when there was a Cathonic Zone, or Dome, separating the Inner from the Outer Earth, had individual markings. Tee-tees were no different in that respect, but their differences were more easily discernible than most animals. Besides the fact they could talk, and that each had a unique tale it could recount vocally, their most notable distinctions were their tails. Not only were they colourful, as if made up of dozens of multicoloured beads or nodes, they could be read as if Celtic knot-writing.

"I'm not very good at that, Tina. You know Jordan Tethys, the Legendarian, the fellow who almost got boiled alive while your masterly Mama Mel was giving you birth on Shenon? He's over there, at the beer pavilion, and he's real good at reading tee-tee tails."

"He's creepy. He bites off their tails and sticks them onto his head. Besides, he always stinks of beer."

"That he does. But tee-tee tails grow back, with a different tale to tell, and who knows, maybe he'll let you keep it."

"And maybe he'll teach me how to read its new tail. Good idea, fat Auntie Wildie. Let's go get gay, Paree."

"I wish you'd stop saying that, Tinny," said Helen, whose nickname was indeed Paree – after Paris, among other things the lover of Helen of Troy in Homer's Iliad. "That was daddy's joke."

"So? Someone around here has to keep having fun. Come on."

As Tina ran off toward the beer pavilion, yelling for her little friends in their pretty party dresses to join her, Helen, who had opted, instead of a dress, for a traditional, Utopian-style neckerchief, cream-coloured jacket, crewneck and pantsuit, the same as the young Illuminaries, paused before following her. She felt the need, which she never would have done prior to the start of Panharmonium, and the end of almost everything else, to apologize for her baby sister's behaviour.

"I'm sorry, Witch. You know how silly Tinny gets when she's excited."

"Better silly than severe, Paree. You're overdue-stopping being such a miserable little Helen-Hellion. You should feel proud wearing one of your daddy's rings."

"They're Percy's now."

"Not all of them, I see."

"It's for protection. Anyone comes at me, up they go. Or out they go. Or down they go. Way up, way out, way down. Too bad they don't work for you, eh?"

"Oh, I don't know. I've lots of other things that do."

========

And so she did: rings and bangles and glowing things off of which she could materialize whatever she kept in her between-space bottomless bag; among them her metallic marigold, as she called the stunted eye-stave Mel gave her months ago when she was only the High Illuminary and the Witch wasn't even pregnant, if only by a day or two.

What she should have said, she reconsidered as Helen went to catch up to Tina, was 'too bad they worked so well for your father'. She could also have said something like 'at least we're both still here'. But today was no more a day for showing off than it was for nastiness. Today was a day for celebrating survival.

And celebrating those who didn't make it. Those like Mel's much younger husband, Harry Zeross, her predecessor as Master of Weir, Saladin Devason, her twin brother, Demios Sarpedon, his wife, Saladin's year younger sister, Morgianna, the White Witch or Morrigan. For celebrating Morg's dead daughters, both of them, Tsishah Twilight and the Zebranid, Andy, Andrea, Andaemyn. For celebrating those whose actions allowed there to be such a celebration in the first place.

As for those whose actions caused the near Armageddon everyone left had survived, their day was coming. She just hoped she'd be there to contribute to the devils' absolute extermination. Those she hadn't already, that is.

========

On Christmas Day 1955, twelve year old Aristotle *'Harry'* Zeross, codenamed Kid Ringo, later to become Ringleader, used his teleportive Gypsium Rings to take himself and ten other supranormals to a tiny atoll in the Aleutian Chain of islands in the North Pacific known as Damnation Isle.

Those he took with him were the six still-active members of KOC (the King's Own Crimefighters): Cerebrus David Ryne, Wildman Dervish Furie, Old Man Power, Radiant Rider and her adopted siblings, the Elemental Twins, Airealist and Sea Goddess. They along with their oft-times comrades in supra-doings: the Untouchable Diver, Blind Sundown, Raven's Head and Wilderwitch herself. He left them there, in the Aleutians, to do what they had to in order to deal, finally, with Saul Ryne, Cyborg Cerebrus's twin brother, the dangerously erratic supra best known as the Magnificent Psycho.

They went at each other so comprehensively their bodies were never found.

========

For those who knew about the 17-year Secret War of Supranormals, who knew about supranormals or supras period, the prevailing theory at the time was their remains had been washed away when a tsunami rolled over the islet. Kid Ringo returned to the Alliance of Man's get-together then going on in Old Vancouver. He was administered amnaesthetics – memory-redacting drugs long used by the Antediluvian Sisterhood of Flowery Anthea, to which the Witch also belonged – and promptly forgot he was the last of the supranormals.

On New Years Day 1956, Loxus Abraham Ryne, the born-with-the-century father of David-Cerebrus and Saul-Psycho, among others, resigned as chairman of New Century Enterprises. Already far richer than Croesus ever was, he intended to devote more time to the philanthropic Alliance of Man, as the Human League was known in those days, its burgeoning Academies of Man, and the Panhumanist cause of Xuthrodism.

Alfredo Sentalli, then not quite thirty, took Ryne's place at NCE and turned it into the most profitable multinational corporation in the world. In late April 1960, Harry Zeross and Belificent D'Angelo, Radiant Rider's decade younger sister, married in Toronto Ontario. Bel was promptly kidnapped and executed by a group calling itself the Worldwide Order with the Right to Life and Death.

In response to WORLD's threat, the Great Man, Loxus Ryne, immediately formed the Alliance of Man for the Extermination of Resisting International Criminal Associations. AMERICA became the vanguard of the anti-terrorist movement of the Sixties and early Seventies. It turned out to be extremely successful. Terrorism was reduced or, in some places, eliminated entirely, at least for the time being.

WORLD lasted until 1970. Before it went down, its leadership, a largely artificial man called Steltsar and a mysteriously faceless woman, a rogue witch known only as Strife, learned the real reason behind AMERICA's success. The Alliance of Man employed supranormals, specifically the King Crimefighters, their four friends, and Magnifico, as Saul-Psycho had begun calling himself.

Their deaths had been a ruse. Instead, apparently with the energetic elder Ryne's full knowledge, they had gone into deep cover. Bel's murder and Harry's subsequent disappearance in 1960 brought them out of virtual retirement. After the destruction of WORLD they resurfaced, though still not as declared supras. Even in 1970 that wouldn't have been acceptable.

Obadiah Melvin Power, then as now a giant of a man with a great grey beard, replaced Ryne Senior as the patriarch of the Illuminated Faith of Xuthros Hor. David Ryne took over from his father as chairman of the Alliance, which he renamed the Human League after the onset of Panharmonium. Saul Ryne assumed his father's role as President of the worldwide Academies of Man.

Thus freed from all other duties, the Great Man redirected his formidable energies toward attaining his lifelong goal, namely to set up a meaningful United Nations in order to oversee the transition to a new, enlightened, war-free New World — the precursor to today's Panharmonium.

Yehudi Cohen, aka the Untouchable Diver, became the Israeli Ambassador to the UN in New York. John Sundown, a blind Cheyenne elder, became the inspirational and very influential spokesperson for the betterment of aboriginal societies throughout the globe. He travelled with his sable-black mare, Raven, and was a frequent guest at universities and on television talk shows. Gloriella D'Angelo Dark, as radiant as ever, resuscitated her career, fifteen years in suspension, as an occasional actress, model and titular chair of Radiant Rainbows Fashion Emporium.

Despite the publicity thus gained, she maintained her role as the devoted wife to the brilliant but crippled, British-born astrophysicist, Dr Immanuel Dark, and mother to their famous, often infamous daughter, Estrella, who eventually married Magnifico. Well into her late forties Gloriel remained one of the most beautiful women in the world. Often cited as the ideal woman, most folks considered her living proof a devout Roman Catholic could be all things to all people. Except, admittedly, one or two fanatical feminists.

Four of the eleven continued to shun the spotlight. Two, Wilderwitch and Dervish Furie, stayed entirely out of sight; the other two, Aires (Airealist) and Thalassa (Sea Goddess) D'Angelo, went to work for Alfredo Sentalli on Centauri Island, off the coast of Maui, Hawaii. The twins didn't age — despite being born in late 1920, without witch-glamours they continued to look like they were in their early twenties. That was hardly all of it.

It wasn't until the events of late November 1980 that the reasons they were so seldom seen became evident. They, like Furie and the Witch, spent next to none of their time on the Outer Earth. In fact, until they were finally reconciled prior to going to the Moon aboard the Liberty, the Elemental Twins spent most of their lives on the Inner Earth, the domain of all devils, and a lot of other things, trying to track down and dispose of Furie and the Witch.

In 1977 something was detected on the Moon. Aliens? A revitalized WORLD? Witches gone technologically savvy? Utopians rediscovering how everything kept on working in their Weirdom and then applying said rediscoveries in a renewed effort to destroy the Moloch Sedon and his hundreds of possessive devils? No one knew for sure, but one thing was certain. Whatever was up there was bombarding the planet with thought-altering mind-beams.

The effects were quickly apparent. Governments began to topple, at first by revolutions, remarkably none of which were overly long, nor particularly bloody, since police the world over kept embracing revolutionaries, then by democratically being voted out of power. Whole armies started laying down their arms and refusing to fight. In the void developed a never-before-seen spirit of global cooperation.

The Soviet Union was the first to voluntarily dismantle its biological, chemical and nuclear weapons development and deployment programs. Public outcry in the States thereupon forced the Democratic President to begin doing likewise. The birth rate, especially in the Third World, dropped precipitously in three years but, correspondingly, the standard of living rose dramatically. Fossil fuels were rejected as untenable, as were nuclear power plants.

Tremendous strides were made, some close to overnight, at replacing them with renewable, non-polluting energy sources such as the windmills and obelisks capped with firestones threatening to make the globe resemble a spiny sea urchin. Lumber and mining companies started switching to agriculture in the theory that anything the planet needed could be grown in a sustainable fashion.

Unemployment skyrocketed initially. Inflation and interest rates plummeted. Banks and leading lending institutions were going out of business on a monthly then weekly basis. There should have been rioting everywhere, and there was, but the authorities did nothing. Sooth said many of them joined those already marching in the streets. Riots turned to peaceful protests to love-ins. The planet was in the grip of a collective form of mass hysteria. Or, as it turned out, mass sanity.

A year after detection, the United Nations formed the Space Council and chose Loxus Ryne, then 78-years old, to head it. With his propensity for anagrams the Great Man renamed it the Society for the Prevention of Alien Control of Earth.

With the cooperation of all the surviving governments on the planet, SPACE funded, built, and sent into moon-orbit the United Nations of Earth Spaceship Liberty.

About a week later, on the thirtieth of November 1980, New Century Enterprises launched a multiplely manned spacecraft of its own from Centauri Island. The Cosmic Express, as it was known, made an unexpected detour somewhere. A few minutes later it reappeared, intact except for one cosmicar. Blasting through the atmosphere it ignited its Gypsium propellant and rocketed towards the stars. Wilderwitch knew it was still out there, still on its way to wherever, but it was what it left behind in its wake, the greatest cataclysm Planet Earth had experienced in nearly six millennia, that mattered the most. And the last for all too extraordinarily many.

By the tenth of December, the Earth was whole again; had an eighth continent and a couple of billion less people. The Hidden Continent of Sedon's Head was no longer hidden. With the dissolution of the Cathonic Dome, dimensions were rent and the North Pacific returned to being largely a landform. The ocean had to go somewhere and it did.

Millenarian fatalists who had bought property in Nevada and Arizona in anticipation of just such an event come the Year 2000 had their waterfront vacation sites twenty years early.

========

*The crowd announced the arrival of Blind Sundown and Raven's Head with the usual, all too obligatory nowadays, oohing and ahhing. Looking up the Witch was tempted to join them.*

*One thing about the two 'Wakinyah' creatures of the cosmos was they knew how to make an entrance.*

========

For a change it was a clear day, still warm as well. Summer was hanging on, though here in what most folks still called British Columbia, even if there was no British Columbian government anymore, nor a Canadian one for that matter, it was more commonly referred to as Indian Summer. All too appropriately given who, and what, they were.

The solitary cloud more like racing in than wafting in from the southeast, too low to the trees to be an actual cloud, was a dead giveaway. Lest there be any doubt about it, it lit up and was almost as immediately vapourized, revealing a truly spectacular sight. High above them, seemingly suspended on nothing except his much more impressive, even miraculous, mount, a native North American raised his Solar Spear, its spearhead flaring like a miniature sun, in a salute for all to see. He was riding … well, Raven's Head had earned her name.

Mostly a horse with a raven-black coat that, upon closer inspection, was more feathers than fur, she had indeed a raven's bird-head. Had as well the very much telescoping horn of a unicorn, or monoceros, extending out of her raven's bird-forehead. As for how she flew, the talarial wings of Mercury fluttered furiously off both sides of her four fetlock ankles. As for how they kept something of her size aloft – Raven wasn't just a big bird, she was a big mare, a nightmare to more than a few very much deserving some – categorizing her as a creature of the cosmos covered that. So did Wakinyah, Thundercloud Being, in their own American Indian mythology.

Raven's rider was not Radiant Rider. That was Gloriella D'Angelo Dark, who was around Hope Haven somewhere and to whom the Witch, even if she was more likely to have a gypsy heritage rather than an Italian one, bore a vague familial resemblance. (According to many, she was more like of the Devils than of the Angels, but Gloriel's long-gone, paternal Aunt Mnemosyne wasn't long gone in 5927, the year Wilderwitch was born.) It was John Sundown.

His eyeholes were covered in a beadwork blindfold. His headdress, what he called his *'issiwun'*, was a de-skulled but still be-furred buffalo's head with its horns turned upwards. His star-cloak was also made of buffalo, its hide rather than its head. It being not quite officially autumn he had it turned fur-side outwards, the better to reflect heat instead of retain it.

Over his otherwise bare chest he wore a washboard vest. Although made primarily of beads, like his blindfold, it featured dozens of animal teeth and claws strung together. His pants and moccasins were as leathern as the Witch's only Radiant Rainbows' designed robe and shawl — she'd had to hire someone to stitch her clothes together since Gloriel's Fashion Emporium refused to work with animal skins or by-products. No war paint, though, she was happy to report.

"Come along, my fine foetal friend. Time for me to get off our shared butt-end and start with the matters not a whit shit. But, hey, maybe we still have enough time to get lucky. Even with you belly-baking in the baby-burden-oven, it's best never to miss an opportunity to go for a Raven-ride."

========

*For Wilderwitch, riding Raven's Head was not the biggest highlight of that day, that dream, that nightmare, the end of the Panharmonium. Neither was the lowlight what Johnny did to the Male Entity not so long after she and Raven came to ground again; though it was one explanation for the explosion that got her giving birth again, for the second time in her life.*

*By the time Hellion Helen brought her fellow prisoners, the Zerosses' Utopian mother, Mel-Illuminatus, and Tina's accurately identified slimy Aunt Fish, via her father's rings through between-space to her side, the Witch was screaming bloody murder.*

*"Where's my baby?" she kept repeating, screeching all the louder every time.*

*"She's still scum-coming, Witch," kept responding Fisherwoman, Scylla Nereid, Lady Achigan, Wilderwitch's nine years' older sister in more than just Flowery Anthea.*

*"Not her, Fucking Fish-face," the Witch spat anew, giving birth yet again. "Fucking him!"*

*"Fucking Hell," muttered Mel-Illuminatus, realizing what had happened. There'd been two after all. And the firstborn, a boy and already missing, was Satan Incarnate.*

********

# Two-Babies: THE WEIRDOM OF CABALARKON

========

**Demetray, 9 Tantalar 5980**

*Antiseptic stench, like smelling salts, awakened her.*

========

Wilderwitch felt herself lying on her back, in a bed and wearing nothing but a linen smock of some sort. A hospital it was then. She did a mental inventory. No bottomless bag, no agates, no studs, nothing off of which she could materialize anything. Nothing internal either. Someone who knew witches had done a thorough job on her. She felt violated. Worse, she felt as vulnerable as she ever did. At least she still had the requisite two arms and two legs, ribs too. God, she hurt.

Opening her eyes she beheld a truly terrifying sight. The Demon glaring down at her was large and powerfully built, bare and barrel-chested, red-skinned, with obvious horns, a forked goatee, a droopy moustache. Bald on the top, he had a pair of almost penile-looking mutton-chops, a long, black ponytail and pointed ears. Half of his right forearm was missing.

***"Yes,"*** said the humanoid horror, ***"I believe you'll do just fine!"***

Demon, hell! That's a fucking devil!

Epiphany came the moment she spotted only two eyes. Except one of them was in the centre of his forehead. Simultaneously came identification. 'God and the Devil both,' she muttered inaudibly. Unless she just imagined herself muttering it. Gratefully she let pain pass and delirium render her insensate again. Should have asked what day it was.

Would have been answered, if the demons' conqueror-king and the devils' father-creator answered inanities, Devauray the 6th of Tantalar.

========

On Sunday the 30th of November 1980, the Cosmic Express was launched from Centauri Island, a mostly manmade Hawaiian island off the coast of Maui dominated by three not exactly towering, but nonetheless distinct, not to mention extinct, volcanoes that once formed the tips of separate islets. Mere seconds after lift-off it was intercepted by the self-proclaimed Worldwide Order with the Right to Life and Death's Kamikaze Craft and blasted into a black space. Pinpricks of light, in their dozens, approached the vessel.

What were they ... stars, faeries, angels? None of the above. Not strictly speaking, though they had aspects of all three. Were above, however, in the night's sky, the Sedon Sphere — above somewhere, an Otherworld, possibly even the Otherworld of the Celts and just about every other indigenous peoples the world over. Weren't, that is to say, below, in the Underworld, where their unkind kind is usually thought to dwell. Nor were they gods; little gods in some Faiths. Not anymore. What they were once, and were still, were devils.

Everything about the Express, including its very existence, was hush-hush. Other than in the highest corporate and national echelons of the Whole Earth, it might be said absolutely nothing was known about it. Yet even in those rarefied strata virtually nothing was known about its secondary fuel system, nor its major component, Gypsium. The Godstuff was teleportive. Seeing what was coming at him, the cosmicommander activated it. Activating its Gypsium fuel fractured the Express, sent its constituent vessels, the hub-craft, shaft and six leech-like cosmicars, rocketing off between-space almost anywhere except this nowhere.

None of its crewmembers died, at least not immediately. All of them were possessed by until then cathonitized devils. At least one cosmicar, designated Cosmicar Four, shot out of the nowhere that was the everywhere in there; shot out comparatively not far from where it went in, Centauri Island, Outer Earth version. Empty of cosmicompanions, but not quite empty of anything else, it landed in the Aleutians, on a deserted, ice-rimed atoll marked on maps, even on Japanese maps, albeit in Japanese, as Damnation Isle.

Twenty-five years earlier it had been the site of the then final act of what was known in those, for the year 1955, selfsame rarefied strata as the Secret War of Supranormals. There, the last six active members of the King's Own Crimefighters, plus four of their oft-times comrades in supra-doings, took on their greatest enemy, Saul Ryne. Codenamed the Magnificent Psycho, the twin brother of KOC's leader, Cerebrus David Ryne, blew his mind. The six Crimefighters, their four comrades and Saul-Psycho were never seen again. Not on the Outer Earth; not before December 1980 anyhow.

Were not seen alive on the Inner Earth again either. Statues of them were; at least apparent statues of them were: in Centurium, replicated Versailles, the central cavern of the Subterranean Realm of Temporis. It lay beneath Sedon's Cranium, in the northern hemisphere of the Hidden Continent of Sedon's Head, as this Otherworld was known to its vastly divergent, sentient life forms; the majority of whom, perhaps surprisingly, were human.

These apparent statues, which stood in one place or another within Centurium for almost a quarter century, were more than just physical representations of the eleven supras otherwise obliterated that Christmas Day. They were their actual bodies hardened, and thereby preserved, by Solidium, what was also called Stopstone. Was a good thing for all concerned because, for some unknown reason, the crewmembers of Cosmicar Four were no longer inside it when it crashed on Damnation Isle. And the one thing decathonitized devils needed to avoid being immediately recathonitized were sentient shells to possess.

That was the whole point of WORLD's Kamikaze Craft intercepting the Cosmic Express and blasting it into Cathonia, the Sedon Sphere that had separated the Inner and Outer Earth since the Great Flood of Genesis in 4000 BC. The Master Deva masterminds behind WORLD wanted to free their devic siblings, cousins and fourth generational devic offspring from the Cathonic Zone. In other words, it was a jailbreak.

Outer Earth Hindus might take offense at Devas, large case, being characterized as devils. After all Devas to them were gods whereas azuras were devils. Then again Zoroastrians considered Devas devils and azuras gods or under-gods to their Great God, the Wise Lord, *'Ahura Mazda'*. (Who, according to the Annals of Anthea, the teachings of her prediluvian sisterhood, may have been Thrygragos Varuna Mithras, the Great God reputedly, and as yet irreversibly, killed on Thrygragon, back in 4376 YD.)

However, as Wilderwitch, if she was conscious, would be aware since she was born and sort of brought up in this Otherworld, other than a few sensitive sorts the Head's devils could care less what anyone called them. They were as happy with Fallen Angels as anything else. Did not particularly quarrel with being classified as the devazur race, either. Helped to explain a few things, sooth said.

The first generation of devazurkind was a solitary individual, the Moloch Sedon, who was resolutely male. The second generation consisted of his parthenogenetically-procreated children, the Six Great Gods and Goddesses, the three Thrygragos Brothers – one of whom, the aforementioned Mithras, was for all intents and purposes dead – and the three Trigregos Sisters, all of whom were as long gone as they were indistinguishable from each other.

Their offspring were labelled Master Devas and, until earlier in this century, the offspring of Master Devas were strictly azuras. Azuras were only spirit beings, like Master Devas had been for most of their multiple millennia of existence. Azuras, though, were so next-to-useless that, unless they were morons or zombies, they could not even dominate those they possessed. Which was something full devils could usually do without much difficulty.

What happened earlier this century was two highborn Mithradite Master Devas somehow or other managed to possess – unless it was the other way around – the time-tumbling Male and Female Entities: Heliosophos and Trans-Time Trigon's miraculous three-thing, the Mnemosyne Machine best remembered as Miracle Maenad.

These were the ever-recurring beings most responsible for creating Dark Sedon in the far-off, long obliterated first Weir System multi-millennia earlier. Through them the lucky Master Devas, whose names were Tantal and Methandra Thanatos, begot ten new devils. Until the following Friday, Lazam as it was delineated on Sedon's Head, the Thanatoids' Night and Day, their Four Elements and Four Elements were the only solid, fourth generational devils ever born.

One Fourth Generation Deva, Antaeor Thanatos, aka Demon Land, attached himself to the cosmicompanions-empty Cosmicar Four and, indispensably for the other six with him, Mithradite Master Devas all, had a very useful attribute. Demon Land found a way to recall from Temporis, densify and thereupon possess, one after another, the bodies of ten of the eleven supras lost here a quarter century earlier. Which was about when the good things stopped happening for the seven devils and started happening for the long lost supras.

The main trouble for the devils was the supranormals' minds, or spirits, had somehow survived separation from their bodies. Had survived in what they had come to think of by then as a Limbo-like state of, at best, semi-consciousness. It was centred right there on Damnation Isle and, once reunited with their bodies, they proved approaching indomitable.

A moderately minor trouble was the sudden appearance of a non-Mithradite. The nearly never-cathonitized Master Deva, one Vayu Maelstrom, Devil Wind, had come outside through the Nagasaki Gap from the Inner Earth to the Outer Earth at the behest of his father, Thrygragos Byron, he whose age it was upon Sedon's Head, and his grandfather, the Demon as well as Devil King Himself. And Devil Wind proved next to unbeatable.

Battles galore were fought that first day after Limbo on Damnation Isle. Be it because of the Outer Earth's air or because, being mostly decathonitized, they simply could not withstand the formidable abilities of the supranormals, the devils, even Devil Wind and Demon Land, were vanquished by twilight. Not that, just as the supras had not done a quarter century before, they left corpses behind.

Individually these supras had names, most had codenames and one had just a codename. That one was Wilderwitch. Three had D'Angelo surnames — although only the Terrible Twins, Aires and Thalassa, codenamed Airealist and Sea Goddess, were definitely related. The third one was Gloriella D'Angelo by then Dark (Gloriel, Glory of the Angels, Radiant Rider, Rainbow, she whose father found Air and Sea on the day she was born in Rome and whose parents adopted them later on in '33). The fourth female was the lone non-visibly-human among them, the ravendoe who somewhat unimaginatively answered to the name of Raven's Head and whose equally unimaginative codename was Raven.

In addition to their leader, Cerebrus David Ryne – Cyborg Cerebrus being his codename – the rest were men. Like Air and Sea, who were identical twins, Gentleman Jervis Murray, Yehudi Cohen and John Sundown, respectively codenamed Wildman Dervish Furie, the Untouchable Diver and Blind Sundown, were Summoning Children. Which indicated they were conceived towards the tail-end of 19/5920's Simultaneous Summonings.

The tenth was Obadiah Melvin Power, codename Old Man Power or simply OMP. No one, not even OMP, knew how old he was but, other than Raven, who may have been even older, every one of them wondered if the near-giant was their father. One of them did know whose father he definitely was — her daughter's. Which was something else the oversized greybeard still did not realize.

Given names, married names, surnames, codenames, made up or legitimate, were one thing. After almost twenty-five years of their minds being stuck in Limbo, and their bodies encased in Stopstone-Solidium overcoats beneath Sedon's Cranium, calling themselves the King's Own Crimefighters, especially since four of them did not belong to KOC in 1955, seemed an out-thing. They needed a group denomination to better reflect their dramatically altered circumstances. Thanks to Cerebrus they got one. Denomination was damnation, as in the Damnation Brigade.

Was nowhere near all they got over the course of the next few days.

========

*Reverie.*

========

Budding, top and bottom; bleeding, menstruation; puberty. Different order? Bloodshed, big hair, bottoming out? Life-loving Ants started early, 13, 14, 15. Not as early as love-loving, Lovely Lady Afrites, surely. Wilderwitch started early. As early as eventual gal-pal Sorciere, Johnny's childhood bride? Surely not. Certainly had no kid of her own till she was 18. Or was she already 19 when the birth-pangs set in? On the cusp of it anyhow. She didn't know the precise date of her own birth, only that it was around the Winter Solstice. Around now, in other words. Assuming it was still December, which she couldn't be absolutely sure of either.

She'd had lots of lovers both before and after the birth of her daughter. Not so much so since Limbo, though. Count none. Except Jerry, who hardly counted at all. He was incapable of having children. Which saved on the birth control. First was the Osiraq Taurson. Then came, and came they did, in no particular order, that wicked Wiccan Fucking Warlock, that pseudo-supra-saviour Jesus Fucking Conquering Christ asshole, Jervis Murray, him so gentlemanly and un-reproductive, a different him, the oversized fucking faerie. All of them stank. Musk was a nicer word. All of them stank individually.

This one stank more so than most. She opened her eyes. He was black as midnight, albeit perhaps not quite as black as most pureblood Utopian males. Also had a beard, which marked him as a definite hybrid. She recognized him less by the musk as by the thrust, though neither had changed much. Recognizing who he was suggested where she was, besides a hospital bed. It was the Weirdom of Cabalarkon. Was he still its Master?

"Good God, Sal, you look like hell."

"Fuck you, Witch."

"Appears I'm leaving that up to you."

It was now, she'd have learned, has she asked, Sedonda, Sunday, the 7th of Tantalar 5980 YD.

========

On Friday the 5th of December, the Damnation Brigade went down to nine members. Despite a quarter century in Limbo; the travails of Damnation Isle; the long trip from there to Vancouver, where D-Brig had begun setting up their new lives the previous Monday; and all that had happened since their arrival there; Thalassa D'Angelo, Sea Goddess, was still in the early months of pregnancy. Was fed up, wanted peace, no strife, no tribulation; wanted to concentrate on having her baby, Cerebrus's baby.

So, alone, she boarded an airplane. Her destination was Los Angeles. They didn't know if she made it or what had become of her afterwards. Nor did they know that, by the time she flew off, D-Brig only had eight members. What they did know, those that knew much of anything, was that, as of that night, Vayu Maelstrom, Devil Wind, was back on the scene.

He was whirl-winding overtop their newly purchased ranch house on the banks of the Fraser River in Vancouver's remarkably still somewhat rural Southlands area. Wasn't alone either. Had three other devils with him. Allowing for his three eyes, Maelstrom was the only one who looked even remotely normal.

Sure, he had blue skin and, when his lower body wasn't a whirlwind, he wore only a fur garment covering his loins. Sure, his skull was mostly shaven and his long topknot glowed with the intensity of Brainrock, what Outer Earthlings had been calling Gypsium since 1948. Still, if he suppressed his third eye and altered his skin colouration he could pass for human. So could the lone woman among them — except Sedona Spellbinder was composed entirely of smoke.

About the only consistent thing about the third one, Chimaera Glimmenmare, was a mace, his Brainrock talisman or power focus. Otherwise he was changing by the minute: an air-strutting centaur, a be-winged Angelyc like something out of the British Museum's Assyrian collection, a Simian Sapient, an ebonite demon, a preying mantis, the variations were endless. The fourth was just a huge, hovering head, completely hairless and with no body in sight; no head in sight some of the time either.

This was Great Byron, their Thrygragos of a father. Maelstrom, Glimmenmare, and Spellbinder were his Primary Nucleoids, which made them his chief enforcers. They were also his second born litter of three — Master Devas, who were as immortal as their fathers and solitary grandfather, were always born in litters of three because their three mothers, the likely, on some planet faraway from the Earth, still existent, three-in-one Trigregos Sisters, always gave birth at the same time.

(It went without saying that Bodiless Byron once wasn't; once had a body and all that went with it. How he lost it, the Witch would have remembered had she been paying attention in class, which she seldom did – having also run away from the Sisterhood Shelter where was she born and brought up at a very early age – was something else recounted in its annals. She did remember it was here on the pre-Flood, hence then Whole Earth, but not much else.)

Together the four of them could form the Byronic Nucleus. Which they did. Which was how D-Brig's remaining members ended up on Sedon's Head. Which was where, below it actually, they reacquired their ninth member. This ninth, OMP, had already found his own way there. Only he wasn't OMP anymore. Well, he was and he wasn't. Was also, put better, the Awesome Akbar, Akbarartha, the titular Kronokronos Supreme of Temporis. Which was a subterranean realm; subcranial, to be just as precise.

Temporis was a devic protectorate, that of Dand Tariqartha. OMP-Akbar was the Dand's half-son, hence Akbarartha. It had at least a thousand caverns, hence the Thousand Caverns of Tariqartha. The Byronic Nucleus dropped the rest of them off above it the night of the 5$^{th}$. Within it, the next day, the 6$^{th}$ of Tantalar Year of the Dome 5980, as they quickly learned to count time beneath the Sedon Sphere, they, reunited, ended up fighting, and sort of winning, the War of the Apocalyptics.

Weren't nine of them left by the end of it, though.

========

*The Witch opened her eyes.*

========

The Utopian glaring down at her was haggard but still handsome. Perhaps six-five and two hundred forty pounds, his beard and moustache poked out from around the surgical mask he was wearing. Otherwise he was dressed modestly, an operating room smock draped over an Arabic or Egyptian style haik. Although turbans, often wrapped such that only slits were left for their eyes, were the most common headgear for men in the Weirdom, he had arranged part of the haik, a simple, oblong piece of unbleached cloth, to form a hood over top of his head.

Besides the Master's Mace, a kind of sceptre, which he held in his right hand, his one concession to Masterly vanity was his personal chain of office. Depending from his neck, it was a necklace of ruby-red bloodstones upon which was attached a golden triangle with a single eye staring out of it. The hardly just ceremonial mace was a stubby eye-stave, the multipurpose weapon of choice amongst the Weirdom's Trinondev Warrior Elite. It consisted of a 3-foot long, unadorned shaft with a smooth, leathern pod, an eyeorb or prison pod, atop it instead of a spiked, metallic-looking Brainrock head like Chimera Glimmenmare, Byron's Stallion, had.

It was old; possibly pre-Earth-old. It was supposed to make him lovable, which it sort of did, though a better word might be adorable. Holding it, being therefore, demonstrably, the Weirdom's Master, made him of necessity entitled to due adulation. You didn't adore, as in worship, your Master virtually nothing worked in Cabalarkon. If you were an inbred idiot, like the majority of the pureblood Utopians living there, you wouldn't be living there for long. You'd be rapidly dying there.

It also served as a Speaking Stick because, supposedly, no one could lie under the influence of its open orb. No not always illusionary gargoyle manifested out of its top. Trinondevs, the Witch recalled from visits to the Weirdom pre-Limbo, liked their gargoyles; took great pride in making them as frightening and ferocious as they could. They especially liked to show them off atop their eye-staves, their consequential labara (plural of *labarum*), during parades. In fact, seldom having much else to do, they loved nothing better than to parade about Cabalarkon City showing off how high and mighty they'd risen. The Master clearly felt he was show enough.

"You look even worse clothed, Sal."

"So you remember last night. I was worried about that. Nothing I can do about it now. Nothing I can do about this, either. Leg's got to go, Witch. Cut it off!"

Which was when, desperation retaining consciousness, the Witch unleashed her fearsome soul-self. Sent it directly into the Master of Weir, jolting him, Saladin Devason, off his feet. Ordinarily, for safety's sake, she'd have already taken herself to a between-space Shelter and sunk into a trance. Didn't have that luxury today.

Even though she was strapped to the operating table, an intravenous drug-drip attached to her left arm, her Doltaur-damaged right leg exposed for amputation from the hip down, the orderlies moved to pin her shoulders back while a male Utopian surgeon raised high her very own cut-anything blade, what she'd had since childhood.

At her calling, her soul-self exited the Master. Outside her, outside anyone, it was visible, monstrous to banshee-behold. Although always intangible, it was a match in terms terrifying to anything even the most twisted of Trinondev could imagine in terms gargoyle. The sounds it emitted were just as illusionary, as were the lights going out in the operating theatre. Didn't mean those in the room thought they hadn't gone out, however.

Soul-self went into the surgeon. He dropped the blade. Someone else barged through the swinging doors into the theatre. That someone was carrying what might be mistaken for a stunted eye-stave of her own; albeit one with non-gargoyle manifestations. While it had much the same capacities, it wasn't just an apparent eye-stave. Had a short pole with an orb atop it, yes, but it was decorated with twin snakes entwined along its shaft and had a pair of highly stylized wings spreading off it around the orb atop it.

It was a caduceus, the traditional symbol of the medical profession. In olden days heralds often held something similar when they went about their duties. In fact, she recalled, seemingly the very person now noisily bursting into the operating room once told her the word itself came from the Doric Greek *'karykion'*, meaning a herald's staff.

She was no herald. At least she hadn't been pre-Limbo. Might be one now of course. She was, however, a doctor; had been the last time the Witch saw her anyhow. Could it really be her, still so comparatively young? Might she be her daughter? No, she looked older than the maximum of twenty-five any daughter she could have had could be. So it had to be her.

Pureblood Utopians, she'd almost forgotten, didn't age at the same rate normal men and women did; normal supranormals, with the exception of the Elemental Twins, Aires and Thalassa, did either. Then again Utopians were not strictly human. They were extraterrestrials; rather their ancestors were when they first came from the stars to the then Whole Earth some six thousand years ago in pursuit of the Sedonshem.

Like all pureblood Utopian women she was white-as-light. And she was pureblood, not a hybrid like the Master. Even if she wasn't whom she appeared to be, the Witch could tell that because she was not so much expressionless as her look of concern seemed chiselled onto her face. Ambulant alabaster, that was how the Diver used to describe her, Melina Sarpedon.

"Illuminatus?"

"High Illuminary now, Witch. Sorry it took so long to get here. Even sorrier it took so long to accept that that was Gloriel there and that she was telling me you were the Witch here."

"Where you been?"

"Being kidnapped. I only just got released and sent back. You others, get out. I'm her attending physician as of right this second."

Saladin was on his feet again. Unlike Utopian women, Utopian men could register expressions instantaneously. His wasn't concern ... concern for others, as opposed to the Weirdom as a whole, wasn't really part of his makeup. For Sal, it was either anger or outrage; more likely, knowing him, the latter.

"It's too late for her, Illuminary. The leg has to go."

"I'll be the judge of that, Master. I am a doctor, remember. Have been for something like 30 years."

"So you are, Dr Zeross. No one better for the job either. Allow me a word or two before I let you get to it. The Witch's knife's sharper than any of ours."

========

*Sort of winning came with a hefty price tag.*

*Which was why at least one of their number hardly knew anything anymore; if he knew even that much. In what amounted to a cruel case of poetic justice, since he was the one who got the seven others still with him in Vancouver on the night of the 5th to join up with Bodiless Byron and his Nucleoids, that one was their leader.*

========

At least Cerebrus David Ryne was still alive, albeit just, but Air (Aires D'Angelo, Airealist) might not be. He'd vanished in Temporis minutes, if not hours, before the usurper, Lakshmi of Lemuria, who had only turned 18 the day before, arrogated the title of Kronokronos Supreme from OMP-Akbar and ejected them upstairs: to Sisert (the Silent Sands of Cathune Bubastis, Sedon's Cranium). That was where Ringleader, Harry Zeross, now 37 or close enough to it that it didn't make much difference, found them just as the sun was going down.

Harry had accidentally observed the Witch and Akbar in action against a devil, one Freespirit Nihila by her own naming, down below in the Faerie Garden of Temporis. He still had the same teleportive Gypsium rings he had when he abandoned them on Damnation Isle in '55. These he used to transport the now again only eight members of D-Brig to the Weirdom of Cabalarkon.

Harry couldn't tarry. Harry was in a hurry. He had a task to perform for the Master of Weir, Saladin born Nauroz. That task was the recovery of the Trigregos Talismans; one of which, the Crimson Corona, the Witch had brought with her from the Outer Earth. She'd lost it, though, in the Faerie Garden.

Lost it to the selfsame, self-named Lazaremist Master Deva, she who also claimed to have once been Datong Harmonia. Which was the name ancient Illuminaries' gave the Unity of Balance; she who answered to Harmony until she was thought obliterated, on her own feast day, around five hundred years earlier. (In the Year of the Dome 5492, to be precise: the same year, on the Outer Earth, that Christopher Columbus sort of 'discovered' the Americas.)

Not so. Harry had taken care of her, whomever this Nihila was in reality. He was the one who lost it. But he knew whom he had lost it to and that was why he was in such a hurry. The bastard he'd lost it to was Vetala's Soldier. He had a name, Dmetri Diomad, and a title, Cosmicaptain of Cosmicar Four. Was a bastard, too: Dem's Dim, the never acknowledged son of Demonites, Harry's dozen years dead, 12-years older brother, and Roxanne nee Heliopolis Kinesis, a Summoning Child slightly longer dead.

This Diomad, Vetala's Soldier, had somehow managed to obtain all three talismans, the two besides the Crimson Corona being the Amateramirror and the Susasword. He'd therefore played and evidently won the Trigregos Gambit; become, as might be expected, a consequential Trigregos Titan, the first in those selfsame, nearly five hundred years. (That one had been a howsoever brief time Master of the Weirdom of Cabalarkon, Melina Tethys become Somata. Mel-Illuminatus was named after her.)

Wasn't endgame yet. Harry could still get them back, what the Utopians of Weir called the three Sacred Objects. Not that they were anywhere near sacred to devils. Were in fact proven effective against them, which of course was why this Master had sent Harry in search of them in the first place. This despite the fact that this Mel (Melina born Sarpedon now Zeross) and her Illuminaries claimed having them ended that Melina, Somata's, life so prematurely.

Utopians of Weir existed to destroy devils, the Moloch Sedon foremost, but also the two still extant Great Gods, Thrygragos Byron and Thrygragos Lazareme, their spawn and the spawn, or offspring, of the third Great God, Thrygragos Varuna Mithras, who at least had the common courtesy to be fifteen hundred dead and, much more importantly, staying that way. (Which was quite an accomplishment for an immortal. Harmony-Nihila evidently hadn't managed it and she was supposedly the first born of the firstborn, Thrygragos Lazareme.)

Ancient Utopians came to the then Whole Earth for that express purpose: to destroy devils and the ever-spreading evil they carried with them like a kind of universal contagion. Came to Planet Earth ten years before the Genesea, the Great Flood of Genesis; stayed here ever since, unable to go anywhere else primarily because little of their originally extraterrestrial science and technology worked the way it was supposed to work anymore.

Oh yes, also unable to go anywhere because the suddenly Inner Earth, where they were stranded, was now covered, over under sideways down, by Cathonia, the Cathonic Dome or Zone. They were thereby isolated in what amounted to another dimension, an Otherworld, whence there was no escape. Not in number and not on their millennial ships, which were stuck beneath the Dome with them. Besides, why would they go anywhere if it meant leaving the devils behind alive and, as the Inner Earth's deities – which many of them had also been on the Outer Earth, until around 2000 years ago – dutifully, even fanatically, worshipped?

Nergal Vetala wasn't just the devic Queen of the Dead. She was the also vampiric Queen of Hadd, where Dead Things walked, animated by Haddazur spirit beings. It was in Hadd, old Iraxas, a south-central region of Sedon's Head – the Hidden Continent being about the size of Africa – that the Corporate State of Greater Godbad, a veritable subcontinent in the Head's south-westernmost corner, Sedon's Mouth, Lower Jaw and Goatee, was currently waging a war between the Living and the Dead.

And, gee, Harry, Ringleader, Rings, their old pal and ever-so-childish mascot, the Ringo Kid, could sure use some supra-duper help fighting the good fight against the bad blight.

When Rings brought them hither, to Sedon's Devic Eye Land (as Cabalarkon was sometimes referred to since the Headword was indeed shaped like a three-eyed devil's head, from the left side perspective), Gloriel had been barely moving, the Witch barely conscious and Cerebrus barely alive. The other five, OMP-Akbar, Dervish Furie, the Diver, Sundown and Raven's Head, were not so much raring as willing to go.

So it was, where once there were eleven supras left, not counting Ringleader, now there were only the three in Cabalarkon.

========

*Wilderwitch was back in the same private hospital room where she'd been before being carted off to have her leg amputated. She wriggled her toes. All ten of them wriggled back.*

*"Thanks, Mel," she said to the only other person in the room with her.*

*The High Illuminary of Weir, Melina born Sarpedon become Zeross, snapped awake — she'd obviously dozed off in her chair. "Huh?"*

*"I said thanks." The Witch could see dawn breaking through the window behind where Melina propped her chair, and herself. It was, to say the least, very illuminating.*

*"Mind telling me what day it is?"*

========

"The morning of Demetray, Tuesday, the 9th of Tantalar, YD 5980. And you're welcome. Mind if I ask you something?"

"Shoot."

"Why aren't you and Gloriel any older?"

"That could take all day."

"Go ahead. You aren't going anywhere."

"Thanks again. Mind if I ask you something first?" Melina nodded. Was, for the Witch, a wonderment her head didn't fall off. Another thing she'd all but forgotten, besides how slowly they aged, was just how literally statuesque full-blooded Utopian women were. "Dr Zeross, as in Dr Harry Zeross?"

"Yeah, and he's one too, a doctor. We've three kids."

"Cradle robber."

"Better than being a grave robber."

"Don't worry, Mel. It's me, still all of barely 28, if that, to boot. Not that, like you just said, I'll be doing much in the way of booting for awhile. I'm not possessed, either. At least I'm not possessed by a Sangazur and, this being the Weirdom of Cabalarkon, I can't be possessed by a devil, can I?"

"Not unless her name's Pyrame Silverstar."

"Or the Moloch Sedon."

"Sedon's resolutely male. He stays out of women. Put better, he doesn't possess them, if you get the distinction."

"Afraid I already have!"

========

The Weirdom of Cabalarkon began its existence in the Year 10 PD, Pre-Dome. Earlier that same year, some 4000 years before the Christian era supposedly began, a contingent of Utopian millennial ships finally traced the Sedonshem to the Whole Earth. The only solid devils way back when, a decade shy of six thousand years ago, were the Moloch Sedon – whose essence had composed the Sedonshem just as it now did the Sed-Sphere, Cathonia – he and the Thrygragos Brothers.

These last were the Headworld's three Great Gods: Unmoving Byron, already bodiless and as of a few days ago once again a star in the night's sky; Lazareme the Libertine, who'd been mostly asleep on Tympani, the Isle of the Undying One, in the middle of the Aural Sea, Sedon's Ear, for approaching half a millennium; and Varuna Mithras, who was fifteen hundred years dead and to date had exhibited no signs of recovering.

At the time the other devils, then numbering many more than the five hundred Illuminaries claimed survived the Great Flood and made it to the Head, were possessive spirit beings. Which made it very difficult for the Utopians' Trinondev Elite, the Warriors of Weir, who were neither all male nor bored-to-tears, gargoyle-manifesting near-sycophants in those bygone millennia, to track down and either capture them in their prison pod eyeorbs or find another way to nullify them.

The millennial ships had not fluked upon the Earth. They were led to this planet by none other than the Male Entity himself, Heliosophos, Helios called Sophos the Wise. For him it was a much later lifetime than the one he spent on the Inner Earth in the first half of this century. (His Eleventh by his own count; six after helping to 'create' Sedon in the first Weir System.) As always, if just as inexplicably as Heliosophos recurring again and again, lifetime after lifetime, whenever and wherever, he was accompanied by Trans-Time Trigon, a tri-peaked land formation imbued with Brainrock.

Also as always, with Helios and Trigon came the latter's innards, the Mnemosyne Machine. Of the three, Machine-Memory had to be by far the most miraculous. Which was why Miracle Memory was the most common name of her human persona. Ironically, given her male counterpart's abiding passion, lifetime after lifetime, whenever and wherever, was to eradicate the entire devazur race, she could only become human if a Master Deva, one of their Great Gods and Great Goddess parents or, as she'd proven in one of their earliest lifetimes together, the devazurs' All-Father, Dark Sedon himself, humanized her. (Earthborn demons worked, too, though they weren't immortal and consequently didn't last as long.)

In the five years pre-Flood he spent on the Whole Earth before being killed again, for the umpteenth time, and consequently tumbling back into the time stream for another howsoever many lifetimes, the Male Entity had no luck finding Sedon and his firstborn sons. He did, however, quickly locate the tub of Cathonic Fluid containing yet another undying one, the Utopian geneticist Cabalarkon who, rightly or wrongly, Sedon regarded as his father. It was buried right here, where Helios and his Utopian followers of that distant era subsequently began construction on the Weirdom of Cabalarkon.

Still was, the tub and Cabalarkon himself, though nowadays it lay in a separate crypt, a tomb-room incorporated within the Catacombs of the Sleepers. Next door, in a crypt and tub of his own, now lay Cerebrus David Ryne. Above the catacombs was the huge central square or plaza of Cabalarkon, the city proper. Massive, Cyclopean stonework structures, interspersed with spiralling obelisks, most of which had pyramid-like caps on them, surrounded the square.

The caps are firestones, Persephone Zeross was telling silver-haired Gloriella D'Angelo Dark, finally at least bordering on full recovery from her own ordeal in Temporis back on the 6th, as they strolled around, the former showing the latter the sites of the city. They're made out of some unknown combination of metallic or crystalline substances, or both. They semi-glowed, like embers in a dying fire, in the near-winter sunshine.

(Actually most of Headworld's sentient inhabitants regarded the winter season as starting on the first of Maruta, November; near-midwinter sunshine, then.)

That absolutely massive, rectangular building's the old palace. Folks still call it the Masters Palace even though the Master, Saladin, lives in Skyrise, that really, really ugly, Outer Earth looking skyscraper looming up over there, behind the really, really pretty old stuff. Lots of officers and higher-ups in the temporarily currently, since the early Fifties, all-male Trinondev Elite live in the old palace along with their wives and families. A significantly large percentage of the officers, their wives and their children living therein are clones. Kind of neat, eh?

Even though it's more museum than anything else, a repository for all sorts of originally extraterrestrial doodads and gewgaws that don't work anymore, we call that there the Grand Cathedral of Light. Utopians don't not have deities so it's not dedicated to any God, gods or goddesses. Certainly isn't dedicated to any devil either, like the terrible Thanatoids of Lathakra who kidnapped me and my mom and my sisters and forced daddy to go to the Moon in order to get back the rest of their kids.

However, those three towers are highly suggestive of Trans-Time Trigon's three hollowed-out spires. So it was undoubtedly built to honour the time-tumbling Dual Entities; one a man and one a woman, as you might expect. Gloriel may have encountered them pre-Limbo, in her youth or teens, since their eleventh lifetime ended in 5950. (She certainly had their arguable templates, her cousin Kadmon Heliopolis and her aunt, his stepmother, Mnemosyne born D'Angelo, who'd died in 1945.)

A third incredibly antique, yet pristinely preserved edifice bordering on the square's over there. That'd be the Citadel of the Thinkers. Many of Mama Mel's Illuminaries and some of the scientocrats of Weir work there. Think of it as the Weirdom's university and you won't be far off the mark, Percy put to her. As for all obelisks, well, no one knows for sure, let alone how, but, due in some measure to the firestones atop them, they provide the power that ran the Weirdom today and had run it for multi-millennia.

Named after a famous figure in Greco-Cretan Mythology, one who was also kidnapped, albeit by a God of the Dead rather than a God of Death, one whom Romans called Proserpine, Persephone was a hybrid: half Utopian, half human. Having been born 16 years ago this month, her youth more so than anything else probably accounted for the fact she was so little the worse for wear after her torment on the Frozen Isle of Lathakra.

It was there, off the east coast of the Head's immense Cattail Peninsula, Sedon's ponytail, where Percy, her mother Melina and two younger sisters, Helen and Athena, spent an entirely unscheduled weekend away from the Weirdom as the very much unwilling guests of the Parents Thanatos. As it turned out, Tantal and Methandra were two of the Master Deva masterminds behind the Cosmic-Express-caused breakout from the Cathonic Zone on the 30th of Maruta. As such, howsoever indirectly, they were as responsible as anyone for the fact she, Gloriel, Radiant Rider, was able to go for a stroll.

Like all those who came back – except for Saul-Psycho, who hadn't come all back and then apparently not for long – she had not aged despite losing twenty-five years in Limbo. That meant, at a physical age of only 22, Gloriel wasn't much older than Percy. She looked and felt rough; much less lively than her guide. Still, as weak and obviously burnt out as she was, she was on her feet again. Glad of it as well.

Would, mere moments later, be radiantly riding again as well. Would be glad of that, too. Provided she could stay away from more of those damnable, but for some reason, not already damned to Hell devils who damn near killed her and the Witch, as good as killed Cerebrus and may have, for all she knew, killed the others wherever Percy's father took them on the 6th.

Had good reason for her iridescent exuberance. Four of them, plus however many Trinondevs came back with them.

========

*A rainbow on a clear day, sunny but cold, arced upwards, away from the square. Went not all that far from it, only as far as the Master's imposing, stunningly mod-*

*ern-looking – as in Outer Earth modern – metal and glass Skyrise. Whereupon it went straight through the window into a private room in the ICU-section of its lower floors.*

*Therein Wilderwitch was resting and Melina, who was too exhausted to rest, was conducting yet another examination of her patient. It resolved itself into her, the once again rainbow-haired Radiant Rider, wearing only the white modesty gown she conjured when she was using her supra-talents.*

*Sounding like a little girl who couldn't contain her excitement, but who could resist a sudden urge to go to the bathroom – Mel's youngest, Tina Zeross, perhaps – Gloriel made the announcement the two witches, the Althean and the Anthean, had been hoping to hear: "They're back!"*

*Then, before either Mel or the Witch could respond with the inevitable 'who?', she caught herself. Now she sounded crushed, defensive.*

*"I mean some of them are back."*

*The two who weren't were Ringleader and the Diver.*

********

# Three-Babies: **HEAD HAUNTERS**

========

**Sedonda, 14 Tantalar 5980**

*Wilderwitch must have given him something, one of her myriad potions from out of her bottomless bag, in order to deaden his death-throes and thus grant him a painless passage to an endlessly unconscious sleep. Only, the next thing he knew that day, what he still thought of as the 6th of December 1980, he found himself immersed in some sort of semi-viscous substance.*

*Buggered up as usual, didn't you, Witch!*

========

Breathing should not have been possible but he was somehow getting air. He, Cerebrus David Ryne, was calm and, although he could not move, he could see through the stuff. A big, bearded black man holding some sort of stubby, mace- or sceptre-like object was dripping blood into his mirror-walled coffin, if that was what it was. He was speaking into his mind.

"I am Saladin, Master of Weir. You are in the Catacombs of the Sleepers, beneath the great central plaza of the Weirdom of Cabalarkon. The liquid you are lying within is known as Cathonic Fluid. It will keep you alive until my scientocrats find a way to rebuild, then rewire, your headplate into your skull. First, though, assuming we can rebuild it, your brain tissue has to regenerate sufficiently for us to have any chance at a successful rewiring operation.

"Happily you are not alone down here. There are literally hundreds of others in the immediate vicinity of your sepulchre; many thousands more lying in the Slopes of the Sleepers that forms a virtually impenetrable wall around the inland periphery of my realm. All suffer from Imminent Death and, to be frank, virtually no one will ever recover.

"You may be more fortunate. Like me, you are what we call a deviant. You have powers, the full extent of which I shall determine in due course. From time to time I will visit you, to see how you are doing. You may wish to do me some favours. I have many enemies but, within the Weirdom, I am next to God Himself.

"Next to the Devil Himself, rather — but only for the nonce!"

========

*In New York City on Monday, December 8, 1980 some deservedly kept nameless, homicidal publicity hound killed John Lennon, arguably the most popular of the former Beatles — the Beatles at one time being by far the most popular pop group in the world, either part of it. On the same day, Mithrada the 8th of Tantalar, 5980 Year of the Dome, the Living won a decisive victory over the Dead on Dustmound, in Hadd, old Iraxas.*

*Demios Sarpedon did not so much miss it as he was in no shape to participate in it.*

========

The reason for that was Melina now Zeross's exiled for 30-years, black-as-midnight twin brother, along with his wife, Morgianna born Nauroz, raised Somata, the Headworld's most celebrated Utopians not living in Cabalarkon, had been through a lot of late, on both sides of the Dome. Mithrada-Monday's final battle only culminated on Dustmound. It raged all over Hadd for hours on top of hours, as it had done for days on top of days before that. Sraddha Isle was only one battle zone but there, within the Sraddhite Monastery, with the Living spilling blood inside and outside the ancient edifice, was where he lay.

As much as he might have wished otherwise, he had no choice except to stay there, in a chamber well-guarded by Godbadian marines armed with splatter packs. Could do little except toss and turn on his cot, fighting off the drugs Godbadian medics gave him to rest. Had to fight off the drugs in case he'd soon have to fight off Dead Thing bursting into it and taking a fancy to his head. Or, possibly after lopping it off, his body. Godbadian drugs were good. Recipes came from the Outer Earth, didn't they? Or, yawn, not!

He wasn't even awake when word came to the monastery the battle for Dustmound was won; that the latest War between the Living and the Dead was as good as over. Neither was Andaemyn, his and Morgianna's zebra-skinned, 27-year old daughter. Truth was he was in much better condition than Andy, who'd barely survived an unconscionable assault upon her person by Morg's year older brother, Andy's maternal uncle, Saladin Devason, on Sedonda, Sunday, the day before the final battle on Dustmound.

Had to be admitted, as he'd only been informed that morning, Demetray-Tuesday, the 9th of Tantalar, they were both in infinitely better shape than Mama Morg. Hard not to be. She was dead. Far worse in some respects, he was told by Thartarre Holgatson, the one-armed, shaven-headed, chocolaty-skinned High Priest of Sraddha, his friend and hers, she'd turned traitor; was fighting alongside the forces of the Dead at the end.

The High Priest also told him she was slain by Blind Sundown, who was not his friend, nor hers, obviously, as she was attempting to kill Wildman Dervish Furie. Some gratitude that. Sedonda-Sunday, the day before Mithrada-Monday's victory, Furie was all that stood between daughter Andy and Saladin finishing her off.

*'Flip a coin, Sal'*, Demios could just hear the Wildman, who was his friend and should have still been hers, say. *'One side's cracked ribs, a broken leg or arm or neck; other side's a permanent disability, lifelong wheelchair at the minimum. Either way Zebra Girl there's going to an infirmary, not a mortuary.'*

Give him credit, taciturn but politic fellow that he was, Thartarre did try to put a positive spin to the grim news of his wife's last seconds At least, he was pleased to report, Morg hadn't gone to her own private morgue only to get up and fight anew. Instead, she managed to wrap herself in a shroud-like chrysalis (presumably) of her nightmare-gargoyle eye-stave's making.

She may have been fighting with the Dead, but she didn't want to fight as one. The woman did have some pride left after all. And it was still there to collect, should he be so inclined.

He was.

========

*Sometime after Melina left her the morning of the 9th, the anaesthesia finally kicked in big time and Wilderwitch was as out of it as she'd been since Harry deposited her in the Weirdom. When next she was aware of her surroundings, she immediately sensed she wasn't in the private ICU room anymore.*

*She was about to open her eyes when she heard voices. Keeping her soul-self invisible she let it come out of her long enough to see who was speaking. The only one in the room with her was Saladin Devason. He wasn't talking to himself, however. It just seemed that way.*

*"Look at that leg. Only thing this Witch will do fine is dying."*

***"I said she'll do just fine, son. I didn't say she couldn't do with refinement."***

*Wisely she recalled her soul-self and chose to go back to sleep. She'd find out the date later.*

========

The Sraddhite monastery, the main headquarters for the forces of the Living, was a Cyclopean structure akin to a Mesopotamian, Tower of Babel ziggurat. It was built early in the Head's history on one of many islands dotting Lake Sedona. Whatever its original name was, it was renamed Sraddha Isle roughly four centuries ago. Which was about the same time it became a bastion of the Living amidst the 360-degrees, lake-surrounding Land of the Dead.

Because of both its strategic and symbolic value, Nergal Vetala, the Vampire Queen of the Dead, made Sraddha Isle, not just its monastery, one of her primary targets. Sent not just her Dead Things and their allies, for the most part afterlife revenants dropped by huge, mutated, fully alive and minimally sentient vultures, ones collectively known as the Cloud of Hadd, against it. Sent her soldier, Trigregos Incarnate by then, against it as well. Which was a good percentage of the reason Demios was confined to a cot when the final battle for Dustmound was fought.

Victory, as far as those who actually needed to breathe were concerned, only partially accomplished, Sraddha Isle remained the occupational forces' HQ. Most of the bigwigs there were from Hadd's territorially immense neighbour to the west, the Subcontinent of Godbad. In spite of it being homeland for Great Byron and his tribe of Byronics, the Sarpedons, including his white-as-light twin sister Melina from long before she married Aristotle Zeross, were members of Alpha Centauri's inner circle.

And Alpha Centauri, the Fatman, through his Centauri Enterprises, effectively controlled Godbad. Which was why, the Fatman being for the most part a straight-shooter, it was officially known as the Corporate State of Greater Godbad. As such, because of their comradeship with the Fatman, Demios was well-known and respected by Godbad's military higher-ups.

Although it took him a couple of days to get mobile, he had no problem convincing Godbadian General Quentin Anvil to transport him to where Morgianna fell. Didn't have to use the coercive capacity of an open eyeorb atop his eye-stave. Which definitely was pre-Earth; may have even been pre New Weir System, it was that old. Probably wouldn't have anyhow. He didn't approve of mind-bending as a matter of basic principle.

Sooth said he was something of an iconoclast when it came to eye-staves and eyeorbs. Unlike Morg, whose favourite gargoyle was a ghostly white mare's head, a nightmare's head she termed it, he didn't approve of the essentially harmless practise of manifesting gargoyles atop them. Said it was pointless, a waste of brain power. Which, brain power, was not only what charged them – eye-staves and their orbs worked best in cities; in fact they quickly ran out of steam outside of populated regions – it was what made eye-staves and eyeorbs do what they did.

Which was quite a lot, all things considered. The Utopians of old Weir System – their Mother Machine as much or more so than their technomages – really were geniuses. Too bad their descendants here on the Earth, especially those living in the Weirdom of Cabalarkon, were mostly congenital idiots.

If pressed, he'd admit the reality of the situation was a tad different. No matter how solid a Trinondev could make them, he disapproved of the practise because his despised brother-in-law approved of it. Nonetheless, the proof was in the proverbial suet pudding. Fat lot of good manifesting gargoyles did the sad sack excuse for a squadron of Weir's Warrior Elite the ordinarily quite capable clone, Golgotha Nauroz, led against the Dead. Their casualty rates were among the highest any band of the Living suffered in Hadd.

Much better to have used the protective, force-shield-like thought bubbles they could project to hurl explosives and other incendiary devices at Haddazur-animated Zombies than to manifest gargoyles. About all gargoyles were good for was making the Ambulatory Dead fall down dead already laughing, those that had mouths left such that they could laugh.

He had yet to see a Dead Thing Walking that wasn't scarier than any goofy gargoyle.

========

Since around the turn of the 56th Century of the Dome Hadd had been covered by thick, sun-blocking, yet remarkably rain-free clouds. That it never rained in Hadd, while the largely impassable Diluvian Mountain Range that formed its northern boundary was the wettest area of the Whole Earth, was of course devil-doing. Using Outer Earth technology the Godbadian Air Force salted the non-vulturous Cloud of Hadd, thereby causing a torrential downpour that swamped the Land of the Dead.

Dustmound was a repository for inanimate corpses; native Iraches for the most part, ironically ones who once worshipped Nergal Vetala as their Life Goddess. These bodies therefore amounted to the Vampire Queen's reserve squads. Most Dead Things could not abide falling rain or running water. It was so bad fresh water actually dissolved the vulnerable ones. Hit by the deluge these reserves were decaying, liquefying, at an unheard of rate. Dustmound itself was in the final stages of collapsing in on itself when Morg was killed. As a result the ground was still so unstable no effort had been made to retrieve her remains at the time.

After over four decades together Demios, who had earned the codename Blackguard while acting as her protective shadow in their years prior to marriage, felt obliged to get hold of Morg's chrysalis-caked corpse before, now that it was drying up again, a Haddazur-occupied abomination broke through her cocoon, took it over and thereafter turned her into a Haddit zombie. After all, wasn't that why, to prevent it happening, she'd used her last gasp, mental might to wrap herself up in the first place?

Would, if she had been taken over, be an indignity to have to kill her more thoroughly, as it were, the next time they met. He, or whoever encountered her shambling corpse, would first have to mutilate it, de-arm and de-leg it in order to stop it from moving, then immolate or otherwise make an ash of its meaty detachments to stop them being stitched together and Haddazur-animated again.

The Godbadians provided him with an armoured, all-terrain vehicle and a driver. They were joined by a couple of Thartarre's Sraddhites, warrior monks fully equipped with splatter packs containing incendiary devices brought from the Outer Earth by brother-in-law Aristotle Zeross, Ringleader, Mel's much younger, wholly human husband, the week before. Once they arrived on what had been Dustmound they discovered, in place of his wife's body, a statue of her, one far too big and heavy to hoist into the back of their ATV.

It had to be a twisted joke. On the Outer Earth, prior to becoming the Ants' superior circa 1953, the Master's year younger sister had been codenamed the White Witch. Even though, as a hybrid, her face did wrinkle and crinkle, albeit very slightly, she was often described as a walking statue. Whoever had replaced her cocooned corpse with a genuine statue must have known that. Whole thing smacked of faerie tricksterism and Demios knew a couple of sick-humoured tricksters capable of pulling off just such an elaborate stunt.

They were Young Life and Young Death, Hush Mannering and Auguste Moirnoir. The former often visited the Fatman, Alpha Centauri, at Centauri Enterprises' headquarters in Aka Godbad City, while the latter actually lived in the Sraddhite Monastery. Before being devil-cursed, covered in faeriedust and morphed into perpetual seven year olds, they believed they were Pandora Mannering and Augustus Nauroz, Sal and Morg's parents.

Regardless of who made it and how it got there, Demios vowed that before he died he would erect it in the central plaza of Cabalarkon, the very heart of the Weirdom. Trouble was erecting this maddeningly mysterious, even mocking statue of his wife there probably couldn't happen until he had overthrown Saladin and become the Master himself. Still, with ever-expanding Godbad's help, he figured it wouldn't take much more than a year to achieve his lifelong goal.

Why shouldn't the Corporate State of Greater Godbad, which in large measure was responsible for the conquest of Hadd – and which was also the most Outer Earth modern civilization on the entire Headworld – add the Weirdom of Cabalarkon, the Head's most ancient one save, perhaps, for that of Corona City on Apple Isle, to its list of satellite states?

That resolved, it was just a matter of convincing the notoriously violence abhorring Fatman that that was the way to go.

========

Looking around he spotted a well-kept woman of indeterminate age, maybe somewhere in her thirties or early forties, on the largest hump of ground in the nearby area; what, because it was just a pimple of its former self, the Sraddhites dubbed Diminished Dustmound. She was dressed like a widow: hooded, veiled, and all in black. Was bending over, intent on sifting through the dirt seemingly looking for something of value.

It wasn't raining but, due primarily to the non-shambling, even graceful way, she moved they figured she couldn't be a Haddazur-animated zombie. Nor, since it was broad daylight, with nary a cloud in the sky, could she be a vampire. While she did have pale, ghost-white skin, that didn't mean much. There were lots of men and women on the Head without much in the way of skin pigmentation; his late wife for one.

Even from this distance they could see it crinkled and wrinkled, so she was no Utopian pureblood. Her clothing and the fact she had jet black hair so long it stuck out underneath her hood and veil and all but covered her upper chest, indicated she was not one of the multinational Warrior Priestesses of Sraddha either. They wore brown robes and, man or woman, invariably shaved their skulls.

That she was dressed as if in mourning might mean she lost a mate, friend or lover in the final battle for Dustmound and, ultimately, all of Hadd. That her complexion was so pale, and her hair so dark, they further agreed she was probably one of the far-ranging, seafaring Pani merchant folk who hailed from Krachla, at the southern dick-tip of the Penile Peninsula, of which Hadd was its shaft. That she was here at all suggested she had come in on a witch's stepping stone

There were plenty of Witch Sisterhoods on the Inner Earth. Most stemmed from the life-loving, so-called Superior Sisterhood of Flowery Anthea, which was named after the wife of Xuthros Hor, the Biblical Noah, and as such claimed to be antediluvian. So did the Hellions, only they claimed to be much older than the Ants and pointed to the fact they worshipped the chthonic, as in earthborn, Mother Goddess, as proof.

Which, while it did make them anti-devil, devils being skyborn or Cathonic, unfortunately tended to make them pro-demon, unsavoury sorts that most demons were — even those who spelled it with an 'a', as in daemon (originally an ancient Greek word for guardian spirit, a demigod).

Then there were the Athenan War Witches. Even though she didn't carry any visible weaponry, that's where they figured this mysterious woman's allegiance lay. Athenans were named after the Olympian Goddess of War and Wisdom. Athena was probably a devil. Of course for all he knew, not having made a study, like sister Melina had, as to which onetime worshipful goddesses were or were not devils, she may just as easily have been a complete myth.

Athenans claimed to be as life-loving as Ants and Alts (Althean witch-healers, also like Mel) but, boy, were they murder on the Ambulatory Dead. And the Undead, most specifically vampires. Battling bats, as they termed it, was their specialty. In their youth both Scylla Nereid (Fisherwoman), who'd been in Hadd fighting at his side, and Sorciere (John Sundown's decades gone wife) were trained primarily as Athenans.

Morg had lots of connections to the War Witch Sisterhood as well; had had, make that. So did Andy. But no one had more of a connection to them than Tsishah Twilight, Morgianna's, albeit not by him, first and only born besides Andy. Tsishah was the Athenan Mother Superior. Was also the retiring Anthean Aortic of Shenon,

Witch Isle. No contradiction there apparently, because War Witches only made war, in the killing sense, on those already not-alive.

Still, Tsishah was never without weaponry. So maybe he'd have Andy, once she was mobile again, break the news of Morg's demise to her. Then again maybe he better do it himself. Andy, who swore she was a Hellion, not an Athenan, and therefore very much more inclined to fight than flee – like father like daughter in that respect – was in no shape to defend herself. Might not even live long enough to leave Hadd alive. And he certainly wasn't going to allow her to walk out of Hadd any other way.

There were of course other kinds of Dead Things on the Head besides ones animated by Haddazurs. Be that as it may, he had no reason to have any similar resolve with respect to this Black Widow, as he was already thinking of her. He was curious what she was looking for, however. Obviously just as curious, and a whole lot more agile than he was, one of the bolder Godbadian servicemen patrolling what was left of Dustmound went up and spoke to her.

When he came back he said she had broken a mirror and was trying to find its pieces so she didn't have any more bad luck. They'd talked for a few minutes and, since she seemed friendly enough, he offered to help. She declined; said it kept her busy, that she had all eternity. Thereafter, since over the course of the next few days she was often seen again, Diminished Dustmound became known as Haunted Dustmound.

Should have called it Demon Mound!

========

*Although he had no idea how long it was between periods of wakefulness, Cerebrus did manage to fight off unconsciousness once in a while.*

========

Usually he opened his eyes and, once he adjusted them for the lightless conditions of his encasement, focused on himself, reflected as he was in the mirrored underside of his stone coffin. Thereupon he would stretch out the tentacles of his mind in an effort to connect with that of the others, become frustrated and promptly go back to sleep.

Sometimes he managed to make an at least tentative contact with the familiar mentalities of his six fellow members of the Damnation Brigade now living within the Weirdom: Gloriel, Furie, Wilderwitch, OMP-Akbar, Johnny and even Raven, absolutely inhuman, if perhaps not so much so inhumane, as she was. As yet he could not communicate with any of them telepathically. Not even the Witch – technically his aunt, Mother Eden being her much older sister – who was by far the most psychically sensitive even without the blood connection.

The experience was unsettling, too much like Limbo. Except he could both see, in the mirrored lid, and sense his body; a body being something he did not have and, therefore, something he could not do in the quarter century his mind or spirit was lost in the Grey. There was another difference. In Limbo he had company. Often Thalassa was there; sometimes one of the others, the Diver or OMP predominantly. They could talk. But here there was no one.

He railed silently against his loneliness, his impotence. He had a body and, Goddamn it!, that should make him stronger than he was in Limbo. Then again, on Damnation Isle back in '55, his headplate had not been damaged. Clearly the

Cathonic Fluid abetted what mental might he still retained. The combination was all that was keeping his brain functioning, albeit at such a low level; all that was preserving his life.

One day he awoke determined to get out. But how? Kid Ringo, Ringleader, wherever he was, assuming he wasn't dead and buried or otherwise disposed of by now, could teleport via his Gypsium rings. Upper level witches like Wilderwitch, the White Witch, Fisherwoman and Sorciere got around the Weird or the Grey, or whatever they were calling between-space these days, on witch-stones. His paternal cousin, the now 27-years' dead Jesus Mandam, aka the Conqueror, King Conqueror or Conquering Christ, could also teleport.

Cerebrus did not have access to rings, witch-stones or howsoever Jesse got about inter-spatially. Wilderwitch, though, had a soul-self. He had seen it, a frightening sight if ever there was one, and he knew from firsthand experience a few of the supranormals he'd come across during the Secret War of same, the roughly ten years he was able to participate in it as a supra and not as a drooling, bed-wetting near-vegetable, could externalize their ectoplasms, as it were. Externalize more than that, too, some of them.

Sedon St Synne – whom he'd learned that first few days out of Limbo back in Vancouver was still somehow alive – wasn't one of the latter but he was his godfather as well as one of the former. He called what he could do Wayfaring in the Wild Weird. Perhaps he, Cyborg Cerebrus, could learn to become a Wayfarer in the Wacky Weirdom.

First, though, he had to concentrate on sending his consciousness, his spirit as he conceived of it, outside the stone sepulchre where his body was stuck. Which he eventually did. Which was when he met the Ghost of Cabalarkon, the one-eyed, undying Utopian born in the far-off planetary system of First Weirworld.

"Lot of us around, Cabby? Spooks, I mean?" Cerebrus inquired familiarly after the ghost, who said he could call him Cabby if he wanted, introduced himself.

"Not as many as you might think considering where we are. It's not that Sleepers don't want to come out and play. Or even just have a look around. It's more like they can't. You see, Sleepers can be awakened with blood. A couple of drops and they'll sit up, take notice and even talk to you. A pint or so and they'll step out of their sepulchres and walk around for a while. But if people don't come to see us, don't drip blood in our vats, we just stay under.

"Our situation is somewhat analogous to why folks leave flowers on their loved ones' graves. They figure if they don't show they still care their loved one's spirit will become moribund; have a more difficult time resurrecting. Neglect atrophies us. In my case, the Master often visits me. In the case of most of these others, no one visits them."

"So they're more dead than sleeping."

"More, yes. But not dead. Many of those within these catacombs would revive if you sacrificed a baby. Some would get out and run a marathon if you cut open your arteries and drained your life's blood into their coffin. But you'd be dead and they wouldn't be running around for long. They'd need more and more blood. And, if they didn't get it, they'd die the Immediate Death, not persist in a semi-permanent state of Imminent Ditto."

"So you, we, are vampires."

"Not really. Without immersing ourselves in Cathonic Fluid, we would certainly die. If we got out and tried to subsist on blood, we wouldn't last very long, either. Our appetite would be insatiable. No, much better to stay in our tubs and wait for Utopian scientocrats to find the key to immortality. Or the cure for our particular disease or physical affliction.

"And that last has happened, although not in Saladin's time as Master. His predecessor, Kyprian Somata, who was also his great-grandmother, was an Anthean, their Mother Superior as it happens, but she was also a patron of both Science and the Arts. She, her Illuminaries, Ants, scientocrats, techno and biomages, actually did come up with cures once in a while; vaccines for example were discovered – more like rediscovered – in the early years of her reign last century.

"This Master, though, is a troubled man. I believe he wants what's best for the Weirdom, but he's cursed by his own heritage. Masters of Cabalarkon, which is the original and only true Weirdom left on the Whole Earth, should not be sons of devils. They should especially not be Pyrame Silverstar's son because that might make him a mortal incarnation of the Moloch Sedon, the Demon King; the devic All-Father who regards me, somewhat inaccurately, as his father.

"This Pyrame, whom her fellow devils considered the Pauper Priestess on account of she has neither a talisman to call her own nor a protectorate to call her home, is an amazingly yet, as far as I'm concerned, inexplicably unique individual. For reasons beyond me, and indeed beyond our Illuminaries, only she can bear mortal sedons, small case.

"However, since she's been gone thirty-odd years, Saladin may be the last Sedon on the Head; although again there's undoubtedly at least one other left beyond the Sedon Sphere. Otherwise, so the Moloch informs me, the Dome would collapse and either the Headworld or lands surrounding the North Pacific Ocean on the Outer Earth would be overwhelmed in the resultant Second Great Flood."

"The Moloch informs you?"

"None other. Every year around this time, the Winter Solstice, he pops by for a visit. Hey, who knows, maybe he'll even say hello to you; emphasis on the Hell."

"Something to look forward to then. How'll I recognize him?"

"Not a problem. Sed isn't the most imaginative of deities and, make no mistake about it, he is a deity in here, the top dog of the top gods. You're an Outer Earth Christian, aren't you?"

"I'm not overly religious. Neither were my parents. My mother was an Outer Earth Ant or Alt-Healer. Along with my sister Aranyani, she disappeared when I was only nine or ten years old. But my father was, and probably still is, the patriarch of the Illuminated Faith of Xuthros Hor. That's the Biblical Noah, by the way."

"We've met."

"Noah or my father?"

"Noah. He once dribbled some blood into my tub. You were saying?" Met Noah, sublimated Cerebrus. Was he really that old? More to the point, did Noah actually exist? Must have.

"Um, right. Christian? Yes. At least I was baptized and brought up a Roman Catholic."

“Then he’ll come to you as you’d know him best. He’ll come to you as Satan.”

========

*The morning of Sedonda, the 14th of Tantalar 5980, General Quentin Anvil authorized a Godbadian helicopter crew to retrieve the hefty statue of Morgianna Sarpedon that someone had left on Diminished Dustmound. Demios Sarpedon, even with the lift supplied by his impossibly old eye-stave still moving slowly, and feeling poorly, a week after his encounter with Vetala’s Soldier on Sraddha Isle, insisted upon being there in order to ensure all went well.*

*It did, though not without a curious incident having nothing to do with statuary.*

========

As the statue was being winched onto the carrier copter, he again spotted the Black Widow, as he and the Godbadians thought of the night-shrouded madwoman who had been as good as haunting Diminished Dustmound for most of that same week. Supposedly she was trying to piece together a mirror broken during the decisive battle for Hadd.

Why would anyone carry a mirror into battle? Could it be the Amateramirror, one of the Three Sacred Objects he, his wife, both her daughters, Ringleader and many another had been trying to find for decades now? Had to be. Masters of call-me-Cabby’s Weirdom brandished a replica of it on important occasions but Vetala’s Soldier, Trigregos Incarnate (Trigregos Titan, to recall an earlier Melina, not his sister, from Illuminary records) had been wielding the long lost original on Sraddha Isle a week ago. It, the original, was gone now. By all accounts OMP, Kronokronos Akbarartha now, had destroyed it the next day.

So was Vetala’s Soldier, again reportedly due to his ill-advisedly tangling with the amazingly alive and apparently unaged membership of the newly christened Damnation Brigade. He, a lifeless, eyeless husk of prematurely decrepit humanity at the end, was buried beneath Dustmound as it collapsed in on itself. There was, however, as Thartarre Holgatson was hardly the only one to report, a tinge or tingle of something else about the whole episode. Like everyone he’d queried on it, though, Thartarre’s memories of what that was exactly were muddled and fast-fading.

Demios decided he’d have to limp over, using his eye-stave to provide some degree of support as well as levitation, and have few words with her. He wanted ask her about the connection, if there was one, between the mirror whose remnant shards she was single-mindedly sifting around in the dirt looking for and the Amateramirror. Might even use the coercive capabilities of his eyeorb to ensure her soothsaying.

First, though, he had to supervise the carrier copter lifting the, to his mind, even more singular statue representing Morgianna aboard it. As he was doing so, he spotted someone speaking with the Black Widow out of the corner of his eye. The man, if man it was, manlike shape anyhow, was dressed similarly to her, entirely in black. Only it, his clothes, if clothes they were – it really was hard to see from this distance, distracted as he was – had dozens of spotlight sparkles glinting off what Demios took to be his all-covering hood and cloak.

Where had he come from, who was he and why did he inspire such an eerie impression of the night’s sky? When he looked again both had vanished.

========

***“You’ll be Gomorrah.”***

*So the male said, by way of introduction. The Black Widow, arrayed as she was in her own self-generated murk of darkness, regarded him in an absentia sort of way.*

*"I was. Partly. But, believe you me, even if you don't believe in me per se, that was a very, very long time ago."*

***"I believe you're Gomorrah, then."***

*"Then believe I've been called many things in my days and many more nights, both before and since. Believe, further, you are trifling with Mother Earth's truest servant, her most loyal daughter. Believe, finally. I am warning you off."*

***"I'd rather warm you up."***

*The Black Widow raised her veil. He was starting to intrigue her. "You look vaguely familiar. Should I know you?"*

***"Down here I'm sometimes known as the Judge."***

*"Sodom?"*

***"Close enough."***

********

# Four-Babies: WITCHES DEMONIZED

=========

**Sedonda, 14 Tantalar 5980**

*Wilderwitch didn't so much figure out where she'd been moved to on the 9th as her faithful physician, Melina now Zeross, Mel-Illuminatus, the High Illuminary of Weir, told her. It was the second to uppermost floor of Skyrise, which the Master had built in the mid-Seventies after a visit to the Subcontinent of Godbad, Mel also informed her. She and her children, whose names were Persephone, Helen and Athena, lived a couple of floors below. As for who lived on the top floor, the penthouse, that was obvious. Apparently he lived there alone as well.*

*Not that he spent most nights there anymore.*

=========

Wilderwitch was still there when Melina popped by for a moderately later than usual first visit of the day most of a week after her move. Astonishingly, given the broken ribs she suffered taking on the Medusa (Mater Matare, Mother Murder, the Apocalyptic of Death) and the smashed, very nearly severed leg caused by Flying Doltaur's harpoon going through her right thigh in the Calvary Cavern of Subterranean Temporis on the 6th, the Witch was conscious, coherent and, for her anyhow, approaching ebullient.

"What news, Mel?"

"It's the 14th."

"Thought it was. See how much better I'm getting? Today's the day you take me off the drug-drip, right? And let me see the others."

"As for the first, maybe. As for the second, we're going shopping first. As for the rest, good, bad or uncertain?"

"Going shopping?"

"It's market day so we're going shopping, all six of us, including Raven's Head. And my daughters. Furie in particular needs some new clothes. Trinondev fighting togs, even when they're covered by robes, just don't suit him and, as for his feet, well, him in sandals is almost as scary as him next to naked, though you'd know that better than me."

"I stay away from Furie, naked or not. I gather he hasn't reverted to Murray."

"Worse, I'd say he's going the other direction, getting closer and closer to the full Furie. I've never seen the full Furie – not sure anyone has – but it's beginning to look like he isn't anything remotely human. Your boy's developing horns."

"My boy, not that he is my boy, nor even my man, is Jervis Murray. We're both a mite free-spirited for monogamy. And I don't think anyone, not even him, has ever seen the full Furie. But if he's coming out, that can't be good. He must be feeling threatened."

"So he turns into an even more threatening monster. Not the friendliest of strategies. Still, given what he's been through, what you've all been through, it's a nice option to have."

"Nice is hardly the word I'd use, all the more so given the above. Look, Mel, they've been back for five days. You're not going to convince me they haven't tried to see me in five days, Furie especially. Gloriel saw me the first day and she's the one who told us the rest of them were back a couple of days later."

"Except for two; two who still aren't back. But you're right. You really aren't wondering why Gloriel hasn't come back to see you again, are you?"

"Sal's keeping them from me."

"The Master's keeping them from you, Witch. And believe me, what God wants, God gets. Think of it this way. Johnny and Raven somehow or other manufacture a nimbus about themselves, right? It keeps them from being spotted by us Normies and Normas when they're flying about ever so high and mightily above. Well, so do the top two or three floors of Skyrise. Except it's the Master doing the manufacturing. Conjuring, make that.

"Might have even got the idea from seeing Raven in action, though I don't think he ever did. I did; have, a number of times, after she showed up in what … '42 or '43?"

"End of '40, at least so I heard. Before my time. And Manitoulin might have been riding her during the Battle of Little Big Horn, sixty-five years earlier; though that might have been a different Raven's Head. Must have been. She can't be that old. But her sort are, aren't they. Xuthros Hor rode the first one, didn't he. Six thousand years or close enough for horseshoes."

Mel gave her one of those 'thought I was the Illuminary looks' but chose to return to the subject at hand, Saladin's evidently quasi-mystical Skyrise. "Funny thing, when you fly into it, the nimbus, the cloud – if you could, which only Gloriel can, if she hadn't had a relapse, since Raven still isn't up to flying yet either – they, Skyrise's top floors, don't so much have a cloud about them as they appear not to be there. You can't be found because you're here and your here isn't their there. Am I making myself clear?"

"Sal's screwing with them. Except, you're here."

"Ah, but right now I'm not there."

The Witch understood. Mel's explanation made perfect sense to her. Saladin had conjured the equivalent of a Witch's between-space Shelter. What didn't make sense was why Sal was keeping the rest of D-Brig away from her. Mel had an explanation for that as well. It amounted to Devason demonstrating who was boss. Her brother-in-law wasn't a great believer in equality of the sexes. Except in bed, it went without saying; though, again, he was more interested in satisfying himself than anyone else.

"Deals have to be struck. I'm striking most of them and so far I've managed not being struck myself. Which is no mean feat when you're dealing with a motley crew of volcanic lava-louts, only one of whom happens to be the Master of Weir. I still haven't convinced him to let them stay in Skyrise instead of that cesspit of an old palace they're bedding down in with Golgotha and Gethsemane Nauroz, their kids, and Golgotha's upper echelon Trinondevs.

"Not that I'd expect him to permit Raven's Head stay here, what with her defecation limitations in terms of toilets. Like I told Akbarartha, who's acting as your D-Brig's spokesperson, even if it's his Homeworld Sceptre doing most of the talking, it's the Master's Weirdom and you've got to make some accommodations if you want to get any decent accommodations."

"The Diver would have been proud of you for that, Mel. Defecation limitations probably came from OMP, though. Sounds like something he'd come up with. Been years, probably more than the twenty-five we were gone, since I heard OMP's cuddly cudgel yapping. I'm almost jealous. What's Sal got against Raven anyways?"

"Like I said – fay-said, more like – it's more a matter of her being resolutely not toilet-trained than anything the Master or anyone else, other than me, has against her. And, as for me, I'm a doctor, I'm hygienically inclined. Besides, it's kept them busy building her a spiffy new barn off the old palace."

"Accommodations for accommodations. Gloriel's doing manual labour?"

"Glory's doing rainbows. Other than, arguably, designing outfits that can never be as fetching on anyone as they are on her, it's what she does best. What's almost as amazing is how supportive they can be. OMP, Johnny and Furie may be three of the strongest supras there ever were but, with her around, their muscles are going to waste."

"Start with the worst then. If there is something worse than the full Furie coming out."

"There might be."

========

*And so there were, Cerebrus's condition worst of all. Were many an uncertain thing as well. But there were also good things. Being a doctor Mel liked good things. So did Wilderwitch.*

*Self-centred as she often was, she especially liked it when they had to do with her.*

========

"If I'm any judge of anything – and I am, by virtue of being a 30-plus years' medical practitioner if nothing else – your danger's passed. It better have. I busted my brain, wore out my eyeballs and ruined my manicure making sure your thigh wasn't infected. Knit it up internally as best I could and redid the stitches God knows how many times before it got to the point where I figured they'd hold. So long as you don't take up strip-teasing or ballroom-dancing anytime soon, that is."

"You don't get manicures, don't even wear makeup, and my days as an ecdysiast, especially in a ballroom, number all of one."

Stuff happens, as they say. The Witch was referring to stuff that happened starting in the Hotel Vancouver's ballroom on or about the Autumnal Equinox of 1952. A good percentage of said-stuff was born the following Midsummer. (Although not anyone by either her or Melina, Illuminatus, who was there that night. Which wasn't odd in her case, since Murray-Furie was infertile, but was in Mel's case. Of course she was a cloistered, seldom-seen Roman Catholic nun in those late days of the Suprawar.)

"Let's hope so. As for the others, I told you we couldn't do anything for Davy. But, while I'm no more a psychiatrist than I am a veterinarian – Raven's Head, please forgive – I reckon the only reason Glory's not radiant-riding today is because Raven's still a little shaky on her pin-wings. Your Angelic Rainbow doesn't want to show her up. Doesn't want to make her look up to her, either. Furie might be developing horns and hooves of his own, but we won't have to cut off either of yours, your pins, hooves, feet, nor anything above them. Thus concludes my diagnosis."

"As you may have noticed a few days ago, no matter how drug-dripped you drip-drug me, I wouldn't have let you. I'm an Inner Earth Anthean, a life-loving Ant. More, I'm a deviant, a supranormal, even if I'm not much of one compared to the others. All due apologies to you and your colleagues, but I was born knowing more about matters medical than any man, or any woman, could ever hope to learn. Another thing I learned a long time ago, my personal long time ago, not yours, is I heal rapidly."

"Then you won't miss your agates."

"I won't what?"

"As *you* may have noticed a few days ago, the Master confiscated them. All of them, your Anthean Agates and any non-Anthean whatever you want to call them. And your bottomless bag, your jewellery, your studs, your cut-anything knife. Upon my return he had me check your teeth. Then he had me x-ray you top to bottom, of your feet, not just your bottom, or your front, just in case you'd swallowed some spares. Or secreted a few wherever, any wherever, that may have escaped my very best colleagues when they first went over you."

"Under his supervision."

"Of course. The Master trusts no one. Not even me. Under his supervision, as well, he let me rummage through your bottomless bag, as you Ants call the things even if the proper word for them is kibisis." She added this last in her best 'see, who's the Illuminary now?' voice. The Witch either didn't pick up on the gauntlet or could care less, probably the latter.

"Didn't realize you could."

"Neither did I. Mind you, when I was growing up Master Kyprian taught me how to get stuff out of hers. Think what you need, she instructed me, then reach in and, if it is there, it'll be there for you to pull out. Only I had no idea what I needed when I looked into yours. Nor did I have any idea they really are as good as bottomless."

Master Kyprian was Sal's predecessor as well as his great-grandmother. The Witch had been in the Weirdom when she died, ever so mysteriously, in 5950. Although she'd been sick for a number of years, she was awfully young for a Utopian to die, barely two hundred. So why, sick as she was, hadn't she had herself immersed in a tub of Cathonic Fluid until a cure was found for whatever was ailing her? Good question; one she'd asked Kyprian before she died. Her answer was because the Weirdom still needed her. Besides, she wasn't that sick.

So, was it murder? Had to be. Was she sleeping with a murderer? Probably not. Would Mel tell her, if she knew, if she was murdered? Only by the Master's will and, for Mel, chances were she still regarded Kyprian as her Master.

"What's in them is mostly between-space."

"Funny, that's exactly what the Master said. Between-space, like All of Incain, is what he said precisely. He's obsessed with the She-Sphinx. Had a dream it, she, would be the death of him. Masters have dreams. Kyprian had them, too. She died in her sleep, you might recall. I do, I was there; was in her bedroom when she died. You know what they say: you dream you're dead, you're dead, end of game."

"You said rummage?"

"So I did. I had no idea all of what you'd hidden inside yours until the Master opened his eyeorb and shone its light into it."

"He shone his eyeorb inside my bottomless bag? You talk about having no idea how much capacity it has, I had no more of an idea he could pull off that kind of stunt than I did you could rummage."

"He is the Master, Witch. And it's a good thing he is because, after doing just that, rummaging around inside it, I pulled out a few of your jars of condiments; mixed them up with some stuff we had here and came up with some medicines we don't have here. They're why your leg's healing; not because you're willing it."

"Just like that?"

Even though her lips and her teeth moved when she spoke; even though the muscles in her face did too; it was only minimally. There was something about her eyes. They flashed, if eyes could flash. For Mel, as with most pureblood Utopian women, her eyes were a sort of semaphore. Right now they were flashing 'back-off'.

"Call it divine inspiration, if you prefer. And there's no question we could do with some divine, as in celestial, heavenly, inspiration on the Head. But, yeah."

"Wouldn't have anything to do with the fact you're a Summoning Child and that your Summoning-heritage is that of a supra-healer?"

"Sorry to disillusion. I'm just intuitive when it comes to meshing medicines."

"Oh, please! Do me a favour, Illuminatus. Please stop denying you're a supra-normal. I remember what you could do with that caduceus of yours. The pole fused with your spine, the prison-pod-slash-eyeorb became your head, the entwined snakes your arms, the wings came out of your shoulder blades. You were a flying fucking Female Fury for awhile."

"Until Electrocretan sorted me out. And she had lightning bolts when she didn't have snaky arms. That was nearly thirty years ago."

"I guess it was."

"No guessing allowed." There was that flash of the eyeballs again. "It was, believe me. Look, Witch, it'd be far better for both of us if you were the one doing me the fucking favour. Let's not talk about our past. It was a long, long time ago, recall? My past more so than yours, granted. Let's concentrate instead on our mutual future. Not good enough? Let's concentrate on your future specifically, then.

"You're my patient and I prescribe patience. Patience isn't just a virtue. Particularly in your case, it's a necessity. That still not good enough? Well, I hate to disillusion you even more, but without your agates you're about as supra as I am now. Nor any of my regular clientele are any day of the week."

Wilderwitch took that as a challenge. There was nothing she liked better than challenges. Other than surviving them, that is. "Don't be too sure of that."

"Come on, Witch. Casting sensory illusions and an ability to externalize your soul-self are only borderline supra-talents to start with. After enough training most old-time witches can do either/or. Other thing is, you can have all the strength and speed of any animal you and your Damnation Brigade damn well please but, with a leg like yours, all you'll do is slow down your recovery exercising it. That's why I brought you this."

Melina now Zeross did not have a bottomless bag as such; nor did she carry a doctor's little black bag. She had brought with her a shoulder satchel, however. Was probably where she'd stashed her caduceus, since she wasn't holding it, let alone waving it about when she was trying to emphasize a point, but her mostly immobile face wouldn't allow it. She picked up the satchel and from it pulled out a rod-like object, one with a Trinondev's eyeorb, or prison pod, attached to one end and a wrist strap to the other.

"Don't tell me. Every witch should have a magic wand."

"Not sure it's witches who have magic wands, Witch. Even if you do, it isn't. It's a sawed-off eye-stave. Like the Master's Mace."

"I know what it is, Mel. You've got one too, your caduceus. Unless you'd care to admit it's a devic power focus." Melina glared at her. The Witch chalked up another minor victory, but didn't press the point. Quite the opposite. "Joking aside, although it wouldn't take much to make up more than a few more, Sal carries his around like a little girl does her dolly, or a little boy his security blanket. Says it's a speaking stick, on account of no one can lie to him when its orb's open."

"They can't."

"Good thing I'm such an honest person then. He's not the only one, either. You all did, back in the early days. You, Morg, Demios, the Trinondevs, and Sal as well, before he won the Challenge of Weir and earned Master Kyprian's Mace. Plus, if memory serves, which it should do given who my mother might have been, Harry's Mama Meg had one as well. Before she got hold of whatever else was left inside the Olympian Tantalus back in whenever, a year or two after the war; the World War, not the Secret War."

"Where I got my caduceus." An admission. Guess Mel knew I knew and didn't feel like disputing it anymore, the Witch reckoned. "Thought we weren't going to talk about the past."

"We weren't. But it's true. That's why we used to call her Meg-aura, not Megaera."

"Wasn't disputing it. You want?"

"I want."

"Good. You're not likely to need it against devils here in the Weirdom. Nor is a mini eye-stave much of an offensive weapon; not to the extent skilled Trinondevs can make of regular eye-staves anyhow. However, you can levitate with it and that should at least get you up and about to the bathroom at the same time it keeps you off your feet."

"Thought-bubble force shield might come in handy, too."

"Only if you're better than the person you're trying to keep away from."

"I was thinking of Furie. Who were you thinking of?"

"I know you were," Actually Mel wasn't so sure of that. After an additional moment's hesitation she decided to verbally venture another reason she was giving it to her.

"Listen, Witch, the Master hates witches; all kinds of witches but Ants most especial. No matter how good your memory is you've probably forgotten, if you ever knew, that his mother was an apprentice Anthean at the time she had him, and became a fully trained one in the years immediately after she had Morgianna. That she – her name was Pandora Mannering – couldn't resist possession by Pyrame Silverstar, and that consequently he's been forever-after tainted by the name Devason, is only part of why he despises witches.

"Now who's talking about the past?"

Melina did a double-take, as if pretending to look for some else in the room. It was an obvious effort at humour. And Mel did have a sense of humour. Seldom laughed at her own jokes, which was just as well. Outsiders like the Witch found a full-blooded Utopian woman clucking away without being able to crack much of a smile very unsettling. Of course, had she been able to crack a normal, howsoever broad, smile her whole face might have cracked off.

"Must be me. Hear me out anyways. You're right. The Master won the Mastery during a Challenge of Weir he issued in 5950. You were here with Fey, your daughter, who was only three or four then. So was I. So were the Nightingales, Eden and Aranyani, Davy and Saul's mother and sister. We were looking after Master Kyprian when it took place.

"Morg, my brother and I weren't allowed to compete because we're Summoning Children. That is to say we were only 29 at the time and rules were you had to be at least thirty in order to qualify for the Challenge because that's the age of your majority here in Cabalarkon. Anyone younger than thirty is still a kid."

"Because Utopians, even if they're not quite purebloods like Morg and Sal, live so much longer than we humans, supras and non-supras alike. I didn't buy it then and don't buy it now. Strikes me as awfully arbitrary, but that's the way it was." (Sal wasn't Fey Woman's father any more than Murray-Furie was, but that didn't mean they weren't intimate long before Limbo.)

"And is to this day. There's more to it than just age of course. There was, rather. We Utopians used to go through years of schooling, asceticism, yogic exercises, meditation training, you know the routine, all in aid of maturing our brain, like a fine wine. Traditionally, Trinondevs couldn't even become Trinondevs until they were thirty. Their brains just weren't sufficiently mature for them to wield their eyestaves properly, don't you know. But that had all gone by the wayside long before we came along; long before Master Kyprian had as well."

"Because Utopians had inbred themselves to the point of idiocy."

"Not all of them obviously. My brother and I, our parents, and many another, we're not imbeciles but we can still call ourselves, themselves, True Utopians. But True Utopians have been concentrated in Cabalarkon for far too long. So, yes, up here we're in the minority in terms of being non-imbeciles.

"As for the rest of the globe, both sides of it, Utopian genes are strong. They're just so mixed up with humanity's it's difficult to tell who has enough left to reinvigorate our race. But that's my job, and that of my Illuminaries. One of them. But I'm straying. We were talking about the Master and the Challenge of Weir."

"The 30-year thing, I remember. You figured that's why Sal issued it then; not because Master Kyprian had been ill for so long even more things than was usual for around here were falling apart."

"That's what Demios figured; figured a few others things as well, rightly or wrongly."

"Such as?"

"Such as, obviously, he'd have easily won the Challenge had it been issued a year later. You see, Ubris Nauroz – Master Kyprian's son-in-law, her favourite, and that of most Utopians in the early years of this century – had bequeathed him his eye-stave, which he still has. Ubris claimed it came from New Weirworld with the original Trinondevs of Weir; that it was the oldest one still extant, which it may well be. The way Demios had it figured that should all-but-guarantee him the Mastery once he came of age. Figured further that's why Master Kyprian was hanging on, refusing to immerse herself in a tub of Cathonic Fluid."

"So she could hand him the Master's Mace on a platter."

"Precisely, though he'd have liked a few heads on it as well. Needless to say Saladin, who's always fancied his head, as I do mine, didn't see it that way. Neither did Master Kyprian, truth told. Even toward the end she did not, shall we say, encourage pretenders to her throne. And, to be fair to Kyprian, things didn't start going really off-kilter until a few years after she became sick."

"Kyprian wanted you and Sal to marry."

"So did Saladin. Me, I wasn't interested. Didn't want to become Master, either. Still don't. Probably neither did Morgianna, not that she can anymore. Nor does that matter anymore; not any more now than it did then. Rules say anyone over thirty can petition for a Challenge of Weir and, the moment he did so, turned thirty, Sal did so; called for a Challenge. Rules don't say you have to be a Utopian, though, and Kyprian appointed a certain Lady Achigan, Scylla Nereid, codenamed Fisherwoman on the Outer Earth, to be her champion."

"Who also just happened to be the estranged wife of the King of Godbad."

"Exotic as well estranged, Witch, as you well recall. A whole lot stranger than you or your other sister via the Dual Entities, Eden Nightingale, as well. And it's ex-King Achigan Auranja nowadays, just in case you were wondering. He and Fish have had so many ups and downs since then, I can't remember if they're back or forth in terms of their marriage right now. Which-witch is almost as weird-in-the-Weirdom as Fish. I'm the High Illuminary. Protocol's supposed to be one of my specialties. It's part of my job to know these things."

"Why is it everyone starts fay-saying when we talk about Fish?"

"Because we're no good at fishifying?"

"Hey, I can spout Fishisms with the best of them, even Her Majestic Cold-Bloodedness. Just don't get me going, okay, or we'll both reef-regret it. So, you're fay-saying Fish's still alive. Thought she might be. Sister's a regular catfish, isn't she?"

"Three or four times, maybe more. Has had more lives than a kitty litter of catfish, has our ever-fishifying Fishwife. Starting to get where I'm going with this?"

"Sal's mother was an Ant. For something like sixty or seventy years before she died, even more mysteriously than how she got sick in the first place, Master Kyprian wasn't just an Ant, she was our Mother Superior. Due to her uncharacteristic carelessness when it came to losing girl-children, Sister Scylla probably shouldn't have been eligible to become one, but Kyprian made the lovely Lady Achigan Auranja her pet-goldfish project and finished Fish's training anyhow.

"Sister Eden became in-here's Mother Superior of our life-loving Superior Sisterhood, that of Flowery Anthea, Noah's wife, after Kyprian died. Morg, Sal's sister, became out-there's Superior a couple of years later. He's demonized her because she married Demios, his nearest and least dearest rival to the Mastery, a man with an eye-stave even older than the Master's Mace. How am I doing so far?"

"The Master didn't demonize her; more like Morg did it herself. Which is why she became known as the Morrigan. But you're forgetting someone."

"Just shy about drawing attention to myself. When I wasn't on the outside I hung out with Eden and Aranyani while I was toting around Fey back in the late Forties. I was hanging with you and the Nightingales right here when Kyprian was dying, yet for some reason refused to resign the Mastery and immerse herself like Sal wanted her to do.

"I fought, mostly on the same side, with his little mother and his little father, if Hush and her Aug the Dog are his devil-cursed parents. Fought alongside Fish, Demios and Morg as well, again mostly on the same side, for years and years. And it's a toss-up as to which one Sal hates more in particular than he hates all witches in general.

"Oh yes, almost didn't forget, Fish isn't just my sister in Flowery Anthea. Like Eden Nightingale was, she's my sister in the recurring Dual Entities; at least so Miracle Memory told us in the late Thirties, when I was about the same age your Helen is now. Got it, Mel. Got all of it. What I don't get is how you think giving me a metallic marigold is going to protect me from the Master?"

"Metallic marigold isn't bad. Better than a mike on a spike, as I think someone – probably the Diver, his English was always pretty good – called mine at the Amsterdam Academy before the Second World War broke out for real. But, you're right, it won't. Not for long, if at all. Might give you a better chance at getting away than having nothing is all."

"You're a witch, too. If he hates all witches, why doesn't he hate you?"

"He does. For lots of reasons, and not just because I jilted him. If it weren't for Harry I'd have been tossed out a long time ago; tossed out again, I should say. I'm only an Althean witch-healer, though. We don't much dabble in esoteric stuff. Besides, I started my medical training on the Outer Earth in the Forties and finished my degree in Godbad when I became a nun in order to avoid the Fatman's sanctions for siding with Fish and Achigan in its civil war."

Greater Godbad's Fatman, the Witch knew, wasn't born Alpha Centauri. Centauri Enterprises founder and presumed main man to this day was born Alfredo Sentalli on the Outer Earth a year or so, or maybe just a matter of months, before her. She also knew he was the sometimes shell of Thrygragos Byron; had been since 1945 out there, 5945 in here. She even recalled Gloriel once telling her that he was the godson of her father, Raphael D'Angelo, this despite the fact that he was born in Toronto and the Family D'Angelo didn't emigrate to Canada until the Forties.

(Regardless of whether or not her birth mother was Miracle Memory humanized by whomever – probably Krepusyl Evenstar, Twilight's Grey Lady, the second-born Lazaremist who was once, over a thousand years earlier once, Mariamne Dawnstar, Daybreak's Bright Lady – she had a good memory. At least she had a good memory in here.)

"I don't use any of the hands-on mumble-jumble Alts are so notorious for when it comes to doing my doctoring. Of course, even if we do trade with them occasionally, albeit through third parties who still pay us what amounts to tribute – hence the x-ray machines and most of the other Outer Earth modern diagnostic equipment we use in the hospital – the Master has no time for Godbadians either.

"Neither did Kyprian, as you'll remember. They worships devils, always have, whereas our reason for being is to obliterate them. That's why our ancestors came to the Whole Earth in first place all those millennia ago. I'd be a qualified physician on the Outer Earth. And the Master has admired Outer Earthlings ever since Master Kyprian sent he and Morg, Demios and I, there to attend the Academy of Man in the late Thirties."

"With Fisherwoman as their only slightly older vanguard."

"Not just Fish. Granny Garuda and her apprentice, your Sorciere, preceded us. Even today, albeit thanks mostly to Harry, they're the key to his continuing Mastery."

"Tell me about it."

"Sort of already did, didn't I? Part of my job, isn't it?"

"Detecting Utopian genes in outsiders. Tell me more about it."

"Oh, I will. You aren't going anywhere for a long while. Certainly not away from Cabalarkon; the territory, if not just the city. Not without agates you aren't. Haven't got to the best of the best yet. Why don't you step outside onto the balcony and see for yourself. It's probably still dark enough."

"Naughty, Mel. Seems to me, keen-eyed medical practitioner that you are, you'll have already noticed I'm not walking so well. Give me a couple of days to master this undersexed lollipop of yours and I might be able to kindly oblige you. In the meantime, why don't you just tell me what I'll see if I did."

"The Sedon Sphere, what else? There's a whole lot less stars up there than there were prior to the Night of the Dark Stars, as the night of the 30th of Maruta has already been recorded in our annals, but there are some new ones in the southwest quadrant. Really bright ones. Don't know how you and your D-Brig pulled it off, assuming it was your bunch who did it, but Bodiless Byron and his Primary Nucleoids are shining away upstairs for the first time in recent memory. There are also four entirely new stars in Constellation Apocalypse. We're pretty sure one of the original ones is still missing, but it beats hell out of where we were on the 30th."

"So why aren't I jumping for joy?"

========

*The launching of the Cosmic Express took place on Centauri Island, on the other side of the Cathonic Dome from Aka Godbad City, on the 30th of November 1980. Two weeks later the War of the Apocalyptics was over, virtually everyone who dared play a Trigregos Gambit had lost, Helios was no longer on the Moon, and Cerebrus David Ryne was a ghost.*

*It could be worse, he supposed. He could be dead.*

========

They – Cabalarkon, the black-skinned, one-eyed ancient in his illusory, royal-purple gown, and Cerebrus, he in his equally illusory muslin robe with its hood pulled up to cover his damaged headplate – spoke of many things this day, the morning of the 14th of Tantalar 5980 as call-me-Cabby told Cerebrus it was under the Dome. Among them, Cerebrus wondered if he, spiritual sort that he now was, could possess other people, like Master Devas did? Cabby said that was impossible. Utopians and humans were very much alike, were even biologically compatible species, but they weren't devils.

"As the Master observed the first day he placed you down here in our company, you are in all likelihood a deviant, one with considerable psychic prowess. You may eventually be able to escape your physical confinement by yourself. Your body isn't the problem; your brain tissue is. And from what the Master told me, so is your headplate. Scientocrats should be able to reconstruct it, once they have a chance to go over it in a lab, except they dare not remove it.

"They do and, fluid or no fluid, you would probably die instantly. I say probably and probably presents too great a risk to you in particular, I'm sure you'd concur. On the other hand, if you knew how your headplate was built, you should be able to telepathically impart that information to them."

"I was shot in the head in '39 and mostly a vegetable until the Christmas Holidays of '46. As for how my headplate was built, all I know is who did it. Who was there when they implanted it, put better. And most of them are dead. Fact is, but for my father, a man named Milo Mind and the Diver, I think all of them are dead."

"Surely there were witches involved. Wilderwitch, as you and I both know her – me from going on thirty years ago, you from as good as yesterday – made it back to the Weirdom at the same time you did. Set your mind's eye on her. See if you can get inside her head. You might be able to pick up something useful."

"I have, from my tub, though only in a scraping-the-surface way. She's not in much better shape than me; seems as out of it as I am most of the time. They must be drugging her, keeping her borderline comatose so as to prevent the pain from completely overwhelming her. About the only one I seem able to get to with any regularity is this Master of yours, Saladin. And if you'll pardon the literary allusion, while I can read him like a book I'm having trouble figuring out what language he's written in."

"Doesn't surprise me. Still, he's the only one who's given you any blood and you couldn't ask for a better place to start expanding your horizons. Try wayfaring to him."

Cerebrus did. Succeeded as well.

========

*Before leaving her to go shopping and, it turned out, a few other things, including welcoming husband Harry and the Diver back to the Weirdom of Cabalarkon, Melina Zeross performed another of her excruciatingly thorough examinations. Pronouncing the Witch in remarkably good condition for someone who'd come within a catfish's whisker of losing her life a week ago, she detached the anaesthetic I.V. and propped her bed-back up such that she could come as close to sitting as she had since arriving in the Weirdom.*

*She stayed in that position most of the morning. If she wasn't napping she was playfully experimenting with the stunted eye-stave, it and its multipurpose eyeorb, Mel had given her. Had pretty much abandoned manifesting grotesque gargoyles and was working on a flowering marigold, albeit one with flabby tentacles instead of pretty petals, when the Master walked in for rare daylight visit.*

*Considerate fellow that he was he brought his own darkness with him.*

========

"Greetings, Witch. Perhaps you can advise me. I'm trying to decide whether I should I call you Cynthemis Dyana or just plain Cynthia."

It was no secret Melina Zeross spoke to Gloriella nee D'Angelo Dark even more often than she did to her; no secret she had been speaking two or three times a day to their fellows in D-Brig ever since their return from Hadd. The Witch was under no illusions Mel didn't report damn near everything she spoke about with any of them to the Master. So Saladin Devason would know she liked to use Cynthia as a kind of nom-de-non-guerre.

Cynthemis Dyana, though, was her secret name, arguably her real name, the one her just as arguable mother claimed she'd given her when she was born. Witches did that sort of thing and the Female Entity, Miracle Memory, if she was her mother, had to have been at least part witch some of the time. She was, after all, part something all of the time; came with being a three-thing. But how could Saladin know it if Mel didn't? Had the darkness he'd brought with him told him? And if so, how had she known it? Oh, oh.

Wilderwitch braved her best bluster. "Don't waste any of your seemingly few and far between little grey cells on that, Sal. I've told you before, or if I haven't, I'll tell you now, Witch will do just fine. Who's your sad excuse for a girlfriend – Murk Mist, Mad for Mud Magpies? She looks likes she could use some brightening up. And I know just the fellow to do that. Got a solar spear tailor-made for the job."

Devason might not have caught the Witch's reference to an oft-told tee-tee tale – oft-told in the Land of Twilight anyhow – of how a Lazaremist Master Deva, Mariamne Dawnstar, she of Daybreak, whom the Romans had as Aurora, came to become Krepusyl Evenstar, she of Crepuscule. (The Aztec equivalent was Tlahuizcalpantecuhtli, except he was a lord, like Lucifer, not a lady.)

May have forgotten it or, if he had never heard it before, didn't let his ignorance ruin his otherwise sunny disposition. In her considerable experience, with a variety of men and women guys like Saladin, never let stupidity spoil their gloating.

"This," he said, introducing his dusky companion, "Is the lovely Lilith. She's a demon queen; make that the Demon Queen. You might have heard of her. She's the mother of Anti-Patriarch Cain, Slayer of Abel, amongst many another. You're going to bear our child; whom I might name Abel simply because Lily's never had an Abel before."

"The fuck I am, Sal." Wilderwitch encased herself in a transparent globe generated by the eyeorb and levitated toward the ceiling. So far so good. Next stop – though she hoped she'd have enough oomph not to stop dead – was the window. Too bad Saladin was carrying the Master's Mace, his 'Speaking Stick'. Not that it spoke. Miss Murkiness did.

"Oh, look, Sodom. Wicked Witchie wants to play ball."

"Not bad, Lily. I was going to say 'the fuck you are, Witch – momentarily!' No, check that, I'll go with Cynthia. And call me Saladin. Sodomy's kind of outré for me."

"Don't be so homophobic, to quote an unfortunately too long a time occupant of mine. Of course she'd more likely just call you an asshole. And Lily strikes me as overly much in the nasal-spray-way of pollinating poetics. So I better go with sinful Cynthia myself."

"You're not a fucking faerie, are you? You're starting to sound like my mother."

"I'm fucking demon with a brain. If that make me a fucking faerie, so be it. I'm the full glass half full with one; filled up with the other. Shall I catch her?"

"Don't bother. She's headed in the right direction. My bed's bouncier. Besides, it's got mirrors."

========

Masterly Mace, even if Saladin did, as often as not, call it a speaking stick, overruled other eye-staves in the Weirdom. Overruled dinky facsimiles of them, too. Like the Witch's metallic marigold, with or without tentacle-petals. Wouldn't have been the Master's Mace if it didn't. As for why Lilith was only partly Gomorrah, a very, very long time ago, that was also partly why Saladin Devason was called Devason; that is, the half son of a possessive devil.

Half-Mama-Devil's name – not that she had a name as such, the name she was most commonly known as then – was Pyrame Silverstar. It was only quite sometime later on, after she ceased being half-Gomorrah, that her fellow devils started calling her the Pauper Priestess. Which was highly ironic in most respects because the assassination attempt, by asteroid, that she and her Sodom escaped by fleeing the Dead Sea's shores in the Outer Earth's Middle East to the Inner Earth's Sedon Peak, on the Cattail Peninsula, in the Year of the Dome 2000, set it off.

The lava that had been flowing there, then as now Tvasitar Smithmonger's home, was molten Brainrock. Wouldn't be devic power foci without it.

Power foci, combined with debrained daemonic bodies, rendered devils individually solid beings. Pyrame, thanks to occupying – and thereafter sublimating – Demon Queen Lilith, had already been independently solid for two thousand years by then. That they called her thusly was due to the fact that she had no Tvasitar-fashioned Brainrock talisman to call her own. To some it sounded rude. Pyrame, Lilith inside rather than outside her, thought it funny. Without her, them, devils would never have any of their own.

Even though she often lived with Sedon-come-to-ground in Grand Elysium, prior to the Atomic Twins rendering it uninhabitable circa 4825 YD, Pyrame had no devic protectorate to call her home, either. Unless it was Incain, All's external domain. Which, being a pristine but extremely isolated beach at the base of an almost vertical mountainside, had no inhabitants. Which made it a waste of space for devils since they thrived on worship.

Pyrame didn't need worshippers. She had Lilith. Then, come 5950, she didn't.

=========

*For Gloriella nee D'Angelo Dark, learning that much of the Headworld was inhabited by devil-worshippers answered the question that had been plaguing her virtually from the moment Demon Land brought her back from Limbo. Why hadn't God Almighty damned these devils to Hell already?*

*He had. Sedon's Head was Hell on Earth!*

********

# Five-Babies: BLUR OF THE MOMENT

========

**Sedonda, 14 Tantalar 5980**

*She was happy with Gloriel; with being addressed as Gloriel, rather. Wasn't very happy about much else. Wasn't even certain she should be happy about being alive.*

========

Gloriel had a reputation for being much more fragile mentally than physically.

A week and a day after her ordeals in Temporis and Sisert, she wasn't doing too well in either department. Neither was Raven's Head. At least she wasn't flying again. Hadn't done so after Temporis on the 6th either, though of necessity she found her second wind and put paid to Nergal Vetala in Hadd on the 8th. Whereupon, not long thereafter, she flew Sundown and OMP-Akbar to the comparative security of Sraddha Isle.

As for whether that was because she couldn't or just wouldn't fly, even her fellow Wakinyah Thundercloud Being, aka Creature of the Cosmos, Blind Sundown, had no way of knowing. Raven simply wasn't telling. Or if she was, Gloriel wasn't understanding her. (Besides Sundown, only Wilderwitch and the irreplaceable Mel-Illuminatus could do that.) She was on her feet, even if they were hooves, however, and graciously allowed Gloriel ride her.

The other three, Dervish Furie, OMP-Akbar (properly Akbarartha, the deposed Kronokronos Supreme of Subcranial Temporis) and her usual rider, John Sundown, the apparent Irache holding Raven's reins such that he could see through her eyes, strolled alongside them. Together, leisurely making their way through the weekly market set up in the great central square of Cabalarkon, these five already legendary devil-fighters made a splendid sight.

Perhaps just as unforgettably, the High Illuminary of Weir and her three half-human daughters were right there walking with them. As always when she was out in public the High Illuminary was carrying her caduceus. Mostly from the way it glowed perhaps too many, of the less than avid celebrity-blinkered, onlookers were like the Witch and suspected it wasn't just a stunted eye-stave, with her manifesting, instead of a gargoyle, the emblem of her medical profession.

Didn't matter to even those suspicious few. She was theirs, not the devil whose power focus she'd somehow purloined. Pureblood Utopians couldn't be possessed.

She additionally was living testimony to the old adage: Doctor, heal herself. Wasn't anything wrong with her, was there. She was about to turn sixty, most knew. Was a Summoning Child like many another still living in the Weirdom; like even more – including his year younger, now reputedly killed-in-Hadd sister, Morgianna, and brother-in-law Demios, the High Illuminary's twin – the Master, whose mother hadn't been a pureblood, exiled after winning the Challenge of Weir in 5950.

Yet, even for a slow-aging pureblood she was exceedingly well-preserved. Was, all agreed, as porcelain beautiful as ever; the Utopian embodiment of female perfection. All in all then, all also agreed, it was as if the gods had deigned to walk amongst them. Was really too bad the one on the raven-doe was so unattractive.

What made it even more enjoyable for the throngs gathering to watch them parade about, as Warriors of Weir were wont to do anyhow, was they had an honour guard of both those selfsame, albeit only mostly male Trinondevs, manifested gargoyles rampant atop their eye-staves, and the High Illuminary's self-evidently not quite so high-up Illuminaries accompanying them. Had to be admitted, mostly by the men amongst the masses, some of whom were drooling – no imbeciles they – that the female Dr Zeross's mostly female Illuminaries were as buff as their skin was seemingly buffed, shiningly so.

True, it was an unseasonably warm Sedonda for Tantalar. True as well, only a week or so before the Winter Solstice – and winters in Cabalarkon could get awfully, well, wintry – the comparative warmth was welcome. But it wasn't just because the weather allowed some of the more adventurous Illuminaries to go about in sleeveless tops and, shockingly, in skirts, which were seldom seen in the Weirdom and then usually only on children or teenage hybrids such as the Zeross girls.

There was a fresh breeze in the air and it wasn't, someone remarked, figuratively speaking, just wafting in from Fearsome Fobbiat. Was an air of, he hoped, refreshing change that had nothing to do with the changing seasons. The outward signs were certainly there. Although some of the Trinondevs on parade were far too young to be proper Trinondevs — after nearly 30 years of an all-male Warrior Elite they were also far too female.

While not very many of the Illuminaries were men – some things never changed – they were at least out and about as a group. Rarely before, at least in recent memory and even then probably not since Master Kyprian's time, had Illuminaries been seen in public as just that, Illuminaries of Weir. Master Saladin must be mellowing. Either that or because these outsiders were supposedly her friends, albeit rumours had it from decades earlier, the High Illuminary was at last evolving from being a mere functionary into an effective, liberalizing counterforce to his publicly proclaimed, ultraconservative opinions on a woman's place in society.

Other than as caregivers, teachers, scientocrats, if their natural aptitudes couldn't be redirected more appropriately, and, on suitable occasions, as arm-candy for his now tragically, Hadd-decimated Trinondevs, he believed women were best seen out of home with their children in tow. He definitely wouldn't approve of sleeveless tops whereas his definition of skirt would be of a dress ending just above the ankle rather than below it.

Had to be said in his favour that he never expressed much interest in what went on behind anyone's closed doors. Of course, notoriously unmarried heterosexual that he was, that was because he didn't like to be perceived as a hypocrite. And, especially over the last couple of decades, what went on behind his closed doors could hardly be construed as ultraconservative in the traditional, Outer Earth sense of the word.

Was, he'd say, more like ambitiously preservative. Was, many an imbecile of Weir did say – without fear of retaliation, since he needed their mindfully enthusiastic support for the Mastery as much as they needed him to keep everything working properly – sheer profligacy. The Master had had dozens of women and they'd had perhaps not quite so many dozens of children, not one of whom had reached the age of twenty as yet.

All were hybrids. Couldn't be anything else given their father was a hybrid himself, but some were more noticeable in that regard than others. Virtually all were as healthy, as in non-idiotic, as he was. All were unacknowledged and to a one lived as if they were non-born clones. Which was to say they had surrogate parents, development teams they were called, like Golgotha and Gethsemane Nauroz – whose children probably were clones – looking after them.

If they acted hoity-toity, haughty, self-important; in other words if they acted as if they belonged to the Master, regardless of whether they were or weren't his offspring, they were punished. It was almost a rule of thumb in the Weirdom, the metropolis of Cabalarkon and its surrounding, remarkably verdant countryside, that if a kid looked unkempt, underfed, under-clothed, at all more deprived than most, chances were he or she was the Master's child.

Liberalization was probably inevitable.

The Master was fanatically reclusive but the Zerosses were anything but. While the youngest, Tina, was a handful for anyone, her parents most especial, the two oldest, Persephone and Helen, were outgoing and friendly. Were, in Outer Earth parlance, approaching the category of teen and preteen pop idols amongst the hybrids. Were almost as popular among regular Utopian boys and girls, both born and non-born, their own ages. As for those in their twenties or early thirties, their admiration for the Zerosses was often equally genuine; only more mutedly so.

The Family Zeross spent a great deal of time travelling. With their father having those astonishing rings of his, they even went to Outer Earth on a fairly regular basis. (Devils couldn't do that, not on their own and not without a tunnel through the Dome like the one that supposedly existed in Aka Godbad City.) Didn't just bring back Outer Earth fashions either. They brought back Outer Earth attitudes.

They were – not that their father had been seen for awhile – the closest thing the Weirdom of Cabalarkon had to a royal family.

These outsiders, though, made for some pretty stiff competition.

========

At perhaps 6½ feet Kronokronos Akbar may not have been as tall as most of the men and some of the Utopian women but, in terms of width and breadth, he was about the size of two or three of them standing back-to-back-to-back, arms-in-arms. His florid face, great beard and shaggy, greying mane suggested an advanced age for a human or near-human. Nonetheless, he appeared perfectly capable of snapping any one of them in two, as if they were matchsticks.

Near-human, in the first place, because he claimed his parents were faeries. Non-human, in the second place, because he made no secret he was a Devason, like their Master of the last 30 years. Rumours being rumours some had already pegged him for Saladin's ... what? Quarter-brother in that they shared the same devic half-mother, Pyrame Silverstar. While that may or may not be true – a certain

High Illuminary of Weir on Earth believed his devic mother was Malar Tzigame, Byron's Butterfly – there was no question he had a devic half-father, Dand Tariqartha, he of his now former devic protectorate, Subcranial Temporis.

The six foot long, rune-carved cudgel he always carried with him ended in a 3-eyed head deliberately fashioned to approximate that of that selfsame Master Deva, Lazareme's Earth Magician, whose star had been shining out of the night's sky since the 6th of Tantalar. Even though Lazaremists were generally considered at least marginally more acceptable than Byronics and Mithradites, a devil was a devil and a Devason was, um, a matter best not mentioned in public places due to walls having Masterly ears in Cabalarkon.

As if to do for the on-looking Utopian women what Mel-Illuminatus and her female Illuminaries were doing for Utopian men, he wore of a tanned tunic that fell to just above his knees. A 50-year old tree trunk would be jealous of legs like that. The rest of his outfit wasn't much to write home about, though.

What little else there was of it consisted of a broad, light green sash about his belly and a long, dark green cape whose ends were clipped together by a globular pendant or medallion that bore upon it a facsimile of Sedon's Head, placed as it was in the Outer Earth's North Pacific Ocean. This pendant or medallion bore a dubious resemblance to the banner used by CE (Centauri Enterprises), the expansionist, for profit, we-make-everything conglomerate that gave the Corporate State of Greater Godbad its (bad) name.

Dubious because the subcontinent's devil-lovers weren't satisfied with their Outer-Earth-derived knowhow. CE had designs on the Weirdom's incredibly ancient, undeniably extraterrestrial technology. Since no one was too sure how anything up here worked, let alone what most of the stuff stored in the Grand Cathedral did, logical sorts argued the Godbadians should be allowed to at least try to figure it out.

'And have them turn it on us?' the vast majority, and not just the Imbeciles of Weir, countered. 'Over their dead bodies, albeit only after cremation and even then only after their ashes were scattered over the sea.'

(The neighbouring, on three sides, Ghostlands were said to be uninhabitable, but that was only true in terms of living beings. Dead Things walked there; hardly all of them were Vetalazurs, who couldn't abide rainy weather; and, even if the azuras animating them supposedly couldn't possess purebloods, no one was too sure that didn't apply to low-watt imbeciles. Consequently nobody wanted to tempt fate by leaving corpses lying around that might get up and go in search of their next meal.)

Like the rest of OMP-Akbar's clothing, the pair of ordinary brown riding boots he wore had seen better days. For many of the women there having difficulty containing their oohs and ahhs, it was almost as if he was saying: 'Ladies, form your line-up over there and bring your needles and thread. The finalists will both get to see me naked but the winner will be the best seamstress.'

Only he'd probably try to fay-say it.

========

Although he had no facial hair and was more than half a foot shorter than his massive companion, John Sundown was also a powerfully built man. Cloaked as he was in buffalo hide – a star blanket he called it – he too presented a magnificent figure. He wasn't just decked out in his star blanket, either. On his head he wore an *'issiwun'*, a de-skulled bison head with its horns pointed upwards while about his empty eyeholes he'd strapped a colourfully-beaded blindfold. A similarly strung-together bead breastplate or chest protector was overtop his embroidered, leather shirt. Leather pants and moccasins completed his ensemble.

Carrying his solar spear, its spearhead giving off the faint but perceptible glow of Brainrock-Gypsium, with his dark hair braided and falling to his chest, all that was really lacking was war paint. Not that anyone in D-Brig was complaining. War paint meant just that, war. As in against the Apocalyptics in Temporis and the Ambulant Dead in Hadd, post-Limbo.

As in when he pursued his Vengeance Quest throughout much of the latter half of '53 and the first half of '54 against the likes of the Warriors of the Writhing Moon and various renegade King and Queen Conquerors after Sorciere was butchered, in June of '53, while she was giving birth. As in on Christmas Day '53, in the midst of his Quest, when he, carrying a Soviet-made H-bomb, rode Raven's Head against the Conquering Christ and The Rache on Salvation Island. As in on all too many occasions even before he was blind; even before the Secret War commenced in early '38.

Right now all any of D-Brig, Raven and Sundown included, were hoping for was an extended time of peace such that if they had to go into battle again, which it seemed like they always did, they'd be sufficiently healed to stand a chance of healing anew later.

========

As for Sundown's beast, although ravendeer had once been native to the relatively nearby Mystic Mountains, Sedon's Crown, not a one of the often extraordinarily long-lived Utopians had seen the likes of Raven's Head. Creatures all but identical to her were the stuff of legend. Melina's underling-Illuminaries had bruited it about over the course of the last few days that devils not only once feared them, they sought to eradicate them.

Which was why there weren't any left in the Mystics, riddled as they were with devic protectorates full of worshipful hunters who like nothing better than the taste of roasted ravendeer. Still and all, what devils feared, even Utopian imbeciles admired. And, well, some of them were clones.

One wonders …

========

Wildman Dervish Furie was not much taller than Sundown. Nor was he particularly broad shouldered or seemingly as muscular. However, he actually had horns of his own; ones that weren't attached to an otherwise boneless bison's head; ones that were starting to curve backwards the longer they grew. Although Africa-born and Jamaica-raised, his skin was somewhat lighter than that of any full-blooded Utopian male. No doubt because of his slight muzzle, bristled beard and sharp, glistening teeth, he exuded an aura of what was often described as animal magnetism.

The way he moved he appeared ready to tear off his borrowed Trinondev robe – a ground-length shirt, *'galabia'* or *'djellaba'* – and pounce, fangs bared, claws extended, at any moment. Not that any of the women disinclined-to-sew, as opposed to receiving seeds sown, watching them go by thought he would rip them apart. Not literally. Close, maybe. They did anticipate needing the services of a top drawer supplier of complete wardrobes afterwards, however. A specialist clothier or seamstress just wouldn't be up to the task.

What Furie reminded them of most was a satyr, a male faun. They all knew what fauns were best at doing and it wasn't wooing.

Unless wooing counted as foreplay.

========

Although riding Raven, Radiant Rider was no Lady Godiva, if only due to the fact she was wearing clothes. With her soft-looking, very lightly olive skin, Caucasian but easily tanned, muscular arms and legs, comparatively moderate breasts and hips, she reminded some there of the Zeross girls; of all too many of the older female hybrids, none of whom were beyond their teen years as yet.

Which was a shame because not a one of them fit the Utopian ideal of beauty. They were simply not bounteously protrusive, ivory-hard and marble-white enough to register very highly on their ethnic thermometer of pulchritude. Which was also a standard complaint amongst the idiots of Weir.

Every month or so, not that he had for awhile what with all the troubles, in Hadd especially, Aristotle Zeross brought in carefully selected outsiders to mate with pureblood male and female Utopians. The High Illuminary made the final selection and, most agreed, it was a pity she didn't spend more time looking in a mirror before she picked the women in particular. Nonetheless, she claimed only those in whom she and her Illuminaries had detected strong Utopian characteristics – evidence of a no matter how recessive, literally unearthly genetic structure went the argument – made the grade.

Problem was the resultant hybrid men, not that any were men yet, were never quite tall enough; were rarely even black enough. As for the women, women-to-be, the theory was of course that, once they grew up and married, they would have children of their own, more intelligent non-imbeciles to restock the Utopian gene pool. Only, how could they attract anyone appropriate to marry when, speaking plainly – imbeciles always spoke plainly, those that could get intelligible words out – they were so burdened with, well, plain ugliness?

The Weirdom would just end up being populated by hybrids of hybrids. Cabalarkon might as well have gone the way of all the other ancient Weirdoms if that happens. And all the Hidden Headworld's other Weirdoms – their Utopian inhabitants, make that – went human. Even more problematic in terms of attractiveness for the one riding the ravendoe was she had that long, sleek, silver hair.

Pureblood Utopian women may have tinsel-white hair, but something that over-the-top silvery was anything except a desirable feature. Far from it. Ill-omened came instantly to mind.

True, the glistening, sheer argental quality of her hair reminded some of the old-timers of Celeste Mannering ... Master Kyprian's beloved, thirty years gone, and thoroughly missed, Anthean adviser from the early decades of this, the Sixtieth Century of the Dome. The Celestial Superior, as Celeste was known as back then, had not been seen in the Weirdom for sixty years or so; maybe less, but probably more. Had, reputedly anyhow, been dead since '23.

(Not that being dead on the Head was necessarily as terminal as it was on the Outer Earth. Not when the Dead could be animated by Azura Spirit Beings and their devic forbearers.)

The Celestial Superior was the odds-on maternal grandmother of the current Master. It was her equally silver-haired daughter, Pandora, who had been possessed by a devil when she bore Saladin Devason. And that devil, some shuddered to recall, also has silver hair. When she had hair at all, that is. And when it was not breathtakingly long and jet black, which it had been during parts of the Teens, Twenties and Thirties when she, masquerading as Miracle Maenad, co-ruled Apple Isle alongside her Taurus, Ulysses Heliopolis, and its resident Master Deva, Cruel Plathon, the Bull of Mithras.

Naturally – or as naturally as devils could get – that devil, the one who was immune to Trinondev eyeorbs and had tried to take over the Weirdom in 5950, had a quadrangular head with a single eye shining out of each of its three uppermost, triangular sides. Had a name, too. Lots of them. Was, however, most commonly individualized as Pyrame Silverstar.

No, seemingly spun-silver for hair was not a good thing to have in the Weirdom of Cabalarkon. Best to cut it off and take it to the bank for deposit before anyone else did it for you, starting at the neck.

Gloriel was dressed in fine, shape-revealing silk or something similar. It was the same near-gossamer material Melina Zeross and her daughters wore under their warm, woollen sweaters and leggings or trousers, except hers was iridescent, all the colours of the rainbow. Even if her hair was an unlucky hue and she was not built to their preferred proportions, with no shoes or underwear they could perceive, many of the more open-minded men could not help having much the same thoughts about her that their non-mending-minded women had about Furie.

Sensual was not the word for either the Wildman or Radiant Rider. Sexual, plain and simple, was!

========

No doubt sensing their prurient interest in her, the former Obadiah Melvin Power (OMP, Akbarartha, the rightful Kronokronos Supreme of Temporis) took off his cape and gave it to Gloriel. There was an audible chorus of good-natured boos and cat-calls from the milling crowd when she draped it around her shoulders. Furie glared, three evil-looking eyes opened in the carven head atop Akbar's sceptre, and Sundown's solar spearhead flared more noticeably, even dangerously. Muted murmuring and a respectable, respectful space was quickly achieved.

Utopians, after multiple generations of inbreeding, were more like Dystopians; not much better than low-browed ignoramuses, at least in terms of appearance. Even some of the clones oozed bodily fluids in an approaching stereotypical manner. For far too many of these unfortunates, Akbar thought perhaps cruelly, what was truly amazing was not so much they were able to clothe and feed themselves – clothes and food being mostly artificially replicated, as if they were still on millennial spacecraft, by means not so much unknown as imperfectly understood.

No, it was that they still recalled how to put one foot in front of the other and call it walking. He doubted they could spell it, though.

========

"So you are Harry's family," Sundown was saying to the Zeross girls. "I had a wife once. And children. Save for the last who, thankfully, was stillborn, mine were all boys, as beautiful in their own way as you are in yours. I trust Harry takes better care of you and your mother than I did my family."

"Old news, Johnny," Furie reprimanded him. "Lighten up. We've a new life ahead of us. Who knows? Meet Miss Right and maybe you'll start another family."

"Unlikely, Dervish, but Raven might. This cloning technology Mel-Illuminatus tells us these scientocrats of hers have perfected strikes us as most promising."

"You're joking." Sundown rarely joked. Was not one for talking much either. "All right," Furie rephrased, not wanting to put the Cheyenne Summoning Child off before he had a chance to get going. Silence for Blind Sundown was akin to green for grass. Truth told he was more often silent than he was sightless. "So you're serious. Whatever for?"

"What we did to the Apocalyptics in Temporis and what Raven did to the Vampire Queen in Hadd can't have been accidents. We're naturals, Beauty and I. If there were many of her and many men and women armed with solar spears like mine, the devils would run in terror at our coming."

"More likely they'd just hide in goddamned shells," growled Furie, who, as Murray was a trained paramedic, had always been more reactive than reflective. That did not mean he approved of Sundown's methods — said methods usually being complete indifference or destructive decisiveness. "And what would you do then?" he wondered, not so much tempting fate as daring the renowned killer to tempt it for them both. "Blast everyone in sight on the off-chance they might be devil-possessed?"

It was a good thing Sundown was as slow to anger as he was; was probably a better thing for Sundown. No one, not even Dervish himself, knew what the full Furie looked like, let alone what he was capable of doing. Not having reverted to his Jervis-Jekyll persona since he and Cerebrus encountered Mars Bellona, Lord Tornado and the Shadow Woman in the Tokugawa Era Cavern of Temporis, on the morning of the 6th, he was beginning to suspect it would be a lot more murderous than anything Sundown or Raven had done in the past.

At least an argument could be made their extreme actions – sanctions, more like – were justifiable. The full Furie might kill for fun.

"Listen, Johnny. I don't mean to preach, but your people and mine have been through Hell on Earth, or at least Hell in North America, over the course of the last few hundred years. And they're still being put through it, especially yours, from what little we saw of them in Vancouver. Our skin colouration makes us easy to spot, but these Master Devas are as invisible as they are damn near anything else they please to be."

"You're quick with the hells and damns, Dervish. We all are; witness what we're calling ourselves. And maybe you're right. But are you so sure we shouldn't make the effort?"

Just then an elderly Utopian woman ran past them, shouting an alarum. "It's on the radio. The Weirdom's under attack," she cried. "From the Elysian Fields!"

========

*The Witch didn't know much else, but she did know the moment seed met egg she was pregnant; this for the second time in her life and, discounting a quarter century in Limbo, the first time in a decade. The never-slavering ghost who'd been watching them go at it was astonished to see himself reflected in the mirror behind their bed.*

*'My God,' he congratulated himself, to himself, howsoever caustically. 'Aren't you are a handsome devil!'*

========

"You're no more god than devil," a voice spoke into his head, insubstantial as it and what was left of his headplate was.

The ghost, Cerebrus David Ryne wayfaring in the Wild Weird for the first time successfully, re-evaluated his reflection; reconnoitred it, put better. A female form seemingly made up of translucent ice superimposed itself, glass on glass, over itself, himself. "Have another peek, Horrite. Try to look deeper, with your middling impressive mind's eye."

"You are?"

"Klannit Thanatos. Pleased to make your acquaintance, such as it is. Don't ask where the name Klannit comes from because, other than four thousand years ago it was a kind of daemon, with an 'a', I neither know nor care. I just assume my parents, or maybe just my mother, came up with it as if out of the air. Which is probably where they think they came up with me as well. Because that's what I mostly am, a somehow sentient shape in the air.

"The Zerosses, and many another, know me as the Thanatoids' Haunted Angel. Thanatoid because my parents, whom Illuminaries of the long ago past named Tantal and Methandra Thanatos, are Master Devas, two of Thrygragos Varuna Mithras's first born of three by the Trigregos Sisters. Angel because, as such, I'm a useless Spirit Being barely able to occupy and thereafter hold onto an icicle homunculus crafted specially for me.

"Haunted not just because that's what I've been doing to my parents ever since my birth, the first azura ever born, decades before the Great Flood of your Genesis, our Genesea. Haunted also because of my desire to become a true devil; not just a devilish wannabe. Today's Illuminaries call me Mirrors on account of my affinity for ... what else? Were we on the Outer Earth thirty, forty years ago, your father might have codenamed me the Mirror Mentalist.

"And maybe he did, because I was out there a few times during your Suprawar. Probably acquired more than one codename. As Speculum, for one, I was even a member of Strife's Sinister Sisterhood, though then I was animating a dead supra calling herself Obsidianna." While Cerebrus drew a blank with Speculum and Obsidianna – must have been before his time – he certainly recalled Faceless Strife. Wilderwitch refused to take any of the D'Angelos through the Weird after Damnation Isle for fear Thalassa or Gloriel might contract her.

"Except I didn't mean me. Or you. I meant them."

What was left of Cyborg Cerebrus did as bade. Saladin Devason finished making love to Wilderwitch with an anticlimactic grunt and the obligatory deep breaths. But there was more, he realized, stretching his mental tendrils such that he could read him, Braille-like, without an interpreter. The Master was not altogether himself. He thought he was making love to some sort of darkness-shrouded succubus, a Black Widow woman, one with only two eyes but one who was not entirely herself either.

The Witch was not possessed, she was coated; rather, her soul-self was. And Saladin was not making love to her, it, the nevertheless effectively possessed spirit. Another horror was. It also had two eyes, only one of them was in its forehead.

(This, coating more so than possessing, Klannit somehow managed to inform him even as he watched them go at it ghostlike, was what demons, whichever way it was spelt, did when they took over someone. Those that there were bright or brainy enough to pull it off, that is, which weren't that many.)

"See what I mean?" said the evidently multitalented reflection that was no longer just Davy's reflection into his mind.

"He really is a regular Satan, isn't he?"

"That he is. Any suggestions as to what we should do about him?"

"Don't imagine there is anything I can do about him. However, I know just the fellow who might. Got a solar spear tailor-made for the job."

"My thoughts exactly, Horrite. I'll be keeping my eyes on you."

"So is he. The one in the centre of his forehead just winked at me."

========

*Weir's Warrior Elite concentrated en masse.*

*Leaving the Zeross girls in the care of Mel's Illuminaries and the inexperienced Trinondevs, a solid thought-balloon of levitating energy formed around the senior Trinondevs, their field leader, Golgotha Nauroz, Melina Zeross and the members of the Brigade — including Gloriel and Raven's Head, who consequently felt no need to fly anywhere on their own.*

*Globular in shape, the psychogenic bubble manifested non-gargoyle, though gargoyle-like wings akin to those atop Mel's caduceus and propelled them eastward.*

*Toward what hadn't been the Elysian Fields for well over a millennium.*

========

After the out-flowing floodwaters of the Genesea left the Archipelago of Pacifica, the Places of Peace, high and dry – save for impressively wide, hence usually navigable, extremely deep canals between what had been islands – devils or more than likely just their approaching all-powerful All-Father terra-formed it such that the now Hidden Continent did indeed resemble Sedon's head, left side perspective. The Weirdom of Cabalarkon was consequently described, geographically speaking, as Sedon's Devic Eye.

Looking for all the world like the winged-globe symbol so commonly found on ancient Assyrian cylinder seals, they were beyond the metropolis of Cabalarkon within a few beats of the manifested wings. It was a long way, two and a half hundred miles, to their destination but, powered by their collective brain power, the Trinondevs covered the distance with perhaps even beyond supranormal speed.

As they did so, those members of D-Brig with them once again marvelled at what not just devils, like the four who made up the Byronic Nucleus, but their worst enemies could do when they put their minds to it. Marvelled as well at the land blurring below them. The farms, fields and ranches didn't look very well tended but they were still moderately green and obviously, come summertime, fairly fertile.

Despite ever-encroaching overgrowth, patches of orchards and vineyards were also perceptible. Although now barren they, like the farms, looked worked. Which suggested, in this cradle-to-grave, yet stunningly tax-free welfare state, there were still some Utopians, be they incompetent twits, borderline cretins or purebloods, not only capable of growing and harvesting their own food or meat but prepared to do so.

The woodlands were surprisingly thick, so chances were there was fresh game to be had as well. So, why did those in the port city and presumably everywhere else in this evidently bounteous land subsist on the crap spewed out of food processors that, Melina told them, were salvaged from their multiple millennia-old generational ships?

It wasn't that everything anyone needed came to them free of charge and effort, though that undoubtedly explained a lot of it. Neither was it corresponding laziness. Why do anything when it's all done for you? Nor, despite the disconcerting images of spoon-fed obesities with guns or even hoes that sprang immediately to mind and were hard to shake, simply a matter of inbred idiocy. What could fools plant except foolishness?

Again according to Mel, who spent the journey in lecture mode, most of it was due to the Weirdom's dangerously diminishing population. Not many died, very few in fact, but far fewer were born. Sex was as popular as ever – more than perhaps was proper, the comparatively brief-time nun added – but when you saw the malformations that made it as far as maternity wards, well, regardless of her Roman Catholic past Mel for one was all in favour of birth control.

"Wait!" cried Gloriel, as they neared the Slopes of the Sleepers. "There are the mounds."

"And beyond them," Mel gasped, realizing it wasn't just the barrow mounds wherein were buried the vast majority of the Weirdom's sacred Sleepers, as well as husks of dozens of their once incredibly massive and majestic millennial ships, to which the still young Angelic was referring. "Celestial God! It is an army."

There was no denying that. Was also no denying a darkness-shrouded, skull-headed, scythe-wielding devil and an odd-looking humanoid with a woman's willowy body, bared breasts and a four-sided tetrahedron of a head, with a solitary eyeball staring out of each of its three uppermost surfaces, were at the forefront of this army.

Yama Nergal, the devic Grim Reaper, and Pyrame Silverstar, the half-mother of Saladin Devason and (just possibly) Akbarartha, among thousands of others, were not leading it. No, between them stood someone who had the Crimson Corona tied around his rubber-hooded forehead, the Amateramirror strapped onto his left arm as a shield and who was brandishing the Susasword in his right hand.

This was not Vetala's Soldier, the Trigregos Titan as was a week ago. It was someone, in addition to the Trigregos Talismans, clad in a sleeveless wetsuit, with Gorgon-goggles for eyeglasses and mud or tar smeared over his otherwise exposed skin. Yehudi Cohen, the Untouchable Diver, led the Inglorious Dead.

Raven's Head, Blind Sundown on her back, burst out of the Trinondevs' winged-globe of mind-manufactured energy. Suddenly there were dozens of her and dozens of him, all armed with solar spears. Then there were hundreds of her and the

Sundowns were Trinondevs carrying eye-staves. The prison pod eyeorbs atop them opened, but the solitary eyes inside them promptly vaporized. Trigregos Diver rose into the sky.

Then he was three, triplets. All were women, all were beautiful, all had something of the dark-haired D'Angelos about them; the likes of Gloriel's sister, Anna Maria, who ran Radiant Rainbows Fashion Emporium on the Outer Earth, their dead sister Nita and their just as dead aunt Mnemosyne. Each had three eyes and wielded one of the Trigregos Talismans.

Dozens of other devils were behind them. Strangely, most looked female. Even more strangely, they started to come together; became a conglomerate devil — a stupendous Sphinx with the wings of a demonic dragon, the serpent-scalped skull, forked tongue and goggle-eyes of a terrifying Gorgon, the body of a hellcat, and the breasts of a beautiful woman whose milk, no one doubted, was bile.

The battle was joined.

The original Raven's Head and Blind Sundown took out the devil armed with the Brainrock scythe; cathonitized the Nergalid Reaper as surely as they had Nakba Ramazar, the Vultyrie and Mater Matare in Temporis. Radiant Rider, the Kronokronos Supreme and the full Furie, a ferocious-looking, iron-hided juggernaut none of them had ever seen before, but all of them, Dervish most of all, feared was always lurking beneath the Wildman's surface, went for the Diver-girls and diverse devils.

They panicked, vanished. So did the female sphinx. The devil with the quadrangular head fled into Samsara, the Weird, the Grey, the universal substance between-space. Raven and Sundown went after her. A few minutes later they returned empty-handed; counting coup for once denied them. And not just for them.

The battlefield was abandoned. No, not abandoned; never had been. No engagement had been fought. Ocular proof aside, there had been no army of the Inglorious Dead. Visible far beyond the Slopes of the Sleepers, the Ghostlands, old Valhalla, the one-time Elysian Fields, still glowed with forbidding radioactivity. It was as if nothing had happened.

As if.

========

*Upon their return to the metropolis of Cabalarkon hours later, none of those who went as far as the Slopes of the Sleepers had any idea what, if anything, went on out there. Helen Zeross, Harry and Melina's twelve year old daughter – whom they nicknamed Paree, as in Gay Paree, after Helen of Troy and the Judgement of Paris – brought them an only partial solution to that mystery a few minutes later.*

*"Daddy's back, mommy, and he's brought some funny looking guy with him. He's all dressed in blubber."*

********

# SIX-BABIES: BLACK GOD – WHITE GODDESS

========

**Sapienda, 14 Tantalar 5980**

*The Thanatoids of Lathakra, Tantal and Methandra, being Master Devas, had a triplet. Antique Illuminaries named him Phantast. His fellow devils called him Dream. His star no longer shone in the night sky. Hadn't since the 30th of last month.*

========

It was already dark by the time Melina Zeross paid the Witch her second visit of the day, the 14th of Tantalar, 5980 Year of the Dome. Sitting in a wicker chair by the French doors to the suite's balcony, she contemplated the heavens, no nimbus over the upper floors of Skyrise now, as she waited for her patient, whom she could hear fussing about next door, to finish her business.

The toilet flushed. Wilderwitch, feet not touching the floor, levitated out of the bathroom and took not to her bed but sat in a chair beside it.

Both looked much different than they had that morning. If anything the Witch seemed brighter, happier, healthier, whereas Melina was the opposite. It was as if the stone sculptor the Witch fancied handled Mel's makeup had decided to replace her usual austerity of expression with one of desperation, even hopelessness, before entering her presence.

"What's wrong, Mel?"

"Seems the Master had a dream."

"That's not all he had."

"What do you mean by that?"

The Witch caught herself. Swiftly improvised a serviceable disclaimer: "Only that he must have had more than one. Or don't Utopians dream?"

"Oh, we dream all right. But this may be the first time we've ever experienced, en masse, simultaneously, not to mention while we're awake, someone else's dream."

"Not getting you?" Mel told her what occurred on the faraway border between the Weirdom and the Ghostlands (old Valhalla, the Elysian Fields). When she was done the Witch was no better off than when she began. "Sounds more like a mass hallucination to me. Supra-superior witches like me can do that sort of thing. Did one in Temporis as a matter of fantastic fact. Saved a lot of lives, too; almost at the cost of my own, you don't have to remind me. But, even if Sal could do a ditto, why would he bother? You sure it didn't happen?"

"The dream? It did. He admitted it. Said it wasn't a Phantast Folly either, on account of, well, he's the Master and Phantast's a devil; a firstborn Thanatoid, as a matter of unfortunately not fantastic fact."

"Not the dream. What he thought he dreamed."

"Ah, but that's the point, isn't it? It couldn't have. Sure, the primary devils we saw were Pyrame Silverstar and Underlord Yama Nergal. There's no doubt of that. There's also no doubt their army was composed of the Nergalid's Inglorious Dead — Death's Angels, they're called. The Master's seen them before; seen Pyrame and the Nergalid as well, back in 5950 if not afterwards. So have you and I; though I still wonder how reliable your memory is, going to and from the Outer Earth as much as you did way before getting stuck in Limbo.

"The She-Sphinx had to be All of Incain. I don't know if you've ever seen her in person, probably have, but you'll have seen pictures of her when you visited us while Master Kyprian was still around. She looks similar to the Egyptian Sphinx except she's got wings and can move. Of course he could too, pre-Flood. She's mostly an over-endowed mandroid, a largely between-space, semi-sentient, and perhaps even semi-daemonic machine constructed by the Dual Entities centuries long before the Great Flood of Genesis, that is to say long before there was a Cathonic Zone, to hold onto daemons. Worked as well on devils, once they came to ground and especially once they started debraining daemons to make themselves independently solid beings.

"Out on the Slopes All became Demogorgon to us, the Unnameable to devils. She's done that before, become the Conglomerate Devil, at least she has according to our annals. On Thrygragon, in 4386 YD, almost 1600 years ago now, is one example; a poor one as reports on that year's Mithramas vary a fay-fairy bit. I told you the Master's terrified of her. He's had a premonition she'll kill him. So maybe that's part of it. He manufactured some strategic mind-games while he was sleeping and then played them out."

"And you saw them."

"We all did. At least we saw the endgame of one."

"You're not persuading me it had to be a dream."

"How about this then? There's only one Sundown and one Raven's Head, not hundreds of her and hundreds of his Solar Spear. And, even if our scientocrats and biomages are successful, chances are it'll be years before there's any more than just her and it."

"Whoa! What am I missing?"

"I'd have got around to telling you eventually. Or preferably let them tell you. It's part of the accommodation for accommodations I was talking about this morning. Raven's Head has decided to let us try to clone her and Johnny's agreed to let us try to duplicate his Solar Spear. So you see it's like the Master was dreaming about the ramifications of their decisions, and his, and came up with the scenario we all witnessed."

"And how would Sal know what the full Furie looks like?"

"There is that, I grant you. But since none of us do, who's to say we saw the full Furie today? He'd certainly know the other participants, even the triplets the Diver split into; I recognized them myself. They're Telepassa of Godbad's eldest: Ino, Agave and Autonoe. Our Helen, Paree, buddied up with their younger sister, Semele, who's around the same age, when we were on Shenon in '74."

"I've heard names like that before. Cretan mythology, right ... King Cadmus and the Greek version of Harmony's get?"

For someone who was born to her abilities, the Witch had managed to learn a few things over the years, possibly by osmosis. Cadmus was the founder and first king of Thebes whereas Harmony was the daughter of War and Peace, Ares and Aphrodite, after whom Lovely Lady Afrites were named.

"Not sure I approve of 'get' but, yeah. More like Theban than Cretan, though."

"Oh, I don't know. Cadmus had a sister, Europa, who Zeus-Mithras, unless it was Zeus-Varuna, kidnapped from Phoenicia and swam to Crete, where she had three children."

"One of whom was named Sarpedon, as in my last name. Truth is ..."

"Know that, too. What about these kids?"

"They're mostly grown now; must be almost 20, and to judge by his dream have become, for humans, gorgeous young women. Their mother's a Quarter Queen of Shenon. She doubles as both the Afrite and Althean Ventricular. Has, as might expect with a brood of four girls, Anthean training as well. This time the truth is, uninterrupted, she's scheduled to take over as the Antheans' Aortic as soon as Tsishah Twilight retires. Which she should have already if you're like me and think a decade ends on a 9 and starts on a 0."

(This was Dome's 60$^{th}$ Century even though its dates might make someone think it was the 59$^{th}$. In the same way that while it was nineteen-hundreds on the Outer Earth, it was its 20$^{th}$ Century.)

"Only problem is there's no obvious candidate to take over the Ventricular position Telepassa's leaving. Not from any of the eligible Sisterhoods anyhow, though there's been plenty of names put forward, including that of any one of her three eldest daughters. They're accomplished Lovely Ladies."

"Witch Isle's troubles selecting a new Quarter Queen don't strike me as relevant to what we were talking about, Mel.

"Maybe not, but they've been on my mind a mite lately. As a high ranking Alt Healer I'm on the selection committee. And it is sort of relevant because that's where the Master met them, when I was there having Tina with Telepassa acting as my midwife, and he came close to being stewed alive."

"Stewed alive? Sounds like another one those stories you'll have to get around to telling me someday. Can't say I recall this Telepassa of Godbad, probably never came across her pre-Limbo, but I am curious about who's in charge of what on Shenon these days. I foresee a long night's conversation ahead of us, Mel. There's something else, though, isn't there? The stone gnome who does your face has got you looking awfully downcast."

Stone gnomes were the catch-all explanation for how everything extraterrestrial in the Weirdom, such as the firestones atop the omnipresent obelisks erected almost everywhere you went, the food processing systems, waste recycling, clothing replacement machines, matter transducers and indeed everything else that still worked up here, still worked.

Supposedly these stone gnomes operated exclusively by the Master's Will. Yet, like Trinondev eye-staves and their orbs, it was the brain-power of the populace that, as it were, maintained their charge. Hence the notion that while the Master could only rule with the people's consent, which came with their contentment as much as it did with their hopes and prayers – if not their outright worship per se – only a Master could hold stone gnomes to task such that everything a Utopian needed to stay alive, especially the ones who were otherwise incapable of fending for themselves, continued to do so.

Might even exist, these stone gnomes. The very young, the very old and the imbecilic majority swore by them. Besides, time-tumblers, one of whom was mainly a machine that could be humanized by devils, devils themselves, azuras, deviants, witches, supranormals, faeries, demons, either spelling, flying sphinxes, man-eating Angelycs, Simian Sapiens, at least three different varieties of the Walking Dead, non-Anthean, anthropomorphic ants known as Myrmidons, sentient Saurs, the Mantels of Temporis, mermen and mermaids, Melusine Piscines and Akans like the fabulous Fisherwoman, strictly water-breathing Lemurian frogmen, amphibious Lemurian frogwomen, they and their mandroid guard-bodies, they all existed. So why shouldn't stone gnomes?

"I'm not staying," Melina said to the Witch. "In fact, for the next little while anyhow, I may have to delegate some of my colleagues to come and do your daily checkups."

"Why? More to the point, how'll they get in?"

"Seems, other than for my colleagues who'll have to learn to breathe Skyrise's rarefied air, that won't be an issue. For some reason the Master's in an even better mood than you seem to be. Not only is he letting your D-Brig fellows move into Skyrise if they want to – minus Raven, like I told you before – but as of tomorrow you can start having unlimited visiting hours."

"That's wonderful. What isn't?"

"Harry and the Diver are back. Yehudi's only wrecked, exhausted, but Harry, well, Harry's what not wonderful. He's wretched, Gypsium sick. Worst ever. I'm afraid he's dying."

"And there's nothing you can do for him?"

"Other than stick him in a tub of Cathonic Fluid for six months to a year and hope the rest cures him, not that I can think of. We'll keep him with us as long as we can, if only so I can perform some tests and try out some meds that might work, but I don't want to leave it too long. Mind if I ask you something?"

"Depends."

"How about I start with why your hair's so straight. Looks darker too."

"Does it? Haven't noticed."

Just then something smashed in the Witch's bathroom. Mel was quickly on her feet, rushed into the room next door and came back seconds later holding a shard from the mirror that evidently no longer hung over the sink. "Must have been a minor earth tremor. We get them sometimes. Dark Sedon getting drunk and falling on his head we say.

"Here, check it out yourself." Mel made to hand the piece of broken mirror to the Witch, looked up as she was about to do so and dropped it, shattering it.

"That's bad luck, Mel."

"Christ, Witch, you're walking!"

"And you said casting illusions wasn't much of a supra-talent."

========

**Sapienda, 25 Tantalar 5980**

*Some nights are memorable, others are forgettable. Some nights you're just glad you survive. Virtually any night of any year, anyplace. anywhere, anytime, some folks don't have the opportunity to say the same thing anymore. Eleven days after his return to the Weirdom of Cabalarkon, what he had called home for two decades, one person hoped he wasn't about to fall into the latter category.*

*He was, however, resigned to the likelihood he wouldn't be saying anything for a very long time.*

========

Mithramas was still celebrated throughout much of the Upper Head. In other parts of the Hidden Continent it wasn't so much remembered as Thrygragos Varuna Mithras's Feast Day as for Thrygragon, his 4376 Death Day; albeit only so far, so good, as his scandalously older (by Outer Earth standards), but both lovely and loving wife often qualified, when the subject came up. By contrast, Zmas Day, a comparatively recently inaugurated, annual affair in the Weirdom of Cabalarkon, more like marked Weir on Earth's Rebirth Day.

By the Master's decree, it was held every Mithramas, the twenty-fifth day of Tantalar, the second month of the Mithradic Tetrad and the tenth month of the Sedonic Year. On the Outer Earth it would be December the 25th, Xmas to those who followed Xuthrodism; Christmas to many people; Saturnalia or the Winter Solstice to not so many others.

(Erroneously, as it happened, except for those who lived during Imperial Roman times when, some say, the solstice did indeed fall on the 25th and when also its legionnaires, at least until Christians seized his Cave Temple on Vatican Hill in the year 376 AD, celebrated the birthday of their deity Sol Invictus, the Head's selfsame Mithras.)

Zmas Day was named after Aristotle Zeross, the Outer Earth supranormal once codenamed Kid Ringo but who had been using Ringleader exclusively since coming to the Inner Earth in May of 1960, Vanalal 5960 YD. Ringleader was the same codename Harry's father Angelo used during the Outer Earth's Secret War of Supranormals.

Prior to, during and after that war, which began in early 1938 and ended in late 1955, Angelo Zeross – Angie to his friends, of whom he counted many – made quite a reputation writing, speaking and publishing philosophical tracts and disputatious polemics wherein he, an avowed anarchist, envisioned a perfect world based on mutual respect and intercommunity cooperation. (Didn't make quite a fortune selling his ruminations but, hey, he already had one of those — in shipping, for the most part, but also in agriculture.)

Angie never came close to realizing much more than a fraction of his dream and that only for the briefest of time on Crete, as the Second World War got going in earnest. By contrast, like Xuthros Hor, Jesus Christ or even Jesus Mandam, Harry was a saviour to his chosen people; in his case, though, he had 'saved' his adopted people, the Utopians of Weir here on Earth.

The elder Zeross was killed in 1968. The Outer Earth Bible claims Hor survived the Great Flood by some 350 years. Believers say Christ rose from the grave and ascended to Heaven wherein he continues to rule as God the Almighty Three-in-One. Which, curiously, many an Anthean and Illuminary believe the Trigregos Sisters, the All-Mothers of Devazurkind, do as well, somewhere in the heavens, as the Three-in-One Goddess.

Mandam – Mary Magdalene born Ryne' son, hence David, Saul and Aranyani Nightingale Ryne's cousin as well as Barsine-Vetala's (arguable) twin brother – was vapourized on Salvation Isle 27 years ago today. If he rose from anything no one noticed. Besides, Jesse was the saviour of supranormalkind only in accordance with his own demented mindset.

Unlike all of them, Rings had never been other than alive.

Still was — barely!

========

The Banquet Hall, which wags called the Hate-Sedon Sphere, a name all of D-Brig had taken up to varying degrees, was a vast, high-domed structure erected in the rectangular Masters' Palace's massive interior courtyard. A two-levelled, square-blocked pyramid, like a mastaba or Mayan temple with an additional layer built on its top, was constructed in the middle of the hall.

The ground level was for the multitude of Weir; the second level, overtop the kitchens, was for scientocrats, Illuminaries and the Trinondev Warrior Elite; the top level, High Table, was where the Master of Weir and his honoured guests – ordinarily select scientocrats, techno- and biomages, Illuminaries, Trinondevs or, like today, visitors from outside the Weirdom – sat. Or would sit, once matters got properly underway.

The second level was accessible from the bottom, floor-level one via external stairways on all four sides. The top level, though, was physically inaccessible to anyone without the know-how. And that, even if they just pretended to have said know-how, was jealously guarded by the Master, his so-called scientocrats, and the Illuminaries of Weir.

High up, near the internal apex of the architecturally impressive, glassine dome was an also glassed-in platform that ran the circumference of the Hate-Sedon Hall. Here, albeit without Wilderwitch and Raven's Head, but with the Diver, what little was left of the Damnation Brigade, together with the Family Zeross, gathered to wait until it was their turn for a grand entrance.

Wildman Dervish Furie, after twenty-minus-one days, no longer had horns. Was no longer outwardly a wild man. Or a fledgling faun, for that matter. Nor was he Dervish Furie anymore, not manifestly anyhow. He did, however, have a huge lump on his head, between where his horns used to be, to match an equally huge headache. Both came from being bonked on his noggin by OMP-Akbar.

Rather, by the latter him batting the former him near enough batty such that he reverted to his not very, if at all, supra-self: the Normie Normalman Wilderwitch professed to love. Only, when he'd gone up to see her in her apartments on the second-to-uppermost storey of Skyrise not long after submitting his Dervish-self to the tough love of Kronokronos Akbar and his Homeworld Sceptre, she'd denied him, aka Gentleman Jervis Murray, the kind of love he'd been looking for.

Had tried to be nice about it. Said, to quote her directly: 'The Moloch Sedon and his remaining devils will make Murray-mincemeat out of you, Jervis. Best thing you can do for both of us is go back to being Dervish Furie. Then you might survive.

Then we all might survive.' Said a few other things as well, did the Witch, none of them particularly pleasant. Even gave him a choice. He could leave voluntarily or she'd throw him out 'marigold metallically', to quote her just as precisely.

When it was completed in 5975, she'd further informed him, Skyrise was twenty-five storeys high, one storey for every year of Sal's Mastery. It thereafter grew, she claimed, one storey of height for every year of his continuing Mastery. That meant it was now thirty storeys high, or close to it. Skyrise, it appeared, would be a work in progress so long as Saladin Devason was the Master of Weir.

He'd be Dervish Furie before he hit ground, no doubt of that. However, she'd questioned, could even the Furie withstand such a drop; withstand it landing on his head especially? Mind you, she'd added, at Mel's insistence, Skyrise had a brand spanking new, Outer Earth modern hospital on its lower floors and she could personally vouch for the quality of care in its ICU.

Murray left of his own accord.. Was, hours later and dressed in a saffron, African-style robe, a loin cloth underneath it, with Ringleader and his three daughters.

Harry was hardly his dashing old self. Nor was he his dashing young self, as far as that went. Instead of his usual plethora of glowing rings, earrings, bracelets, anklets, chains, and so on so circularly, his one piece of jewellery was his wedding ring. And it did not even glimmer, which may or may not mean it was one of his teleportals, as he sometimes called his rings.

He was sitting in a hand-cranked, mechanized wheelchair and, beneath his fur-frilled, burgundy dressing gown, wore silk pyjamas and slippers. Beside him, tears quelled for the time being, his hybrid daughters had pinkish-white skin and very blonde hair. Also had colour in their cheeks, flesh that looked warm to the touch and, miracle of miracles, expressive faces — ones that lined when they winked, frowned or grinned.

They were each wearing bright red party dresses that on the youngest was sweet; on the budding, middle one dainty; yet, on the eldest, looked inappropriate for a fully-developed and already very attractive, recently turned 16-year old sweetheart. (As the Diver observed, quoting Neil Sedaka, one of a large number of pop stars he'd discovered upon their return from Limbo most of month ago.)

They were by the matter transducers they would use to transport themselves to High Table – matter transducers being perhaps not so remarkably still functional leftovers from the much more than 6,000 year old generational spacecraft Utopians used to crisscross the cosmos in pursuit of the Sedonshem; this before it finally came to ground on the Whole Earth centuries pre-Genesea.

The girls had been terrified of Dervish Furie, with his horns and fangs, but had taken an immediate liking to Jervis Murray, he with his darkish, though not altogether jet-black skin and still thick but now trimmed beard. They were in charm-mode; were competing with each other trying to tell him how matter transducers kept working despite the fact no one in Cabalarkon knew how to make, let alone service, one anymore. He was distracted, was forever looking around for Wilderwitch, who had yet to show up, and missed most of what Harry's youngest, Athena, was saying.

"What was that again, Tina? What're stone gnomes?"

"Gnomes made of stone, silly," the 6-year old repeated.

"They're what keeps everything going, Uncle Monster," elaborated 12-year old Helen, who liked to sound superior and could be quite rude. "Tinny thinks she saw one this morning in the old palace." (The Diver had said something about her, too. Playing on her given name, it was along the lines of 'her nickname may be Paree, but I bet she already has lots of little Parises lined up to tie her shoelaces'.)

Although the Diver had chosen to bunk down in the one-time Masters' Palace and Raven now had a laboratory-cum-stable built off it, the other members of D-Brig now stayed in Skyrise, in guest quarters reserved for visitors. Most Utopians still regarded the old palace as the hub of the Weirdom. Understandably so. Until barely five years earlier, Masters of Weir and their court always lived there, hence its name.

It was from there, not Skyrise, that the underground ducts and tubing that kept the majority of the imbeciles of Weir living in the metropolis supplied with food and clothing originated. As for why the Diver opted for the old palace, he wasn't saying. However, at least part of the reason anything extraterrestrial still worked had to have as much to do with the nearness of one of the Weirdom's self-renewing, barely dribbling springs or fountains (more so than outright geysers) of molten Brainrock-Gypsium as it did any hypothetical stone gnomes.

And, after a chance encounter on Sraddha Isle earlier in the month with an old love of his from the very late Thirties, a certain amphibious – because she had gills behind her ears – exotic Piscine, the ever-fishifying Fisherwoman, the Diver discovered he could metabolize the Godstuff. In all likelihood this newfound ability of his was making him far more impressive than he ever had been before.

Then again most of D-Brig felt they were stronger beneath the Dome than they had been beyond it.

"I did!" the child insisted. "It was making ice cream."

"Tinny's seen a lot of things," commented Persephone, the eldest and, as such, considered herself her parents' proxy. "Mom used to say she was pixilated, fairy-touched, but now she says we shouldn't talk about it. Weird things like pixies don't seem so cute any more. Stop trying to upset your father, Tinny."

"Stop calling Tina Tinny, Percy," Harry requested weakly.

"Yeah," added Helen, supportively, if just as guiltily. "Her name's Athena, after the Mediterranean Goddess of Athens, not the War Witch Sisterhood Aunt Morg was running in Hadd." Someone must have told the girls Sundown killed Morgianna Sarpedon while she was in the process of working her wonders on the Dervish, trying to turn him back into the Jervis presumably so she could slay him. Murray was so scatterbrained himself he did not even notice the past tense.

"Oh, do be quiet, Paree," commanded the older girl imperiously. Not only had Percy noticed the past tense she also knew her sister was wrong. Athenans were named after Mediterranean Athena, who was the Olympian gods' Virgin Goddess of War as well as Wisdom. (Virgin because no man had conquered her, just as no man would ever counter Athens in its Golden Age. Except, apparently, some sort of AIDS-like plague that ended it.)

She did not want the conversation to continue in that direction. For a very good reason. Old-time Illuminaries returning from the Outer Earth in the Dome's Thirtieth Century believed its gods and goddesses, even many of its demons and monsters, were devils who'd somehow breached the Dome hundreds of years earlier. They combined Mediterranean and Athena to come up with Methandra, Mithras's one-time, long-time Virgin.

After their time on Lathakra, as hostages of the Scarlet Empress, her brother-husband, King Cold, Tantal Thanatos, and their so-called Haunted Angel, their usually unjustly unacknowledged azura-daughter – a Spirit Being that animated ice statuary fashioned by their youngest devic offspring, Sedunihas, who appeared to be about Tina's age – if either of her sisters heard that baleful name again they would probably have conniptions.

Fortunately her middle sister was more interested in having a spat than a fit. "And my name's Helen. I didn't even like the awful Eiffel Tower, Persephone." The intense sibling rivalry between Harry's oldest daughters was approaching scratches-to-face tangible even to someone who had as little experience as Jervis Murray, being an infertile, only child, did with kids.

"Hey! What's going on now?" Murray pointed to the floor, trying to defuse some of the heightening tension.

A procession of mostly jet-black men in white robes and a lesser amount of alabaster white women in black ones, both sexes wearing colour-matching turbans, but without their veils drawn, were making their way through the multitude and climbing the stairways to the second level. The female Trinondevs present were mostly older; had probably retired immediately after Master Kyprian's death thirty years earlier when Saladin decreed an all-male corps. Nonetheless, those that had them were proudly brandishing their eye-staves, a multitude of individualized gargoyles manifest and rampant.

"That's an honour guard of Trinondev Warrior Elite," said Ringleader. "Except for Golgotha, a few of his closest confederates and some of the younger men who saw Nergal Vetala in Hadd, for the most part they're imbeciles. Wouldn't recognize a devil if it was letting its third eye shine forth and eyefire-burning what little is left of their little grey cells to crispy critters."

Zeross, as sickly as he was, was making no effort to hide his scorn. "Doesn't stop them trying to put on a show of their own, though. They think they're making an inspirational arrival. I think they're making bigger fools of themselves than they already are. A circus parade of clowns and freaks waving banners of bloated buffoons in motley would be less ludicrous."

Harry had been brought up an anarchist; someone completely contemptuous of silver-spoon, elite any things. Seemed he was going to die one, too. Or at least be submerged as one.

Harry's wife Melina, Mel-Illuminatus, flanked by Akbarartha and a grim-looking Blind Sundown came up to them. Today was both Mel and Sundown's 60th birthdays. Neither was celebrating it for reasons obvious. Following them were Yehudi Cohen, the Untouchable Diver, and Gloriel, Gloriella D'Angelo Dark; radiant as ever, thought Murray, whose 60th, like that of the Diver – unless it was just their 35th – was still some days away.

Both women were dressed in strapless evening gowns. Mel's was beige or off-white, like the pantsuits, usually with sleeves and no skirts, so uniform amongst her fellow female Illuminaries. For her part, as always when she wasn't just in the opaque modesty gown she conjured while using her rainbow abilities, Gloriel's was multicoloured.

Their outfits, if you could call them outfits and not skin-fits, looked more spray-painted on than anything else. Were clearly, almost scandalously so, inspired by fashion magazines, not all of them published by Hugh Hefner (of the early 1950s' Playboy fame), extremely popular on the western Outer Earth when D-Brig was there last – in Vancouver, for not even a week – at the beginning of the month.

Gloriel would have seen them, might have designed their gowns, but as to where she got the material and who did the sewing, that was something Murray made a mental note to find out. Perhaps, contrary to what he'd said to John Sundown that morning at breakfast, neither needles nor mirrors were banned in the Weirdom after all.

Mel-Illuminatus hugged her daughters one by one then held a long, tight embrace with her game, but already exhausted husband. She was whispering something into his ear. Gloriel turned to the Diver, whose hearing was as acute as his goggles-enhanced eyesight and who, she knew, was also skilled at lip-reading in a number of different languages. "I know it's none of my business, but what's she saying?"

"As it happens it's all of our business, Glory," the Diver told her. Mel had spoken at some length to OMP-Akbar, Sundown and himself, both separately and together, a few minutes ago. He didn't need to be much of a lip-reader to realize she was repeating much the same thing to her husband now.

"The Master has priorities. They're for the best, she says. And Hubby Harry, like you and I and the rest of us, have to keep our non-Lathakran cool. She was making a joke, by the way. Other than the temperature there's nothing cool about the Frozen Isle. Her and her kids were held captive there until Rings promised to deliver the remaining Thanatoids from the Moon. Which he did. Which is why he's so sick. Which is also why she was keeping her voice down.

"Mel and hubby's girls are terrified King Cold will come back for them. Tina, who's hyper at the best of times, had a near-breakdown earlier today when she got hold of one of Harry's rings and popped over here, to the old palace, in order to get some ice cream. Mel says the refrigerator's chill didn't just remind the poor kid of Lathakra; it very nearly made her hypothermic.

"So much so she didn't do the sensible thing and use daddy's rings to take her back to safety. She froze up, all too damn near almost literally. Fortunately one of the chefs – one of the guys who can cook without immolating himself, rather – found her and hauled her out the freezer just in time. Apparently, just by the by, Utopians call refrigerators glacials."

Gloriel, who had no idea anyone except Harry could use his rings, shook her head sympathetically. "And to think I was brought up believing Air and Sea weren't just my adopted brother and sister; that they were my cousins, live Aunt Dolores or dead Aunt Celestine's Summoning Children. Mountaintop tip of irony, isn't it? I'm a nominal angel. So were they. Except they turned out to be devils."

Upon his return to Cabalarkon, the Weirdom and the city proper, Harry reported what had become of Aires and Thalassa to the others. Because he could get through the Dome whereas she couldn't, the day before he went to the moon, on the Tenth of Tantalar, he helped Mama Methandra bring Sea Goddess in from the Outer Earth, perhaps saving her life in the process.

Earlier, on the Sixth, Papa Tantal, King Cold, had hauled, unasked, a very much unwilling Airealist to Lathakra directly from Temporis. Until then, D-Brig had no notion what had become of their comrade. He'd last been seen with Sundown and Raven's Head about to take on Catastrophe (Nakba Ramazar, the Headless Apocalyptic of Sudden Destruction) and the lowborn, nearly mindless – despite having two heads – Vultyrie.

(Mel-Illuminatus claimed the Vultyrie, before she was cathonitized, was worshipped by birds. Which explained her near mindlessness – birds were, after all, birdbrains. She may or may not have been trying to funny. She was deadly serious awhile ago when she disclaimed Gloriel's notion that the Hidden Headworld was Hell on Earth. It wasn't; rather, only part of it was. Showed them too, on a map of Head, one of dozens she had.

(There it was called Satanwyck whereas its capital city was aptly named Pandemonium. Not just because of what it was, but where it was, she also called it Sedon's Temple. Said that it was one place that if you went into, you could never leave. Whereupon the Diver, who'd made a five-day study of mostly English and North American pop music popular while they were lost in Limbo, started humming the Eagles' biggest ever hit 'Hotel California'.)

Upon hearing of the Elemental Twins' true heritage, the Diver made some stupid remark about it being no wonder they called themselves the Damnation Brigade. It wasn't the first time no one laughed at one of his cracks. As if to make amends for it, he actually apologized at least for the degree of its tastelessness.

"Be that as it may," he unapologetically proclaimed this time, very much recidivist-Diver wittily, "According to both of our Faiths, not that my faith in mine is anywhere near as fine as your faith in yours, Gloriel, devils are Fallen Angels. Though I suppose that's just a euphemistic way of avoiding the real question of whether they jumped or were pushed."

The Angelic, as Gloriel and her family were often referred to, usually didn't string together words like 'mountaintop tip of irony'. However, she'd been hanging out with OMP-Akbar of late and the old man was prawn-prone to whimsical fay-saying. Indeed, with the near-giant in rainbow-tow, she'd flown to the tip of a mountaintop in the Mystics Mountain range, Sedon's Crown, hundreds of miles north of the Weirdom proper, that very morning.

They'd gone that far not just so Gloriel could prove to the old man, whom she regarded as kind of surrogate father figure, that she'd fully recovered her game, as it were. They'd also gone as if to demonstrate that they could leave the Weirdom anytime they pleased, with or without the Master's permission. Somewhat unexpectedly they'd there encountered yet another variety of Headworld angel.

Mel had warned them about the be-winged primitives who lived in the equivalent of eyries throughout the Mystics. (All very eerie, the Diver would have said, if he was around when Mel was telling them about them. Which, fortunately for the obligatory groan factor, he wasn't.) Although they were called Angelycs, she said the winged humanoids with eagle heads, date palms and, yes, watering cans, were once worshipped in Assyria as, believe it, spirits or demigods of agriculture known as Nisrail (rhymes with Israel); their god being Nisroch.

It wasn't just eagle heads those who touched down sported, either; albeit only the Nisrail did that. There were lions, tigers, wolves, bears, all manner of traditionally powerful beasts, though by far the most common were human, male and female. Weren't shape shifters, so they weren't demons, any spelling. Looked extremely strong, could fly carrying major loads, Mel had told them, and as such were often employed as builders much as Poseidon's Cyclopes were said to have built the famous, well, cyclopean structures of antiquity not just here on the Head.

While, to the best of Mel's considerable knowledge, there wasn't a Master Deva known as Nisroch, the Trumpeter – Thrygragos Varuna Mithras's lion-headed Heliodromus (sun-runner) or messenger to the gods – was very similar in appearance to these Angelycs; may have been their deity or devic Dand, in fact.

Devils, she'd added, often called the Trumpeter the Masochist, due to his proclivity for getting beat up, especially by Dark Sedon, who apparently hated him bringing messages while he was altogether in Cathonia. Antique Illuminaries had him as Djinn Domitian in part because he liked to be dominated. (You weren't supposed to shoot the messenger in polite society, but this Djinn, who hadn't been reported, let alone seen, in decades, seemed to welcome it. Made him feel worthy of attention.)

Regardless of their size, sex, or the head they were born with, she further noted, they reminded her more of the man-eating harpies found in Greek mythology than any angel, celestial or fallen, in the traditions of Judaism, Zoroastrianism, or Manichaeism. Nor any of the later on established, monotheistic religions like Christianity or Islam, for that matter.

One look at their teeth, fangs more like – had to be filed in order to get that sharp, Gloriel reckoned – pretty much cinched know-it-all Mel's claim as to what they ate — raw flesh. Worse, to judge by way they looked at them, Gloriel and Akbar, they doubtless had every intention of making their next meal their, hers and his, raw flesh. Needless to say, the D-Brig 2 weren't Trumpeters, weren't masochists; decided not stick around to sample the cuisine.

"That's another thing I was brought up believing," she contributed as they awaited the go-ahead signal. "Only it probably never occurred to my father, my mother, nor any of their fathers and mothers before them, exactly how true it was. I mean, they're extraterrestrials and where else would you fall from except Heaven, the heavens?" (Actually it probably had, given her maternal grandfather had 'invented' something called the devil-ray whereas her paternal aunt Celestine had initiated the Simultaneous Summonings of 1920.)

"Still, it seems so easy for Mel to say; so matter-of-fact. Dare I say … so cold-blooded? Guess I just did. Don't these Utopian women ever perspire?"

"They've got as much emotions as you or I do, Rainbow. They're just genetically incapable of showing them moment by moment. Pay attention. Protocol's very important here."

Melina finished instructing the other Illuminaries. They, men – also in western-style pantsuits instead of the far more common-for-males' Arabic, African or eastern-style robes – and significantly more women than men, all bare-faced and wearing headscarves or turbans, nodded dutifully. Lined up in front of various matter transducers and awaited her next command. She turned to her husband, her daughters and D-Brig.

"The Illuminaries and my family are familiar with these proceedings, but you newcomers are not. So listen carefully and please don't deviate from what I'm telling you. What you're about to behold – and be a significant part of, I might add – is not just sound and light, signifying nothing, to quote Master Kyprian's favourite writer. What the Master does signifies everything to these people. As offensive as it is to some of us, he's as good as their god."

"And what God wants," the Diver started to say.

"Shut up, UD," Sundown silenced him. Did his spearhead just flare?

========

*If a High Illuminary of anywhere, including Weir, asked you to jump off a bridge or, maybe, Niagara Falls, would you? Unless it was just for fun, any self-respecting member of a supra-group still ever-so-ill-advisedly calling itself the Damnation Brigade would likely say no. If the High Illuminary of Weir asked you to step into a Brainrock-Gypsium-fuelled matter transducer, a fellow like the Diver, who learned he could inhume the stuff in Hadd, might have said: 'About time. I'm famished.'*

*Instead he said: "You ladies go first. By All means."*

========

After the Illuminaries did what amounted to a test run, if only to demonstrate they could teleport safely, OMP-Akbar and Gloriel stepped into the first available transducer. Persephone and an unconvinced, still trepidation-beset Diver thereupon stepped into the second. As Jervis Murray moved to join Helen in the third one, John Sundown placed an iron grip on his arm.

The native American's cosmic aura was such that, so long as he was within even a yard's distance, Gentleman Jervis Murray could not become Wildman Dervish Furie any more than the Diver could become untouchable or Gloriel rainbow-radiant, let alone rainbow-ride. Unescorted, Helen and Athena Zeross went into the third transducer.

"What's going on?" demanded Murray.

"There's been a change in plan, Jervis," explained Sundown unhappily. (At least he hadn't just grunted and shrugged his shoulders noncommittally.) "I'm told it's for everyone's good that Dervish Furie stays under your skin during supper. Myself, I suspect it's for the good of two specific people."

"Wait a minute. Where's Witchie?"

"Let's go." prodded Sundown. He easily ushered Murray into the fourth transducer. Supported by his wife, Ringleader joined her in the last one.

=========

The Diver didn't do a very good job emphasizing the 'a' in All such that anyone he realized was there realized he was referring to All of Incain. He thought, as usual, it was kind of clever, her being mostly a machine, yet one able to get around between-space as if she was a self-contained matter transducer. Someone who was there, even if the Diver didn't realize it, albeit only because he was damn near ubiquitous, did catch the inference.

Didn't like it either. Particularly didn't like All the self-proclaimed invincible she-sphinx of Incain, the Prison Beach thereof. Other than the Dual Entities, said She-Sphinx, usually capitalized, who was known as Ginny the Gynosphinx pre-Flood, was about all he stayed away from on the Hidden Continent. At least the Male Entity could be killed. In fact he had been, for the hundredth time, very recently on the Moon.

And when Helios dies, he goes back into the time stream, carrying All's creator, the Female Entity, with him, and her carrying Trans-Time Trigon with them both. If only All was that easy. Short of being hit by a Brainrock asteroid she seemed, and probably was, as indestructible as she was self-sustaining.

Was now and was then, when she first ate Primordial Lilith then, centuries later, munched Pyrame Silverstar before she even named herself.

=========

*This someone was visible every night above the Head; was visible as a star, hence dark during the day, an eye in the sky, as it were, looking down upon everyone living or at least awake and moving throughout the Inner Earth. This eye, and it was an eye, had a mouth for a pupil. It, the mouth, had lips in its pupil. These lips formed a grimace rather than a grin.*

*It was the right time of year. Was past time to go downstairs, actually. Was, as well, once again, time to remind these pestiferous, so-called supranormal blowhards who was not so much the teacher to their pupils as who was the school principal, the boss, the guy with the strap. That he could leave his office, Cathonia, while still maintaining it, was one more example of his near-omnipotence on in or under this, his Hidden Headworld.*

*He didn't mind being the proof in the Zmas pudding.*

=========

Five spectacular balls of a transparent, membranous material that magnified those inside them came out of the dome above the Banquet Hall. The populace, idiots, borderline imbecilic caregivers, teenage hybrids, non-born clones, scientocrats, Trinondevs, Illuminaries, everyone in attendance, was treated to an unprecedented exhibition of flash and fancy.

The spheroids shot over top of them, passing by time and time again so that everyone could get a glimpse, possibly for the last time, of their acknowledged saviour, Aristotle Zeross, with his wife, their family and their friends, the devil-fighters; at least one of whom was also a proven re-cathonitizer if not a for sure a devil-slayer. Finally the balls settled on High Table level and the ten people within them stepped out. The spheroids vanished.

With Sundown sticking right beside Furie; Akbar, Gloriel and the Diver with the three Zeross children; and Melina helping her husband; they took the chairs Mel's Illuminaries indicated were intended for them. After Harry was seated at one head of the table Mel herself joined Golgotha Nauroz, the skeletal, too tall, black-as-midnight, skull-faced leader of the Trinondev Warrior Elite – the people's hero, as she'd previously described him – on the edge of the upper level and beamed brightly.

In voices amplified by his eye-stave, his microphone on a staff, Golgotha and Melina raised their hands and pronounced in unison: "Let the Master come!"

The dome lit up almost as luminously as the sun. It coalesced, dimming only slightly less blindingly so, around a figure suddenly standing as if on nothing except the air itself. Thus appeared Saladin born Nauroz, the Master of Weir since 5950.

Large, powerfully built, bearded, both bare- and barrel-chested; not quite as black-skinned as Golgotha and the rest of the non-hybrid male Utopians; he was in full Masterly regalia. That consisted of a headdress made of ostrich feathers from which protruded a single rhinoceros horn; a sleeveless cloak made of fur from a white gorilla; a reindeer-leathern kilt belted about his waist; it, the belt, composed of an intricately held-together assemblage of ivory tusks taken from elephants or woolly mammoths, boars, walruses or narwhals; gauntlets that looked like bear paws and boots that looked like tiger paws.

About his neck he sported his chain of office: a corona of ruby-red bloodstones off of which depended a medallion shaped like a golden triangle with a single eye staring out of it. In one hand he raised a curved, Saracen-style sword. In his other he raised the Master's Mace, what he as often referred to as his 'Speaking Stick' and what someone else had described as a mike on a spike. On that arm he brandished a shield so shiny it reflected like a mirror.

Just about everything on him gleamed, parti-coloured, with the unmistakeable glow of Brainrock-Gypsium. No more so than he did — he may or may not be a Creature of the Cosmos or a Wakinyah Thunder Being, but the halo surrounding him imparted the aura of a radiating Celestial; a definitely non-fallen angel. (His grandfather, Ubris Nauroz, had been the so-called Nubian who, along with Celeste Mannering, the Celestial Superior, called the Simultaneous Summonings in February-Balek 19/5920/1.)

Murray struggled to get out of Sundown's grasp. "Let me go, Johnny." When the American aboriginal resisted, the Africa-born, Jamaica-raised Summoning Child tried futilely to become Furie. "Look through my eyes, Fuckhead," he raged, denied the opportunity to growl or snarl anymore ferociously. "He's got the Trigregos Talismans, the same as Vetala's cursed soldier had in Hadd and the dream-sent Diver we saw out on the Slopes did ten days ago."

Instead of releasing him, Sundown edged over to Ringleader and had Murray repeat his assertion. Zeross shook his head regretfully. "I wish they were. I was tracking down the real ones when I came across you in Sisert. Those are fakes; made of Brainrock, sure, but fakes nonetheless. UD took care of the originals."

(OMP-Akbar once believed he'd done a ditto during the final battle on by then Drenched Dustmound. According to the Diver, though, his Homeworld Sceptre leaked. Luckily he was in position to get hold of them before anyone else could. He'd subsequently melted them out of existence in the lava lake crater of Sedon's Peak, filled as it was with molten Brainrock, on the shores of which he came across Harry Zeross, altogether the worse for wear, on the Fourteenth.)

"Jesus! Jervis, Johnny, look at that!" (Because they were in direct contact, Sundown could see through Murray's eyes.)

Saladin was growing huge, immensely huge. His shape was filling the entire hall. Then, abruptly, there was a clap of thunder and he was standing on High Table level, his normal, mostly non-glowing self again. A woman appeared beside him. At least it looked to be a woman. Her clothing made it difficult to tell.

She was cloaked from head to foot in a boxy, snow-white burqa, a deliberately all-concealing costume usually only seen in the most fundamentalist areas of the Muslim world beyond the Cathonic Dome. Even her eyes were veiled. Murray squirmed nervously. Sundown tightened his grip.

The chanting began: "HAIL, SALADIN! HAIL, MASTER! ALL HAIL!"

Saladin reached his arm upwards. The sword, the shield, the chain of crimson stones, with its triangular medallion so reminiscent of the pyramidal eye on the back of the American dollar bill, lifted off him. As they vanished as if into the night's sky, which could be seen through the hall's glass dome, Star Sedon looking down, he embraced his escort.

In one motion she tore off her unappealing garment and kissed him on the lips. The cheering immediately quelled. Were the people sucking in their collective breath; were they shocked by what they had just seen her do to their reclusive, witch-hating Master;; or were they simply stunned by the woman herself? Probably the last.

She was undeniably as statuesque as any female pureblood in the Weirdom. Broad at the shoulder, tight in the bosom, waist and hips, she was wearing a diaphanous outfit as white as her skin and so clinging it was difficult to tell where the outfit stopped and the skin began. A white skull-cap covered all of her hair; no mean feat that. Two rabbit ears of cloth stretched out of her just-below-knee-length skirt, hid her breasts, and were tied around the back of her neck. That was it, no shoes, leggings, jewellery, makeup, nor any other ornamentation.

She was the perfect compliment to the Master. If he was the black god, she was the white goddess.

"Finally figured out why I'm holding onto you so tightly, Jerry?" Sundown queried sardonically. Due to contact with Murray's arm, the Cheyenne Creature of the Cosmos could see as well as Jervis could. Put better, since they were using the same set of eyeballs, he could see exactly what Jervis saw.

Murray grunted in understanding. "Didn't think it had anything to do with love, Johnny."

"Not on my part it doesn't."

"Nor on mine; not anymore."

========

*The awkward pause passed and, perhaps appropriately, the tumult grew so deafeningly no one but Sundown heard Jervis Murray gag on his mashed potatoes.*

*The black god's white goddess was Wilderwitch.*

********

# Seven-Babies: DAMNATION DISAPPEARING

=========

**Boxed-In Boxing Day 5980**

*"Not same as Saul. Not same as Psycho." Those were the last conscious thoughts of Cerebrus David Ryne before he, on the 6th of Tantalar – like his twin brother had nearly a quarter of a century earlier – literally blew his mind. (As well as, in his case, disconnected his headplate, what made him a cyborg.)*

*Cerebrus was wrenched out of oblivion as much by an irreducible terror as by droplets of blood plopping into the liquid in which his entire body was submerged. Like the Diver, on a day-to-day basis, he felt no need to breathe whilst immersed in Cathonic Fluid. During his twenty-five years in Limbo he had never felt any need to breathe either. Then again he did not have a body in Limbo. Did now, a useless one.*

*Next to useless, make that. He opened his eyes.*

=========

Due to an anomalous outcropping (puddle?, spring?) of Brainrock-Gypsium nearby, the Citadel of the Thinkers was the oldest building still standing in the Weirdom of Cabalarkon, Sedon's Devic Eye-Land. Although they were constructed off the same enormous, obelisk-bestrewn square at the heart of the metropolis, it predated the old Masters' Palace and the so-called Grand Cathedral by a few decades, perhaps even a few centuries.

The Citadel was built by the Dual Entities shortly after the Whole Earth's original contingent of Trinondevs, led by Heliosophos, Helios called Sophos the Wise, the Male Entity himself, came to ground a, to-date, final time. That meant the Citadel had been in existence since no more than a decade before Xuthros Hor caused the Great Flood of Genesis some sixty extremely eventful centuries past.

In catacombs underneath the city's vast, central square, its firestone-capped obelisks and its Cyclopean structures, underneath a large part of the metropolis itself, lay many dozens of sepulchres filled with Cathonic Fluid. In these stone coffins *'slept'* virtually every one-time Master of Weir who had not quite died during the last six millennia.

The Citadel, the tri-towered Grand Cathedral, the old palace and the catacombs were not built to house these past notables. They being here was more or less an afterthought. The lone notable they were built to house, at least underground, enjoyed company. Cabalarkon, call-me-Cabby, had told him so himself, ghost to ghost, sometime ago. Had also told him he had one special visitor who came to see him around this time every year.

"Hi," Cyborg Cerebrus gurgled, doing his best to fain fearlessness. It wasn't working and he wasn't the only one who realized it.

As Cabalarkon predicted, the visage staring down at him could only be described as Satanic. The scarlet-skinned man was entirely naked and playing with himself. He had a knotty erection, thicker and much longer than the horns protruding out of either side of his forehead. Except for a tail-like tuft of hair growing out of the back of his skull, his gnarly head was shaved bald.

His ears were peaked and pierced, though he wore no earrings. In addition to the ponytail he had a thin moustache and a forked goatee. His right arm was cut off just below the elbow. It was from this stump that the blood dripped into the tub of Cathonic Fluid within which Cerebrus was immersed. His two eyes bore through him, constricting his very soul.

Cabalarkon's warning he might be coming round, his Satanic seeming, the fact one of his eyes was in his forehead, none of that gave away his identity. Cerebrus had seen him before, with his mind's eye — his *'phant'* or *'phantasia'*, as it was technically known in not just mystical circles. (The word *'aphantasia'* was an actual condition, one defined as a blind or absent mind's eye that resulted in those afflicted being unable to form mental images.)

The humanoid horror was inside the Master when he was making love to Wilderwitch while, at the same time, a supposedly fantastical Trigregos Diver was launching the apparently just as illusionary assault on the Weirdom from out of the Ghostlands on the 14th. Miserable Moloch must be here to finish me off now that I can't do anything about it.

***"Calm yourself, Horrite. I only wanted to see what manner of being could infantilize a Master Deva the calibre of the Apocalyptic of War. Oh, yes, you got your man — but he got his too. Pleasant dreams, pathetic little would-be patriarch. I doubt you'll recover sufficiently to cause me or mine any more bother.***

***"Though I am about to start causing you and yours more trouble than humanity could possibly begin to imagine!"***

He smiled suitably evilly, revealing mandatory, shark-sharp or barracuda-like teeth. The grandfather of all Master Devas effortlessly drew the heavy stone lid back over the tub. As it slammed shut Cerebrus David Ryne was once again faced with oblivion.

Except, why did oblivion look like him? Then why did look it like a female face made up of translucent ice?

"Thought everyone saved their visits for Boxing Day, Klannit?"

"No need to think so loudly, cyborg," said the reflection. Although, upon further reflection, of his own, he decided Klannit Thanatos, the Mirror Mentalist as she'd self-codenamed herself, couldn't be a reflection as such. She had to be ... what? A sending?

"A telecasting," she offered, alternatively. "I like to far-speak face to face."

"Don't suppose you'd listen if I told you to get out of my mind."

"Of course I'd listen. I just wouldn't pay it any more attention than if you told me to get out of your face." Seeing an icicle woman smiling, no doubt thinking it was warming, even fetching, for a fetch, didn't really work for Cerebrus, but he held his peace so well Klannit didn't even interrupt herself to comment upon it.

"But, far-speaking of listening, you and I and your pal with the solar spear have some killing to do."

"Can't you just get to him like you get to me?"

"With a name like Blind Sundown, you think he gazes into a mirror very often?"

"He can see through others."

"Isn't others I want compelling."

"Not sure I can help you. I mean, aside from ethically, I'm not sure I could compel anyone given the shape I'm in."

"Neither am I. Still, you know what they say about two heads being better than one."

"Don't need two heads, Klannit. I'd be happy with one that does what it's supposed to do, mine. Besides, you just said you're useless when it come to getting to Johnny."

"Wasn't my head I was referring to but, given the shape you're both in, I catch your drift. How about two brains being better than one, then — yours and one that nearly matches yours?"

"Not getting you."

"Still missing the point, aren't you? Isn't me you're supposed to get. By the way, it's after midnight. Which makes it Boxing Day. Which makes it okay to have visitors, right? I sure hope so because there's someone here you are supposed to get and, funnily enough, he's as much in a box as you are; only his is way smaller."

Cerebrus finally got her. Got him, too.

========

*It was quite the night for everyone in the Weirdom, not just Cerebrus and not just those at High Table. Sooth said, for those at High Table, High Table was just the beginning.*

========

First the Diver was caught near the kitchen glacials, their refrigerators, off the floor level and beneath the second level of the mastaba. He was trying to ingest his meal privately, away from prying eyes. Ingesting for the Diver involved particlyzing his dinner, plate and all, inserting it into his gut, inverting the plate, shaking it off, pulling it out, whistle-clean, and starting to digest what he'd dumped inside himself.

Some of the time he burped and most of the time he did so breathing. Which he had to remind himself to do as he had no need of air; hadn't had since '38. Air just came to him if not exactly supernaturally then at least supranormally. Then, probably because, despite his best efforts not to be seen, he'd been spotted coming through the floor; was understandably given where he was, mistaken for a devil.

Then the Master made all six members of D-Brig there in attendance submit to being eyeorb-probed for devic possession. Which they did, five of them did anyhow: Murray, the Diver, Gloriel, Akbar and Sundown. And which they passed, though admittedly, first Jervis Murray then John Sundown stomped off before the Master got around to testing Wilderwitch. Who couldn't possibly be a devil, could she?

An hour or so later, postponing for just a little while longer the inevitably sad and drawn out fare-thee-wells to Ringleader, Harry Zeross, all of those at High Table, save the guest Illuminaries, fulfilled a promise they'd made to Raven's Head and reconvened in her newly completed stable-cum-laboratory. Which D-Brig, with some unseen and not always overnight help, had built off the old palace. Whereupon the high feelings at High Table bubbled over anew.

This time, in full view of Harry, Mel-Illuminatus, their hybrid daughters, the Master, his Trinondev escorts and their leader, Black Skull-Face, Golgotha Nauroz (Ubris's clone), Wilderwitch – who could have been and was, even if she didn't realize it, daemonic as opposed to devic – and Dervish Furie, not Jervis Murray, went at each other viciously, tooth and nail, fang and claw, no holds barred, though thankfully no overly bloody holes caused.

The Witch, back to her non-illusionary, non-altogether-white, gypsy-self, was wearing a short but expensive sarong salvaged from her bottomless bag by Mel so she could look her best for Raven. (The Wakinyah Thunder Creature liked colourful clothes on those she sometimes let ride her.) The sarong didn't fare as well as she did. In fact, hobbled as she still was by her Doltaur-damaged thigh, blood from which wound was seeping through her expertly, Mel-applied bandages, the Witch gave a remarkable accounting of herself.

She really was very good with that metallic marigold of hers, it had to be said. To the detriment of the walls in Raven's new digs, it also had to be said. Ah well, they all said, eventually, re-plastering the walls would give D-Brig something to do come the morrow besides having breakfast with each other.

While Akbarartha more so than anyone else was sorting them out with his Homeworld Sceptre, eyeorbs – including the ones atop the Witch's undersexed lollipop and the Master's mike-on-a-spike Speaking Stick – automatically triggered and, as if magnets to metal, rocketed off eye-staves throughout the nearby area. They'd detected the presence of the Moloch Sedon down below in the catacombs, where he was visiting his putative father, the ever-undying, one-eyed Utopian after whom the Weirdom was named.

Eyeorbs in their dozens were consequently chestnut-roasted unto so much crumbly ash. D-Brig, those who got to call-me-Cabby's private crypt in time, were flattened, Furie all the way back to Murray yet again. And Gloriel, who got down below first, came face to face with the greatest evil she could imagine — the greatest evil of her Faith dirty-dog-ditto, if indeed Sedon was Satan.

She lived to tell the tale. For now. They all did. Even if it once took them nearly 25-years to be in position to tell anyone other than each other anything, they mostly always did. That is to say, with the exception of those who didn't, back in the days of either the Society of Saints or the King's Own Crimefighters, and there were many of them. D-Brig, though, seemed blessed. Had to be because of their name, the Diver said.

It was not a tale any of them would repeat with pride, however. The Moloch Sedon was just so absolutely beyond anything in their experience, even Hiroshima, which both the Diver and OMP (and his wife, Corona Power, who was wearing the real Crimson Corona) survived relatively unruffled, it defied all logic to even think of ever taking him on.

Then …

========

*Athena Zeross didn't so much refuse to settle as refused to settle in bed with her mother. The 6-year old might even have blamed Mama Mel for what had just happened to her father. She chose instead to settle in Helen's bed. Which was where Persephone found them. The middle sister was snoozing away contentedly, evidently without a care in the world, but Tina was awake almost from the moment her eldest sister walked into the bedroom. Percy wasn't alone.*

*"Holy spit," Tina exclaimed, recognizing who was with her. "Boy, you sure must have eaten a lot at supper, Auntie Wildie."*

========

Blind Sundown was not in contact with anyone that morning at breakfast when Persephone and Helen Zeross tossed three of their father's rings at the feet of Gloriella D'Angelo Dark, Gentleman Jervis Murray and Kronokronos Akbarartha, thereby sending them elsewhere. Nevertheless he, Thundercloud Creature of the Cosmos that he was, sensed something terrible had just occurred. He was on his feet, solar spear in hand, its spearhead already flaring, in a instant. He could have immolated the two girls before they caught another breath.

"Don't get mad, Mr Sundown," Percy pleaded, her voice breaking. "Auntie Wildie told us to do it. She said they wanted to leave."

For some reason he hesitated. Maybe crisping a couple of teenage or near teenage girls was beyond even his capacity for unbridled slaughter. More likely he apprehended that, if he killed them now, he might never find out what they had done to his companions, let alone why they had done it. Most likely he realized that, since he could kill them any time he felt the need, there was no urgency to retaliate immediately.

Besides, when it came time to exact appropriate retribution, it would not be, could not be, on a couple of children. "Did she really? Too bad. I'm rather fond of the Witch."

Ringleader, Aristotle Zeross, their father, was an irreligious anarchist. At least he had been brought up to be such prior to D-Brig being sent into Limbo thanks to, and along with, Saul Ryne, the Magnificent Psycho. However, the Cheyenne Summoning Child recalled hearing from Gloriel that their Utopian Summoning Child of a mother, Melina born Sarpedon, had become a Roman Catholic nun while they were, as it were, away. Given her own upbringing, the Angelic had been delighted to report as much to him.

Sundown despised organized religions; due to constantly running away from a nun- and priest-ridden boarding school(s) throughout the late Twenties, early Thirties, none more so than Catholicism. Howsoever he hated to admit it, though, even he had to acknowledge, not very loudly, nor very often, they did sometimes have some educational and/or moral value.

That thought, he still had no way of telling just how much in the way of fear of Hellfire and Damnation, both of which he personified, Mel had instilled in her children. He expected they knew the difference between the speculative and the certain. (Apparently this Satanwyck place, Sedon's Temple, that know-it-all Mel showed them on a map a few days earlier was not full of just that, Hellfire anyhow. Somewhat shockingly she'd added that demons, mostly spelled without the 'a', which it was full of, were extremely inflammable. Which he already knew from Hadd.)

He was right about their upbringing. Just by looking at him the girls must have ascertained precisely how close they were coming to greeting their father in the Afterlife long before Daddy Harry got that far. Whereupon Helen, regaining her tongue, very nearly blew their opportunity for any chance at momentary longevity.

"Who isn't?" she ventured.

"Have to find that out, won't we?"

========

As its name suggested, Skyrise was a 30-storey skyscraper constructed of glass and gleaming metal. Rings must have brought the makings for it from the Outer Earth. He'd brought in many things from there: fine wine, properly tooled machinery, Radiant Rainbow fashions and, Sundown didn't doubt after seeing, through various eyes, most of the preteen and teenage hybrids gathered in the Weirdom for Zmas, highly fertile architects, trades people and labourers to help build it.

Once she left them in the catacombs Wilderwitch must have moved up to Saladin's private apartments on Skyrise's uppermost level. Since its top few floors were once again inaccessible by elevators or stairs, Sundown marched the two girls to their mother and traded their unburned hide, still eminently burnable, for the code to the matter transducer that could take him to the top level.

Given he was so important to the Master's plans and, more importantly, quite capable of turning her daughters into flaming shish kebabs before she could blink either of her eyes, the High Illuminary felt she had no other choice except to oblige. That he knew there had to be a functional matter transducer up there, well, it made sense — this even if what he told her and the girls confirmed, both ways, didn't; not to her anyhow.

When he emerged on the Master's floor he asked one of the newly-appointed female Trinondevs there where he could find the Witch. The young attendant sounded like a non-hybrid and seemed remarkably competent for a Utopian pureblood; not that either the Master or the High Illuminary would employ an imbecile of Weir. (Imbeciles mostly came from families who'd been in Cabalarkon for millennia. Sarpedons like her had only been here for a couple of thousand years whereas Somatas like Master Kyprian's clan had only been in the Weirdom for under half a millennium.)

She pointed out her recently renovated suite of rooms but warned him Wilderwitch did not want to be disturbed. He assured her that, like she would be herself, the Witch would much prefer being attached and disturbed than detached and disintegrated. Although she couldn't look into his eyes, they being blindfolded, she raised no further objections, thus proving her mental competency.

Once again imagining where it was as much as anything else, he found her antechamber and inclined his head upwards. He had a feeling Wilderwitch was creepy-crawling, spider-like, along the ceiling. "Get down here, Witch," he demanded. "And tell me what you did to those children." Wilderwitch dropped off the ceiling, did an elementary somersault, and landed on her one good leg in front of the blind man. He waved his spear at her. It flared briefly and the Witch vanished in a puff of smoke. "Quit wasting my time."

"You're as amazingly aware of your surroundings and as quick to react as ever," admired the conceivably real Witch, wheeling out of her illusion of invisibility. She was wearing a dressing, a dressing gown, and nothing else. Last night's tussles with the Dervish reopened her wound so she'd had her injured thigh re-bandaged and gone back to using a wheelchair "Not everyone can see through a glamour let alone dispel one."

"I didn't see through anything, Witch. Can't, as you should know full well, having known me as I am longer than any member of this D-Brig of ours. Not without holding onto someone else I can't. If anything I sensed through it. And don't flatter yourself by attempting to flatter me. You should know better than trying to fool a blind man, especially one who's a...."

"Thundercloud Creature of the Cosmos. Yeah, yeah, I know your spiel. So what are you doing here? Not come to give me a lecture on monogamy I trust."

Actually, other than Sea Goddess, who was only monogamous in terms of having just one lover at a time, and Gloriel, who seemingly wasn't all that interested in sex, especially not for pleasure, Sundown was about the only one of them who could give her such a lecture. To the best of her knowledge, he'd known, in the Biblical sense, only one woman during his entire lifetime. That'd be her closest female friend ever, possibly her only friend ever: his long dead childhood bride, twice over, Solace Sunrise, Sorciere.

"Gloriel told me at breakfast the Diver disappeared from his room in the old palace overnight. That's the what and the when of that. She told it to me just before Harry's two eldest disappeared her, Rainbow, OMP and Murray. So I know the what, when, and who of that. What I want to know is the where and the why of any of this, though I can guess a good part of the last. You see, the Zeross girls claim there's more than just the two 'who' of them involved in all of it." For him, that was a speech.

"Harry's horrors said I put them up to it?" the Witch grasped. Sundown nodded. Her verbal expression of surprise struck him as genuine. Good thing for her. "Well, it wasn't me."

He wasn't so sure about her expression of innocence. But, he'd heard as a preteen youth in the early Thirties – at the Catholic boarding school Manitoulin forced him and Solace to attend, like most children in their Rocky Mountain village – that when it came to witches it was always better to let them erect their own stake, preferably on a wagon of straw, before setting it ablaze.

"This is the Headworld, Witch. How can you be so sure?"

"I'd know, Johnny."

"You'd think the girls would, too."

"There is that, I grant you. Does the Master know?"

"Mel knows so, if he doesn't already, he will soon. Unless ..."

"Unless?"

"Unless, like I said, he knows already."

"I see. Guess we'll have to see about that then."

"Not a matter of guessing. We will."

"Want to hold my hand?"

"Only until I get hold of his neck."

"If needs be, leave that to me."

"Maybe you better let me hold your hand."

She did. He took it … tightly. As good as she was with sensory illusions, even tactile ones, he didn't need to be a Creature of the Cosmos to realize it was real. His solar spear flared. She swore, only belatedly realizing that she was within his exclusion zone and he wasn't about to let her leave it.

"You bastard!"

"Adopted bastard," he corrected her.

Shamanitoulin, as even Shaman Manitoulin, the Cheyenne medicine man who raised both John Sundown and Solace Sunrise from infancy after the Summoning of 1920, sometimes referred to himself, never did acknowledge he was either of theirs father. Then again he never denied it, either. He had after all raised Solace's definite mother, Louise born Riel eventually St Synne, who died having her, and it wouldn't do to admit even a semblance of incest.

They disappeared.

========

*"How?"*

*"That isn't a 'w'-question, Witch."*

*"No, it's a 'h'-one, asshole."*

*"I've been practising."*

========

Melina came out of daughter Tina's bedroom in the floor-wide apartments she lived with her children, and hubby Harry prior to him being put down, as in immersed in a tub of Cathonic Fluid, as he now was and would be for the foreseeable future. Sundown had been there before, when he traded Percy and Paree to her in return for the code to the Master's matter transducer.

Which, that he'd been here, not the matter transducer, was how he managed to travel back via the Grey. Had to know where you were going before you went there. He'd told the Diver that when he first started practising short-hop teleportation in Vancouver, the night of the 5$^{th}$, and the only thing that had changed in that regard was he was getting quicker at it.

Mel-Illuminatus took one look at whom Sundown had brought with him, between-space, which until then she hadn't realized the Cheyenne Summoning Child could pass through without Raven's Head, and charged at them both. Like a mother hen protecting her chicks, she did so screaming.

"You fucking bitch!" Whereupon she was repelled, ass-backwards, halfway across the room. Where she landed, ass-cushioned, on the floor. Skyrise had sumptuous carpets.

"That's fucking Witch, Mel-bitch," Wilderwitch reprimanded her. Despite last night's close encounter with the Moloch Sedon in call-me-Cabby's private crypt, which resulted in her all but having to beg the Master for a new eyeorb to fit atop it, she really was good with her metallic marigold.

Unfortunately Blind Sundown still had her in a grip that wouldn't have been out of place in a metalwork shop. There wasn't much she could do about him, not when he was inside her sphere of influence, as it were. She simply hadn't got that far in terms of narrowing the effectiveness of the force shield her undersexed lollipop projected about her to exclude someone already holding onto her hand.

"What's going on?" cried Tina, rushing out of her bedroom in reaction to the commotion going on in their living room. She went straight for her mother, then stopped herself as if on a dime, which they didn't have in the Weirdom, and gaped at the Witch and Sundown in evident amazement. Gaped more so at the former than the latter, it seemed to him, he who was the latter holding hands with the former. Not that she could have had any idea how they got here.

"Holy poop, Auntie Wildie. You really must have had a big time dump."

The High Illuminary, from her undignified position on the floor, looked about to reflexively blast her youngest for using foul language. She must have thought better of it and instead glared at Wilderwitch. For her part, the Witch's eyes never left Tina. Which was fine with Sundown. He already knew what he looked like.

"What's that supposed to mean, Athena," the Witch demanded of the little girl, presumably feeling now was not the time for diminutives.

"Only you were so much fatter this morning when you woke me up."

This time the Witch did look at him. "Let me go, Johnny. I've got to sit down."

"And why exactly would I do that?" he asked, half-admiring how deadly he looked. He really should have combed out his braids better before he redid them.

"Because I can feel my leg starting to haemorrhage again and because I all of a sudden think I know who was here this morning."

"And who might that be, other than, all of a sudden, not you?"

"My daughter," the Witch responded. "Fey Girl, Fey Woman by now, was a big baby." Was also born in here, though she was conceived out there by a father whom she never told was said daughter's father; never told anyone, not even Fey. "That didn't change as she grew up. And out, in all directions. When she wasn't much older than Tina is today she was, like, Tina-times-two size-wise."

"And now she's more like you-times-three," said Melina. "Or was, last time I saw her."

The Witch instantly shifted her glance to the High Illuminary. Mel raised herself as far as a kneeling position and inelegantly began rubbing feeling back into her aching bum. Tina ran into her arms. She was crying now, her eyes darting between the Witch and Sundown like the terrified child she had to be by now.

"Why haven't you ever told me how she's doing?" Wilderwitch sounded accusatory. Sundown still wasn't letting go of her.

"You never asked and it never occurred to me you'd be interested. I mean, you're an Anthean and Antheans aren't supposed to care anything special about their daughters. They're just little sisters, right? Besides …"

"Besides?"

"Besides, last time I saw her she was doing …" Mel glanced at the daughter in her arms, "Um, well. Well, yes, that's it. Was also doing fat well. Really well."

"Let's try again, shall we? Besides?"

"She was doing, well, like you're doing, Witch. With the Master. Only it wasn't really well. It wasn't working out. Fey's infertile."

"Now I really need to sit down, Johnny."

"Where's your pretty little box, skinny Auntie Wildie?" wondered Tina, tears under control now that she felt, howsoever erroneously, safe in her mother's arms.

Sundown let Wilderwitch go. Thought better of it immediately, picked her up bodily just as she started to swoon and carried her over to the nearest available sofa. Whereupon he laid her down, stepped back and let Mel deal with redressing the seepage-drenched bandage around her right thigh.

He didn't feel bad about her. Didn't fell bad about what he'd been intending to do to her ever since Percy begged for her life by blaming the Witch. He felt bad for them, all of them, for himself as much as for her and everyone else, what was left of the Family Zeross and their just-this-morning, four lost fellows in D-Brig.

He knew what fit into a little lacquered box. The remnants of Psycho's brain!

========

*They, Wilderwitch and Blind Sundown, went to Raven's Head's stable-cum-laboratory, its walls still as much of a mess as they were after the Witch and Furie went at each other so viciously the night before. It was Boxing Day after all and where they came from – rather, where they had spent most of their time pre-Limbo – Boxing Day was visiting day.*

*It wasn't just Raven they came to visit, though they did that. It was more a matter of gathering her up such that the three of them could visit Cerebrus David Ryne. The others, Murray-Furie, Radiant-Gloriel, OMP-Akbar, and UD-Yehudi, said that's what they were going to do, after they all helped put Rings, Harry, down last night. They should have, too.*

*Would have as well. Had not other issues come to the forefront, the Witch going off with the Master foremost, Sundown and Raven going off on their own, albeit with Golgotha Nauroz, second-most, if only to avert another, offensive to the Master, display of pique. It was a bad night, last night. Had been a lot worse next day so far.*

*Raven's Head neigh-cawed a query.*

========

"So it was Aranyani Ryne who came to get Psycho's brain on Damnation Isle?"

"I understand Raven as well as you do, Johnny," insisted the Witch, who was back in her wheelchair again and wearing a neck-to-toe drapery, complete with headscarf or *'hijab'*, rather than the far more immodest sarong she put on after High Table the night before. "And, motherly-speaking, it's Aranyani Nightingale, just by the by. She's my niece, Eden's daughter. And, yes, that makes David and Saul my nephews, but you'd know that already."

"And Eden Nightingale's your sister in more than just Flowery Anthea."

"As is Fish, Fisherwoman, Scylla Nereid. Heliosophos's fellow time-tumbler, the Female Entity, Miracle Memory, claimed we were hers, hers in the sense she bore us all the way to birth. As opposed to all the other hers, whom she somehow managed to pawn off on someone else to do the birthing bit. Starting with Eden in '09 and ending with me, in '27, we were born nine years apart. Seems there's something mystical about the Number Nine."

"There's something a lot more than just mystical about this Female Entity of yours. Gloriel's aunt, Mnemosyne D'Angelo, married a Heliopolis, Agenor. Had a kid by him, too: Europa, not Kadmon. I tried to kill him once, Agenor, not his kids. Well, okay, I tried to kill him more than once. No more than he tried to kill me."

Raven's whinnied an objection. Agenor Heliopolis, the first Olympian, he who rode a Pegasus psychopomp – more correctly known as a pterippus – between-space and was expert with Zeus's bolts of lightning, had tried to kill her, too. Sundown allowed she was right; as always. "We do have a long and almost always bitter history – her-story, as you'd have it, Raven – about us, don't we?"

They were in the catacombs of the Sleepers. The wall torches the Master had insisted be lit the night before – Sal enjoyed melodramatics – were out but the obelisk-powered, electric lights were on. As if Thundercloud Creatures needed light to see by; as if Wilderwitch did either. They found the crypt, and the stone sepulchre wherein Cerebrus lay, immersed as he was in Cathonic Fluid. Raven volunteered to provide the blood necessary to wake him up.

The Witch, now that they were friends again, employed that double-entendre-laden way of speaking she often used to make light of a potentially desperately serious situation. Suggested one Creature of the Cosmos shouldn't prick another Creature of the Cosmos. All the more so when they were incompatible species.

Raven's Head whinnied an observation. The Witch and Sundown had heard them coming, too. There was nowhere near as much time as they'd like. Sundown easily flipped open the stone coffin's hinged lid. Cerebrus looked fine. Or as fine as someone with a bent out of shape, stress-cracked and in spots gorily ruptured headplate could look. At least none of his brains had visibly spilled out into the tub.

"Interesting," said the Witch.

"Interesting?" Sundown as much as echoed, albeit quizzically.

"The lid and sides are mirrored."

"This is interesting?"

"Sal's drawn the drapes about his bed."

"Which have a mirrored lid and sides?"

"A mirrored roof, Johnny. And sides, yes. Not anymore, though."

"Now that sounds interesting."

"Only in terms of their absence. Oh, look who's here."

"Raven and I are Creatures of the …" Raven's latest sound, a sharp, nearly inaudible whistle, shut Sundown up. Lit his spearhead up as well, although he quickly dulled it mentally.

It wasn't Golgotha Nauroz and a bunch of older Trinondevs, veterans of Hadd, coming to take them to the Master of Weir. It was a bunch of Trinondevs much younger than the grizzled veterans who usually accompanied Golgotha. They didn't know the two females but they'd been introduced to their male leader previously; Sundown and Raven shortly after their arrival in the Weirdom to stay on the 9$^{th}$, the Witch within a day or two of her emerging from her enforced seclusion on the 15$^{th}$ of Tantalar, December.

(Did December have Ides? Someone had asked Mel. Yes, she'd answered, no doubt after pressing her invisible know-it-all button, but wasn't it on the 13$^{th}$?)

He was, according to Melina, a non-born clone named Capputis. She further gave them to understand that, even though he was still in his late teens and had only recently moved up from what passed for cadetship in the Weirdom, he was one of the Master's favourites. One thing he wasn't, this Capputis, was pretty. Not by any stretch of the imagination.

For a clone his skin wasn't even all that jet-black. Facially he was both pockmarked and pimply, simultaneously looking both oily and rough, almost scaly, to the touch. He had an overly large head – a sign of hydrocephalus, water on the brain, Sundown recalled Melina telling them at the same time, and probably on the same day, that Ides just meant the middle of the month; that there was noting foreboding about it, this in reference to events out on the border that turned out to be the Master's Dream; his Phantast Folly, as some whispered.

That did not necessarily mean he was mentally deficient, she assured them. In fact, she insisted, he was quite intelligent. He was certainly smart enough to stay away from Utopian barbers. His hair was long, hastily tied back with a strip of leather, tangled and wet. He must have just come from a having a shower because today was the first time any of them had seen him without a loosely knit, toque-like headpiece, with earflaps strapped underneath his chin, that resembled a Peruvian *'chullo'* or French Canadian head muff, albeit without the facial covering.

That the Master now allowed women, unsuccessful Illuminaries for the most part, to become Trinondevs was one of Mel's most recent victories. That so many of Golgotha's then all-male Warriors of Weir perished in Hadd made it an afterthought-wise decision. That, as evinced by the parade of fools they witnessed the night before in the Hate-Sedon Sphere, a likely majority of Cabalarkon's population were inbred idiots had a lot more to do with it. It was no wonder a few hundred dead in Hadd put such a crimp in the Trinondev replacement pond.

You didn't have to be particularly intelligent to become a Warrior of Weir; not like you did a scientocrat or even an Illuminary. You just had to be fit and at least borderline competent. And there were as many fit and borderline competent female Utopians as there were male ones. Were an extraordinary amount of fit Utopians, plain and simple, emphasis on simple, as well. Whatever came out of the Weirdom's food replication systems had to be good for you. Too bad it tasted like recycled crud.

Which of course was what it was. Utopians recycled everything, even their own waste. Even if it had been six thousand years since they'd ridden millennial ships, for countless generations upon countless generations, old habits died hard. And, admirably if counter-intuitively, so did Utopians.

Raven squawked some more.

"What's that?" muttered Sundown, who had only just that moment decided not to toast Capputis.

As far as the Cheyenne Summoning Child was concerned the teenager had been following him around a fair bit more than mere curiosity warranted. Once, not long after he came back to the Weirdom from Hadd, Capputis had even asked to hold his solar spear. Sundown let him. As he'd proved in Hadd, he didn't have to be holding it in order to activate it. (Neither did OMP-Akbar his Homeworld Sceptre. Facts that many an overconfident enemy had learned the hard way — and not just in Hadd.)

"What's he got behind his ears?"

=========

*Hybrids had lived in the Weirdom of Cabalarkon for generations. It could even be argued that the Somatas, the family from whence hailed secretly hated great-grandmother Kyprian, his predecessor as Master, were hybrids. They originally came from the Weirdom of Kanin, on the outskirts of the Gregarian Fields, Sedon's Mole, and Kanin had no tradition of maintaining any form of ethnic purity even amongst its ruling class.*

*They lived a good long time, did most of them, Master Kyprian only being somewhat of an exception. (One famous short term Master, very long term High Illuminary, Jordan 'Quoits' Tethys by name, was a millennial child, born circa 5000 YD. She very nearly made it to her 500th birthday. Of course, being a Tethys, she was probably also a deviant – had a devic half-mother, likely Dame Chance, Wintry Moira – and deviants did tend to outlive their birth contemporaries. They also tended to get themselves killed at a young age by boasting about it.)*

*So maybe there was something to the theory that it was stone gnome slop, not unearthly genetics, that kept Utopians up here going and going and going. One thing was certain. Saladin Devason wasn't taking any chances. He ate the recycled crud spewed out of the food processors, but he also exercised fanatically.*

*Wasn't one for sports, however. Didn't even play board games. But he recognized when one was afoot. It was a Sedonplay and he had to admit, even if he was a mostly unwitting participant, it was proceeding rather well. Where once there were ten, then eight, now there were only four. He trusted the countdown would continue, that soon there'd be none.*

*He further trusted lascivious Lily counted the same way he did. If not, well, he'd had some thoughts on that as well.*

********

# Eight-Babies: **D-BRIG 4**

========

**Lazam, 25 Tantalar 5980**

*In deference to Raven's Head, Saladin Devason chose to meet with them in the throne room used by previous Masters of Weir on Earth. It was in the old, but impressively vast, four-winged, rectangular-shaped Masters Palace, Hate-Sedon Sphere in its central courtyard, not far from her stable-cum-laboratory.*

*His rationale must have been, one, she wouldn't have far to go if she chose to go and, two, if she chose to go on the spot, this particular area of the old palace, as smelly as it was ancient and decrepit, still hadn't been hosed down after last night's debauch. Imbeciles, like many an Outer Earthling, of any age, definitely knew how to party.*

*Weren't, also like all too many an Outer Earth teenager, too keen on cleaning up after themselves, however.*

========

It wasn't just Wilderwitch, Raven and Sundown he'd summoned. All three of the Zeross children were there, as were their onetime supranormal mother, Golgotha Nauroz and, oddly, his wife and fellow clone, Gethsemane. A number of Golgotha's Trinondevs and Melina's Illuminaries were as well. Capputis, now wearing his loosely knit chullo, or whatever it was called, earflaps secured beneath his chin, and the other young Trinondevs who escorted them to the throne room stayed, too.

Veils drawn such that only their ever-watchful eyes were visible, eye-staves bolt upright against the floor, manifested gargoyles looking ready to pounce atop them, they took position behind the Master. The latter sat in a throne, an unoccupied, backless footstool in front of him. Sundown figured Sal wanted all these comparative outsiders here in order to ensure the appearance of an impartial hearing. He had a solar spear to ensure an impartial hearing.

Like Wilderwitch had to her metallic marigold, Sal had attached a fresh eyeorb to the top of his Speaking Stick, his Master's Mace, which everyone already knew was anything except ceremonial. Persephone Zeross sat on the stool first. His eyeorb opened, an otherwise disembodied eyeball poked out of it on what might have passed for a prehensile, albeit organic, coat-hanger and bathed her in a kaleidoscopic radiance it emitted.

"It certainly looked like her," Persephone confirmed, under its hide-nothing influence, once she finished relating everything that had happened to her just after dawn that morning, and what she and Helen did on her, the Witch's, instructions an hour or so thereafter.

"Who else could it have been?" wondered Helen, when it was her turn to undergo the same truth-extracting, psychic probing.

Neither girl knew anything of what had become of the Diver and no amount of questioning could get them to say where they sent the other three. Which was as peculiar as it was indicative. Most there realized that, in order to work Harry's rings, you first had to visualize what they were to do before you deployed them.

If the girls hadn't envisaged where they were sending them, they couldn't have sent them anywhere. Yet they had. Ergo, they had to have had somewhere specific in their *phant*, their mind's eye. How could they not recall where it was, especially under the glare of the open eyeorb atop the Master's Mace? It was as if they'd been blanked, redacted, and, as the Master was quick to point out, everyone knew what that meant. Witchcraft!

Which left Wilderwitch without any choice but to submit herself to an identical grilling. "If it was witch-work it wasn't this Witch's work," she stated, incapable of lying even if she so desired. "Couldn't be. To coerce anyone, even children, into doing anything, this Witch needs agates. To blank or redact anyone afterwards, this Witch needs a dot for that ditto.

"Might the Mighty Master be able to advise this courtroom where her dittoing dots might be? And might he as well advise this court where this Witch was during the relevant time period, who she was with and what they were diddling-doing, dot-ditto? Besides not teleporting anyone anywhere."

"Your sarcasm isn't impressing anyone, Cynthia," said the Master. "However, I can verify for all here to hear that I did indeed confiscate your Anthean Agates, as well as your bottomless bag and every article of weaponry or jewellery, and every scrap of clothing you had on you, the moment Dr Aristotle Zeross left for Hadd after depositing you in our care. I can also verify they are still there, where I locked them up, in a safe made of Stopstone, which blocks Brainrock, in my quarters.

"You do not know where this safe is but someone besides myself, someone who is in this hearing room, does. I have allowed that same someone access to your enchantments in recent weeks. Your enchantments would include these selfsame witch stones. High Illuminary of Weir, you shall now submit yourself for examination."

"As the Master wills," said Melina, moving to take her turn on the hot seat.

She'd been asleep, having cried herself that way within an hour of them putting hubby Harry to rest. She wasn't a deviant; couldn't be because she was a pureblood. Her caduceus was just a manifested gargoyle. Even if it was a devic power focus, as many believed, she wouldn't know how to make it work as a teleportive device.

As for her dreams, yes, she was aware that Phantast Thanatos, the devic Dream Weaver, his star, no longer shone in the night's sky and, yes, she and her hybrid daughters had been kidnapped and held against their will in Frozen Lathakra, the devic protectorate of his triplet brother and sister, Tantal and Methandra, but she wasn't under their influence.

She'd be happy to recount them in detail, if the Master so desired, which he did. Suffice it to say tears were not the only thing wet about her last night.

Everyone left the old throne room scratching their heads. The Diver had just vanished, possibly of his own freewill, but the two eldest Zeross girls had not acted of theirs. They were no more certain as to whose freewill they acted on behalf of than they were where they sent the Angelic, Uncle Monster, as Helen referred to the Wildman, and the exiled Kronokronos, OMP-Akbar. Whoever put it into their minds to get rid of them, and to where, took it out again.

Wilderwitch couldn't have been in two places at once or, if she could, she hadn't volunteered that information while under eyeorb-probe. Despite the training Master Kyprian gave her years earlier, Melina was no good with agates, never had been. Not for casting glamours, stepping between-space on them, or using them for purposes coercive.

The bit about her caduceus not being a power focus she pulled out of the Olympian Tantalus decades ago didn't count as a lie because the Master was happy to let her claim otherwise. The Trigregos Talismans he'd sent Ringleader in search of were devic power foci, too, as were – according to some anyhow – the facsimiles he wore as part of his regalia. Wouldn't do to tarnish her reputation, or his, by association, by forcing her to admit too much in the way of borderline devic doings.

No mention was made of the possibility the early morning visitor first Persephone, then Tina and Helen had, with Percy in tow, might have been Fey Woman, Wilderwitch's overweight, by now 34-year old, lookalike daughter by whomever — the Witch had never told anyone, not even her, the identity of Fey's father. No mention was made of the lacquered box Tina said Fey, if it was Fey, was carrying.

Was it a pretty prop? A deliberate misdirection? Why had Capputis and his Trinondevs shown up just before they, the Witch, Sundown and Raven, had a chance to awaken Cerebrus? Because that was the obvious answer, wasn't it? Mind-control! Oh, yes, one other thing. There were other witches, weren't there?

Not to mention psychopomps that could travel inter-spatially, even through the Weird into the Weirdom.

========

"So if it was witchcraft, like Sal says it was," Sundown suggested to the Witch after the hearing concluded. They, her in her wheelchair, him pushing it with one hand and with Raven's reins wrapped around his other hand, the one he was also using to hold onto his Solar Spear, were returning to Raven's nearby stable-cum-laboratory.

"And if it wasn't your witchcraft and, even if she can get stuff out of your bottomless bag, Mel's no good with witch-stones, why does it have to be Fey's witchcraft? You know any witches who can get about in the Grey, the Weird, Shadowland or whatever else it's called today, without agates?"

"There are lots of other Sisterhoods, Johnny. Fey may or may not be infertile, which means she may or may not be an Ant, but Fish, for one, belonged to a whole convention of covens. So did Sorciere, your Solace, and she could use any witch's stepping stones. Was great with illusions too, the best I ever saw."

"Thanks for the memory, Witch."

"Sorry."

Raven's Head made a scold, more of a chirp of chastisement than a whiny whinny. "No I'm not getting morose or morbid, Beauty. All I'm saying is the Master supposedly doesn't allow any witch-stones in the Weirdom, other than the ones he keeps locked up in this Solidium safe he was boasting about."

"There are other ways to traverse the Weird," said the Witch, only now beginning to apprehend where he was heading.

"So there are. But, ask me, that only widens the field of suspects. For example, both Fish and Solace sometimes rode psychopomps – which it seems you are too, Raven – to get about between-space. Fish had a few. Delphi comes to mind for one; that psycho-bicycle the Diver said she had in Hadd for another. Plus, back in the Forties, Solace had Aquilla, a half-brained … what did she call him? A Garuda, that's it."

Psychopomps, another one being Agenor Heliopolis's Pegasus, what first came out of the Olympian Tantalus at least as early as the late Thirties, could traverse the Weird. They had nothing to do with the Magnificent Psycho. In the lexicon of the late White Witch, Superior Sarpedon, the Morrigan, they were related to demons. (As Sundown, after three weeks on the Head, now knew, demons were chthonic or earthborn creatures whereas devils were Cathonic or skyborn, as in extraterrestrial. Some could teleport. Morgianna wore one of these last for awhile. Didn't do her any good in the long term.)

"So did Eden," said Wilderwitch. "Hers was a nightingale, appropriately enough. Name of Medici, also appropriately enough, since the Medicis ruled in Florence, Italy."

"As in also Nightingale, got you. That young fellow with the big head, the one always running the Master's errands, Capputis, he's supposed to be a clone, right?"

"So I understand. What of it?"

"You noticed any other clones with gills behind their ears?"

Wilderwitch was still silently cogitating on that news when they arrived at Raven's digs. She wasn't as swift as Johnny or Raven were to realize the walls were no longer the mess she and Furie had made of them; were in fact back to being as good as new. Was barely swift enough to pick up on the significance of Raven's exclamatory squawks. Wash that birdbrain's mouth out with soapstone she was thinking when Sundown made another observation.

"And if they're demons, they're shape-shifters."

"Wait a minute there," the Witch protested. "You're suggesting I'm a demon?"

"Not at all," said Sundown, regarding her querulously, through Raven's eyes and with her perspective. "Should we have been?"

"Of course not. What were you saying then? I must have missed it."

"Only that stone gnomes must have fixed the walls and stone gnomes have to be demons. Demons are shape-shifters. If they wanted to look like your Fey, to cast suspicion on you; wanted to have pretty little box with them, to cast suspicion on Psycho; who's to stop them? More to the point, if stone gnomes are what keeps everything going in Cabalarkon; and the Weirdom's akin to a devic protectorate, which Mel says it is; who keeps everything going? Sal's who!"

"Curiouser and curiouser cried Alice," said the Witch. "I'd say you're fixated on Sal, but I'm getting that way, too. Come on, Johnny. You too, Raven, once you've taken care of your business." Raven's Head declined. Said, in her inimitable voice, that if the stone gnomes could fix her walls without being seen, they could at least fix them the way she wanted them to be seen. Besides, she wasn't ready to do her business quite yet. Unless it was with stone gnomes.

Sundown said he'd go with her; had just one question first. "Where?"

"To tea of course. You said it yourself, 'this is the Headworld, Witch'. Maybe it's Wonderland, too."

"And Golgotha's turban was made by the Mad Hatter?"

"No, but his looking glass might have been. Why do you keep looking at me like that? I'm not going Mad Hatter myself."

"I'm not, Raven is. But, um, since you asked, why did you think we were talking about you when we were talking about demons?"

"I misunderstood you is all. Wasn't really paying attention. I was still mulling over your notion that Capputis might be Fish's son." Raven said something. "What's how straight my hair's becoming got to do with anything?" Raven responded. "Then you don't know diddle about the things. Some of them might eat their moms in uterus but none of them possess anyone. They coat. Do I look coated?"

"You're sounding awfully defensive, Witch?"

"And you're both starting to piss me off again."

"I'll add that to my list of coyotes."

When Sundown was having difficulty understanding something he called it a coyote of a conundrum. Had done as long as she'd known him. As for the eldritch earthborn, daemons or demons were hardly just native to Satanwyck, Sedon's Temple; unholy heaps of the soulless, sometimes man-eating, denizens of depravity hailed from Hadd's north-western neighbour, the Forbidden Forest of Kala Tal, where they were best known as Indescribables.

They came in all sorts of shapes and sizes, from all over the Hidden Headworld, even from underneath it. Indeed, that's where the majority of them came from: Temporis's Mantels were related, as were the guard-bodies worn by Lemurian Frogwomen like Fish's step sister, Aortic Amphitrite of Shenon.

The so-called Hell-Well of the World, aka Absudyl, the subterranean realm of mandroid mush, lay directly beneath Cabalarkon's Weirdom whereas whimsy-prone faeries, like OMP-Akbar claimed to be, even had otherwise fully functional brains. That some of them ate their mothers, while still in the womb, was something of an exaggeration. Most of them waited until they were born to eat their moms.

Which of course explained why fucking faeries stole babies. Why bother having them if they'd just eat you?

"All right. If you have to know, it's the shampoo I'm using. Let's go see Melina."

========

*He opened his eyes. Two visages, only one of whom he recognized, glared down at him. "Can I help you?" he asked telepathically.*

========

Saladin Devason had also declined the Naurozes' invitation to tea at their apartments elsewhere in the old palace. Instead, accompanied by the hydrocephalic 'clone' currently at issue with the three remaining members of D-Brig in the Weirdom, he ventured into the catacombs of the Sleepers, to the crypt between Cabalarkon's and Ringleader's separate resting places. It was the teenager's blood, not his own, that awakened Cerebrus David Ryne.

"Quite the contrary," said the Master, "You can cease helping me. I told you once you might feel like doing me some favours someday. I did not tell you that you could do them without me telling you to do them. Capputis, destroy the mirrors."

"What's that behind your ears?" he wondered, as the teenage Trinondev, having removed his knit cap so it wouldn't get in the way, bent over him to do the Master's bidding.

The question, which he simultaneously thought-transmitted to his two latest visitors this busy Boxing Day, elicited no response, neither verbally nor telepathically. This wasn't surprising in the case of the latter. As the Master of Weir, Sal had to have developed, over the decades, a strong, perhaps even beyond supranormal defence system against matters mental made manifest or merely subliminally submitted, to use some of OMP-Akbar's alliterative phrasing.

Cyborg Cerebrus couldn't help but be impressed with the clone's ability to block him. Somehow or other this Capputis fellow was managing to ignore him as thoroughly as he, using the butt-end of his eye-stave, went about smashing and removing every scrap of glass on the insides of the stone sepulchre.

He was just as assiduous when it came to catching every cracked-off shard in a force shield cast by its eyeorb. Nary a speck nor a fleck of mirror dropped into the tub, filled as it was with, besides Cerebrus, Cathonic Fluid. Once he was satisfied with the job done the Master slammed shut the lid atop his stone sepulchre.

Sal must be feeling super-stressed, thought Cerebrus. He didn't even bother gloating as to how immune he was to my mind-mining magnificence.

========

*"Capputis is a clone," said Klannit Thanatos, far-speaking to him without the visuals. "At least everyone, including himself, thinks he's a clone. They're gills."*

*"You! How the ...?"*

*"Aren't you glad I didn't get out of your mind?"*

*"Who do you want Johnny to kill?*

*"Other than Dark Sedon, you mean? Who do you think?"*

========

The ice-statuary-animating azura finished instructing him as to what she, Klannit, and her devic parents, Tantal and Methandra Thanatos, King Cold and his Scarlet Empress – who were also Air and Sea's parents, she added for the first time – wanted him to do. The manipulative Mirror Mentalist had obviously been holding back that information on purpose; in hopes it would sway him to their cause, that of the Thanatoids of Lathakra.

Although eight years older than him, he and Thalassa were an item, as they said on the Outer Earth. She'd had a few boyfriends in her day, starting with Cousin Jess when they were barely 17, but she only had one boyfriend at a time and, so long as it lasted, made for a very loyal girlfriend. They had never married, mostly because she didn't believe in marriage, but also because she was officially dead; had been since '43.

That didn't stop them from being very Biblical with each other. In fact, some while after they'd been in Limbo, Sea told him she'd been pregnant. Which was a horrible thing to admit when she'd just lost her body, if not her mind, with a baby inside it, the moment Psycho blew his mind, theirs, and all of their bodies apart.

Not that either of them dared mention it again after that first time but for 25 years he, possibly more so than she, was tormented by thoughts of what might have been. Daddy Davy had a nice reverb to it. Still did, on Damnation Isle and once they'd returned to Vancouver. She claimed her persistent pregnancy was the main reason she had to go away the night of the 5th.

She'd turned to water and back any number of times since their return from Limbo. The foetus had presumably turned to water and back with her. That didn't mean it was in any way safe, let alone sensible, to stick with D-Brig. Cerebrus was determined to thrust them right back into it. There was the perceived menace on the Moon for one thing. Boiled – something else she could do with her state-shifting supra-gifts – down to she just wasn't prepared to take the risk.

Klannit, the Thanatoids' Haunted Angel, told him Thalassa was doing fine. Didn't know if she was still pregnant; at least so she insisted. She could find out. Her parents were not known for their open-mindedness. Still, do as she instructed and they'd likely come around to the notion of having a supra son-in-law.

Consequently too churned up emotionally to return to oblivion after she finally let him be, Cerebrus sent his spectral self outside his stone coffin. As he hoped, the Ghost of Cabalarkon was somehow sitting on his own sepulchre in the crypt next door. It was almost as if he was awaiting him.

Was a minor miracle them being here, let alone not slipping through the floors or ceiling.

========

"Haven't seen you for awhile," said the one-eyed Utopian revenant. "The Master's clearly been neglecting you. How'd you get with it?"

"His bodyguard, at least I assume he's his bodyguard, got me up. So to speak. Name's Capputis. He's gills behind his ears."

"Does he really? Hmm."

"My hmm exactly. You have any idea why they'd clone an amphibian?"

"A few actually. There are amphibians on the Head. What aren't there? Other than once they get too old for air and have to stay underwater for good, Lemurian Frogwomen are amphibious. So are Akadan Piscines, I think; some of them, anyhow. They certainly were at one time. Plenty of mermen and mermaids around the coasts as well. Red-capped Merrows and changeling Selkies are found in comparative abundance off Crepuscule, the Land of Twilight.

"A lot don't have fishtails and, if they've one thing in common with the Master, it's most of them hate Godbadian Imperialism. Could be the Master's breeding amphibious ambassadors in a renewed effort to gain some allies and thereafter restore the Godbadian monarchy, which he reckons would be more on his side than Centauri Enterprises. Despite pretensions to being a democracy, that's the company that runs the Corporate State of Greater Godbad. He reckons it's after our technology."

"Is it?"

"Indubitably. Might even have the wherewithal to figure out how everything extraterrestrial we have left works too. Aka Godbad City's linked to the Outer Earth. But you know that. You told me the Byronic Nucleus brought you through the Dome using the Nag Gap, Nag for Nagasaki, which is accessible from the Outer Earth's Centauri Island."

"Hence the Inner Earth's Centauri Enterprises."

"Hence exactly. Hence also the Outer Earth's equivalent, New Century Enterprises, I'm told. Its Cosmic Express was mostly our technology I'm to gather, thanks to our new neighbour. What did Capputis wake you for? I'm surprised he could even move your lid, let alone lift it. It doesn't have a crank."

"He didn't, the Master did. Could be Sal's become as paranoid about giving me blood as he is about these Godbadians you just mentioned. He had Capputis smash all the mirrors in my coffin. You have any other ideas as to why that is?"

"I might. Remind me to tell you about the Thanatoids' Haunted Angel."

"I'll do that. Had some other visitors as well."

"Anyone I know?"

"What do you think?"

"You mean you can't read me?"

"Seems my readings are restricted to those who give me blood. You haven't, assuming you have any left to bleed."

"I'm as flesh and blood as you or our newest neighbour. You are aware Harry Zeross was deposited next door to you last night, aren't you? And his tub has a crank to open it."

"Am now. He never gave me any blood either. Why would you think I could read you?"

"Because my Sedon of a Sed-son has. He came to see me last night."

"So why ask what you already know?"

"You said visitors. That's plural."

"So it is. All right, you might as well know. No point keeping secrets from each other, is there? Saul, my twin brother, was here last night. He's travelling with a woman named Faith McBride. She's some kind of supra who can pass through Samsara, the Universal Substance, solely by will alone it seems.

"Can do the same when it comes to the Dome – get through it, I mean – which even devils can't do. That's why the Byronic Nucleus needed to use the Nag Gap."

"And friend Harry had to do the Thanatoids' rescue work beyond it, if *you* have to know."

"I didn't, but do now, thanks to you. Anyhow, Saul raised the lid of my coffin telekinetically; had her drip some blood into my tub. Probably wanted to boast about how much better he was than I was now; this despite the fact she still carries around his brain in a box. But I got hold of him mentally. Tried to force what he knew about my headplate out of him."

"You succeed?" He queried, presumably having determined that that was a better opening question than what this Psycho's brain was doing in a box, let alone how could it be functioning?

"Couldn't hold onto him long enough. More's the pity. He wasn't as strong as he used to be. Not even as strong as he was when he tried to take me over in Vancouver a few weeks ago. I stopped him then, with some help, and I thought Wilderwitch had finished him off, what was left of him, shortly thereafter.

"Mind you, she thought Johnny and Raven had. Or at least that's what I picked up from her when I read her back in Vancouver, on the Thursday before the Byronic Nucleus brought us inside, when she was still too weak to resist my probes. Maybe I should go back to mind-reading literacy school."

"What was left of him being his brain in a box?"

"Something happened to Demon Land before he could bring Saul all the way back like he did the rest of us. I've my suspicions I know what it was, too. He overloaded psychically bringing back his own siblings. Did you know Aires and Thalassa D'Angelo were Aires and Thalassa Thanatos, a pair of fourth generation devils?"

"I knew there were an Aires and Thalassa Thanatos. Master Kyprian was always worried about what became of them. Their stars never made it to the night's sky; not like most of their other siblings did, after a batch of top level Byronics waylaid them coming down from Sedon's Peak back in '33. You were saying, about your twin?"

"Most of Saul's body's missing. Fact is, except for some of his little grey cells, a portion of his brain that is to say, which is fading fast, all of it still is. I think that's what he was here for; to find someone to help him retrieve it. It was a wasted trip. For both of us. This Faith managed to extract him before either of us could get anything useful out of either of us."

"Guess that explains that then."

"Explains what?"

"The Master popped by to see me before he went to see you a few minutes ago. Plopped by to talk to me, rather. That is to say he used his own blood. This Capputis was nowhere to be seen. Something's happened, cyborg. Four of your buddies in this Damnation Brigade of yours have vanished."

Cerebrus was incredulous. His immediate reaction, he said, upon hearing everything the Master told Cabalarkon – everything call-me-Cabby chose to tell him, make that – was Wilderwitch was behind it. With her soul-self she sort of could be in two places at the same time and Furie, the Wildman-side of Jervis Murray, was a jealous so-and-so. Might have hunted the Master down; done him serious injury. Sal and the Witch racing in wheelchairs was an interesting image.

"Except, it can't be. Wilderwitch sinks into a trance once she unleashes her soul-self. Except also, her soul-self's as mute as it's intangible. Except, assuming she can, and except for Saul we're all more powerful post-Limbo than we were pre-Limbo, why would she take on the form of a fat daughter? Why wouldn't she appear to the Zeross girls as, well, you name it, instead of the one witch, other than herself, who would draw attention to herself?"

"The Master's thoughts exactly," the Ghost of Cabalarkon responded to the Ghost of Cerebrus. "He had it down to mind-control. Which is why he came to see me, then you, after he was finished with the hearing. Figured it had to be you with the controlling mind. Me, I wasn't so sure it couldn't be Melina, the witch he first tried to finger for it in the hearing. She's the kids' mother. She's a Sarpedon. She's ..."

"Stop right there. Melina Sarpedon's still alive? Illuminatus is here, in the Weirdom?"

"Thought you knew that already."

"So you can't read me any more than I can read you."

"Books I can read, though they tend to get terribly soggy awfully quickly in a tub full of Cathonic Fluid. Minds I can't. Why?"

"Mel-Illuminatus is one of the ones who put together my headplate over the Xmas Season of '46-'47. I've got to find a way to get to her."

"You got a diamond drill?"

"What's that supposed to mean?"

"Not a great deal. Just repeating one of your Rings, Harry Zeross's most tasteless jokes is all. Outer Earthlings have a problem with full-blooded Utopian women. Call them ambulatory alabaster, among other things. The cretins. As soon as he gets ectoplasm-walkabout, I'll be sure to ask that particular Cretan cretin to have her plop by your coffin for a visit."

"You were waiting for him, weren't you? You weren't waiting for me."

"Why would I? My Sed-son of a Sedon says you're a waste of space. Says it won't be long before I have another neighbour kicking and spitting in your stall."

Cerebrus withdrew his ghost to the sanctity, if it could be considered such, of his own crypt, of his own stone sepulchre.

========

*Ethics, the notion members of D-Brig, like the members of SOS, KOC, and the King and Queen Conquerors before it – like ever so lofty, and superior, and so far beyond everyone else Wakinyah Creatures of the Cosmos – should never kill, let alone be encouraged to kill, no longer plagued Cerebrus. Neither did Klannit's enticements to the effect she could look after Thalassa and, implicitly, their unborn child if he did as she, and Mirrors' parents, firstborn Mithradite Master Devas the pair of them, insisted he did.*

*Thinking rationally, as if for the first time since being stuck under – unless he was just rationalizing the abandonment of his ethical convictions – how was he to know Thalassa, once D'Angelo but apparently always Thanatos, was still pregnant? How was he to know she, Sea, a duplicitous devil as was now evident, ever had been anyhow? When it came right down to it, how was he to know she was even alive, let alone on the Frozen Isle of Lathakra?*

*'Other than the Moloch Sedon, who do you think?' Klannit had far-asked him.*

*'Enlighten me,' he'd far-responded.*

*'What keeps him going, his father, Cabalarkon!'*

********

# Nine-Babies: **FAY TAILS**

========

**Lazam, 26 Tantalar 5980**

*Tea was done. The minor disaster of Tina Zeross pushing one of Golgotha and Gethsemane's cloned or non-born 'sons' against a sharp table-edge had been sorted with, of all things, a plastic band-aid imported from the Corporate State of Greater Godbad. Blind Sundown had gone off to wherever he'd gone off to, in accordance with Dr Mel-Mom's prescription to take a fucking walk, for fuck's sake.*

*Wilderwitch was looking at herself in a body mirror, a pair of them, on wheels, in the Naurozes' apartment.*

========

For some reason Saladin Devason, if it was Sal, or done on his orders, had neglected to remove or cover up the mirrors here in the old palace the same as he had inside Skyrise. What he had against mirrors, if he had anything against mirrors, especially since he'd once been so enamoured of them he'd surrounded his bed, roof and sides, with the things, was one of her personal coyotes of a conundrum.

She'd figure it out eventually, she supposed. First things first, though. And the first thing for her was finding out how culpable Master Foetal Father was when it came to getting rid of her four fellows in D-Brig. Felt she'd come up with a typically perverse angle on how to do just that as well.

She was nude and on her feet. Despite the herbal-ointment-lathered bandage wrapped about her right thigh, by her own reckoning she looked damn good for someone who, ego-bolstering bluster aside, but for the undeniable expertise of her friendly physician should have been a corpse. Or, at best, a peg-leg-ambulatory amputee by now.

She finished combing out her mess of hair, which, disturbingly, was indeed both straighter and darker than usual – what was it about the Weirdom's shampoo anyways? – and mouthed a silent prayer of thanks no spiders, or worse, had fallen out. For her part Mel was more pleased the comb she'd lent her survived the abuse.

Said dutiful doctor rolled up the other full-length dressers' mirror. For a variety of reasons, not the least of which two of her daughters almost being fried alive for doing something someone who either was the Witch, or who looked remarkably like her, put them up to doing, Dr Melina Zeross was nowhere near as friendly to her anymore. Still, she wasn't calling her a fucking bitch anymore either. Was probably thinking it, though.

"Is this necessary, Witch?" asked the High Illuminary of Weir, frowning in that bizarre, alabaster-white, wrinkle-free way that so unsettled non-Utopians. (They could raise eyebrows, and dilate eyes, but that was about it for face-to-face demonstrativeness, if that was a word. "I don't want to call you a narcissist, or sound like a prude, but I really don't think my kids need to see you buck naked."

"Let's not be overprotective, Mel. Percy's 16 and Paree's 12. I don't think the sight of a woman without any clothes on is going to offend them. Besides, I want to get this right."

"But they're so innocent."

"Innocents, maybe. But it's too late to plead their innocence. Even if they blanked as to where, they admitted what they did."

"Under the influence of the Master's Speaking Stick."

"And to you, hours before that, albeit with Johnny right there beside you ready to red-hot-poker them." The Witch regarded her backside. Lost weight indeed, she huffed to herself. There had never been anything to lose. Fat and her were not even nodding acquaintances; never had been. Well, other than the last time she was in the family way.

"Look, even though they deny it, they might be responsible for getting rid of the Diver, too. Besides, even if they're innocent of that much, innocents don't use their father's rings to send three of my oldest friends God knows where. I'm no different than Johnny and Raven, Mel. I want to know who put them up to it, I want to know why and, most importantly, I want to know where they sent them. Oh, yes, I want to know right now!"

"Then what?"

"Johnny, Raven and I'll figure some way to get them back. Or, if they don't want to, then at least give them a choice we all can live with. I'll give you a three or four letter hint how we'll do that, too. In descending order they're 'p', 'h' and either 'a' or 't' — and that doesn't spell PHAT Auntie Wildie."

"No, it spells Persephone, Helen and either Athena or Tina. But Percy and Paree have no notion where they sent them. They were working under some kind of spell or, most likely, some sort of brain-boggling, got-no-choice, psychic-puppeteer, string-pulling." Stringing words together via hyphenation was an academic trick Mel had always fancied, even on the Outer Earth where, howsoever perversely, Wilderwitch first got to know her.

"Question is whose, isn't it? You heard Johnny at teatime. He may be all over the place when it comes to tossing blame around, but every one of his scenarios has some degree of validity. How would Fey get here? Does she have a psychopomp? And even if she is carrying Psycho's boggle-brain in a box, how would they know your kids can use Harry's rings?"

"I'd have thought that obvious. If it was Saul, he must have read them. Or read any number of others. It's no secret Percy and Paree went beyond the Dome to get Harry a Christmas Tree and Tina was caught screaming in the glacials yesterday, after she used one of his rings to go there for some ice cream."

"He couldn't have got any of that out of me. I only just heard about them at tea. And if it wasn't Saul, but whoever it was knew what had become of him, well, you have to admit that if speaking sticks can get memories out of people chances are they have to be able to put ideas into them. That's why torture's useless. The victims will say anything to get them to stop."

"So you agree with Johnny. You think it was the Master who put them up to it, using his Mace?"

"I think it's awfully convenient he's the one who conducted their interrogation – all of our interrogations. That's how you got away with that waffle about your caduceus. If it is a devic power focus I don't know how it works, my taut butt! All a matter of willpower, isn't it. If I was any better at using my metallic marigold, I'd have eyeorb-probed them myself."

"I am. My caduceus is. I did."

"Before or after Sal got to them?"

"Does it matter?"

"Only if you want to take his place at the top of the hit list."

"Watch it, Witch. I'm still the one conducting your physicals."

"And you signed a hypocrite's oath, not a Hippocratic one?"

"Touché. And I'm sorry."

"So am I. We're sounding like a couple of old hens who've lost their roosters."

"We have. Except you weren't interested in Murray anymore. Why should you be? You've got the Master now."

"Not if his cock's a speaking stick coming through from the opposite end."

"God, you're crude."

"Part of my charm, Mel." Wilderwitch did something with her fingers then moved away from the two mirrors. Her front and back images stayed in them. She pulled on a robe then sat in her wheelchair. A few more rotations of her hands and a simulacrum of herself formed between the mirrors. She caused it to parade around the room like a fashion model.

Satisfied, she said to Melina: "Okay, bring in the kids. Once we get them to adjust the hair, put a few dozen pounds of bags and sags in the proper places, get the clothes right and work out the sound of her voice, I'll soon find out if Sal's responsible for fat Auntie Wildie."

========

*Blind Sundown was not at OMP-Akbararthas level when it came to truly extraordinary, as in far beyond standard, supranormal strength. No one was, not even Dervish Furie, who was likely next-in-line in that regard. But he could probably come close to matching the Master in a barbell tossing-and-catching contest.*

*For the second time that day had no problem hoisting open, on its hinges, the lid to Cerebrus David Ryne's stone sepulchre. The plop, plop, plop of blood did its usual trick.*

*This time Cerebrus didn't just open his eyes; he sat up.*

========

"About time you came to see me, Johnny. It still Boxing Day?"

"So I'm told. What is it, Ryne? You've been giving me headaches for it seems like days now."

"Probably because it has been. I need you to do something for me, for everyone. I want you to go to the crypt next door and kill Cabalarkon."

"And why would I do that?"

"You kill Cabalarkon, you kill the Moloch Sedon."

"And the reason no one's tried to do that before would be?"

"Ah, but there's no one like you. No one who's such a great killer and especially no one with a solar spear like yours."

"Except there has been, a man named Manitoulin for one. Not that he was a killer. And probably a few thousand men like Manitoulin before him; many of whom might have been."

"And all of whom spent their lives on the outside."

"I wouldn't be too sure of that. Fact is, I'd be surprised if most of them hadn't been under the Dome at one time or another. They were shamans, wise men; in tune with the Otherworld. And this is the Otherworld. The Witch and OMP are from in here and where do you think Raven's Head could have come from?"

"North American Indian mythology after the coming of the White Man and his horses, I'd have said. And just did. Call it an experiment then. Indulge me, just this once. You've next-to-nothing to lose, I've already lost most everything I had to lose, and the entire cosmos would be a vastly better place if we managed to lose Dark Sedon. Permanently!"

"There's where I agree with you. Still don't see, if killing Cabalarkon means killing Sedon, why no one hasn't done it yet. And don't tell me it's because I'm blind. Even I'm tired of making that joke. Feel like a radio announcer too idiotic to say speak to you next time instead of see you later."

"Maybe he's just damn hard to kill. Which should make killing him a great challenge for a great killer like you. Think, Johnny, there has to be a reason Sedon carted Cabalarkon across the cosmos for multiple millennia in his Sedonshem. Has to be a reason he's kept him protected down here, in a realm where no devil dares venture for fear of being sucked into a Trinondev's prison pod, ever since landing on the Whole Earth howsoever many more millennia ago. Cabalarkon's what keeps him alive. Has to be."

"Maybe he does. And maybe I will. Think, that is. Just don't try to do it for me, okay. You aren't so hard to kill. Hell, like you say, you're most of the way gone already. There's something you don't know."

"The Diver's disappeared and two of the Zeross girls used their daddy's rings to send ..."

"Where?"

"I was going to say somewhere. I don't know where. Saul did it, though. Don't know about the Diver. To read him, he's been vanishing a lot since he found out he can metabolize Gypsium; kind of just drifts into between-space. Might just drift back again anytime. Psycho, though, he must have sent the others to look for the rest of his body. He's travelling with someone name Faith McBride, by the way. She's a supra, specializes in self-teleportation."

"A self-psychopomp, like Harry's aunt, one way or another: Roxanne Kinesis, Slipper. Guess that's one coyote I can put to bed. Faith must be the name she uses on an everyday basis. Wilderwitch calls her Fey Girl or Fey Woman. Says she's her daughter from the late Forties. Had her during one of her famous walkabouts back then. One guess where she went."

"Is she indeed? More grist for the mind-mill. And the Witch hightailing it off to the Hidden Headworld without any us – mostly me – being any the wiser. Guess it's my turn to guess why she's always been so opaque to me. Tell you what, you go next door and par-broil Cabalarkon. Meantime I'll do what I can to track this Fey down. She gave me blood, so we've a link."

"You do that. You find her, read her, find out where she had the girls send the others, give me another headache or two, and we'll talk again."

"Goddamn it, Johnny! Just do it. You gave me blood, too. I can compel you."

"Did I? You mean this." He held up a teacup that still contained a few droplets of blood. "There's this fellow named Golgotha. He's a clone. He and his wife, who's also a clone, raise clones as if they're their kids. Which I guess they are, in the adoptive sense. Call themselves a husband and wife development team. Their kids are what they're developing. Into fine and upstanding, Utopian Hate-Sedons like them, I imagine.

"One of them got in the way of a table's edge rather awkwardly and cut himself while we were having tea with their parents awhile ago. Mel – you remember Illuminatus, don't you? You must, you've been sending her headaches, too; today, if not for days like you've been doing to me. As if she needs any more headaches, today especially. Anyhow, she's a doctor and whilst she was sticking a band-aid on this kid's cut she squeezed some of his blood into this here cup then asked me to go see what the fuck you wanted, to quote her directly."

"You're all so clever, aren't you?"

"Not as clever as whomever made sure the only crypt next door to yours belongs to Harry, brain boy. The other side of yours is just a solid wall. Isn't anything there except bricks, more bricks and even more, even thicker bricks. I just checked. Guess that means I had the same thought as you. Great minds and all that."

"Either that or you were holding onto someone when they looked in a mirror."

"Huh?"

========

*Saladin Devason stepped out of the shower that night in Skyrise. He positively tingled with anticipation.*

*Although he still wept for his traitorous sister – who was reputedly killed in Hadd by Blind Sundown while fighting alongside the Dead against the Living – and for Harry-Ringleader's indefinite loss; although he still inwardly fumed at the Diver for destroying the three Sacred Objects; and at Furie for preventing him killing his black-striped, black-hearted, would-be assassin of a niece, Andaemyn Sarpedon, on Dustmound; things were decidedly looking up.*

*And not just looking!*

========

After not just drying himself off, he sprayed on some scent his little mother gave him a year or so before he permanently banished her, devil-cursed, demon-sprinkled, faerie fart that she was now. Throwing on a dressing gown, only loosely tying it, he went into the bedroom. Cynthia, the name Wilderwitch answered to when she was with him, was already sleeping.

He went over to the bed, whose roof was draped over and whose mirrored sides he'd had collapsed like an accordion then taken down altogether and stored away from Skyrise. If Melina and her daughters had indeed been kidnapped by the Thanatoids of Lathakra, as all the Zerosses, even Harry, claimed, then it made no sense to as good invite their Haunted Angel, who'd been plaguing the Weirdom for decades, into his home, let alone his bedroom.

Witch Cynthia had been on the verge of death when Rings brought her, Glory of the Angels and Cyborg Cerebrus to his Weirdom most of a month, less a week, earlier. Her recovery had been nothing less than phenomenal. Astonishing what a little demonic bonding could do besides a daemonic binding of flesh and bone ripped nigh unto shreds by a devil's talisman; an Apocalyptic Nucleoid's Brainrock harpoon, no less.

Possession by devils, even their azuras, was supposed to be even more healthful but, save Sedon, they couldn't last long in a proper Weirdom; not without being detected and automatically sucked into eyeorbs. That should happen with demons, too. After all, devils occupied debrained daemonic bodies and both, spirit and body, vacuumed into eyeorbs; rather, into the between-space microverse they generated within themselves.

(And they did, though hardly automatically. Demons were tricky things; full of quirks and quarks, as Harry used to put it. Worse than ants, of the creepy-crawly variety; you really had work at getting rid of them.)

Still, demonic bonding or no daemonic binding, miserable Ants were like that, trained for resilience. Not that their superb training, or even their Superior Nightingale hierarchy, had been able to save Copperhead, Kyprian Somata, his officially beloved, yet privately despised, predecessor as Master of Weir here on Earth.

Nonetheless, he admired Cynthia's spunk. Could not have been more pleased when he saw her knocking about her erstwhile lover, Dervish Furie, last night in the supranormal ravendoe's stone-gnome-reinforced manger. Even if he detested witches as a matter of conviction, he genuinely hoped they would be together a long time.

And if they weren't, well, daddy provided. He'd provided his Mastery.

========

*Saladin pulled back the covers. She turned towards him. He gasped. It wasn't her.*

*"Fey!"*

*"You bastard! You know me, don't you?" she screeched, leaping to her feet.*

========

He stumbled backwards reflexively, crumbling into the chair on his side of their thusly emptied bed. "What are you ranting about? Of course I know you."

Fey Woman stayed up, started prowling the room like a wounded panther. She was wearing one of the expansive – all the more so on her, because she needed it to be so expansive – all-covering, from the neck down, earth-toned *'granny'* dresses so often seen in the Weirdom. Cynthia, albeit with a headscarf or *'hijab'*, had on something like it at the hearing earlier today.

"Why'd you make me do it?"

"Do what?" Although he was sure he had to be dreaming, the Master strove mightily to keep himself under control. Slumped deeper into the chair as if to force docility upon himself.

"Don't come the fool with me, Saladin. You're no inbred imbecile like the majority of your people, no non-born clone like all too many of your Trinondev Elite. You used an eye-stave, your Master's Mace, to bring me to heel. Used it to mesmerize Melina's kids into sending Diver, Rider, Murray and the old man away. And let me tell you why."

"Please do." He sat up attentively. Had only just realized Fey was Cynthia-Wilderwitch's daughter. The long, wildly crinkly hair and facial resemblance, more so than the choice of spacious clothing, was too strong for her to be otherwise. Mel might have warned him. Then again Mel might have married him, years ago. Saved him from having to bed suchlike hellcats.

"Because they're beyond you; too popular for you to rein in and too powerful for you to take on, man to man. Or Master to Rainbow, in the Angel's case."

Docility wasn't working. He was quickly losing his patience. Much more of this outrage and in ten seconds he'd start applauding her performance, briefly. It would only take a couple of claps of the hands and he'd have this Maenad of a madwoman on her knees begging to do anything except die. Ten, Nine, Eight ....

"Sundown and Raven are as well, but they're different. They're devil-slayers, recathonitizers at the very least. And they've promised to help make you more solar spears and ankle-winged, horny-headed ravendeer. Then there's the Witch, my mother and, in comparatively short order, the mother of your child ..."

"She's pregnant?" Eight, Nine, Ten ....

"Of course she is. Speaking Stick or no Speaking Stick, she wouldn't have gone to bed with you if that hadn't been her intention. She likes strong men and she's as fertile as her sisters, Eden Nightingale and Scylla Nereid. But you couldn't take it... having two of my mother's former lovers under the same roof as you and her?"

"Two?" Ten, Nine, Eight, Seven ....

"And you know the Witch has always fancied Gloriel."

"She has?" Six, Five, Four ....

"Admit it, asshole. You couldn't take the competition. Envy blinded you more so than Sundown's ever been. My mother's not only bisexual, she's a very bad Anthean but, by God and the Devil, your god and your devil simultaneously, she was going to have your child and stay here to raise it. You didn't have to use me to get rid of her friends. They were no threat to you."

Three, Two ....

"Where'd you have them sent?" Fey had been stomping closer and closer to him. She was leaning over and breathing in his face now. That was about as far as dignity would allow. One!

"Listen, woman, all of what you've said is as fascinating as it's instructive." His tone was cold; intentionally chilling. "I'd heard your mother was a creature of unpredictable moods, but no one ever said she was insane. You, however, are a complete lunatic." Zero! He clapped his hands together. "Be gone!"

She looked at him confusedly. "What did you say?"

He did it again. She was still there. How was this possible?

"What are you doing? This is no time to be playing at being the Puerile Potentate of Poppycock's Principality."

"I'm the Master of Weir," he clapped his hands together one more time. She still stood there, eyeing him in a perplexed manner. "I tell you to be gone you should be gone!"

"Sorry, my fault." She vanished.

========

Wilderwitch stirred on the couch across the room. "What's going on, Sal?"

Still in his dressing gown, but without his mace, which he'd left with the rest of his Masterly regalia in the adjacent wardrobe alcove, he went over to her, loomed over her.

"Were you here all this time? When all that was happening?"

"Fell asleep reading," she yawned and, just to complete the illusory experience for him, blinked sleep out of her eyes.

She was convinced of his innocence. Other than unknown, where that left her and her four missing companions, she had no more of an idea now than she had when she, her soul-self in Fey's guise and she throwing Fey's voice like a super-adept ventriloquist from the couch, started her creative charade.

"When all what happened?"

"I just had the strangest dream; visitation, more like. It was your daughter, Fey Woman. She is your daughter, isn't she?"

"I've a daughter by that name. Fey's a few years older than me now but, yes. You know her?" (Wilderwitch reckoned herself twenty-eight, Fey thirty-four.)

Saladin was in no mood to recommence all that crap. "Who by? Sundown, the Diver? No, it has to be the fucking faerie, Kronokronos Akbar, doesn't it? Fey's a big girl."

"Why does it have to be any of them? Could be the Man in the Moon for all anyone except me knows. Not that Helios was on the moon thirty-five years ago, and not that I've ever been into incest in any case. No one else, not daughter, not daddy, knows who he was and, sorry, Sal, as much as we're bed-buddies these nights, I'm not about to change that now. Some things are best left to a woman and her reproductive system."

"Oh, really," said the Master, angering incrementally, albeit not overboard-angry; not look out, time to jump out the window angry … yet. "Perhaps we should see about that."

Had she just blown it? Should she even think such a thing around him? Could he mind-mine her? Riling a lava-lout, to use Mel's term, as volatile as Saladin Devason might make for a decent death-wish but it was hardly the witch-wisest of strategies. Too late now, if he could. She hadn't got far last time she tried to get away from him. Only got as far as right here, as it happened, and look what that got her: baby bun baking in the oven.

She was becoming antsy-anxious. Was even fretting in the fay-saying way she, like Fish, Fisherwoman, Scylla Nereid, was prone to when things were sliding toward that slippery slope of no-climbing-back. The drugs Mel gave her for pain must be adversely affecting her capacity for precision premeditation of her wicked words as well as her devious deeds.

"Flabby bag of belfry-bats called me a Puerile Potentate of Poppycock's Principality. He any relation to Murk Mist, Mad for Mud Magpies?"

Where did Sal come up with that? Did he fay-say just because his little mother, whom she remembered best as Hush, not Pandora, Mannering, did? Or was it contagious? "Not that I know of. They're both characters in tee-tee tales I used to tell Fey as a child." Maybe she was stretching, but she figured she could recognize an opportunity for a non-window-out when one presented itself.

Sal was over sixty years old, far beyond foetal, but in many respects he was still a big baby. So she tried on some not-yet-with-the-breast, savage-beast-soothing, voice-work. Such that she could remember it, gave him a simpleton's synopsis of said sad story: "Back when she was a fairy princess, Godda, of the Land of Daybreak, used to make mud magpies all the time.

"Had a thing about ravens, I heard, and there weren't any ravens, especially ones that talked, left in Daybreak anymore. So that's why she made mud magpies, to approximate them. Got her dainty dresses so filthy dirty her fairy queen mother, Maboberon, turned her into Murk Miss and moved Daybreak all the way west, across the world, to where it became the Land of Shadows, and no one could see how soiled her dresses were anymore."

Sal gave her a look most grown or growing men never gave her. A lot of little boys, intrigued as they were by not such different sorts of things, one-eyed trouser-snakes, fishy snails, fishier whales and tee-tee tails amongst them, had, however. Deciding she was onto a good thing, she kept it up.

"Murk Miss's Miss Mist, Thrygragos Lazareme's Venus. Non-feeorin call her Krepusyl Evenstar these days; or did the last time I was beneath the Dome. Her protectorate's Crepuscule, the Inner Earth's dreary, drizzly Land of Twilight, on the far West Coast, howsoever hundreds of miles it is south of here.

"The tee-tee tale alludes to how, when the Head was something like 1200 years younger and Evenstar was Mariamne Dawnstar, she annoyed Dark Sedon so much so he switched her protectorate, which was the Land of Daybreak, in the Headworld's occipital regions, with that of the Byron Spawn, Yati, on the other side of the world, in Sedon's Mouth, just north of the Subcontinent of Aka Godbad.

"Yati's Bodiless Byron's Dragon. His protectorate was Samarand, and maybe it still is, but back then it was Sedon's Tongue. Only, Sedon was so drunk with power when he moved Daybreak, he missed his mouth entirely and Twilight became Sedon's Outer Nose. That's why some of the little people, the indigenous feeorin who were moved with Daybreak, sometimes jokingly call themselves the lickspittle people."

"Always wondered how that came about," said Saladin.

Rage spent, he'd sat on the edge of the bed; had become so calm so fingers-snapping-fast Wilderwitch had a notion to change her name to Scheherazade, she of the Thousand and One Arabian Nights fame. She made a place for him on the couch. He came over and sat down beside her. Instead of lapping out of her lap, which was the other way she could have played it, she had him lapping out of her hand, albeit only the proverbial sense.

"And Prince Poppycock?"

"He was so fat and lazy, rather than get up and get anything for himself, he used to clap his hands together whenever he wanted his servants to bring him something. One day they were so slow to see to his desires he clapped so hard both his hands fell off. So he started screaming, only he yelled so much he expelled his tongue straight through his front teeth and altogether out of his mouth. Now he could neither speak nor bite."

"Then," Saladin picked up, "He had a little bell attached to a wrist-stump. Only he rang it so loud it vibrated off the rest of his arm and he became deaf. So he had a signal light attached to his other stump. Only he flashed it so brightly his other arm burned up and he became blind. So, having finally learned his lesson, he started getting things for himself. I've heard it."

"Not my version of it. You see, which he didn't anymore, when he got up to get what he wanted both his legs fell off from under-use so his servants had no choice but to do everything for him. They didn't, he'd die, and they'd lose their jobs. It's a happy ending. Poppycock got whatever he wanted without having to do anything ever again."

"She made the most extraordinary allegations."

Oh, oh. Must be time for another stratagem. "Like I was pregnant?"

"That was one of them."

"I am."

Turned out lapping out of her lap was the way to tame the savage beast.

========

Somewhere on the Outer Earth someone could no longer say she was pregnant. Reason for that was she had just given birth. Her mate was delighted. Both sets of their parents were as well. After some initial misgivings, they had come to terms with their offspring's choice of life's partners. Wasn't like miscegenation – racially mixed marriage – was a rare, let alone punitively illegal, event in these, the latter decades of the Twentieth Century.

Although the man was not the baby's father, which they didn't realize because it never occurred to any of them to verify his paternity, they should have been even more delighted than they were. Harry Zeross was no longer out and about. Consequently, he was no longer using his miraculous Brainrock rings to traverse not only the Weird under the Dome but the Cathonic Zone itself and, thence, wherever he desired anywhere on the planet.

Not to mention above it, as far as the Moon, which was why he was now in a tub of Cathonic Fluid. Had he been it would only be a matter of a few weeks or months before the newborn was found dead in his or her crib, an apparent victim of always-heart-wrenching SIDS (Sudden Infant Death Syndrome).

Apparent because the baby would still be alive. Not that, in all likelihood, they would ever discover the reality of the matter. Ringleader exchanged live infants for dead clones, ones 'developed' specifically for the, to most folks, unconscionable task needing done in order to save his adopted people: the hate-Sedon, originally extraterrestrial, Utopians here on Earth.

And, as much as he personally might wish to do so, he never reunited those he took back to Cabalarkon with their birth mothers. Neither would his successors.

========

*If Saladin Devason got his way, which he usually did, with daddy's help, neither would Persephone Zeross. He anticipated her mother would see it the same way he did. If not, well, he'd had some thoughts on that as well. Lascivious Lily, Black Widow that she was, had certainly looked good as an illusory white goddess.*

*He expected she'd look better not having to concentrate on maintaining a glamour.*

********

# Ten-Babies: SEEING-EYE SUNDOWN

========

**Devauray, 27 Tantalar 5980**

*One of the peculiar things about Damnation Isle was that virtually every combatant in the Outer Earth's Second World War, North Pacific battlefield (battle-ocean?) called it just that, albeit in their own language. Had done so for hundreds of years. Which of course meant they got the name from the native Aleuts.*

*They stayed away from it, the Aleuts; believed the misty, ice-rimed little islet, with its three volcanically inactive spouts, more so than peaks, was the entrance to what passed for their Afterlife Otherworld. The Japanese, who took it over in May 1942, held onto it tenaciously until mid-1943; in both cases at tremendous cost in terms of men and materiel.*

*What was so important about it? In December 1955 Wilderwitch thought she knew. It was an entranceway — the Aleuts' Otherworld was Sedon's Head.*

*They didn't get a chance to use it the day they were thrust into Limbo; not altogether successfully anyhow. Was it the way Fey used to pass through the Dome? She made a mental note to ask her daughter that when their inevitable reunion took place. She just hoped she got to ask her first. Before Johnny and Raven did.*

*Thundercloud Creatures of the Cosmos rarely took notes.*

========

"The Master and Fey," Dr Melina Zeross, the High Illuminary of Weir, was telling the Witch and Blind Sundown at breakfast the next morning, the 27th of Tantalar 5980, "Had a fling that ended about ten years ago. I sort of put him up to it, as it happens. Regardless of whether he is or he isn't, it isn't healthy for a Master to be thought of as a heartless womanizer.

"While he's hardly childless, not that the throne is passed down hereditarily in any case, it also isn't healthy for a Master to have all these uppity young bastards, male or female, running around without a mother's steadying hand. It got so bad, their attempting to lord or lady it over everyone else, we had to send most of them into the countryside, away from Cabalarkon City, to be raised by husband and wife Development Teams as if they were non-born clones."

"How is the Mastery handed down?" wondered Sundown.

"Someone issues a Challenge of Weir," said Wilderwitch. "Like Sal did in 5950. Winner takes all and if it isn't the reigning Master then he or she has to retire."

"Actually it's more complicated than that, Witch," said Mel, who didn't take much to warm to a subject, any subject. She felt it her obligation to illuminate the ignorant. Came with the title and job description. "It starts with what amounts to a fitness test, the same as the early dynasties of Egyptian Pharaohs had to go through starting on the thirtieth anniversary of Pharaoh's reign, then repeating every five years thereafter. The ancient Egyptians called it, wait for it, the Sed Ceremony."

"Surely not after the Moloch Sedon?" said Sundown.

"There've always been gaps in the Cathonic Zone, Johnny. They're caused by cataclysm; until Atomics came along on the Outer Earth, mostly by the eruption of volcanoes. They rarely endure for more than a human generation or so, more often than not nowhere near that long, but Dark Sedon doesn't need one to go to the other side. Why would he? He is Cathonia. So, yes, I believe it is named after him.

"In fact if you ever go to the Cairo Museum you can see a big, framed print of an aerial photograph of the Giza Plateau in one of the Old Kingdom rooms, though they might have moved it by now. The photo was taken in the Twenties or Thirties and, just below and to the right of the pyramids, where there's now a parking lot, you can spot a shape that might pass for a facsimile of the Headworld."

"I've seen it," the Witch verified. "The Egyptian sphinx was once, and probably still is, an entranceway to the Head. But don't let me interrupt, Mel."

"I didn't," Sundown observed. "You took it upon yourself."

"No matter," said Mel, by now used to the verbal sparring the various members of D-Brig seemed to take delight in, almost like children in a classroom. Although neither of them were members of KOC: the King's Own Crimefighters (she was, at least of the early on, immediately post-war group), many of the others were; SOS: the Society of Saints before them, ditto.

"Not that that matters anymore. Let's call it a fitness test and leave it at that."

"One that Sal's predecessor failed, I take it."

"Her name was Kyprian Somata, Johnny. Though I expect you'll have heard that by now. She wasn't very old by our standards, not much more than a couple of hundred, if that, but she fell gravely ill in the mid-Forties and never really recovered. Still, everything kept on working the way it was supposed to and that's the litmus test we Illuminaries, whose duty it is to approve a Challenge of Weir, have traditionally looked for when we decide if a Master's fit to continue being the Master."

"So Sal didn't issue the Challenge?" interrupted the Witch, albeit studiously.

"Ah, but he did. Unlike some of the other Weirdoms, of which Cabalarkon's is the last ethnically pristine one left, albeit only by comparison with the others, ours has no history of having what you might think of as a hereditary right of succession. However, it does have a form of aristocracy, a noble class that at least theoretically ensures the retention of its privileged status by assuring the wellbeing of its people.

"Although he was only Master Kyprian's great-grandson, Saladin counted as a member of that aristocracy. He waited until he was about to turn thirty, which is the youngest age anyone's allowed to become Master, then he petitioned the then-Illuminaries to have Kyprian declared incompetent. Which, curiously enough, was about when things began to cease working the way they were supposed to work."

"Cried Alice," Sundown inserted.

"That's curiouser, not curiously," Wilderwitch objected.

"Whatever," said Sundown, using one of Persephone's favourite words.

"It began with the toilets backing up," said Melina. She tried to skew her nose but decided the effort was more trouble than the end-result warranted. "And when they weren't fixed adequately, we had ourselves a plague of rats. Which the children found delightful because a lesser contagion of them turned out to be tee-tees and every tee-tee has two tales to tell." Sundown knew what tee-tees were by then.

"Only both their tails, which have to be read, and the tales they told out loud, grew more and more doom and gloomy. Once our local murder of crows grew bigger, were in fact supplanted by ravens, presumably from the Land of Twilight where ravens, like faeries and even the occasional genuine demon, roam freely, Utopians became increasingly distressed. That was enough for Kyprian. She was the High Illuminary as well as most everything else in those days. So she sanctioned Saladin issuing the Challenge of Weir."

"With one proviso," Wilderwitch recalled. "She demanded the right to appoint a champion, someone who would answer the challenge on her behalf. Enter my fishy sister."

"Whom the Master to this day thinks Kyprian brought in to be his bride after I rejected him, and her, for the umpteenth time."

"Except Fish was already married."

"To Achigan Auranja, the Summoning Child, then-King of Godbad. Wouldn't have made any difference anyhow. A Weirdom's strength derives directly from its people. The people, no matter how inbred imbecilic most of them are these days, and were in those days, especially the aristocrats, funnel their strength into the Master and, quite frankly, Kyprian had lost the faith of her people. By hook or by crook – how's that for an Alice reference, if it is one? – Saladin defeated all comers and became the Master of Weir."

"Not before Master Kyprian died, though, howsoever mysteriously."

"No more mysteriously than how she became ill in the first place," Mel reminded them. She and the Witch had been there, the latter with Fey Girl, but it was all news for Sundown. He nevertheless had the sense Mel was remaking this last point more for the Witch than him. "Then again there are those who construe the disastrous series of events that led up to her dying, and him assuming the Mastery, as manifestations of Divine Will."

"*'In Nomine Patris, et Filii Dei, et Spiritus Sancti'*," Sundown recited very much by reviled rote. (Even if he and Solace, not Sorciere, kept running away from Catholic residential schools, some stuff stuck.) "*'Dei', 'Deus', 'devs'*, diva, God, gods, goddess, divine, devil, deva, they come from the same source. In here, under the Dome!"

"I prefer to believe otherwise," said Melina, fingering her crucifix, which Gloriel, Glory of the Angels, was the first to tell him she, Mel-Illuminatus, habitually wore on a sometimes glowing chain around her neck. (Sundown despised nuns as much as he did priests and the laymen who supervised his dormitories. "But you're right, Johnny. Divine Will may well equal Sedon's Will."

"Thanks for that at least," said Sundown, growing tired of Mel's monologue. He rolled up the left sleeve of his leathern shirt and pretended to look at his wristwatch, which he no more could see than he was wearing one. "Didn't you tell me you had an appointment with a gynaecological Gynarch, Witch?"

"Aortic Amphitrite, Lakshmi of Lemuria's mother, is a gynarch," said Melina. "No matter how dictatorial my patients might regard me, I'm just a physician."

"Are we to expect an announcement soon?"

"That's almost clever, Johnny," said the Witch. "Expect, expecting." He looked at her blankly. Rather, with a cloth blindfold covering his eyeholes – he kept his colourfully beaded blindfold aside for special occasions, like when he was about to kill someone – he inclined his head in her direction, a blank expression on his face.

"If it was, it was unintentional. Like your pregnancy."

"It wasn't," she protested, unconvincingly to his mind. "I wanted it."

"Says she," said Melina, approaching scornfully. "She who's been so out of it since Temporis she's even persuaded herself she likes the Master."

"We've been over that already, Mel. I do — just don't expect me to say that in public. Or even in private. I'm not about to get involved in any chattel marriage."

The whole notion of marriage was anathema to the Witch. Two people expressing undying love for, and devotion to, each other in a formalized ritual, one most couples took as confirmation they had thus magically become each other's exclusive property, struck her as true perversion. Human beings weren't anyone's property except their own.

Besides, monogamy was for the birds; and them only for a few species. (All right, a few more than a few.) It had no more to do with marriage than having or raising kids did. Although, even if her Sisterhood held men weren't necessary when it came to raising girls, she felt you needed two to successfully do both, firstly and long afterwards, marriage was not a prerequisite for either.

She changed the subject. "And what's your day shaping up to, Johnny?"

"Got to go impregnate Raven," he said then, realizing that hadn't come out very well, quickly added: "Help impregnate her, make that. Don't ask me to explain the process. Sal's hotshot smart-asses, these embryonic engineers of his – biomages he called them – used a bunch of militaristic terms like nuclear ovum, blast-cyst sites, cellular stem-guns and even they didn't seem too sure what else.

"Simple sort that I am I still don't understand how, if she's the last of her kind, she can even become pregnant. But they think they've synthesized the male bits necessary to fertilize Raven's eggs, so I'll be there when they try to stick one of them back into her. Then it's my spear's turn."

"Don't go anywhere near that, Witch" Melina cautioned her.

"Hard to resist," said Wilderwitch. Whereupon she proceeded to try – ever-so-valiantly for her – to comply with her just-that-moment-made, new day's resolution. "So long as they don't ask you to donate any blasting-cap cells yourself, Johnny, I wish you both well. Tell Raven I'll come by later. Mind telling me what they're going to do with your spermato-zoom spear? Sorry."

"Knew you couldn't resist for long," said Sundown. "Sal called this lot technomages. The shaft's nothing special so they're going to subject its head to a spectroscopic analysis, find out what it's made of, which they've pretty much already determined is mostly Brainrock, what Harry called Gypsium, and then try to duplicate the process.

"I'm told these technomages have access to some millennia-ancient, even pre-Earth machinery that automatically manufacture eye-staves and eyeorbs, as well as most everything else the Weirdom needs. The hope is, once they feed the data into these somehow still functioning artefacts, stone gnomes will do the rest."

"Never underestimate the capability of a stone gnome," Melina advised him.

"I'd be happy just seeing one," said the Witch.

"So would I," Mel agreed.

=========

By the time Sundown arrived at her stable-cum-laboratory Raven's Head was already in a snit. Some of the Trinondevs in attendance, notably Capputis, the pock-marked teenage clone who never seemed far from action central, were so worried about her emotional state they and the scientocrats, who weren't, were debating whether it might be best to postpone the insertion.

She doesn't have to carry the foetus, Capputis reminded him unnecessarily. The Master's biomages, specialists in embryonic engineering, had explained as much to he and Raven any number of times of late. Utopian clones are grown in developmental tanks, what amount to artificial wombs external to the egg-donor. The overnight addition to the lab came so equipped.

The other thing it came equipped with was the gadgetry another set of scientocrats, ones known by the equally quaint rubric as technomages, were going to use to analyze his Solar Spear. Even after re-emphasizing said-soothing encouragement, it took him awhile to get her quelled such that she could explain what was so upsetting her.

Turned out it wasn't the procedure she was about to have. It was, irrespective of how valid its purpose, that the laboratory aspect of her domicile had expanded overnight, with her lying in her manger sleeping through it. The situation was intolerable, she told him. She was going to kick it down around her ears, and theirs, if someone didn't shut down these, these, these ... whatever they were.

"Are," said Capputis, having understood her verbal vitriol thanks to his eye-stave. "Stone gnomes are mandroids. That's the easiest way to think of them anyhow. They were, are, the Weirdom Mother Machine's operatives, if you will. You may have heard of nanotechnology or even of interlocking nanites — nan or nano just means one-billionth. But stone gnomes are more nebulous than that. Has to do with ether; rather, Utopians conception and manipulations of it."

Sundown was doing it again. Giving him the evil eye despite wearing a blindfold. He decided to pull a Wilderwitch, not that he did so consciously, and tell him a story.

"Ancient Utopian astronauts travelled for multiple multi-millennia on approaching asteroid-sized millennial or generational ships. There were dozens of them, maybe even hundreds of them, and, as vast as they were, inbreeding was always a worry. So the populace of the ships got together every few generations such that they could exchange personnel, intermingle and, as one might expect, interbreed.

"Inevitably some ships were lost and some ships simply got separated from the rest of the pack, as it were, sometimes for thousands of years at a time. Equally inevitably, therefore, inbreeding did happen. Fortunately the designers of the ships installed automated failsafe devices that in effect took over the ships' operations. When they needed hands-on, um, operatives they automatically manufactured operatives with hands, the mandroids."

"Demons," said Sundown, having already made the connection.

"We prefer stone gnomes, sir, for the sake of the children and simpletons of Weir, but you're welcome to say mandroids, upper or lower case. Or golems, for that matter, since the Outer Earth folklore regarding golems is based on very much ramped-down Utopian designs. As for saying demons, we discourage that — and not just for the sake of children and simpletons.

"Demons are disgusting, nasty things. All body and no soul, though contrary to what you may have heard, some have fully functional, individualized brains – which mandroids, being automatons, don't really – and those that do are attuned for atrocity. I've even heard that if you know a demon's name you can both conjure and control him. For a price of course; your firstborn, perhaps, and a jar of catsup. Besides, demons are chthonic, earthborn. They were here long before we Utopians or even Sedon's devils came to the Whole Earth."

"In generational ships."

"Us, yes. Or millennial ships. After a lengthy hiatus on the Moon, during some of which time Thrygragos Lazareme led an exploratory party down here, the Sedon Spawn arrived on the Sedonshem. It was compositionally identical to the Cathonic Zone in that both are, were, made up the Moloch's own essence.

"Think of it as a spiritual spaceship given solidity as needed and you'd be bang on. It's all detailed in the Annals of the Illuminaries by the way, if you'd care to verify any of this. Assuming you could read it of course. Me, I've only read the shortened version: 'Forever and Forty Days', it's called. Has nice pictures."

"These ships of yours, where are they nowadays?"

"Decommissioned and buried, but you know that already. Their husks form part of the Weirdom's inland boundary, the Slopes of the Sleepers."

"I meant all of them," Sundown clarified. He'd been to the Slopes, part of them anyhow. Trinondevs took him out there on the 14th, when the Master had his dream of an invasion, coming from the Ghostlands and initially led by Trigregos Diver, that most everyone in Cabalarkon somehow experienced as if it was a real event. "The ones out there can't be all of them, can they? There are other Weirdoms."

"Plenty of them. Ours is the last; the last, pardon me, pure one, at any rate. But to answer your question, to the best of our knowledge every millennial ship that made it as far as this planetary system landed here, where the Slopes are now. The other Weirdoms, including ones we established on the Outer Earth once we regained access to the Kore Gap, which went through the Dome from Apple Isle in the late Thirties, were satellites of Cabalarkon's. Used shuttles sometimes called vimanas or cosmicars, some of them quite large, to get around."

"What became of them?"

"Don't forget we're talking a very long time here; back in the era of the ten patriarchs of Golden Age Humanity. Sedon raised the Dome nearly 6000 years ago, to prevent the archipelago of Pacifica from being overwhelmed in the Genesea, which ended this Golden Age after not much more than fifteen hundred years. No one knows when the Kore Gap came open. Maybe until relatively recently it never wasn't open. But we didn't start using it until around 4000 years ago, when it exited on the island of Crete in your Middle Sea, the Mediterranean.

"The opening of what's called the SAG Gap, which has been known to wander, but most of the time remains stationary in the vicinity of Sedon's Peak, on the

Cattail Peninsula, Sedon's Ponytail, can be dated to about the same time period. As for the link between Egypt's he-sphinx and Incain's she-sphinx, that's been there as long as they've been there. Which might have been pre-Genesea, according to some theories I've read.

"As you can probably appreciate given that sort of timeframe, over the millennia the populations of other Weirdoms were … what? Assimilated, I guess that's the word. Their founding fathers, and mothers, interbred themselves into the slurry of humanity and Utopians ceased being a distinctive species everywhere but here.

"Their extraterrestrial machinery, shuttles included, everything salvaged from our derelict millennial ships, must have shut down due to a lack of enough Utopian willpower to keep their mandroid maintenance workers from atrophying. With very few exceptions, and then only a few reasonably well preserved buildings still in use, there's nothing left of them now except ruins."

"Slurry is like mud, right?"

"It's a liquid full of sediment. The liquid dries and it becomes hard as stone. Hence the stone gnomes."

Capputis was trying to be funny. Sundown just wanted to know what slurry meant. Had a few other questions as well. "How is it their work just appears?"

"That's what I meant by nanites nebulously. Any pre-construction's done between-space workshops akin to your Witch's Shelter, likely so as to eliminate distractions. When it's ready it's installed, very quickly. Rather, when it's ready it just sort of ceases to be between-space and materializes in place. Very handy that. None of this two seasons business like on the Outer Earth: winter and construction. Anything else, sir?"

"The designers of the millennial ships were the Dual Entities?"

"Designers might be giving them too much credit, sir. The Male Entity is Brainrock-blessed, that's why he time-tumbles and how he manages to take the Female Entity and Trans-Time Trigon with him when he does so. But virtually everything else about them derives from First Weirworld's Mother Machine, which Sedon destroyed a few centuries after they created him. Fact is our Illuminaries have long believed most everything about the Female Entity is the Mother Machine. She is mostly a machine, you know."

"So Illuminatus tells me, the Mnemosyne Machine, Machine-Memory. Devils humanize her. That's when she becomes Miracle Memory."

"Demons, too, some say. And it's 'humanized' her, past tense. They're gone. Tumbled back into the time stream for something like the hundredth time when Outer Earthlings destroyed their base on the Moon a couple of weeks ago. Dr Zeross – the human Dr Zeross, not our High Illuminary – must have told you that. Our Dr Zeross believes her husband, with his Gypsium rings, precipitated that event, but I'm not so sure. Outer Earthlings have a tremendous talent for destruction without any help from the not so much unknown as unknowable Godstuff."

"So we do. Where do stone gnomes get their raw material?"

"Ah, as to that, our Illuminaries claim, without a shred of evidence to back them up as far as I'm concerned, that deep beneath the Weirdom there's a huge depression filled with just that, their raw material. Illuminatus sometimes calls it the Hell Well but most of us less esoterically inclined Utopians refer to it as Absudyl, the Subterranean Land of the Mandroids, mostly because the whole notion of it strikes us as an absurdity. How can their raw material be themselves?"

"Simple," ventured Sundown. "Mandroids are oil."

"Well, they probably are carbon-based, if that's any consolation. Can't say I've ever seen one. Guess my mindset's too practicality-oriented."

"You sure this Absudyl of theirs doesn't go by another name? Say, oh I don't know, say, Temporis?"

"Temporis," Capputis obliged. Although at times obsequious to the point he verged on condescension, he clearly felt himself somewhat of a wag. However, all this particular display of puckish wit earned him was a cautionary frown from Blind Sundown. Very disturbing, especially to one used to Utopian woman, whose spontaneous reaction came mostly via their eyes.

"It's conceivable," the hydrocephalic said, apprehending Sundown only tolerated jocularity from his friends. "Originally, so Illuminaries instruct us, mantel half-lifers were – and therefore still are – mandroid-variants. Dand Tariqartha, the Master Deva whose star now shines in the Lazaremist Quadrant of the night's sky, was an Earth Magician.

"He could both mould and program them as he pleased, but he could also somehow give them flesh and blood; make them as free-thinking individuals as you or I. We in Cabalarkon know that for a fact. Fully alive mantels were amongst those who attacked us during the last Challenge of Weir, thirty years ago, and we killed enough of them to be sure of that."

"We?"

"Put better, my Trinondev predecessors killed enough of them to be sure of that. Sorry for the inaccuracy, sir. Shall we get to it?" Capputis asked Raven's Head point-blank.

Him mentioning the last Challenge of Weir must have rang a bell. She responded with a squealing query of her own. "I have met this Fish-person," he responded. "Her name is Scylla Nereid and her correct title is Lady Achigan, though she was once the Queen of Godbad. But, no, I'm not her son. I was cloned with gills behind my ears because the Master wishes me to become his ambassador to the amphibious and solely water-breathing races of the Head."

Raven had another query. "While that's true," Capputis acknowledged, "Water-breathers do communicate telepathically, as well as through tactile methods and visual ones such as sign language, I anticipate no problem in that regard. You'd be amazed what eye-staves can do. Couldn't understand what you're saying without one, could I?"

"Would that I could see through them," said Sundown, uncharacteristically wistfully for him. Raven did glare at him, silently. Capputis took that as a go.

"Have you tried?"

========

Raven's Head had the procedure.

It wasn't just her dignity that was affronted by it, either. She took to the pile of straw laid out for her in the manger and was still asleep when Wilderwitch, Muslim hooded and veiled like the Master and her both seemed to prefer she be when out in public, wheeled by for a visit later that day.

"Getting knocked up sure did knock her out," Sundown put to the Witch.

"Did that eyeorb you're holding just wink at me?" she responded. Then it suddenly dawned on her what was going on. "My God, Johnny. You can see!"

"Yeah," he responded. "Though it's giving me a headache."

"Sure that's not Cerebrus wanting to meet us again?"

"Maybe it is. I know just the fellow who should give him blood, too. There's something about that Capputis know-it-all that rubs me the wrong way. The Cerebrus-way, if you catch my drift." The Witch nodded. Even if he was her nephew, she'd never been overly found of their erstwhile leader. Mind-control was a despicable ability as far as she was concerned.

Came in handy once in awhile, though, she had to admit. When she had her agates she'd been known to employ it herself, as a last resort. Had even tried to milk, then redact Cyborg Cerebrus's own memories that fateful first, and final, Friday in Vancouver only three weeks and a day past. In that, if not much else, especially recuperative abilities, he was still better than her.

"Could be," mused Sundown, "He deserves to bleed. Bloodily!"

========

*Even if Sundown was only expressing his frustrations figuratively, Wilderwitch did not approve of him expressing them so graphically. He might actually mean it. He could certainly make them happen. So could her sister in more than just Flowery Anthea. And Codenamed Fisherwoman was reputedly far more than just prawn-prone to expiring her anemone-enemies.*

*She, Fish, had sometimes been accused of hate-hake-eating them.*

========

Sedon's starry eye-mouth didn't just look down on his Headworld, drooling in the form of rain or snow. Or not so much so precipitously. Sometimes it looked to the heavens, desirously so. Looked to the higher heavens, to Outer Space; to the Outer Earth's Outer Space for wordsmiths who enjoyed mincing words, not just hamburger meat, and insisted the Outer Earth was the Inner Earth's outer spaces.

He was hoping to spot then, eye-mouth-tongue extended like that of a frog – and that of a Lemurian frogwoman – snare and subsequently hurl at Incain's Prison Beach the Brainrock asteroid he felt certain would destroy All the maybe-not-so Invincible. Brainrock asteroids didn't just come as called. They did come, though, once in a very long while; unfortunately almost always in the form of Trans-Time Trigon returning with the Dual Entities to pester him anew.

So it was he stayed away from All. Wasn't too worried about her, sooth said. The She-Sphinx didn't contain enough raw material, Stopstone-Solidium, to do him any lasting harm. Somewhere did, however. Reversed mountaintop tip of irony that it was, it was also his Head's little grey cells of potentially the Grey, the Stopstone so prevalent sub-cranially in places like Absudyl and Temporis.

He might have been undisputed king of his Hidden Headworld but its undersides, its veins and arteries, were the Hell-Well of the World.

========

*The usurper, Lakshmi Arthadot, had been Kronokronos Supreme of the subcranial latter for barely three weeks. Right now she was in Centurium's replicated Palace of Ver-*

*sailles. Was observing, not disinterestedly, Caverns Calvary, 1492 and pre-Columbian Plainsland America splat into a splash of not-immediately-solidifying Solidium slurry.*

*"I knew you could do it," congratulated her Summoning Child gynarch of a mother, Aortic Amphitrite, a Quarter Queen of Shenon and a Lemurian frogwoman with one of those amazing tongues of theirs. Fish's Treat had as well. In many respects it was her idea. Lakshmi was barely eighteen. Was at heart as ruthless as her mother, just not so much in practise.*

*"Hey," complained Tsishah Twilight, Shenon's other Aortic, seemingly unimpressed. "Even I might have been able to pull that off if I had Dand Tariqartha's Power Sceptre."*

*"Except you don't and I do," Lakshmi reminded her, as full of youth as she was of concomitant overconfidence.*

========

Tsishah was the late Morgianna born Nauroz, become Somata, then Sarpedon's daughter by the likely not at all late faerie type Tom-Tiddly Taddletale. (Faerie types didn't so much die as they switched underlying bodies when they, the ones who'd been carrying them around, did die, as Tsishah's daddy, who was born Tammuz Rhymer of Dukkha, had done decades ago.)

That she had reddish-brown skin, and as a result looked more like an Irache than anything else, belied her parentage. Even though a hybrid, like her year older brother Saladin Devason due to identical parentage, Mama Morg had been white-as-light whereas Tom-Tiddly Daddy had blue skin — very fay that.

Like most upper level witch-deviants – maternally she may have been Wilderwitch's half-sister (quarter-sister?) in that they both could have had the same devic half-mother: the Grey Lady, Miss Mist, Krepusyl of Crepuscule – Tsishah was a skilled illusionist. Her Irache skin-colouring was no glamour, though; no aural, as in aura, manipulation.

While she may have inherited faerie blood from her father, she hadn't so much inherited a debrained demon from her mother as she'd acquired it, her, in the very early Sixties, via her mother's connections as the demon-loving Hellions' Morrigan. It was the demon who had Irache skin-colouring.

Was quite the her-story was Tsishah Twilight. All of them there at that moment were quite the her-stories. Although she swore she was like mother, like daughter, more of a Hecate-Hellion than anything else, she was also Shenon's other Aortic; the Anthean as well as the Mariamnic and Athenan Quarter Queen. Not for much longer, she hoped. Better not be. She was having a lousy year.

In accordance with Shenon tradition, as someone born in the Thirties she was scheduled to resign at the end of the year. Which, howsoever controversially, was the coming Spring's Equinox Eve on most of the Head. Her replacement, albeit as a junior Quarter Queen, a Ventricular, was supposed to be a teenager or young woman barely into her twenties, if that, someone therefore born in the Sixties.

Things weren't going as planned, however. When it came right down to it, nothing was anymore. The person chosen to take her place as the senior non-Lemurian Quarter Queen was Telepassa of Godbad, a fully trained Ant as well as a pinnacle-level Althean healer and Lovely Lady Afrite. Since Telepassa was already the Forties' born Ventricular, someone had to replace her. The odds-on favourite to do that was one of Telepassa's three triplets, Lovely Ladies all.

Tsishah was so sure the succession was set, she left her aorta or atrium on Witch Isle nine months ago; on the day of the last Spring Equinox, to be precise. Which was when those, like her, who believed a decade ended with a Nine (9) instead of a Zero (0) felt she should leave. Initially she went back to the Irache enclave in the Northwest Cattail, not all that far from Shenon as the bat flew, to try and patch things up with her estranged mate, the father of her four children, one Mani-Balam by name; Jester-Jaguar by designation.

When that, to say the least, didn't work out, she moved to the other side and other end of the Cattail, to the Zebranid Leper colony, in the Southeast Whiplash Range overlooking the Prison Beach of Incain, far, far below it. There, for a time, she lived with Mama Morg, Step-Daddy Demios and their daughter, her half-sister, Andaemyn, Andy. (No doubt due to both Demios and Morgianna knowing the fullness of Tsishah's sad sack story, Andaemyn's name meant 'without demons'.)

Since none of them, particularly Andy, were around very often, most everyone there soon began deferring to her. Thus, whilst still nominally in charge on Shenon, she added the responsibility of running the Zebranid Leper Colony. Added also, therefore, responsibility for (publically) head-manning, as it were, the witches' latter day revival of the Panharmonium Project; which inordinately relied on All of Incain to get its agents to the Outer Earth as close to at will as she could.

Now they'd lost contact with said operatives, notably Sharkczar (as the latest Steltsar styled himself), Crystallion (once Crystal St Synne, OMP-Akbar's by default step-daughter), her Hell's Horsemen and their Atomic Firedrakes. (Who wouldn't be Sharkczar-Steltsar, Crystallion, Hell's Horsemen and atomic firedrakes without all the preliminary work clandestinely done by rogue techno- and biomages under her auspices on Shenon.)

Done a ditto with their outside puppeteers, Korant other-Ventricular Balkis (Sheba Faerie Flight) and her twin brother, Solomon 'Boom-Boom' Mandam (the Outer Earth's latest Daemonicus). Any and all of them could well be dead. Mother Morg was as good as. Had, probably too late to forestall the inevitable, cocooned herself after falling-failing to acquire the Trigregos Talismans in Hadd, where Demios and Andy were still laid up.

Now Miracle Memory – the real mastermind behind the Panharmonium Project – was thrust back into the time-stream; her Herr Hel Helios's latest fiasco having ended as they always did, with him getting himself killed; this time on the Moon of all places. Now as well, she'd only just learned her designated successor, Ventricular Telepassa, along with all four of her daughters, had vanished off the face of the Inner Earth; at least as far she and her various sisterhood contacts had been able to thus far determine.

So too had Pyrame Silverstar, only recently decathonitized and whom she'd allowed, after considerable hesitation, to share her demon-coated body for the briefest of periods two weeks ago. Thought she had, rather. Had her demon back, but didn't think she still had the devil. Then again, Master Devas were renowned for their ability to hide themselves away within their shells without said-shells realizing they were being possessed. Were also renowned for not leaving memories behind.

She should know. She'd spent the better part of two decades being possessed by one, hence her adopted last name, and didn't recall boo about it. Only knew she had been, because others had told her so. And now she was here, in replicated Versailles. The show must go on, said Fish (Lady Achigan, one of those who told her about her previously possessed past; helped get her dispossessed as well, truth be known).

Didn't say so in so many words of course. She'd fishified instead: *'Haul your bass-ass to Centurium, sea-saw. Tadpole's prematurely scupper-scooped up the dandy Dand's penile pole and wants us to come schmooze with some ooze.'*

Was about to say something else, was Fish. Right this minnow-moment.

========

She hadn't been herself of late so, as well and as long as she'd known her, Tsishah just hoped she was still up the task of understanding her form of fishy fay-saying.

"We all abysmal-depths-did, Treat," fishified Amphitrite's stepsister. (So far so good, Tsishah reckoned.) "Quay-question remains. Can Lack-scruples here oozify enough non-living caverns to do the trickle-up trick? We don't want to become mass murderous krill-killers if we can auk-avoid it."

"Nor," non-fishified Fish's stepsister, Lakshmi Arthadot's mother. (Treat's own mother Merthetis brought her up alongside Fish for most of her first dozen years – until she 'donated' her to Cabalarkon's Master Kyprian – and so didn't need an interpreter.) "Do we necessarily want to liquefy all the caverns containing non-living replicates. Some of them, some of the replicates, might yet prove useful."

"Abalone-abominations, the splish-splash-splat of them," countered the one-time Queen of Godbad, Wilderwitch's sister in the Dual Entities.

Fish had made the mistake of going against her better judgement by supporting her kingly husband when he allied with demons, including an earlier Steltsar, during Godbad's Civil War in the late Fifties, early Sixties. Still counted herself fortunate to have survived that debacle. Even if it meant joining forces with usurpatious Godbadian despoilers, had been fighting against them and theirs ever since.

"I say, and have always fay-fucking-said, mallet-mush them into a mess of mash then add them to No-lack-bluster's fish-soup."

"Lady Achigan's a point, mom," said Lakshmi of Lemuria, Fish's No-lack-bluster as well as her Lack-scruples. "And I don't mean at the tips of her teeth."

Fisherwoman – ex-Queen Scylla of Godbad, nowadays Lady Achigan (Amphitrite's mother, Aortic Merthetis, the then Lemurian Quarter Queen of Witch Isle, named her Scylla Nereid after she found Fish in the belly of the beast, Island Leviathan, shortly after her birth in 5918) – was an exotic in many respects; a human, which could nevertheless pass for, in most other respects.

Generically genetically, even though she couldn't materialize a fishtail out of the Weird and thereby become an actual mermaid, she was a Melusine Piscine. Once had a daughter she named just that, Melusine, not Piscine … once, as in no longer. Still had always matted, never combed, vaguely reddish hair; definitely greenish-tinged skin; distinct gills behind the ears and what appeared to be an extra layer of shark-sharp teeth.

Her usual scant, navel-baring clothing was more blubbery than cottony or wetsuit rubbery. Had – and this was as recent addition as far as Lakshmi could recall – a dark, spotted cloak that upon closer inspection looked fishy in every respect. It was her latest psychopomp and, yes, it had once been just that, a fish; an eagle ray, to be absolutely accurate. How she'd come by it, got it demon-coated and revenant-raised, was amongst her very latest her-stories.

Although she never showed much respect to anyone – least of all her own Summoning Child of a husband, even when Achigan Auranja was King of Godbad – she'd earned a great deal of respect for herself over the decades. Part of that was because she was found at birth with three devic power foci that she still had.

The two she most commonly used were her gaffing hook and fishnet, while the third, her bellybutton bauble, or Vesica Piscis, supposedly made it impossible for devils to occupy her. That hadn't prevented her being fused with, as opposed to being possessed by, Freespirit Nihila on Raised Dustmound, Vetala's Middle Finger Salute to the Sedon Sphere, the night of Sedonda, the Seventh of Tantalar.

Hard to beat that. All the more so when they'd apparently parted, quite literally, as friends on the 8th, shortly after the Living, with next to no help from her/them, won their already Headworld-legendary victory over the Dead on what was by then Diminished Dustmound.

Doubly hard to beat when one considered who Nihila purported to be — none other than Datong Harmonia, a Lazaremist firstborn, the first Master Deva ever born of the three Great Goddesses (by a matter of seconds), the Unity of Balance as well as, in effect, the patron saint of the witches' Panharmonium Project.

By contrast, while she was an unscrupulous opportunist and tended to blow her own horn, as it were, Lakshmi was hardly lacklustre. Not today anyhow. Neither, despite what many believed, was she an illusionist. She took a smattering of pride that she could pass for human, not just from a distance but from relatively close by. She nevertheless wore a deliberately thin-skinned, entirely non-sentient mandroid guard-body that was not only mentally malleable (solely by her), it could shape-shift, within her size limits, her inside it.

Many a Lemurian frogwoman, her far less human-looking mother included, did the same thing. Indeed, although it was of necessity much thicker and hence nowhere near as malleable nowadays, Amphitrite wore a very similar guard-body; one that, upon intimate inspection, let her pass for human, at least for awhile. (Said while starting when she was as young as Lakshmi and first living on the Outer Earth, alongside Fisherwoman, as the aquatic supranormal codenamed, appropriately, Lady Lemurian.)

Frogwomen did so not just for protection, though that was the main reason. They also did so because most non-Lemurians found Lemurians unsightly and Lakshmi didn't want to look even vaguely unsightly. Was, then and there, practising to appear very much non-unsightly for her upcoming wedding announcement.

Her latest wedding announcement, make that.

========

Devils could only procreate Azura Spirit Beings with each other, true. But many, probably most of them, at least occasionally occupied sentient individuals and, through them, had half-children; deviants, in Headworld parlance. Dand Tariqartha was one of the most prolific in this regard. (His biological prowess was most of the reason Lakshmi could look so human even without wearing her protective guard-body.)

His half-sons and half-daughters grew to become Kronokronoi. At Dand the Dad's insistence – and with her ambitious mother's wholehearted approval – Lakshmi agreed to marry a certain Centurion Sophiscient on Tantalar the 6th, the day after her 18th birthday. This centurion was the son of none other than Kronokronos Akbarartha, the rightful Kronokronos Supreme.

Born in the late Thirties he was more than a twinge old for her. He knew it as well, loved someone else, as did she, but the Dand was adamant. The Awesome Akbar was his favourite half-son. Gone thirty-five years plus by then, Tariqartha nevertheless felt their wedding – hers and Sophiscient's – would be an ever so appropriate way to mark his 4,000th birthday. (Or, more accurately, the 4,000th anniversary of the day he became individually solid.)

Only, on the 5th of Tantalar, her actual 18th birthday, the day before their scheduled wedding, Akbar himself (for some reason calling himself Obadiah Melvin Power, rather than Kronokronos Akbarartha — Artha, as in Arthadot, being her last name as well) reappeared in Temporis, spoiling her bath as he did so. Suddenly, albeit perfectly reasonably, the Dand was more interested in her marrying him than his, Akbar's, son.

The events mostly of the 6th took over from there. The Dand self-cathonitized. Just as he did, she got hold of his power sceptre, which was a facsimile of his own head, on a pole, and which was therefore akin to Akbar's Homeworld Sceptre in almost every way. Since that was what Amphitrite had assigned her to obtain, chances were long before her conception, she had no further need of marrying anyone in order to get close to Tariqartha.

So, not needing him, nor Sophiscient, she promptly booted OMP-Akbar out of Temporis, he along with the rest of what was left of this Damnation Brigade of his. Whereupon, with her first decree, she confirmed the devic Dand's prior declaration: namely, that her engagement to Sophiscient was null and not so much void as happily avoided.

Finally, love will out, she was free to marry the man of her heart's choice; the man both her mother and her mother's stepsister – who was almost more of a mother to her than Amphitrite – had intended her to marry all along. And Centurion Sophiscient, now newly appointed Senator Sophiscient and duly made Lakshmi's main go-between with the various Cavern Headmen and Headwomen, not all of whom were Kronokronoi, was only too pleased to arrange it. Even if he had to leave Temporis to do so.

The proclamation of their banns was going to take place, hers in his place, his in her place, a few days from now, the 1st of Yamana still 5980 on much of the Head; the 1st of January 1981, New Years Day, in large parts of the Outer Earth. They'd personally be in both places for both announcements. And, as both mothers had emphasized, their physical appearances were at least as important as them appearing personally.

Couldn't be in both places simultaneously of course, but near enough. Matter transducers didn't just work in Call-me-Cabby's Weirdom.

========

The teenage deviant – half-children of devils were always known as deviants – wasn't happy with her look for ahead, only four days ahead. Dutiful lass that she was, she currently had her guard-body going with the positively porcelain pretty, even lustrous. Her shiny whiteness was a concession to her mother — Amphitrite tended to think strategically. Now that she was Kronokronos Supreme, Lakshmi wasn't so sure she had to think so obligingly similarly.

For one thing she had no intention of hiding the gills behind her ears. Fish never did. Claimed she didn't wear glamours any more either, though how someone in the 63rd year of an absolutely amazing life could look as good as she did without wearing glamours remained a mystery to Lakshmi. Still, as exotic and undeniably old as she was, most humans found Fish pleasing to behold; so long as she didn't smile too often, it almost always had to be added.

Didn't her mother, though. Thought her monstrous. And she was, looked so much like one of the transforming frog creatures depicted on the Fountain of Latona, which they could see from the windows of the long, purpose-built room they were in, it was a wonderment the Marsy Brothers, who cast the Outer Earth originals, didn't have any Lemurians for models.

Except they didn't. Lakshmi did. Her model was her idol, Fisherwoman. Which was why she personally preferred her guard-body jade-green and texturally scaly rather than polished alabastrine. Did prefer her hair tinsel-silvery, which Fish's wasn't. Was more akin to reddish seaweed or fire coral. Lakshmi had to show some individuality.

She'd also prefer it if her mother didn't Treat-treat her like a child. Fish was married and had Winifred-Wave before she turned 18. Lakshmi vowed she wouldn't be far behind.

"We've already agreed," she asserted, trying not to echo much-loved-Fish's nonetheless grating condescension, "We can't risk evacuating everyone out of the Living Caverns. So, how can we risk evacuating the ones we merely find interesting out of the non-living ones? I mean, we don't even know if they could survive beyond Temporis. It's not like they've ever led a normal life; not like Kronokronos Mikoto and his Two Thousand had been doing for decades before their final rebellion. They just endlessly repeat what the Dand programmed them to do."

Kronokronos Lakshmi – and she was a Kronokronos, a half-daughter of Dand Tariqartha, Thrygragos Lazareme's only recently self-cathonitized Earth Magician – had done her bit to become the Kronokronos Supreme of Temporis. Even if she hadn't done it quite according to the long-term Panharmonium plan of her elders, she was more than prepared to follow through to the next level. Which was to give All the Invincible such a severe case of indigestion the She-Sphinx had to do-due-diarrhoea all over a certain eye-mouth in the sky.

"We could find out," suggested Tsishah, who was quite fond of Temporis, visited it often, especially after her coregent had Lakshmi. "You could choose one and, if you can without Tariqartha, alter its conditions to that of a Living Cavern. I mean Centurium's alive, so is the Faerie Garden and the Shogun's Cavern. Your mother didn't seduce Dand Neptune in Cretan Cavern 2000 YD without it being at least partially alive, otherwise you wouldn't be here."

"And if they can," considered Aortic Amphitrite, "Then what? Turn them loose to fend for themselves? Where? Upstairs, in the Silent Sands? No one survives there for long."

"Not to the sun-slurping surface of Sisert, we cod-can't," Fish reaffirmed. "The mighty mollusc in the sky would speckle-spot them for sure if we did sprat-that, tadpole."

"Nevertheless," Witch Isle's still acting Aortic argued, "As Lady Lemurian II just demonstrated, we've got the raw material we'll need anytime we need it. And in All we've got the delivery system, again anytime we need it. We've your wedding announcements to make, but not for a few days. So where's the harm in experimenting? We don't have to send them anywhere once they've transformed, not immediately, but we could. Dependent on where we got them from, somewhere in the Cheeks or on the occipital side, perhaps."

Fisherwoman eely-eyed her. So it seemed did her latest psychopomp, whom Fish was once again calling Eagle Ray Revenant after both Tsishah and adoptive sister Amphitrite prevailed on her to stop calling it (him?) Ronnie Ray-Bum after the USA's president-elect, Ronald Reagan. (Both Fish and Amphitrite had been to Hollywood in the Forties. Neither could believe Americans had elected Ronnie Ray-ban. Not to the presidency anyhow: Jimmy Stewart, maybe; Reagan, never.)

"You're not trying to dugong-duck out of anything avian, are you, sea-saw?"

Once in a very long while, especially when she was growing serious, Fish had been known to stop fishifying altogether. She was implying the aging Aortic thought there might a useful replacement down here to do stuff she, the Irache lookalike, perhaps ill-advisedly had agreed to do up there. Way up there.

"Hey," said Tsishah, Fish's Sea-saw, not needing a translation. "I'm as willing as ever to take Herr Hel's place in the Stopstone saddle and ride the slurry She-Sphinx through the night's sky, chasing down after dark's biggest eye. I'm just saying, what's the hurry? I mean, for another thing we still don't have any way to get Fish's mighty mollusc to stand still long enough to get dumped upon. There's no harm taking an inventory."

They were in the Hall of Mirrors, the perfect place to do an inventory of what caverns held mantel-what, or mantel-who, albeit in repetitive, endlessly cyclical mode. One who wasn't a Hall, nor an All, but who like them all was ally of All, was also a mobile mirror. "It may not come to that," Klannit Thanatos, who'd been quietly listening to all they'd been saying, told them. "Seems I've managed the miraculous and made see the sightless."

"You did the squid?" queried Fish, not necessarily trying to be fin-funny; this despite what she was wearing on her back.

(Eagle rays couldn't fly as such, not even between-space, though they could shoot out of the water and splat back in. It was already a dead thing animated – an Indescribable – when it did that then tried to splat Fish as she was leisurely swimming off Hadd in the aftermath of the final battle over ulimately Drenched Dustmound. Got itself psycho-popped as a consequence. She needed a replacement for her psycho-bicycle anyways.)

"Well," reconsidered the Thanatoids' wannabe devilish Ice Queen, trying to be funnier, "To be an honest haunt, your son did the lid." Rather than groaning, the Lemurian Aortic pointed a webbed finger at the mirror pane that, as if a Godbadian television set, had only minutes earlier broadcast the collapse of the non-living cavern called Calvary.

"You can't manage the miraculous, azura. That was His job."

========

*It was joke worthy of the Untouchable Diver, a former lover of both hers and Fish's from the days of the Outer Earth's Suprawar.*

*One presumably worthy of even a Mantel-Diver.*

********

# Eleven-Babies: **CEREBRAL INCINERATION**

========

**Sapienda, 1 Yamana 5980**

*For the next three nights and three days, not-so-blind-anymore John Sundown rarely left Raven's stable.*

========

Hooded and veiled Wilderwitch wheeled by, sometimes three or four times a day and usually stayed for an hour or two at a time. Melina Zeross did as well, albeit walking. She often came with the Witch, though sometimes she showed up with one, two or all three of her daughters in tow. Only Persephone visited on her own. Sometimes, Raven imparted to Sundown, there was a perceptible, non-Gypsium glow about her.

Might the 16-year old be suffering a bad case of puppy love? Might the first name of the puppy she was in love with be Johnny, even if you prefer John?

Golgotha and Gethsemane Nauroz, neither in veils and never with any of their cloned charges, were almost as frequent visitors. Since he wouldn't touch the mush Utopian crud-recycling space-machinery spewed forth, the latter had taken it upon herself to bring him handpicked, baked, butchered and properly cooked, terrestrial food. Suchlike edibles were remarkably plentiful in the near hinterlands, where many of the farmers and their functionaries still belonged to the so-called Sarpedon underclass whence hailed Mel's extended family.

Another daily visitor was Capputis. Sometimes he didn't wear the loosely knit toque, even if it was a chullo, it with its earflaps pulled down to hide the gills behind his ears. He seemed, all of a sudden, almost proud of being an amphibian. There was a reason for that, D-Brig-3 speculated, albeit without corroboration. A non-born clone, he wasn't. Yet another of the Witch's nephews he might be.

The Master never came by, which was fine with Sundown. He was balking at sticking his spear into a replication system that, as usual, was just there one morning. Didn't want stone gnomes using it as a shish to skewer rock marshmallows or whatever they roasted when they did a kebab, assuming these howsoever billionth bitty bits ate.

Finally, on the 31st of Tantalar, what would be New Years Eve on much of the Outer Earth, Raven's Head rejected the implantation. Made quite a mess doing so. Felt much better for it too, she said. The mess especially. Let stone gnomes clean that up. Except of course they wouldn't, not if it meant being seen.

Then it was Wilderwitch's turn to be in a snit.

========

"You look troubled, Witch," Sundown observed, via the open eyeorb atop the eye-stave Capputis supplied him after he discovered he could see through the things.

Moderately mid-barrel imbeciles of Weir had finished cleaning up Raven's filth and left the three of them alone in her stable-cum-laboratory. He was sitting cross-legged on the cot he had set up in the lab, his spear across his lap and holding the eye-stave like a collapsed telescope in front of his cloth blindfold. Raven was up on all fours, tentatively testing out her legs after three days off them.

The Witch was in her wheelchair. Significantly absent from her usual accoutrements, which never amounted to less than her all-covering clothing and, of late, one other thing, was that one other thing. Her metallic marigold wasn't even in the chair's back or side slots. She wasn't too pleased to see Sundown holding onto his seeing-eye stick, as he called the eye-stave, either. She didn't want any mikes on spikes broadcasting what she came by to request.

"Do me a favour, Johnny. Take that thing into the bathroom, stick it in the sink and leave the water running over top it."

"I doubt it'd fit in a sink."

"Then detach the orb or stick the whole thing in the tub."

"There's only a shower."

"Johnny!"

When he returned, Blind Sundown again, leaving the water running behind him, he made another mistake. "Not having cranial cramps, are you?"

"You ever use the 'cramp' word with Solace?"

"I wouldn't have dared."

"Then show me the same courtesy."

"I meant Cerebral cramps," he said, not backing down. Even mentioning his long dead wife's name, any of them, got his danger-dander up. "I have."

"Well, I haven't. Stayed away from him as well. On your instructions too, I might add. No way anyone else is going to get a shot at playing mind-games with me right how. You want to hear what I want to tell you or am I just going to go race go-carts with the Nauroz kids? It gets stale after awhile. My chair's my cart, so I usually win. But it's more entertaining that picking my nose. Or my scabs."

"Anyone else?" he asked, sitting on the cot again. Sightless he may be but he was still a Wakinyah Thunder Being. Even if new equipment had a tendency to show up without anyone apparently delivering it, he didn't need an eyeorb to find his way around the manger-cum-lab's by now familiar territory.

"Sal's going to announce it anyhow. Says the pressure's on for him to do the right thing. Which of course is exactly the wrong thing as far as I'm concerned."

"Announce what? Your pregnancy?"

"No, our marriage. The one we aren't going to have. You up to flying both of us, and my wheelchair, out of here, Raven?"

Johnny's Beauty, not caring if she was joking or not, said she was still too whacked to even contemplate the attempt; that she'd count herself fortunate to get herself aloft, let alone carrying anyone. Sundown, though, unstrung the wampum pouch he wore on his belt and began rummaging around in it with his fingers.

"There might be another way," he smiled, finding what he was feeling for.

He pulled them out, showed them what he had, what he'd kept since the morning of the 26th. They were the three Brainrock rings the two oldest Zeross girls used to send their comrades, Gloriel, Furie, and OMP-Akbar for sure, to wherever. He even had a good idea where that wherever was. Had, these last few days, had a lot of time to do some profound pondering on the subject. Plus, he'd been having these hellacious headaches.

Had to be Temporis. Big duh, that. Their bodies were there, covered in Stop-stone-Solidium, for a quarter century; therefore so should that of Saul 'Psycho' Ryne. Akbarartha, once he displaced Lakshmi Arthadot and reclaimed his birthright as Kronokronos Supreme, shouldn't have any trouble locating it via Centurium's Hall of Mirrors.

Because, according to Mel-Illuminatus and, surprisingly, Capputis, who'd apparently spent a lot of time there while he growing up, that's what it's good at, beside reflecting everyone there. (D-Brig 3 knew that already of course. On the night of the 5th Dand Tariqartha had taken all nine of them, even Raven's Head, into what he also called his observation room in order to show them what the Apocalyptics and their allies were doing to his precious caverns since OMP-Akbar started sending them there on their Monday, his Mithrada.)

"Think you can get them to work for you? I've tried. They don't work for me." He handed Harry's dishwater dull rings to her.

"Sorry to disappoint," she said, taking them. "But they're no more glowing for me than they were for you. Oh well, there's always that boat."

"What boat?" He asked, taking the rings back and replacing them in his pouch.

"The Tribute Ship. Mel tells me there's all sorts of places on the Head that send all sorts of stuff to the Weirdom, via Pani Merchant ships, in hopes of securing … what shall I call it? Fatal forbearance? Celestial intercession? Divine goodwill? You get the idea. Apparently it's a tradition that goes back thousands of years, to long before the Ghostlands were forever-after contaminated thanks to the famous Death's Head Hellion and the powers that be then – and be now, in truth – held court at Grand Elysium.."

"Sedon's goodwill."

"So she doesn't tell me."

"But everyone knows it's true."

"Be that as it may," she dodged, albeit only verbally. The Witch didn't move very well yet. In fact, now that he thought of it, he hadn't seen her out of her wheelchair since Zmas Night when, admittedly mostly due to the force shield bubble she cast about herself via her metallic marigold, she had been so comparatively agile.

Had she overextended herself so much so then she had a setback? Or had she just no reason to flaunt her recuperative supra-heritage anymore?

"Mel also says she's had far-spoken conversations with various of her spies – sorry, Weir's ambassadors – up and down the west coast. Apparently this ship's bringing an old friend of hers from the Subcontinent of Godbad. We're to assume he isn't devil-possessed, otherwise he'd be dispossessed the instant he came into the Weirdom's territory, and being a he, he also isn't a witch, so the Master will likely let him come ashore. Might not hear him out but Mel will, that's her job."

"And what's yours, Witch? Why are you really here?"

"This is hard, Johnny."

"He's given you an option, hasn't he?" the apparent Inner Earth Irache said, showing his humanity if not his sensitive side, which he ordinarily had no difficulty suppressing. "The bastard! That's why you didn't bring your undersexed lollipop. That's why you had me douse the eye-stave Capputis brought me. You don't want him to overhear my reaction to what you're here to ask me to do."

"He isn't a bastard."

"No, he's a Deva-son and not just the devic half-son of this triangle-headed Pyrame Silverstar we saw out by the Slopes of the Sleepers two weeks ago. I'm right, aren't I?"

"I wasn't there, but since when does a Creature of the Cosmos need an affirmation of something he knows already?"

"Since when does a Master of Weir need eyeorbs to listen in on something? The walls have ears in this Weirdom, Witch. They belong to stone gnomes."

"I'd get down on my knees if I thought I could ever get up again."

"You love him?"

"I love our child-to-come. And I'm crippled. And I'm not healing very fast at all. And I really don't fancy a long sea voyage south. But, like I said, I won't beg you."

Raven finally pipe-whistled something. "You don't mean that," gasped the Witch. "You do fancy a long sea voyage?" There came a response. "I imagine so. I could ask Melina, but I'm sure there's room somewhere onboard for someone like you. Swabbing the deck's what sailors do most of the time. You'd leave me?"

"We'd both leave you, Witch," said Sundown. "And Raven's welcome to go. Me, I'm staying."

"You'll do it?"

"It's been forty years, or thereabouts, including Limbo, since I've been able to see. At least with eyes of my own. You tell Sal, he doesn't force you to formally marry him, he does what I did and he can have my solar spear." She couldn't believe her ears. Then she remembered what Sundown did all those years ago. Now who was being a bastard?

"What you did was pluck out your eyeballs and give them to Manitoulin. Sal would never agree to do that."

"Replicate it then." Raven whinnied something new, so new even Wilderwitch didn't understand her.

"What was that?"

"You heard me and our guess is so did he. Raven was just clearing her craw."

========

Sure enough, as day became afternoon became sunset – which in terms of geography, the Weirdom being well north of Vancouver Canada, came not all that long after lunchtime at this time of year – Capputis popped by Raven's stable-cum-laboratory. The amphibious clone carried with him a box. It was no 'cista mystica', did not contain Psycho's brain, or what was left of it. It contained an issiwun, perhaps even Sundown's own issiwun, his buffalo-head headdress, skull removed and with its horns turned upright. Sundown felt along the latter two to the horns' ends.

"What's this?"

As always Capputis was as deferential as he was a know-it-all. "I believe the technical term is '*ommatophore*', sir. They are bone-stalks, kind of like antennae, that end in …"

"Eyeorbs. Not quite what I had in mind."

"But they will do." Wasn't a question; was a statement. "Please, go take a look."

He did. The bathroom off the lab had a mirror as well as a sink and shower stall. He put it on. The stone-gnome-made issiwun let him see himself. Let him see a reflection overtop of his own, howsoever handsome, reflection as well. That reflection spoke not to his reflection; it spoke to him. He returned to the outer lab.

"Not bad," Sundown told Capputis.

"The receptacle for your spear is over there, sir."

"So it is. Let's wait until tomorrow. I'd like to hear the announcement first."

"At the reception for the outsiders?"

"For those onboard the Tribute Ship, so I understand."

"It'll be for more than just them, sir. But you already know Cynthia-Wilder-witch is pregnant. Past time the Weirdom did, too."

"The marriage announcement. Rather, the lack thereof."

"Lack thereof? That's why there's going to be so many other outsiders here. There is to be a marriage announcement — mine to Lakshmi Arthadot."

"Yours to who?"

"The Kronokronos Supreme of Temporis. Surely Mistress Cynthia or the High Illuminary has mentioned it to you."

"Now that you mention it, no. There's a reason for that."

"So they have mentioned. Please appreciate, sir, Lakshmi and I have known each other since we were babes at breasts. Which is something else I haven't been able to share with you, mostly because I didn't know myself; not for sure. We're so in love we should have married ourselves, by ourselves, as soon as we reached puberty."

"Watch it, Capputis."

After running away from yet another Catholic boarding school for aboriginals, John Sundown and Solace Sunrise did marry themselves. Did so by themselves, with no one else around, on their 13th birthdays, Christmas Day 1933. This non-born clone seemed to know that. Seemed to know all too much about them as far as Sundown was concerned. Loose lips sank ships was an old saying. Was Capputis attempting to provoke him? And, if he was, whose ship was he trying to sink? Was he suicidal?

"I am trying, sir. It's just that spearhead of yours keeping flaring." The hydro-cephalic was visibly sweating. So far it seemed only because of the heat. Could he sweat out grey cells? Would Big Head's big head consequently diminish in size? Sundown's spearhead flared all the hotter. He was curious. Cried Alice.

Raven's Head interposed a whinny of warning, a cautionary squawk. Sundown smiled. Perhaps because of the stress he was then currently feeling, Capputis missed its import. One Creature of the Cosmos obligingly interpreted for the other. "She says, you were saying? You're in love with lack-thereof …"

"So I was, am, but, alas, Lakshmi is much prized. First she was betrothed to Centurion Sophiscient, whom you will have met in Centurium. Then she was to marry, well, we dare not talk about that, dare we? As you might imagine, should you be so inclined, everything changed when her devic half-father, Lazareme's Earth Magician, self-cathonitized. Or aren't we supposed to talk about that either?"

"Depends on how much you enjoy talking to yourself?" Sundown dulled his spearhead deliberately.

"Thanks for that, sir. I'll make it quick. My never-lack-there-of Love's mother contacted the Master and he accepted her hand on my behalf. I've been waiting, ever so anxiously, for the High Illuminary to confirm the details with this Sophiscient fellow, who's now a senator, but it appears all is finally in order."

"You did say *'alas*?"

"I did."

"So now it's an *'at last'*."

"Ah, I see, as in finally. And so do you; see, that is. You outworlders certainly have a way with words."

"And it seems you've a way with women."

"Only the one, alas. Um, at last. Yes, at last. Eventually. After our wedding. Sorry, I'm, um, stumble-tonguing. Just a little less bright, that flare. Thanks. Let's just say so many things can go wrong when it comes to affairs of state, as well as affairs of the heart, it's a great relief when something finally goes right. And by that I don't just mean Dand Tariqartha's, um, ascension a few weeks ago."

"Don't doubt that for a minute. As for my spear, I still prefer to wait until they're made, the announcements."

"The Master will be appreciative of your preferences. Might I ask why?"

"You might and I might even answer you."

Sundown wasn't trying to be obstructionist. He wasn't even trying to sound as unenthusiastic as he undoubtedly did, putting it mildly. He kind of liked Capputis; very much couldn't stand Lakshmi. If she hadn't expelled them from Temporis after all they'd done for her father; after all they'd lost, well …

Would he kill her as soon as she showed her face at the reception? Why were they tempting fate?

"First, though, I better recharge it. Wouldn't want your Master to get a dull dick rather than a livewire stick for your stone gnomes to toothpick."

"That rhymes. Are you making another pun? The Master's warned me about punning."

"Sal should have warned you about those who make puns instead."

========

That night, more like early the next morning, New Years Day on a good part of the western Outer Earth, Blind Sundown came through the Grey into the unlit Catacombs of the Sleepers. His spear was fully charged. He wore no stone-gnome-crafted issiwun. Was wearing his real one. Was also wearing war paint and his beaded blindfold.

No matter how thick the brickwork was; no matter how much it wasn't supposed to be there anymore; he'd been in call-me-Cabby's personal crypt before — the Zmas night Dark Sedon chestnut-roasted, unto ash, dozens of eyeorbs and basically, by humiliating D-Brig, demon-demonstrated who was the Weirdom's real boss.

Sundown thought of everything he'd sensed there then, and seen through whomever's eyeballs. Whereupon his Brainrock-laden spearhead on a spear-shaft took him through between-space. It was still there, the crypt and the equally stone tomb – which, given its constituency probably didn't qualify as either a coffin or a sarcophagus, though he'd never been too sure of the distinction between the two.

No matter where it was in relation to mundane space, lifting the approaching impossibly heavy slab off Cabby's sepulchre was no more an effort for him than it had been lifting off that of Cerebrus David Ryne's on Boxing Day. Driving his Solar Spear through the Ultimate Sleeper's heart was even easier.

Except nothing happened.

Not immediately anyhow. The roof of the catacombs did not collapse. Neither did the Cathonic Dome. The Great Flood of Genesis did not tsunami for a return engagement. The Hidden Continent of Sedon's Head did not sink into the deepest depths of the North Pacific Ocean, where it belonged. Sundown was not finished yet. Not by a long shot.

He hauled the one-eyed Sleeper's consequential corpse out of its tub of Cathonic Fluid, thoroughly slashed and mutilated it, then incinerated what was left.

Still nothing untoward occurred.

The Wakinyah Creature of the Cosmos sensed someone else in the crypt with him; his shade, more like. Despite not being overly aware psychically, he had no doubt who was there. "Seems that," he railed at the felt, but unseen, silent presence, "Thanks to you, Cerebrus, I just slaughtered an innocent Sleeper. Next time you get hold of me, have something constructive for me to do."

That said, that exclaimed, Sundown took himself out of the crypt the same way he came in, via between-space. Using his solar spear as a blind man's cane, he tap-tap-strolled out of the catacombs.

========

Even though Raven's Head felt fine again, and presumably would until, if the Weirdom's embryonic engineers got their way, they repeated the procedure in the not too distant future, he returned to her digs instead of his own suite of rooms in Skyrise. Raven was waiting, standing upright, neither squealing nor whinnying a thing. Was she ready to fly already? Another no matter; he wasn't. Went into the bathroom instead. She followed. Funny how a man-sized doorway can become a very-big-horse-sized one with a few well-placed, back-hoof, buck-kicks from a certain Creature of the Cosmos.

Holding onto Raven's reins he stared at the two of them patiently. Did so until it was no longer just them he was staring at in the mirror. When Klannit manifested herself, he smiled. Had been doing that a fair bit lately. She reciprocated, did likewise. Then he clinked his spearhead against the mirror. She stopped smiling. He didn't. He fired his solar spear.

The mirror didn't shatter. The glass didn't even melt. She did, though, howsoever many thousands of miles away she was high atop the Frozen Isle of Lathakra's Labrys Mountain Range, if that was even where she was. Screamed too, long and loud. He found her screaming far more satisfying than the silence with which Cabalarkon greeted his death, dismemberment and subsequent cremation.

When the screaming ceased, he let go of Raven's reins. She backed out of the bathroom. Blind again, he stayed behind; undid his beaded blindfold; replaced it with his ordinary cloth one; took off his issiwun; carefully, almost reverentially, placed it on the toilet seat; ran the water and washed the war paint off his face.

Tomorrow had the makings of another busy day but he figured neither Lakshmi of Lemuria, nor the stone gnomes, deserved the honour of him painting his face for them.

========

*The Tribute Ship came into Cabalarkon City's harbour the next morning.*

========

It was the 1st of Yamana, still 5980. (New Years Day, 1981, in large swathes of the Outer Earth but, like many on the Headworld, Utopians celebrated New Years Day on the Spring Equinox.) There was a Godbadian emissary onboard it. Melina knew him. They were friends, she told the Witch. Didn't say if their friendship was Biblical or not, but Mel stopped being a nun before she came across 17-year old Harry in 19/5960.

Cynthia-Wilderwitch, veiled and burqa-boxed-in, clothing-wise, was dockside with her, Mel-Illuminatus. They were waiting for this non-Illuminary-emissary friend of Mel's to get off the ship and subsequently be welcomed to the Weirdom formally. His name was Gomez Niarchos, this Godbadian emissary. They'd been familiar, to use Mel's term, with each other for more years than either of them cared to remember; him doubtlessly more so than her.

"How so?"

"It's quite a long, involved, and at times grisly tale, Witch," the High Illuminary of Weir forewarned her. "Suffice it to say we were on Apple Isle in '64. I was pregnant with Percy. Was due, overdue. Was going without birth-pangs. Whereupon I went seriously unconscious, like I was having a stroke instead of a baby. After that things got even hairier and Harry, well, he got shorn of his gorgeous curly locks.

"You see, there was this one-eyed Cyclops of a devil, a miserable Mithradite by the name of Trawl the …"

"Gotcha, Mel. It's one of those her-stories of yours you never get around to story-telling me. Save it for later. I think they're coming out."

"Okay. Just one thing. It's not his fault he smells like a perfumery. It's ours. Gomez got all heroic and saved our lives. Unfortunately we were unable to return the favour."

"He's dead?"

Mel nodded, as ever a disconcerting sight. "In his own way, hence the smell. Better than rot, he always tells me."

"But it's raining," the Witch protested.

She knew Haddit Zombies dissolved in rainfall. Notwithstanding the efforts of her now mostly missing fellows in D-Brig, that was part of the reason the Living won their greatest victory over the Dead in something like 500 years three weeks earlier. The Godbadian Air Force seeded the devil-emplaced Cloud of Hadd and thereby started a torrential downpour.

"Different kind of Dead Thing."

========

*It was Capputis's big day so it was not the hydrocephalic clone who came to collect John Sundown from Raven's digs. Was, instead, Golgotha Nauroz, Black Skull-Face, the leader of Weir's Trinondev Warrior Elite. He was hardly alone, Sundown didn't need to be wearing his stone-gnome-manufactured issiwun to apprehend.*

*He was, though. Was also dressed in his cleanest leathers, washboard chest-protector, star blanket and beaded blindfold.*

*Innocence, thy name is appearing innocent.*

========

Golgotha hadn't brought along Gethsemane this time; just a dozen male Trinondevs, all of whom Sundown and Raven recognized from Hadd. These were therefore amongst the toughest of the toughest and that alone should have set off his alarm bells. He wasn't worried. Even if Raven was still somewhat whacked out, as she put it, what could they do against two Thunder Creatures?

Except, as Golgotha was quick to inform them, only one of them was going to be allowed to attend the afternoon luncheon where the announcements of the Witch's pregnancy and the betrothal of Capputis to Lakshmi of Lemuria were scheduled to be made. One of them wasn't … guess who?

"Why isn't Sal going to do it here?" Sundown wanted to know. Raven did, too. "The old palace would make more sense, either at High Table, in the Hate-Sedon Sphere, or in the throne room, where he held that farcical hearing of his into our friends' disappearance last week?" He could have, replaced 'farcical' with 'rigged' but chose not to — didn't fit with innocence.

"You know the rules, Johnny," Golgotha replied, looking and sounding more concerned than he should. "It is, as always in Cabalarkon, what the Master wills."

"And what God wants, God gets."

"Precisely."

Black Skull-Face was his codename during the Suprawars. He was eighty years old. Even though he didn't look anywhere near that in human terms, clones didn't age as slowly as pureblood Utopians. Had seen and done a great deal, on both sides of the Dome, during that time. Which wore him out ever further. Believed it wasn't just possible, but extremely likely, the Master could tap into eye-staves such that he could overhear their conversation.

"However, to put your mind at ease – not that it should need doing so – balconies outside the old palace are where the Master and his chosen ones can oversee massive gatherings in the grand square for Utopians in their tens of thousands. Inside it, like you said, groups of people in their dozens, sometimes even in their hundreds, can come together and celebrate a public occasion such as Zmas Night.

"But the Master rarely uses it for smaller affairs of state anymore. Indeed, virtually all formal functions have been held in Skyrise since its completion."

"It isn't growing another storey, is it? "

"As to that …"

"No, don't tell me. It is as the Master wills."

"Just so."

"What else does he will, besides Raven not being there?"

Raven neigh-cawed words to the effect it was just as well she wasn't invited. While she could control her bowels and bladder as well as any other sentient being – certainly better than most of the idiots of Weir – as soon as she saw Lakshmi Arthadot again she'd be severely tempted to control them all over the 18-year old

Lemurian deviant, another one with gills behind her ears, who expelled them from Temporis on the 6th.

"Which is why," said Golgotha, not happily, "The Master has additionally decided to hold the luncheon between-space. The physical site will be inside Skyrise but, as its upper storeys were when we returned from Temporis on the 9th, the particular area of Skyrise where it's to be held will only be accessible via matter transducers."

"Those things give me the heebie-jeebies. Can't the Master just will me up there?"

"There is that possibility, I suppose. More conventional transportation could be made available. Or you're welcome to miss the engagement altogether."

"Engagement or engagements?"

"There is only the one to be announced. My understanding is the High Illuminary has prevailed upon the Master not to, um, insist upon Cynthia-Wilderwitch joining him in an official capacity. Between you and I, it's my opinion the Master was delighted to acquiesce. He shares, dare I say it, more than just his bed with your Witch."

Raven made a vocalization. Golgotha missed it. Sundown didn't. Did correct her. "That's curiouser and curiouser, Beauty, not curious and more curious."

"There is just one other thing, Johnny."

"Knew there'd be. What is it?"

"You agreed to turn over your solar spear to the Master for replication if he didn't insist upon a state marriage with your Wilderwitch. Which he won't. As to whether he would have, that is no longer an issue. However, with respect to the issue of conventional transportation, it can be arranged, yes; stairs or an elevator, whichever you prefer."

He was waffling. Got one of those sightless glares that so upset Capputis; that and a brief flare from his solar spear. Got the point, figuratively. (Wouldn't have survived the point, literally.) Finished delivering his message: "It's just that, prior to either/or, or any other alternative method of transport becoming available, he requests you turn it over to me."

"Because?"

"Because it really wouldn't do for you to immolate Lakshmi on the spot."

"I wasn't going to."

"No, I expect you were going to wait until she told you what she did to your pals. Then you were going to do it; do her. She doesn't have them. The Zeross girls didn't send them to Temporis. Or if they did, Lakshmi has no knowledge of it. The High Illuminary has confirmed that herself. With corroboration from her mother and friends, one of whom you know very well from both before and after Limbo. So nothing's changed in that regard. We still don't know where they sent them. No one does; not even them, her daughters."

"You're talking about Fish. She'll be there?"

"That I can't say, because I don't know, but her mother likely will be. Aortic Amphitrite, whom you may recall was the supra codenamed Lady Lemurian, is a Quarter Queen of Shenon. As you may have also heard, from the High Illuminary, Shenon's a heart-shaped island in the Interior Ocean of Akadan, just off the northwest coast of the Cattail Peninsula, Sedon's ponytail. It's a witch stronghold, true. Wouldn't be also known as Witch Isle if it wasn't. But Lemurians and their queen, their gynarch, hate devils as much as the Master does.

"At the Aortic's urging, her deviant daughter, the Kronokronos Supreme of Temporis, has declared the Thousand Caverns a devil-free zone. While this is to the Master's liking he had to be sure she, Lakshmi, has no, um, ulterior motives when it comes to uniting their two realms as well as their two families."

Raven interrupted, with a squawk of surprise. For his part Sundown was glad he'd secured the manufactured issiwun under his chin with its straps. Otherwise he'd be winching his jaw up from the floor by now. Golgotha raised his eye-stave, signalling a desire to finish what he was saying. Magnanimously, the two Thunder Creatures allowed him to do just that.

"Consequently, the Master has spoken to the undeniably ambitious young woman at some length, in her mother's presence and with his Speaking Stick in hand, just so they thoroughly understand each other, if you known what I mean. They touched on many subjects, including the whereabouts of your missing pals. He is satisfied she is as innocent of having anything to do with their disappearance as she is ignorant of where they might be.

"Furthermore, he is persuaded she shares with him, her mother, her adoptive sister, Capputis's mother, and we in the Weirdom an abiding hatred for Dark Sedon; an all-consuming passion, if you will, toward seeing the Moloch destroyed. And that is why he has agreed to allow his finally acknowledged firstborn to marry her."

They took the stairs.

========

*Alarm bells not ringing yet, nary a headache wracking his skull even though he was wearing the stone gnomes' issiwun, he arrived in time for the start of the late luncheon on the 5th floor of Skyrise. He hadn't altogether given up his solar spear but, as Mel-Illuminatus had lectured them at some length on the 25th, and Golgotha had reiterated any number of times, on any number of topics, on the way over, appearances were all-important here in the Weirdom.*

*So it was John Sundown walked in arm-in-arm with Black Skull-Face, Golgotha Nauroz. He wasn't holding onto his solar spear, Golgotha was, but he wasn't far from it.*

*Never was.*

********

# Twelve-Babies: **CYNTHIA MASTERWIFE**

========

**New Years Day, 1981**

*What did set off the chimes of no-longer-quite-blind Sundown's alarm bells, alas and at last, was the altar-like mechanism set up toward the front of the room.*

========

It looked identical to the stone-gnomes-construct that had, as if by magic, appeared in Raven's digs a few days ago. It was a replication unit. Only one guess allowed as to what it was there to start replicating. Sundown didn't need that much. It was hardly all that had been grating on him these last few days of pondering, most profoundly, but Sal's obsession with getting hold of his Solar Spear really was becoming almost as annoying as the headaches.

On a hidden continent containing all manner of bad bogies, any sensible Master should be far more circumspect when it came to wishing for what was his, Sundown's, to give, but wasn't necessarily his, the Master's, right to receive. Not without tendering a proper price paid, that was for sure.

Then again when you're on a roll like Sal had been, what with everything and everyone rolling his way, especially the Witch, in the hay, why rollover and feign patience? God might be able to get what God wants but God could yet get what God deserves.

========

*Capputis grabbed his hand and shook it as he entered the space, which may or not have been between-space by then.*

*"Glad you could make it, Mr Sundown. Sorry about Raven's Head not being allowed in Skyrise, sir. You're not going to incinerate my fiancée, are you?"*

========

As befit the occasion Capputis was scrupulously dressed in a spick-and-span white under-gown or djellaba and an off-white, approaching beige, long-sleeved over-gown or djebba. Nice embroidery too, thought Sundown. Stone gnome seamstresses (presumably) could turn out some decent work when someone programmed them properly.

There wasn't much you could do about his scurfy, even scabrous skin except give it a good scrubbing – preferably with sandpaper and caustic soda – then peel off what came loose. There was absolutely nothing you could do about the hydrocephalic head. Which, its size, Golgotha having delineated the teenager's newly revealed parentage on the walk over here, occurred to Sundown had more to do with containing his ego than it did water on the brain.

Mel-Illuminatus had once told him how the Master's offspring were so uppity and unruly most of them were sent to the countryside to be raised. Mind you, upon sober reflection, Capputis had more likely been sent to the ocean side to be raised. Even though he'd been warming to him lately, it was no wonder he'd had such an instinctive dislike for the boy.

Even if they'd been allies in Hadd – aside from the aberration she'd become at the end – and many, many times long before that, pre-Limbo, he never much liked his mother either. For a couple of years in the late Thirties, back when he still had eyes of his own, he tended to blame Fisherwoman, Scylla Nereid, for keeping him and Solace apart.

It wasn't just his clothes and rasped skin that made Capputis seem not quite so ugly. For once his head was bare and someone had gone to tremendous lengths to gussy up his great mane of hair. It was clean and shiny, true, but he'd also had a 'do', one calculated to emphasize his ears and what was behind them. Long side-tufts of it had been clustered together and combed forward, as straight as they would go. Intricate braids had been wound up and tied behind his head to prevent the rest of his hair from obscuring what were now his proudest features.

The reason for that was pretty obvious, as obvious as they were. He wouldn't be the only one in the room with gills behind his ears. Lakshmi Arthadot, when she showed up, had them too. So did their mothers and to think, back during the Secret Wars, Sundown always thought Lady Lemurian wore some sort of frog-suit or witch-glamour in order to appear the way she did. He never suspected she was an actual frogwoman.

Golgotha told him on the way over he wasn't sure whether said Lady Lemurian of far too many years gone by (Aortic Amphitrite), or Lady Achigan (Scylla Nereid, Codenamed Fisherwoman), or both, intended to be here for the big announcement. He doubted it. Regardless of their witch backgrounds, the Master didn't get along with either of them.

Their decades of dalliances aside – and it was decades, Fish and the Master went back to their teens – she was Master Kyprian's champion during 5950's Challenge of Weir. Might have won it if she hadn't been forced to withdraw from the distinctly unfriendly contest after Kyprian's mandatory, ever-so-mysterious death.

As for Amphitrite, even if it was largely her that prevented it, the Master never quite got over her frogwomen trying to stew him alive back in 5974 on Witch Isle.

========

"Jumping the gun again, aren't you? You lied to me, you're no clone."

"So I've only just found out. Yes, it now appears my mother was the Queen of Godbad whereas my father was Saladin Nauroz, the mighty Master of Weir. Lady Achigan, as she prefers nowadays, was raised from shortly after birth, to her very early teens, by Merthetis, the twenty years' late Gynarch of Lemuria. She has a stepsister, a Summoning Child like you, Witch Isle's current Lemurian Aortic. Her name is Amphitrite and she is my beloved's mother. By the Master's Will we're uniting Hate-Sedon dynasties.

"You aren't, are you? You're a devaslayer. You can't be."

"Look at my eyes, boy."

"You don't have any eyes, sir. You're wearing a blindfold. Nice beadwork by the way, very stylish. Oh, you mean those … what's the word again?"

"Ommatophores, isn't it? That's what you called them."

"You see? I never lie. Not deliberately. Promise you won't incinerate her."

"Only by the Master's Will."

"Thank you, sir. There's something else I didn't tell you."

"There always is. What is it?"

"I've just seen some mandroids, stone gnomes. First time ever, I swear. Although, if you were to ask me, they're hardly very gnome-like. Got squat little legs but their heads are almost as big as their torsos. Put together they're both bigger than you or I. Got huge yellow eyes that I'd swear were garnet or pumice implants, except they move like real eyes; boxer's mashed noses, slits for mouths, and protrusions for ears that look like handles except they're closed, so you couldn't get a proper grip.

"Most of them have hats that look like bricks. They're tilted so far forward on their heads it's a wonderment they don't fall off, heads with them. They all have these huge thick arms; a couple even have them coming off their heads, not their bodies. And they're shape-shifters, like some faeries and daemons. Lakshmi tells me she's wearing one.

"Calls them guard-bodies but more than anything else they remind me of those ancestral statues on your Easter Isle; Moai, the High Illuminary says. She's surrounded by them."

"To stop me from incinerating her."

"Will it work?"

Sundown chose to ignore the amphibious, ever-so-irritating, teenage prodigy with a big head, fancy hairdo and bad skin. "Hand me my spear, Golgotha."

"Can't do that, Johnny."

"The spear." Despite Golgotha holding onto it, the Cheyenne talisman flared. Capputis stepped back, Golgotha didn't. Did hand him his spear, however.

"Now show me to my seat. And don't worry about your lady love, boy. She's safe, you've my word. You, too, Golgotha. I'll give it to Sal when the time comes."

========

*That time would come soon enough.*

========

Except for the crystal chandeliers above it, the room itself was a not particularly lavishly decorated ballroom converted to a banquet hall. There were lots of four-person tables, most of which were already occupied, roughly arranged in a U-shape. Many of the occupants had to be from Temporis. Where else would you see such a diverse ethnic, colourfully costumed mix gathered in one place?

Certainly not in Cabalarkon. With the lone exceptions of him, Raven, of course, and Wilderwitch, who, when she wasn't in white goddess mode, had about her a gypsy air, every Utopian, even the few teenage hybrids in attendance, was either a white woman or a black man. Temporites, though, came in all shapes and sizes, some straight out of Outer Earth storybooks and folktales, even movies and television shows.

Evidently one was even a satyr, like Furie was becoming before OMP-Akbar clouted him on Zmas Eve; except this one was voluptuous, very much female. (In an almost non sequitur form of fever flash, he recalled Melina telling them, not all that many days ago, that female satyrs were known as fauna in here. Fauna were not to confused with the general term for animals, though their passions were, in addition to exceedingly passionate, bordering on animalistic; in a very much loving way, she added, bordering on prudishly.)

At the mouth of the U-shape was an empty table also set for four. Only the occupants of this table would face outwards, toward everyone else instead of each other. The table Golgotha led him to, at the tip of one arm of the U-shape, was somewhat different in that it had just the three chairs and settings. One was for him, another was for Golgotha, while the third, surprisingly, was for Persephone Zeross.

She nodded pleasantly as he and Golgotha sat down. Raven had been joking about that puppy love crap, hadn't she?

Opposite them, on the extremity of the other arm of the U were her two sisters, Helen and Athena. That was where Golgotha's wife Gethsemane had positioned herself, the better to attend to the ever-active Tina more so than to Helen, who seemed to be glaring at him. Which was only tit for tat in a way. He'd been glaring at Percy. Rather, the stalks ending in eyeorbs atop his faux-buffalo-headpiece were glaring at her.

Sure, as always, she was demurely dressed; more so than he was. There was only a hint of bare skin visible between her long-sleeved shirt and her floor-length skirt, whereas all he had on underneath his star blanket, in the way of a shirt anyhow, was a beaded, washboard vest. But why was she wearing leathers like him? Leathers embroidered with beads like his? Was it for him? Where was her mother?

As if in answer, Capputis having personally greeted the last of the late arrivals and gone elsewhere, no doubt to await a more ostentatious introduction of his own, she, the female Dr Zeross, Melina born Sarpedon, the High Illuminary of Weir, caduceus in hand, stepped from a cleverly concealed, curtained entrance behind the empty head table. Was there a Matter Transducer back there? Had to be.

Were probably a few, if the hall was indeed between-space. Unless, and this was a thought, the room itself waited to be filled before it took itself into the Grey.

"Ladies and Gentlemen, distinguished guests from Subcranial Temporis, newly proclaimed devil-free land like Cabalarkon has always been, and always shall be, visitors from even further afar, may I present the Master of Weir and his just-this-morning-avowed consort for life, Cynthia Masterwife!"

"Huh?" gasped John Sundown, about the only one in the place who dared say anything. And he hardly audibly.

Persephone reached across the table and took his hand, the one not holding his solar spear. "It's all right, Uncle Johnny. Skinny Auntie Wildie says she wanted to marry him. Don't you see, it's her way of winning. She's wants the Weirdom to have an heir, a legitimate heir, not some bastard Fish-spawn."

He suddenly sensed a hollowness in the pit of his stomach. No, not there, in his wampum pouch. He regarded Persephone anew. Why hadn't he noticed before she was wearing three of her father's rings? They were glowing. She was glowing, albeit slightly less so. What was that Crazy Horse supposedly said at the Battle for Little Bighorn?

"Oh," he said instead.

========

*Raven's Head had lain down again for a nap. Shouldn't have, hadn't really intended to, had just felt tired all of a sudden.*

*She snapped awake; was on her feet, her winged hooves, in a instant. They'd done it again, fixed her stable-cum-laboratory whilst she rested. Except this time the bloody stone gnomes had sealed it off entirely, her in it. Reflexively she flapped her talarial wings of Mercury. Didn't go anywhere she wanted. Worse, her legs sank into the floor, as if it was quicksand, up past her cannons almost as high as her knees before they hit solid ground.*

*"Couldn't stop with cement horseshoes. Not when you've those cute little feathery things down there. How do you like the full overshoes treatment, Raven?"*

*Someone appeared in front of her. It was the god-cursed, stone-helmeted, cape-draped Conqueror, Jesus fucking Mandam. Except it couldn't be. Blind Sundown, riding her, had dropped a Soviet-made H-Bomb (that he had actually provided them) atop him, he nailed to a cross, two years (for them) and over a quarter century earlier on a Salvation Isle Golgotha.*

*She said nothing, so he said more. Never could shut up, could Jess: "You've been itching to meet some stone gnomes. Meet me instead."*

========

The Master of Weir strode in from the back of the room. He was arm-in-arm with his splendid, this time dark-haired, white-skinned goddess. Unless her skin was just powdered with talc or some such, it was a glamour she wore when she went about without a bulky, deliberately shape-concealing drapery, hood-like hijab and face-hiding veil. At least Wilderwitch more like limped in, Sundown was moderately pleased to see.

There was no extravagant spectacle marking their entrance. No attempt to come close to the display they, the Witch more so than the Master, put on Zmas Night in the Hate-Sedon Sphere. No lightshow, no thunderous music, no tectonic applause, just a brief trumpet fanfare and restrained clapping. Which the glorious couple acknowledged with gracious nods of the head before taking their seats.

They were glorious to behold, though. He, the black god, was in full Masterly regalia. No shirt — for a sixty year old man he had great abs, did the Master, proud of them, too; ostrich-feathered headdress, it with its solitary rhinoceros horn; white, sleeveless, fur cloak; kilt, be-tusked belt, gauntlets, boots, phoney Crimson Corona chain of office (golden triangle medallion with its single eye staring out of it); sheathed, pseudo-Susasword; reflective, Amateramirror-approximation on right arm like a kind of narrow, ovular buckler; save for his Master's Mace, which wouldn't be far away, the works.

She hadn't bothered with the boxy, all-covering burqa this time. Wasn't much all-covering about her, Sundown was even more pleased to see. What she did have about her was all white, to match her skin's seeming, and East Indian in inspiration. A sleeveless bodice or half-shirt that bared her midriff – the Witch had even better abs than Sal – a shawl that might be called a sari, except it wasn't very long or very broad, and a pair of knee-length … what? Trousers with a slip of a skirt, about mid-thigh-length, overtop them.

She likely wouldn't have bothered with the pants if she hadn't had a massive bandage and horrific stitching to hide. Still, what she was and wasn't hiding was perfectly fine with him. What she wore wasn't his decision to make. He'd already made it, his decision; had next to nothing to do with clothing, however.

She might or might not have been wearing sandals. The stone gnomes hadn't provided Sundown with x-ray vision such that he could see beneath the table, but she definitely was not wearing any jewellery. Which really was a shame. Lots of nifty stuff came off the studs and bangles and other accoutrements she'd ordinarily be sporting. Some were quite lethal.

Not that he'd ever known the Witch to kill anything except the occasional dinner, albeit not without first asking her meal-to-be for permission. Oh, all right, if she could she'd have killed Mater Matare, Mother Murder, the self-proclaimed Apocalyptic of Death, in Temporis back on the 6^th^. Then again the Medusa would have killed her too.

And Master Devas were no more supposed to kill than supranormals; as supras affiliated with the western Allied powers, himself not included, by much later day choice, more accurately. It was a tossup who came closest to killing whom in Temporis. Nonetheless, it was a decidedly good thing he and Raven burst into the Calvary Cavern when they did because Matare wasn't alone and the Witch pretty much was by then. Hence the nearly severed leg.

He found it significant Sal still didn't trust her with much of anything, perhaps not even clothes, from her bottomless bag. He had to wonder if she did as well: find it significant Sal didn't trust her with her enchantments, as he called them at the hearing. Probably not. She was less focused on getting better herself than she was on bearing the Master a healthy child.

At least Sal – he who had entrusted her with doing just that, having his baby – let her wear her hair down, and out, all wild and rat's-nest-like, neither darkened nor lightened, and not overly straight like it had been becoming more and more so of late. Maybe she'd finally switched shampoos.

He hadn't really been expecting any help from her quarter anyways. Was fully prepared to do without Raven's as well. Nevertheless, the Witch wouldn't be a bad sight to go out on.

It was a good day for dying.

========

*Almost predictably the Conqueror kept nattering on and on.*

========

"Oh, I know what you're thinking, Raven. Know you can think, too. That you're not just a birdbrain. Know you can talk as well, after a fashion. Hell's teeth, what with all the doodads and thingamajigs built in my boulder brain I might even be able to understand you. What say you to that?" She resolutely held her peace; did so even as she felt the stone gnome goo trickle upwards, closer to her knees.

"Nothing? Not even a peep of anxiety? Guess you've realized there's nothing you can do. You're not stuck for words; you're just plain stuck. And it's up to me whether you stay that way or not, isn't it? Well, don't hold your breath. Or do, if you think it'll quicken your end. And end it will be. And it's not because you helped kill me. You didn't, you know. I'm not that Conqueror. I'm not Jesus Mandam."

She couldn't hold back a very much unladylike squawk of astonishment. Underneath his stony headgear – his helmet didn't glow but did have brain-like striations that left it featureless facially – whoever was masquerading as Boulder Brain, as members of SOS, and KOC after them, sometimes referred to him, might have been smiling. There was no disguising the mirth in his voice.

"I'm not the other one either; the one your Johnny shot up on Aegean Trigon back in '38, years before he traded his eyesight for his spear and the right to ride you." Her own eyes must have boggled at that. Nothing else did, though the viscous, still rising, pebbly encumbrance did tickle a tad tackily.

"Oh, you didn't know there were two; didn't know the real Conqueror was Ulysses Heliopolis. Did you know his nephew Kadmon finally did kill him back in 1950? No, evidently not. Didn't know he wasn't really Kad's uncle either, I'm supposing; that he was really Kad in his eleventh lifetime and that Miracle Memory couldn't do anything to stop him.

"Well, she could have … but how could she kill the Male Entity almost twenty years before he had a chance to become the Male Entity?"

He had her with that; that plus the fact that the sticky slurry had reached her knees and showed no sign of slowing down. The sound she made still didn't sound anywhere near human but there was no mistaking its meaning. "Glad you asked," he said, as if he completely understood her.

"You see, the Master has a real clever niece. Not Andy, the striped one who tried to assassinate him in Hadd. The older one, the one who's only a quarter Utopian but half faerie, so no surprise re the cleverness. They're natural-born tricksters. Her name's Tsishah Twilight by the way – at least that's the name she goes by these days – and she had this real bright idea while she was in Temporis a few days ago …"

Even as the immobilizing, between-space paste surmounted her knees and slipped toward her belly, Raven's Head listened attentively.

Thundercloud Creatures did make notes after all.

========

*So did Tsishah Twilight. Also, occasionally, though not here, conducted inventories.*

========

Fisherwoman and fellow Aortic Amphitrite hadn't altogether abandoned Tsishah. They were what amounted to backstage with their offspring, Capputis and Lakshmi, awaiting their big moment; their children's big moment, rather. Knowing her fragile state as well as the Master's ongoing, to their mind irrational fear of witches, their enchantments and especially their witch-stones, she was seemingly unprotected. They hadn't left her alone, however.

Sitting beside her, both on mandroid guard-bodies in the shape of the chairs they were sitting on, was the goatish Traveller, Pusan Wanderlust, a Wayfarer in the Wild Weird if ever there was one; had no need of dreams to send herself anywhere except beyond the Dome. A recurring deviant – one of only two left, the other being Jordan 'Quill' Tethys, the legendary 30-Year Man (who'd saved the Master from Andaemyn Sarpedon on Dustmound) – her devic half-mother was a Byronic, not a Lazaremist like Jordy, the Witch or Tsishah herself.

Like the Legendarian, whose Brainrock quill once belonged to his devic half-father, Rumour of Lazareme, her devic mother's power focus, a pedum or Shepherd's Crook, went with her from lifetime to lifetime. Had been doing so for coming up to 4,000 years, Unlike Tethys, who'd only been around for half that time, she always came back female.

Also unlike him, she may well have once been her mother, a devic suicide, Deneb Makara by three thousand years bygone Illuminaries' given name, one of Byron's Winter Zodiacals, Capricorn the Goatfish. Like Fish and Treat, Pusan knew who Tsishah wore; knew her when she wasn't wearable to boot. Knew many of those there. And their forbearers, going back centuries, even millennia.

Was as per usual around here; was quite the her-story, was the Goat.

========

Bare-faced, wearing a headscarf shaped like something an Egyptian pharaoh might have on his head, and a pale, long-sleeved djellaba similar in style to what Capputis had on, so was Melina born Sarpedon Zeross. Was, in keeping with her second place status in the Weirdom, nowhere near as splendiferous in her choice of costume as the Witch.

Of course, Sundown imagined – which he did do once in a while – the Witch wasn't about to be upstaged by Lakshmi of Lemuria in the nuptial department, let alone in the looks department. By contrast Mel, epitome of ideal Utopian femininity that she was, had probably been under instructions not to draw undue attention to herself.

Another one with no jewellery in sight, not even a wedding ring, and with her altogether white, tinsel-hair obscured by the scarf, she was doing a damn good job of meshing with the backdrop. Even kept her caduceus – which he'd sometimes seen glow, through eyes not his own – dull as the overcast sky outside Skyrise. Had a riveting voice, however, and piercing eyes, both of which she now applied to him.

"Prior to the arrival of our other special couple, I would like to take this opportunity to formally recognize and thank our Outer Earth guest, mine and Cynthia Masterwife's old friend and frequent comrade-in-arms, for his efforts on behalf of every non-devil and every non devic adherent on this oft-afflicted continent of ours. Ladies and gentlemen please, I give you Mr John Sundown."

As polite applause and a modicum of table thumping answered her introduction, Golgotha elbowed him in the ribs. "That's your cue, Johnny. Stand up and take it like a man."

The lead Trinondev, who was a genuine clone, not a pretend one, had prepared him for this moment. He rose to his feet and, as the noise level increased, made his way to the replication device in the mouth of the U. There he couldn't resist raising his solar spear and letting its spearhead flare, howsoever briefly. This initially drew a loud sucking sound from the audience as it collectively inhaled and held its breath, as if dreading what he would do next.

Smiling not so much wickedly as in apparent pleasure, he dimmed the spearhead and then, according to script, laid it on top of the device. "By the Master's Will, I present my spear to this Weirdom. My hope is that it will be successfully replicated, over and over again, and that its replicates will be used by the Trinondev Warrior Elite in their endless strivings to eradicate the blight of devazurkind throughout the cosmos."

This brought forth the tumult, much applause, much table thumping, a standing ovation so boisterous it drowned out the whirr of the machinery as it conveyed his spear into its maw and, thence, out of sight into its interior workings. (Had someone just squealed, more so than yelped, 'Daddy!'?)

Sundown watched as it went away. Didn't even acknowledge the cheers of the crowd. Then the pain hit. It was like the stone gnomes' issiwun was swallowing his head, chewing his skull and slurping his brain as it did so. He could still see, though. And through it, through its ommatophores, he saw the Master of Weir on Earth get to his feet.

As that same instant he himself was raised off his feet into the air, enclosed by a Trinondev thought-bubble; perhaps a few of them, not just one cast by Saladin Devason, who seemingly didn't need his Master's Mace visible in order to project force shields. Maybe it was true; maybe he, as Master, was a living eye-stave.

They'd set the trap so well. Planned everything to perfection. Then came a new wrinkle, one neither he nor Raven had anticipated. He felt Persephone's rings form around his ankles, holding them together, and about both his wrists, pulling his arms apart. So much for Puppy John. They wanted a Pulpy John. Reflexively his exclusion zone pushed back. To no avail.

He must have looked like a crucified man, minus the cross, encased in a transparent beach ball floating in midair. Was it his imagination or did the Irache sitting beside the Goat Woman just … what? Jump not so much to her feet as her skin nearly did so independently; nearly jumped off her under-body while the rest of her remained seated, put better.

At which point the fauna materialized a … what now? A bishop's crosier? Something a faerie godmother might tote around? Looked like it. Took them both elsewhere.

Everything was happening too quickly. He was losing his mind. So was the gathered assembly. Their cheers approached crescendo. Reached it, got as high as they would go. Another etherealist – so much for the apparent ability to 'make ether real' being a devic trick learned by witches – the Master had raised his Speaking Stick, his Master's Mace, as if out of nowhere. Whereupon the immediately ensuing silence was positively deafening.

"With that spear," intoned Saladin Devason, in a bass-baritone, "You slew my beloved sister, Morgianna Somata. I have heard the calumnies that she was fighting alongside the Dead of Hadd at that time and, while that might have been the outward take of the matter, she was fighting to obtain the Trigregos Talismans for me, for our Weirdom. Her murder can neither be overlooked nor in any way condoned. Vengeance is not mine. Justice is!"

Sundown could hear the crowd rumbling in approval. Wilderwitch, Cynthia Masterwife, just sat there, to the Master's left, not quite impassively, not quite doing nothing. He could move his head slightly, enough to see Persephone Zeross and Golgotha Nauroz at their table. Golgotha had drawn his facial veil, bad sign that, but the eyeorb atop his eye-stave was not lit up. The one atop the Witch's metallic marigold was, brightly. That, not Sal's Speaking Stick, was from whence came the globe enclosing him; the first layer of it anyways.

He'd expected it of Golgotha, he followed the Master's orders, but why did she have be against him, too?

Percy was pointing her right arm, hand extended, in his direction. She was visibly concentrating. Her fingers no longer had Harry's rings on them. Understandably. He could feel them tightening around his ankles and two wrists. Her father had dismembered more than a few Haddit Zombies that same way. It was only him straining his exclusion zone to its limits that kept them from doing that to him.

On the other side of the U he spotted Gethsemane ushering Helen and Athena away from their table. In the front of the room, Melina still stood beside head table. Capputis came out from behind the curtain. He had in his hands a box that did not strike him as either particularly pretty nor even necessarily lacquered. Was made of wood, however. So that was it, the incredible headaches, why he was finding it so difficult to think straight. The Magnificent Psycho was back, brain in a box, a 'cista mystica'. If he'd ever left; if what was left of him had ever left Weir, make that.

Was Melina the one wearing the glamour of Fey Woman Boxing Day morning after all? Had her story of crying herself to sleep just been to keep him, Raven and the Witch off-guard, so they wouldn't do anything then nor since? So elaborate, so unnecessary. Why hadn't she just had her daughters send him away as well? Was it because the Master wanted his hide for him killing the Morrigan in Hadd?

Answer was, Sal was about to verify, yes! "You are a great killer, John Sundown. So many have died because of you. My friend, my ally in the cause of devic devastation, Wiccan Warlock, whom you knew best as the Conqueror or Conquering Christ, but who was born Jesus Mandam, being only one of your victims; my sister being merely one of your last.

"Oh, yes, I know what you did last night. Cynthia Masterwife brought the information to me. Her soul-self saw everything; impotent to stop anything. But do you know you failed to add the undying Utopian after whom this Weirdom is named to your list; that you wholly failed to destroy the Ultimate Sleeper, Cabalarkon Himself? I thought not. But it was not for lack of trying. Bring that box to me, High Illuminary of Weir."

Melina did so. Took it from Capputis and placed it on the table in front of the Witch and the Master. It was the former, Sal's white goddess, who now stood, the former who handed her metallic marigold, eyeorb open, its tendril-outstretched-eyeball glowing, to the High Illuminary to hold for the nonce, the former who unclosed the box and spilled out its contents.

"You had no right to kill Cerebrus, Johnny," the Witch all but spat at him.

Amongst the ashen contents of the box were the charred remains of Cerebrus David Ryne's headplate, even more fractured than they had been before.

"You have tremendous power," declared Saladin Devason. "Too much power to permit a trial, let alone any thought of mercy. I sentence you, John Sundown, to Immediate Death!"

=========

*"You see," the replicate Conqueror concluded chattily, "It was all about Sed-sons. Jesse, Wiccan Warlock, had been killing them off for years. Now there were only two left out there, his ancient foster father, Sedon St Synne – a septuagenarian then, a centenarian now – and the Sundowns' newborn; who was a boy, not a girl. That was just a stillborn they left behind for your Johnny to find, a deliberate diversion from the full*

*import of the horror, probably a faerie stock or stone gnome facsimile given the semblance of onetime life.*

*"Dark Sedon knew that. Had come to collect the living babe in person. Had his Rache followers, led by the Baphomet Headsman, crucify Jesse just to make it easier for him to gloat. Which was when you two arrived, according to plan. The H-Bomb didn't kill the mighty Moloch, just left him twenty-five years nearly dead. Killed everyone else, though, except you and Sundown, which Jesse didn't expect.*

*"You're not unkillable. Fact is you're about to follow Johnny. Really is a waste, you know. As Tsishah would have told you, if she wasn't so terrified you'd find out her demon's identity, there are plenty of ravendeer – ravenbucks, more to the penile point – where she lives these days, in the high mountains way down south at the bottom of the Cattail.*

*"You could have had the start of many more like you. Gotten laid a few times while you were at it."*

*That didn't make her shiver. Her proving herself a self-psychopomp did.*

=========

He had an exclusion zone.

It neutralized supra talents. But Harry's rings were insensate Brainrock and even if Persephone inherited the talent to wield them, she was too far away for it to affect her. He had confirmed psychopomp abilities – could get about the Weird in near-space terms – but he'd never gone anywhere without holding onto his spear. Did he need to hold onto it? Was that just a crux of a crutch, as OMP-Akbar might put it? It was comparatively close by. He tried, not for the first time. No go, possibly for the last time.

Couldn't teleport without it, not even in his most desperate moments. Or couldn't teleport because he couldn't think straight due the stone gnomes' crablike eye stalks. Or couldn't teleport because he was encased in a mind-globe, conceivably more than one, that might have first emanated from the Witch's metallic marigold. Which Illuminatus, Percy's mom, now held presumably because she was better at handling the things than Wilderwitch.

Yet the helmet was a modified eye-stave complete with open eyeorbs, two of them, on stalks not poles, put together by technomages. His exclusion zone couldn't counter technology, just supra talents. He had been frantically seeking to expand it anyhow; must be why his head retained it wholeness even if the brain (mind?) within it wasn't running right. Spirit was willing sort of thing; just too scrambled to function properly.

Plus, the Master controlled them, the eyes on stalks, even the Witch's, with his overriding Master's Mace, if he even needed that much. Those were the source of his headaches, not Cerebrus or Psycho. Raven had tried to warn him against putting it on; was afraid it'd interfere with, if not out and out nullify, their cosmic aura.

He hadn't ignored her so much as welcomed the attention. Told her as much. Wasn't a horse-whisperer; was a raven-whisperer.

Oh well, he was always going to go that way anyway.

========

*"No one said she could do that," the Conqueror replicate muttered to himself the moment Raven's Head, vibrating intensely, as psychopomps were wont to do, vanished.*

========

Unlike OMP-Akbar with his Homeworld Sceptre, Sundown didn't have an invisible mental string about his spear that he could reverse-twang to like a yoyo.

In Hadd, which Golgotha Nauroz or one of his Trinondev elite might have noticed – if they weren't so busy forming the Wyvern of Weir at the time, then taking out Mars Bellona and/or whoever was animating the by then mostly senseless devil – he hadn't attracted his spear back into his grip as if metal to magnet.

He'd fired it from a slight distance, like an inverted roman candle; caused it to shoot out of the pit it was sinking into, along with Morgianna's cocooning body. Luckily it had enough residual power left to make it as far as his outstretched hand, he on Raven, as she swooped by, low to ever more diminishing Dustmound, drenched as it was by then. If it hadn't had, he'd have had to get off her and risk sliding into the same downpour-fracturing ground as Morg, in her cocoon.

Didn't need residual power today; was totally charged. And they knew it. Should have known much more than that, too.

Sal, Mel or the Witch, if she was the mastermind, should have realized Sundown didn't need to be in contact with his spear to make it erupt. They should have seen to it that, as soon as he placed it in the replication unit, the stone gnomes took it to a different location between-space. Unless they couldn't; maybe there's no such thing as another between-space place once you're already inside the Weird or the Grey or whatever they called it today.

That was his self-devised test of their trustworthiness. He'd have sensed it if they tried to snatch it away; sensed it before they could and acted immediately. That, they might have realized; must be why they'd been piling on impediments, like the daemonic Indescribables did in Hadd (many of whom had been brought there by Morg and her one-armed man, Alastor Molorchus). This way they only delayed the inevitable.

Roman candle … fireball … target Saladin … too late. He wasn't just quick with the fending-off mind-globe, he was instantaneous. On second thought, probably always had it up; ditto the Witch. Or whoever kept straightening her hair; letting her walk on what had to be a supplemental overset of actually serviceable legs; kept messing with her mind. Let alone his mind, if it wasn't Sal or Mel doing it. Unless they shared protection.

Spear blazes through unit, blasts Sal. Force shield dissipates blast, though not uselessly. Spear blaze melts unit; roars out of unit. Roasts Witch — would have, should have, deflects domino-ditto. Does disrupt focus Mel-Illuminatus, the next one over, needs to keep him enclosed with force field projections; hers interior-most one anyway. Cracks spread outwards, splintering overlays. It's a start.

Spearhead fires downwards. Stands itself up. Spearhead fires backwards, up and sideways. He's a Wakinyah Creature of the Cosmos. Spear's sunfire can't harm him. Can and does obliterate ommatophorous helmet. Persephone due in the queue. No need. He isn't only Thundercloud Creature in Weirdom and she's a legit psychopomp; can think, home in on him, and thereafter act independently. Doesn't require wiggly wings frantically flapping ankle-ward to get away.

He hits ground upright, unbending. Spear rockets into hands; spews flames. Room thumps out of between-space defensively, jerking environment disorientingly. Steady on, Sundown; plenty of solar muscle left. Keeps spraying straight-space

Skyrise with said (setting) sunfire. Sprinklers go off, walls resist, briefly; pipes not so much so. (Stone gnomes cutting corners on insulation, replicating cheap metal?) Water cascades, turns to steam, scalds. People running everywhere. Panic an extreme understatement; chaos order of the moment.

Lets everyone survive. Rather, targets no one directly; gives everyone a consequential (non) shot at survival. Rather again, they, he and his Beauty, give them a better shot at survival by buggering off instead of intensifying heat, fire, flames, sun on a stick. He sort of hopes the Witch does; Golgotha, Gethsemane, all four of the Zerosses, too. Even Fish and Lady Lemurian if they really were around behind the nowhere near fire-resistant curtains.

Is altogether ambivalent when it came to the Master or Capputis and, even though he couldn't be sure she was ever in the Weirdom, held some measure of optimism Lakshmi of Lemuria had been crushed or burnt to death when he set Skyrise ablaze both before and beyond between-space. Really was a shame about Cerebrus, though. Doubly so that it wasn't his shade there when he thought he was killing Cabalarkon exactly as he wanted him to; that it was the Witch's mute and always intangible soul-self.

A cosmic aura, a not-altogether-neutralized exclusion zone – as he first thought of his original supranormal ability – was a fabulous gift to have. Especially when you could expand it such that even a stone-gnome-issiwun devouring his skull, causing him massive headaches, could be at least held off, if not outright repelled.

Persephone manifesting her father's Brainrock rings out of this own wampum pouch was unexpected. (Even if anyone had presupposed she could pull that off, who would have anticipated anything so back-stabbing-nasty from such an insouciant sweetheart?) He was pretty sure his aura would have held off their potentially limbs-severing squeeze-play long enough for him to burn free but ... overconfidence never yet begot invulnerability. (Ask Cyborg Cerebrus about that. How could he have ever hoped to best an Apocalyptic, here on the Head, mind to mind?)

Raven's Head coming out of one Weird into another, like the psychopomp she was, at least in part – they always seemed to know precisely where the other one was – and bulling Percy off her game, with a head butt, unicorn horn retracted, saw to it he didn't need to expend much more mental energy in that direction. Meant instead he could zone in all the more to rendering Skyrise the slag it warranted.

He'd have loved to send more than a few stone gnomes the way of the Thanatoids of Lathakra's Haunted Angel. Now that was a sight to behold. And so was this, if anyone was watching – save the Sedonic Eye-Mouth, up there in the sky above his Hidden Headworld – as he and Raven took their leave of Cabalarkon.

========

*After showing off her transcendental credentials from, as it were, a standing in cement overshoes start, Raven didn't have much left, but they both wanted to make a fabulous exit, the stuff of legend. He, riding her, real issiwun on his head, unrestrained hair and star blanket breezing backwards, solar spearhead afire like a miniature star on a staff. She, flying on talarial wings, unicorn horn fully extended, a blazing blade pointed directly at the heart of the Sedon Sphere, at the Moloch Himself.*

*They both heading off into the setting sun!*

********

# POST-BABIES: DAEMONIC DEPRAVATION

========

**Sapienda, 1 Yamana 5981**

*The sky had cleared. Was, Skyrise going up like an infernal torch, all hellfire and, yes, damnation, as if the clouds had vapourized.*

========

"You think they'll survive?" wondered Melina long Zeross.

Using their mikes on spikes, caduceus and marigold – what had saved their hash in the first place, well before it got overcooked – Wilderwitch and the Althean Witch Healer once codenamed Illuminatus had levitated themselves as far as the harbour just as Fearsome Fobbiat, the Headworld's western ocean, was swallowing the last rays of the dying sun. Had all but already swallowed the specks that were Blind Sundown and Raven's Head.

"Isn't much out there, Mel. Not westward. Only the Cathonic Zone and I doubt Raven could make it far enough to even try to break through that. They bear south or north and make it to the Ghostlands, the radiation will kill them. Still, they are Creatures of the Cosmos. They lived through Salvation Island back in '53 and that was a hydrogen bomb that went off far below them. Made it all the way to Centauri Island as well. You never told me Sal knew Wiccan Warlock."

"Must have slipped my mind. Why'd you agree to marry him?"

"It was the only bargaining chip I had left. I was there, Mel. Sort of. I saw Johnny open his sepulchre and kill Cerebrus; saw him pull out his corpse, cut him apart and furnace-blast him into cinders. He was acting the monomaniac, in a frenzy of bloodlust blindness, as if he had to do an absolutely thorough job.

"I couldn't do anything about any of it. My soul-self's as mute as it's intangible; never could make it anything but. And, at that kind of distance, double-duty, voice-casting, ventriloquist trickery's impossible. But Johnny somehow sensed me, it, watching him. Even spoke to me, though he apparently mistook my soul-self for Davy's … what? His ghost, I guess. He thought he was killing Cabalarkon and Cerebrus had somehow put him up to it."

"Because killing Cabalarkon would kill Sedon."

"Would it?"

"It would certainly strike him a serious blow, but I don't see how it'd be anything more than psychologically. Cabalarkon may not be impossibly old but he is possibly the oldest continually alive mortal in the entire cosmos. Sedon regards him as his father. He's spent multiple multi-millennia protecting him. Could be that's just filial loyalty; that's my take on it anyway. He can do it, so why not do it?

"So, yes, it might dishearten him. But kill him, no. Otherwise Masters of Weir or the Dual Entities would have killed Cabby an exceedingly long, long time ago."

"Masters of Weir are not John Sundown. Neither are the Dual Entities. I've met them, remember. They're supposedly my parents, not that they've ever helped me like you'd expect parents to do. As strange as Miracle Memory might be, Heliosophos is just a recurring human; not an undying immortal like Eye-Sky Guy. If killing Cabalarkon stood a chance of killing the Moloch Sedon, Johnny's who I'd have picked for the job."

"Maybe so, but what really gets is me is, from the sounds of things, Davy didn't do anything to save his own life."

"Don't you mean what was left of it?"

"His life, you mean? You're saying Immediate Death's an improvement on being submerged in a tub of Cathonic Fluid."

"Aren't you? There is such a thing as assisted suicide."

"Oh ye of little faith. That headplate was our technology, Witch. I recognized it right away, all those years ago, when Droid Dulles, Mr Automatic, brought it to us. Of course it took the boulder-brain Conqueror to get it working, and Johnny killed Jesse a few years later, but all we needed was time to figure out how to make him a new one."

"Or have your technomages' stone gnomes do it for you."

"Which they would have, if they'd had a chance to analyze and replicate it. But I didn't think it was safe to detach yet. Davy wasn't going anywhere anytime soon."

"Except he did. Someone moved his sepulchre to Cabalarkon's crypt. That must have been why he'd been trying so hard to reach us, to tell us where he was, but neither Johnny nor I would give him any blood. We were afraid he'd use it in order to establish a mind-to-mind link such that he could start compelling us into doing things we ordinarily wouldn't have done."

"Such as?"

"Never got that far but, in hindsight, killing Cabalarkon's the obvious one."

"Sed's Daddy Cabby's more useful as a hostage. Back when devils still called her Providence, the Pauper Priestess, Pyrame Silverstar, did that once, through her shell, Morgan Abyss, the Melusine Master of Weir, whom you'll more likely recall from your lessons as the Death's Head Hellion. That is if you were paying attention in class. Which-witch you probably weren't, knowing you, Auntie Wildie."

"I did when Sister Eden or Master Kyprian was handling instruction duty. Pyrame can function in the Weirdom because she humanized Miracle Memory very early on in the Head's sub-Dome history. As a sort of payback she prevailed on Memory's Mnemosyne Machine aspect to re-jig eye-staves such that they wouldn't work on her; ditto Incain's Gynosphinx, All the Invincible, who'd imprisoned her for hundreds of years pre-Dome.

"And that Morg, the Melusine Master, is the one who might have been Fish's ancestor, if she ever had any kids. Fish fry, I should say."

Mel resisted the urge to clap sarcastically. Observed, albeit just as sarcastically: "And so you just did. And she probably did have kids, little Sed-sons if Pyrame was involved. That's her gift; her hold over Sedon. For some reason, heaven and hell come together when she beds Sed on both sides of the Dome. Only she can half-have the deviant little buggers."

"One-third-have … and she didn't."

The Pauper Priestess was so-called because she didn't have a devic protectorate to make her home, nor a Tvasitar talisman to call her own. She was the first Master Deva to gain individual solidity, however, fully two millennia before any of the others did, so she never needed either/or.

Which meant she'd acquired a debrained demon that selfsame, very early on in the Head's existence. Reputedly, though she always denied it, got expelled from All on Incain already holding onto one — a biggie, none other than Primeval Lilith, the Demon Queen of the Night. So the Witch's qualification made sense.

Even though there was no irrefutable reason for it, there was no denying Pyrame was the only known (one-third) mother of the sedons, small case. It was a nevertheless fiddly assertion in many respects. No third generational devil had ever become the half-parent of a deviant like the Witch, Pusan Wanderlust, Jordan Tethys, Fish, and the rest, without first occupying a debrained demon.

Indeed, Klannit Thanatos, the world's first azura, came into existence pre-Flood, when her devic parents were thoroughly subsumed by bebrained demons. Didn't realize they'd had her until thousands of years later, sooth said. Plus, if the Sundowns had Sed-sons, they couldn't have had another after 5950 since that was when Pyrame was cathonitized the last time.

"No, and how might you know that? You weren't there." The two exchanged glances. The Witch didn't say 'boo' and Mel, who was anything except stupid, didn't say 'oh'. Said instead: "Anyway, Pyrame must have liked the leverage because she tried it again, hundreds of years later, when she was on the outs with her mighty eye-mouth in the sky, forever friend after killing the real Eden Nightingale in 5916."

"She didn't kill anyone. It was a ploy. That was Tralalorn in the Totem Pool."

(Ostensibly Trala, the perpetual devil child also known as the White Dwarf in part because she refuse to grow up, was Pyrame's brood sister in Mithras's Ninth, the one besides Drought, Cathune Bubastis, she of Sisert. Was still around; never hadn't been. Was, arguably, even more of a Headworld constant than Pyrame and her uncountable many mortal Sed-sons. Curiously, to Illuminaries and devils both, there was no record of the little horror pre-Dome.)

(And why would there be, Pyrame would protest protectively. Devils were just Spirit Beings pre-Earth. In literal aeons of existence, only Sedon and the six Great Gods had names to go along with consistent forms and personalities. Their female companions – Pyrame having always been Sedon's main squeeze – were actually conglomerate beings, with as much distinctiveness as there were components.)

"So they'd like you to believe," Mel noted, having heard various versions of the same story, including the one that claimed the Eden who showed up during the Simultaneous Summonings of 19/5920 was actually a de-cocooned faerie by the name of Meroudys Artha, none other than OMP-Akbar's thought lost sister from decades earlier.

(The Trigregos Triplets, Eden Nightingale, Cybele St Synne and Mnemosyne D'Angelo, were supposed to be the great balancers: incarnations of the long lost goddesses, Demeter, Sapiendev and Devaura, Body, Soul and Mind, the collective mothers of third generational devils. Would have been, rather, had they been allowed to reach maturity. Which Cybele, who was still alive, and Memory were … but there had to be three, not two, and killing the real Eden on their seventh birthday rendered the other two merely normal Normas.)

"Master Devas can't lie but that may or may not apply to Dark Sedon. On top of that, there's a provable psychological phenomenon that if you have an unwavering belief that a lie's the truth then it becomes just that, the truth, at least as far as you're thereafter concerned.

"At any rate, something got her decathonitized a few years later, just in time to take over Pandora Mannering and half-mother Saladin Nauroz, that is for sure. Point being Pyrame was still at it, decades later, when she moved on the Weirdom during our time, and got recathonitized for her troubles."

"Because she was a threat to Cabalarkon. Maybe he was onto something."

"Let's not start that again. Can't say as I blame you. I wouldn't give him blood, either. Mind control's about the worst supranormal ability anyone can have. It's so insidious, so base evil, so devic. But the Master did and so did Capputis. That's why the Master had the containers switched. He figured if Cerebrus was between-space he'd stop sending them headaches."

"So it was as innocent as all that."

"Seems so."

"You'll pardon me for being sceptical, Mel, but, other than he likes massages and bedtime stories, there's very little innocent about Saladin Devason. He wasn't supposed to sentence Johnny to die. He was supposed to banish him, send him away on that Tribute Ship over there. Even had you buy passage on it for them, so he told me."

"I did."

"One less lie then. Raven was thinking about getting on it anyhow and now so am I."

"You're Cynthia Masterwife, Witch. He'd never let you go."

"Then he shouldn't have lied to me."

"And he shouldn't have got Percy involved. But he did. And he is the Master."

"That was a load of self-serving codswallop about his 'beloved' sister Morgianna, Superior Sarpedon. Everyone who was there, the Diver, OMP-Akbar, Golgotha, his Trinondevs, said Morg was fighting on the side of the Dead at the end. She was going to kill Furie as soon as she reverted him to Murray-mode. Was using some residue of the Morrigan's demonic talents to do just that. Johnny had to kill her. Besides, even if she got hold of the Trigregos Talismans she'd have kept them for herself, or given them to your brother. I know her. Knew her, rather."

"So do I, did. So does the Master, a did-ditto. And you're probably right. But she was still family and appearances have to be maintained. He has spies everywhere; a lot of them are the same ones I employ. They keep their ears to the ground and their mouths shut. There've been mutterings of discontent everywhere you went in the city for days now. Ever since Zmas Night, if you have to know. I heard them just by walking the streets and you would have too, if that hood you wear when you're out and about didn't muffle murmurs.

"Wild talk. How can the Moloch Sedon just pop down here anytime he pleases? This even though he's been doing so for literally thousands of years. How could the Master not have prevented the loss of the Outer Earth devaslayers, the Angelic and her friends? This despite the fact your D-Brig didn't kill anyone, just got Bodiless Byron and the rest stuck in the night's sky, mostly because of each other.

"If I were Golgotha I'd issue a Challenge of Weir. Why would he bother? He's no more interested in the Mastery than I am. Stuff like that. Every Master has to have his fingers on the pulse of the people. He can't look weak in front of them. He does, things might stop working and that would never do.

"I'd like to think it's water under the bridge. But if it can happen to Master Kyprian, it'll happen to him, howsoever belatedly. Skyrise is smouldering. My daughter's hurt. The Master's humiliated, yet again. And I'm afraid it's only going to get worse after today's disgrace." Her voice trailed away. Both let their thoughts collect silently. Finally Melina spoke again.

"The sun's gone, Witch. So are Johnny and Raven. You coming back in?"

"What for? You talk as if everything's about to collapse about our ears."

"Already done a fair bit of that today, wouldn't you say? But, hey, sounding despondent is part of my job. Look at it from the other perspective. It isn't the end of the world. The sun's sunk but it'll be back tomorrow. Might bring some winter weather with it but Sedon's still in his sphere, Cabalarkon's still as alive as he ever gets, my Harry's still with us, sort of, you're still pregnant and the Master does love his Cynthia Masterwife. Especially the stories she tells him at beddy-byes. Before and after the massages."

"Don't dissemble, Mel."

"Who's dissembling? The middle floors of Skyrise are a mess; even stone gnomes will have to work overtime for weeks on end to repair the damage done, assuming their circuits aren't completely fried; a late luncheon's a later dinner in the Hate-Sedon Sphere; the Master has to hear out Gomez Niarchos and we've still an announcement to make.

"Two announcements: the local populace still doesn't know you're pregnant, and we wouldn't want to waste that fancy *'doo'* Helen gave Capputis, would we? Might have to use the balcony on the great square for that; reassure the people all is well at the same time, even if it isn't. Two? Better make that three, come to think of it. I have to represent the Master in Temporis when we announce their betrothal there tonight."

"You go ahead. I'll be along directly. You're right about the winter weather. Might be time to trade in the sandals and saris for mukluks and parkas, as least outdoors."

"Come see me in Master Kyprian's old quarters in the Masters' Palace and I'll see what I can do about having stone gnomes whip you up a couple sets of both."

"Maybe I will. Tomorrow. Not tonight. Wouldn't want to waste my outfit, or lack thereof, any more than you would Capputis's *'doo'*, would I? Not just for the sake of warmth."

"Look, Witch. Don't mock me when I say this, but I don't want you to leave. Desperation be declared, I'm praying you'll stay. Without Harry and with my daughters, especially Percy, under the Master's thumb, you're about all that's anchoring me. Tell you what, we get through tonight without any more disasters then, as soon as they finish unloading the Tribute Ship tomorrow, we'll gather up my girls and head out to the coast for some overdue rest and relaxation."

"Not afraid of being kidnapped by Master Devas again?"

"Actually, after this last week or two, that might be a relief."

"Only after this last week or two? I'd have said last two and a half decades."

"Ah, but you're not me. I couldn't have lasted that long."

"Yet you did. Without the buffer of Limbo and near-mindlessness. You're tough stuff, Melina born Sarpedon."

"Thanks. Maybe I am."

"Comes with the territory."

"Which, Witch, belongs to the Master, not to me."

"For now."

========

*"What was all that crispy critters crap in Cabalarkon, Fish?" asked the trail-blazing Traveler, Pusan Wanderlust, who was as fond of curse words as she was of fay-saying.*

========

They were sitting in torchlight outside the replicated chateau of Versailles overlooking the backside of the Latona fountain, a favourite of Fish even though the transitioning frogs depicted affronted her fosterage sister, Amphitrite. Were too close to what she was becoming too rapidly — at sixty Treat would soon have to take herself into the sea permanently, the same as Lemurian men always were.

"Mel, if not Sal, should know better than to mess with Blind Sundown."

"Don't dugong know, Goatfish. Doubt the nunnish non-ninny had anything to do with it, though the shoal. Sea-saw must have finny found something inventory-intriguing down here in the fingerling's Netherlands. That's my flense of the whaledreck anyhow. Trickle Treat's been teetering on telling me what it is ever since.

"Wouldn't surprise me if the tipsy tadpole's spilled the spume with Capsicum Cappy. Lovesick lampreys are back and frothy forth on the up-down radiophone nearly non-stop since I got the sprat herring-here earlier in the winkle week. And if she's told him then he's told the manatee Master, you can bet your bottom feeders on that."

"Have to ask them then. Here they come. What's with the new-look guardbody? Head hunk's more brain-coral than Moai?"

"Brain coral snake's Moai seamount like it."

(The Moai seamount was an undersea volcano off the coast of the Outer Earth's Easter Island. Coral snakes were among the most poisonous serpents on either side of the Sedon Sphere.)

"That's Barracuda Boulder Brain back from the abysmal depths of death."

========

*Disaster Number One in Cabalarkon City: Persephone showed up at the engagement dinner with her arm, broken, in a cast and her shoulder, maybe separated, but probably only momentarily immobilized by a sling. The Raven's Head monoceros hadn't been gentle with her, but she hadn't been lethal either.*

*The Witch didn't care. Percy was the one hurting.*

========

Disaster Number Two: Lakshmi of Lemuria didn't show up at the engagement dinner, had bolted the moment Capputis was summoned beyond the curtains, box in hand, cerebral ash and headplate inside it. Took herself, the mandroid guard-bodies and her entire entourage of no doubt ardent admirers back with her to what should have been OMP-Akbar's court in Centurium, replicated Versailles.

The majority did so via matter transducers; not so the main guests of honour. Like Pusan had Tsishah Twilight, Fisherwoman didn't wait for permission; took Lakshmi Arthadot and her mother, adoptive sister Amphitrite, safely away via Eagle Ray Revenant the moment the Master started spouting that suicidal nonsense with Blind Sundown.

Not that that mattered to Wilderwitch, either. Didn't matter that Mel-Illuminatus had to chase after them as soon they were done with the Godbadians; she was heading to Temporis anyhow. Truth told, the Witch wasn't looking forward to an extended reunion with Fish — they'd only exchanged token nods prior to her and Sal entering the banquet hall that afternoon.

Had actually advised Sal against letting Fish in particular into the Weirdom ... and it wasn't out of jealousy. Her sister in more than just Flowery Anthea had always been very perceptive. Very dangerous, too. The best witch left, Mel once told her. Trained by the best witch ever, Master Kyprian, she added.

Plus, Fish detested demons; had done since the Godbadian Civil War, if not before. (Headworld-trained Athenan War Witches didn't just target vampires.) Wouldn't take long for her to divine, if that was the right word, that the Muslim-style apparel she'd taken up wearing since her release from the hospital was daemonic. Much worse, even though she might be dead without it (her), it (she) was be-brained daemonic; a royal, no less.

Fish also had those three devic power foci she'd never leave behind just to come back to Cabalarkon for whatever reason. What she could do, at least potentially, with that soul-net of hers frankly terrified her. One part of her, put better ... the part that wanted to be all of her. And, in her weaker moments, either physically or mentally, sometimes got hold of most of her, at least for a while.

Notwithstanding any of that, Capputis – who was both her nephew, by Fish, his mother, and her stepson due to self-declared marriage to the Master, his father – was the one in despair. At least he was still alive. Couldn't say the same about another nephew, one by long dead Eden, her other sister in more than just Anthea. Those John Sundown killed stayed dead. Cerebrus would not be back.

Disaster Number Three: First she had to endure Sal reaming out Gomez Niarchos, who increasingly did smell of rotting flesh, for even daring to suggest Cabalarkon, the Weirdom, should consider entering into even the most modest of political and/or economic friendship treaties with the Corporate State of Greater Godbad. Then she had to sit back and watch as Golgotha Nauroz, in indigo-blue, Tuaregs-of-Algeria-like costume, facial veil drawn, with just his eyes showing, cut off the Godbadian's head.

This she did care about. But only because Niarchos voided himself the moment blade met neck and, as a consequence, stank even worse that he did already. The man was dead after all. He was possessed by a Sangazur Spirit Being, the kind of symbiotic devazur that, in addition to immunizing their now shared body to rainfall, allowed the original's mind, its consciousness, its spirit, to coexist with that of the Sang.

To his credit, other than noisomely Gomez took decapitation reasonably well. Saladin promised to keep his body from corrupting any more than it already was while his head was away, delivering his message to the Fatman, Alpha Centauri. He could come back and retrieve it any time Centauri was prepared to restore the Godbadian monarchy and enter into a formal union with Cabalarkon. With Sal the Master of both, it went without saying. Though he made a point of repeating it a number of times anyhow.

One other good thing was the Godbadian's head fit nicely into the box wherein they'd placed what was left of Cerebrus David Ryne's ashes and headplate after Sundown killed, dismembered and incinerated what was left of his body the night before. Another good thing was his – the Godbadian's – headless body found a readymade home in the altogether late cyborg's tub of Cathonic Fluid.

*'Waste not, want not'* was one of the Weirdom's favourite sayings.

The Witch didn't care about much of anything anymore, except for the stench, because – as she'd semi-intentionally let drop in her conversation with Mel-Illuminatus out on the dock – the Witch wasn't all there herself. Hadn't been since the 14th. Which-witch was most of the reason she hadn't preceded Cerebrus into the Afterlife by two weeks.

To some ironically, demons were almost as good as devils were when it came to keeping their shells (underlays, more like) alive and relatively healthy.

========

*"Well, all in all I'd say today went rather well, Cynthia," did say the Master of Weir as he came to bed, naked and ready to romp, that night.*

========

Unlike everyone else in Skyrise, including the Zerosses and the patients on the hospital levels, they hadn't abandoned the – due to Blind Sundown and his solar spear – howsoever temporarily, structurally unsound skyscraper. When your area of it was mostly between-space already, what did you have to worry about the rest of it collapsing around your ears?

"We've itty-bitty Raven's Heads swimming around in developmental tanks. We've all the analyses we'll need to replicate Johnny's spear stored in our techno-mages' databanks. Too bad we couldn't hold onto the real thing but, upon reflective hindsight, he deserved some reward for killing my two-faced sister. Might take them a while to get over their hot-stuff huff and get to replicating it, in the numbers we'll need, but it was more important to show the stone gnomes who's boss around here. Same for the High Illuminary.

"Too bad Percy wasn't killed. Still, she is pert, game, and ever so dutiful, like her father. I suppose Raven didn't have to kill her and, if we have to look on the bright side, she can die any time we please. Besides, her survival might yet prove beneficial, so long as we marry her off soon and sensibly.

"Capputis has been. Or will be, come Azky, so long as the High Illuminary smoothes out a few of those ruffled feathers we earned by going after Fish's fiery friends. Or scales, as the case may be. Seems to me Miracle Maenad, Ap Isle's Corn Queen of all Corn Queens, has a few eligible sons, grandsons or whatever left unmarried." (The Korant Sisterhood's long-serving Miracle Maenad was born Cybele St Synne. She was the last of 19/5908 Trigregos Triplets.)

"Solomon Taurson would be ideal, if he wasn't so old and, um, explosive. Must be almost as old as you are, not including Limbo."

"As the Witch is, Sal," said her overlay, asserting herself over the exhausted witch beneath her. "Me, I'm older than the hills, the Slopes of the Sleepers at any rate, though maybe not quite so old as the wreckage that makes up most of them. I wouldn't be so quick to dismiss Persephone, either. While Helen and her can-do personality may ultimately turn out to be more useful to us, I for one wouldn't want to alienate her mother any more than necessary.

"Mel might yet prove herself invaluable to me, personally. She is, after all, a thoroughly, um, illuminated doctor. And by that I mean about as knowledgeable on daemonic physiology as anyone up here. You may not realize this but, even after all those lifetimes of being irrevocably locked into Miracle Memory, being devil-free, while simultaneously being pregnant, is entirely new to me.

"Besides, you're forgetting something."

"I am?"

He looked up. He looked sideways. He looked at himself looking every which way there were ways to look. Looked at her, too. She had nicely straighter, nicely darker hair tonight. Just what he liked in a demon; besides all that white-as-light skin. Actually, considering where she came from, where the sun didn't shine, except in certain devic protectorates like Satanwyck and Temporis – which technically was now a devil-free zone, but where it nonetheless somehow still did – better make that chalky white skin.

"Oh, you mean the mirrors. That's what I meant about reflective hindsight. I missed them as much as you did. I guess that's the problem with Thundercloud Creatures of the Cosmos. There's so few of them it really doesn't do to kill them off willy-nilly. Who'd have thought Sundown could abolish the Mirror Mentalist, Klannit Thanatos, a simple Spirit Being granted, especially from so faraway?"

"Other than me, you mean."

"Must be a premature echo in here. I was just going to say just that."

"So, you think they survived?"

"They better have. Do you know what it costs to book passage on a Pani Tribute Ship?"

========

*The Weirdom had another saying. It began with the word 'What' and ended with the word 'gets'.*

********

# WILDERWITCH'S BABIES 5980/1

## – "Decimation Damnation" –

=========

# CHARACTER COMPANION

(Extracted and adapted specifically for this mini-novel from a capsulated character companion for the open-ended saga of *'Wilderwitch's Babies'*)

## Index

1. **The Damnation Brigade**: Blind Sundown, Cyborg Cerebrus, OMP-Akbar, Radiant Rider, Raven's Head, Untouchable Diver, Wildman Dervish Furie, Wilderwitch
2. **The Dual Entities**: Heliosophos, Miracle Memory
3. **The Shining Ones:** First, Second Third and Fourth Generation Devakind
   - **The Moloch Sedon**
   - **The Six Great Gods and Goddesses**: the Thrygragos Brothers (Lazareme, Byron & Varuna Mithras) and the Trigregos Sisters (Demeter, Devaura & Sapiendev)
   - **Master Devas**
     - The Firstborn Unities of Lazareme: Freespirit Nihila, claims she was once the Unity of Balance as well as Panharmonium
     - Thanatoids of Lathakra: Tantal, Methandra, Klannit, Aires, Constantin, Thalassa & Sedunihas
     - More Mithradites: Pyrame Silverstar, King Harvest, Phantast Thanatos, Mater 'Mundane Death' Matare, Flying Doltaur, White Dwarf Tralalorn, Cathune 'Drought' Bubastis, Mars 'War' Bellona, Diluvia 'Flood' Ran, Domdaniel-Pride, Leontocephalic Trumpeter, Sinistral Sloth of Satanwyck
     - More Lazaremists: Krepusyl Evenstar, Amal-Althea Brand, Irisiel 'Speedy' Mercherm, Unholy Abaddon, Lord Order, Anvil Craftsman, Battle Babe, Rumour of Lazareme, Bright Enlightenment of Lazareme
     - Byronics: APM All-Eyes, Pyçonja Volant, Deneb Makara, Malar Tzigame
4. **Deviants, Demons, Faeries and a Mandroid Mother Machine**

- **Demons** (Primeval Lilith, Daemonicus, Shahiyeda)
- **Definite Deviants** (Fisherwoman, Eden Nightingale, Pusan Wanderlust, Tsishah Twilight, Lakshmi Arthadot, the Legendarian, Miracle Maenad)
- **Probable Deviants** (The Molech Xibalba, Night Owl, Jester Jaguar, Solomon and Balkis Mandam)
- **Mandroids** (Steltsar/Sharkczar, All of Incain, Utopian Stone Gnomes)
- **Outer Earth Supranormals other than the Damnation Brigade** (Sorciere, Fey Woman, Saul 'Psycho' Ryne, Lady Lemurian, 'Boulder-Brain' Conqueror, Mirror Black Obsidianna, Speculum, Faceless Strife)

5. **Mortal Descendants of Original Extraterrestrials**
   - **Utopians of Weir** on Earth, idiots of Weir, scientocrats (biomages, technomages), Illuminaries, Trinondevs, Development Teams
   - **Pure U-Bloods** (Cabby the Daddy, Melina born Sarpedon become Zeross, Demios Sarpedon, Ubris and Augustus Nauroz)
   - **Hybrid Utopians** (Saladin called Devason Nauroz, Morgianna born Nauroz become Somata then Sarpedon, Persephone, Helen & Athena Zeross, Thobruk Grudal)
   - **Utopian clones** (Golgotha and Gethsemane Nauroz, their 'non-born' children, amphibious Capputis)
6. **Norman & Norma Notables**
   - Pandora 'Hush' Mannering become Nauroz, Alpha Centauri, Janna St Peche-Montressor, Yataghan Montressor, Achigan Auranja, Godbadian Ambassador-at-Large Gomez Niarchos, Jesus 'Jesse' Mandam, twin sister Barsine born Mandam Holgat-wife, Sraddhite High Priest Thartarre Sraddha Holgatson, Godbadian General Quentin Anvil, Senator Sophiscient, Telepassa of Godbad, her four daughters, Aranyani Nightingale born Ryne

========

## 1. The Damnation Brigade in Cabalarkon

- **Blind Sundown**:
  - real name: John Sundown, most of his fellow D-Brig members seem to call him Johnny;
  - Summoning Child native North American, a Cheyenne, though he calls his tribe the Tis-Tsis-Tas or Human Beings;
  - considers himself a Creature of the Cosmos; also calls himself a Wakinyah Thunder Being or, sometimes, a Thundercloud Creature;
  - wasn't always blind; in the early 1940s traded his sight to a Cheyenne Medicine Man (Shaman Manitoulin) for his solar spear and the right to ride Raven's Head, his fellow Wakinyah Thunder Creature;
  - original supranormal ability: an exclusion zone that seemingly protects him from being harmed by projectiles, but also negates the powers of other supras with whom he is direct contact;
  - can see through others' eyes when he is in direct contact with them;
  - brought up with Solace 'Sorciere' Sunrise, another orphaned Summoning Child, whom he married (twice) at an early age; together they had a number of children, none of whom survived past their seventh birthdays;

- **Cyborg Cerebrus**:
  - born in late 1920s, son of Loxus Abraham Ryne and Eden Nightingale; twin brother of Saul 'Psycho' Ryne; older brother of Aranyani Nightingale, among a number of others, all of whom (save Aran) are twins;
  - lived through being accidentally shot in the head by the Silver Arrow assassin codenamed Sagitta in late 1930s;
  - headplate installed during the Christmas Holiday Season of 1946/7 turns out to be of Utopian design;
  - submerged in a tub of Cathonic Fluid within the Catacombs of the Sleepers, beneath the Grand Central Square of Cabalarkon City, after (barely) surviving an encounter with Mars Bellona, the Apocalyptic of War, in Temporis on the 6$^{th}$ of Tantalar 5980;
- **OMP-Akbar**:
  - on the Outer Earth went by the name of Obadiah Melvin Power; evidently an amnesiac unknown until spotted walking out of Hiroshima's Ground Zero with his then wife, Corona Power, in August 1945;
  - apparently ageless near-giant codenamed OMP (Old Man Power) when he became a member of the postwar KOC: the King's Own Crimefighters;
  - still has his rune-carved Homeworld Sceptre, but his so-called regalia, which he intentionally destroyed at the beginning of December 1980, turned out to be the Thrygragos Talismans from (mostly) 2008's "Feeling Theocidal" (FEEL THEO) — the Mask of Byron, the mutable Spear of Mithras and Lazareme's Cloak of Many Colours;
  - on the Inner Earth of Sedon's Head proved to be Akbarartha; in the midst of "The War of the Apocalyptics" (WAR-POX), became revealed as the eldest half-son of Dand (Devalord) Tariqartha, Lazareme's Persian or Earth Magician and, therefore, the rightful Kronokronos Supreme of Temporis;
  - booted out of Temporis, along with the rest of D-Brig (but for Airealist, who'd vanished), by the freshly turned 18-year old usurper Lakshmi Arthadot, she of Lemuria, whom he was supposed to marry later on the 6th of Tantalar 5980;
  - no one seems too sure as to the identity of his devic half-mother, if he had one: the Pauper Priestess, Pyrame Silverstar, is one possibility; another is Malar Tzigame, Byron's Butterfly;
  - his sister Meroudys may have become the future Eden Nightingale during 1920's Simultaneous Summonings;
- **Radiant Rider:**
  - birth name: Gloriella D'Angelo; married surname: Dark; codename Radiant Rider; also known as Rainbow, Gloriel, Glory of the Angels;
  - born on Good Friday 1933 (April 14), the same day as Aranyani Nightingale and Thea Mandam; that might make her a Great Goddess reincarnate if she'd passed the Totem Pool test, which she ended up never taking due to Thea's unavailability after apparently never being born;
  - a materialist, also known as an etherealist (as in 'make ether real'); flies on rainbow hair and casts solid rainbows; had been known to project her 'little

angels', which may be azuras (the offspring of Master Devas by themselves, without possessing anyone);
- blames her Big Angel for killing Mr Brilliant, whom she came to consider Lucifer Incarnate (Domdaniel-Pride) after he, possessing Dr Immanuel Dark – a thereafter wheelchair-bound cripple – killed her brother Gabriel (Codename Klarion, the supra Trumpeter), in 1953;
- seems devils cannot possess her; causing some to believe she's a reborn Celestial like her Aunt Celestine, once the Anthean sisterhood's Celestial Superior (who may still exist, albeit as Gloriel's Big Angel);
- another possibility is that she somehow gained Castella Thanatos's power focus when she was shorn of it on the same day, albeit on the Inner Earth, that Gloriel was born;
- four of her older siblings (Nita, Peter, Claudia and Leandro) seem to have gained abilities similar to some of the fourth generational Thanatoids cathonitized on the same day she was born (Ereba, Antaeor, Auraura and Constantin);
- has a daughter named Estrella (Star) whose father was Doc Dark; both are still alive beyond the Dome, as are her parents and three of her once ten strong siblings;
- given twenty-five years lost in Limbo, with her body separated from her mind, Gloriel is still 22 whereas Star Dark is 27 while Doc Dark is a Summoning Child (therefore soon to turn 60 at outset of the mini-novel);

- **Raven's Head**:
  - inhuman, possibly ageless, hybrid creature akin to something out of native Indian mythology or trickster folklore, albeit after the arrival of Wasichus (the White Man) and his horses;
  - considers herself a Creature of the Cosmos like her usual rider, Blind Sundown; also calls herself a Wakinyah Thunder Being or, sometimes, a Thundercloud Creature;
  - not a thunderbird, though could be its inspiration (if it isn't a pterodactyl native to the Head's Floodlands); has a raven's head, a horse's feathered body, talarial wings akin to Mercury's on both sides of her four upper hooves;
  - despite being altogether alive, at least partially a self-psychopomp or spirit-carrier, meaning she can get about between-space (the Weird, the Grey, the dark grey universal substance of Samsara);
  - develops a unicorn horn when in the vicinity of devils; it along with Sundown's Solar Spear forms a binary weapon that can cathonitize Master Devas; probably can't kill them, though Utopians of Weir believe she and Sundown are devaslayers (devil-slayers);
  - also together with Sundown, forms an obscuring cloud about herself when on the Outer Earth;
  - not a shape-shifter, when she appears on the Outer Earth it's under the (hated) glamour of a horse;
  - unclear who set up the glamour (aural manipulation); might have been Shaman Manitoulin or one of his predecessors, could have been Sorciere or even Wilderwitch, but activates it herself as required;

- intelligent, can sort of speak, though not many can understand the sounds she makes;
- not the last of her kind, though she doesn't realize that;
- a solitary Raven's Head was pictured on the cover of 1990's release of Phantacea Publications' "Forever & 40 Days — the Genesis of *PHANTACEA*" {'4Ever40'}, which ended in 4000 BC;

• **Untouchable Diver**:
- real name: Yehudi Cohen;
- German born, probably only half-Jewish Summoning Child whose father may have been the old Baron Tyrtod von Alptraum, the Prussian nobleman who formed the basis for the various, mostly postwar Steltsars, on both sides of the Dome, and 1980's Sharkczar (from "Nuclear Dragons" {Nuke} and "Helios on the Moon" {Helmoon});
- gained the ability to make himself untouchable at will while dressed in a rubber wetsuit of his own making in 1938; can also render those he's in contact with just as intangible;
- he found his Gorgon Goggles – what allow him a degree of far-sight and the ability to see through the ground while soil-swimming – in the Roman Colosseum a few weeks prior to becoming the Diver;
- discovers he's not only Brainrock-blessed but can feed off the miraculous substance also called Gypsium-Godstuff during "Goddess Gambit" (Gambit);
- as such has become a self-psychopomp (spirit-carrier), meaning he can travel between-space by himself, without using the equivalent of a devil's Tvasitar talisman, Ringleader's rings or witch stones;
- unfortunately, when he does so he tends to 'blip' (become unconscious, sometimes for long periods of time — hours, even days)
- wife Rachel, yet another Summoning Child, is still alive on the Outer Earth in December 1980; so are two of their four children;
- seems he also had a son by Fisherwoman (Scylla Nereid) in the late Thirties, early Forties, who grew up to become Chthlonius 'Tiger' Tiecher, one of Kadmon Helios's Trigon Spartae, all of whom apparently died with Heliopolis on Aegean Trigon in 1968;

• **Wildman Dervish Furie**:
- real name (Gentleman) Jervis Murray;
- a Summoning Child like the Elemental Twins (Aires and Thalassa, now believed to be Thanatoids of Lathakra), the Diver and Blind Sundown;
- as such only a few days or weeks short of his $60^{th}$ birthday ($35^{th}$, discounting Limbo) at start of mini-novel;
- no one seems to know what the full Furie looks like, though it appears it might be akin to a rabid faun or satyr;
- the Dervish is a hairy, juggernaut of sheer raw power with impervious skin who, as a teenager and young adult, was sometimes referred to as a Werewolf in Shorts;
- as Jervis Murray he was Wilderwitch's long time lover; wasn't Fey Woman's father, however, as he's infertile;

- he has some sort of relationship with Young Death (Augustus Nauroz on the Hidden Continent of Sedon's Head, the revenant supra Bokor, magician or Voodoo Child known as Auguste Moirnoir beyond the Dome), who calls him 'son' for some reason;
- it's beginning to look like the Furie is a devil, possibly Lemolo Wildwyck (a Lazaremist), who hasn't been seen on the Head for many generations;
- Morgianna 'Morg' Sarpedon, the Hellion's Morrigan until events on Diminished (later Drenched) Dustmound on the 8th of Tantalar, was using aspects of her devil-eating daemonic heritage to draw him out of Murray;
- without the Dervish's engine (namely, the Furie), Jervis Murray would likely be entirely human, possibly even a dead human (see 'Sister Grandmother', a short story that rounded out 4EVER40);

- **Wilderwitch**:
  - born around the Winter Solstice or Mithramas Day, Tantalar 5927, purportedly of the Dual Entities, though who was humanizing Miracle Memory is unclear;
  - devic half-mother might have been Krepusyl Evenstar, Twilight's Grey Lady, which would make her Tsishah Twilight's quarter-sister as Miss Mist was occupying Morgianna not yet Sarpedon when she conceived her a few years later, in 5933;
  - the Witch, capitalized, claims she doesn't have a real name, though it may be Cynthemis Dyana, which Murray-Furie thinks it is, or possibly Cynthia, which Saladin Devason comes to call her;
  - had one child pre-Limbo, a daughter (nowadays Fey Woman), born in 1946, but keeps the identity of her father secret;
  - Fey (Faith McBride beyond the Dome, self-named Phaedra within the universal substance of Samsara, seemingly her natural habitat) was raised exclusively by the Anthean Sisterhood, so the Witch properly regards her more as a younger sister than a daughter;
  - given twenty-five years lost in Limbo, with her body separated from her mind, the Witch is 28, or soon will be, whereas Fey is 34;
  - possibly the weakest member of D-Brig, her major supranormal attribute is that she was born able to do anything a fully trained Anthean witch can do;
  - does have above average strength and speed as well as an affinity for forest animals, especially wolves, who may have raised her;
  - her soul-self is mute but horrible to behold; she cannot solidify it and has to use her natural born ability to cast sensory glamours to make it seem like she can;
  - Freespirit Nihila once claimed she was her Harmony-self reincarnated;

========

## 2. The Dual Entities

- **Heliosophos**:
  - Helios called Sophos the Wise, the Male Entity;
  - Brainrock-blessed time-tumbler (as opposed to 'controlled' time traveller, none of whom exist in **the Phantacea Mythos** due to contextual impossibility);

- at outset of mini-novel, believed decapitated and killed (for the 100th time) on the Moon in early-to-mid December 1980;
- thinks he was Kadmon Heliopolis in his first lifetime;
- many others reckon he was originally Anti-Patriarch Cain, Slayer of Abel, and therefore the son of Primeval Lilith and the second Biblical Adam (the golden-apple-eating first patriarch Alorus Ptah, who had blue skin and golden hair, the same look Helios and Thrygragos Lazareme often affect);

• **Miracle Memory**:
- the Mnemosyne Machine, Machine-Memory, the Mnemosyne 3-Thing, the Female Entity;
- at outset of mini-novel, believed thrust back into the time-stream along with Trans-Time Trigon when the Male Entity was killed on the Moon in early-to-mid December 1980;
- believes she's an amalgamation of First Weirworld's original Mother Machine, Mnemosyne D'Angelo (Human Memory, Kadmon Heliopolis's long dead stepmom from his first lifetime), and Datong Harmonia (Harmony), the Unity of Balance, from his second lifetime;
- can only be fully humanized by Master Devas (devils), prominently Pyrame Silverstar, the Harmony Unity or Methandra Thanatos;
- demons seem to have much the same solidifying effect on her, but are dull-witted and weak compared to devils; evidently she can't conceive when solely solidified by demons;
- as per 4EVER40, was once humanized by the three Great Goddesses (Trigregos Demeter, Trigregos Devaura and Trigregos Sapiendev); with whom, as per HELMOON, she keeps in touch;

========

## 3. Shining Ones: First, Second and Third Generation Devils

• **The Moloch Sedon**:
- seemingly immortal, tremendously powerful, but nowhere-near-almighty All-Father of Devazurkind; likes to appear to Westerners in particular as the Devil Himself, capitalized;
- a dark star above the Hidden Headworld during the day, hence Dark Sedon, his essence makes up Cathonia (the Cathonic Zone or Dome, also the Sedon Sphere);
- there, as seen as early as 1977's **Phantacea One**, it takes the form of the Mighty Eye-Mouth in the Sky, a fact that devils, Illuminaries of Weir and a number of witches seem to know;
- as per 4EVER40, believes the Undying Utopian Cabalarkon is his father/creator, thus denying any contribution from the time-tumbling Dual Entities in Helios's Fifth Lifetime on the first Weirworld some two hundred light years earlier;

• **The Six Great Gods and Goddesses**:
- the Thrygragos Brothers and Trigregos Sisters comprise the entirety of the second generation of devakind;
- the Three Great Gods are:

» **Thrygragos Lazareme** (aka sometimes the Lackland Libertine, but most commonly Thrygragos Everyman), who sees himself as having blue skin and golden hair; in other words, a three-eyed version of Alorus Ptah (the Male Entity in his 61st lifetime); those who behold him think they're seeing their idea of what God looks like;

» **Thrygragos Byron** (aka both Bodiless Byron and the Unmoving One due to that fact that he's all head, with his facial features frozen in the same expression, not because he can't transport himself wherever he wants on the Inner Earth); and

» **Thrygragos Varuna Mithras**, who, as per FEEL THEO, may well have also been Uranus, Kronos and Zeus, in that order, as well as many another pantheon's God the Father prior to circa 1500 BC (2500 YD, Year of the Dome);

- at outset of mini-novel, Byron is the brightest star in the south-western quadrant of the night's sky; Varuna Mithras has been dead, apparently irredeemably, since the 44th Century of the Dome, and no one seems to know what's become of Lazareme;
- circa 2000 YD (2000 BC) Anvil the Artificer (Tvasitar Smithmonger, the devic smithy) crafted the Thrygragos Talismans for the Thrygragos Brothers; they are (or were): the Mask of Byron, the mutable Spear of Mithras and Lazareme's Cloak of Many Colours

» the often three-in-one Great Goddesses are Trigregos **Devaura** (the Spirit or Soul), Trigregos **Demeter** (the Body), and Trigregos **Sapiendev** (the Mind or Individual Consciousness);

- they appeared in 4EVER40 and, much more prominently, throughout HELMOON, but do not appear in the mini-novel;
- neither do their terrible talismans, which the devic smithy crafted for the Master Devas' simultaneous mothers; they are (or were): the Amateramirror, the Crimson Corona and the Susasword;
- at least they don't appear for sure in the mini-novel;

• **Master Devas**

- dictionaries often define '*devas*' or '*daevas*' as '*the shining ones*'; hence also the English word '*devils*', meaning '*little gods*';
- Master Devas compose the third generation of devazurkind; the Trigregos Sisters always bore them simultaneously, in threesomes;
- they believe their fathers are one or another of the Thrygragos Brothers; hence why it's accepted that there are only three devic tribes: the Lazaremists, the Byronics and the Mithradites;
- when Master Devas, whose bodies are debrained daemons, interact sexually, without possessing anyone, all they can produce are azura spirit beings;
- a fourth generation of devakind (as opposed to devazurkind) began coming into existence during the second, third and fifth decade of the Dome's 60th Century; as of late Maruta 5980 YD, every known member of the 4th Generation has been born as a twin instead of a triplet;
- thereafter, on the 5th of Tantalar 5980, the Quadrang or, less accurately, Apocalyptic Nucleoids (Jah Dreadlock, Hatchethands, Mandragora Gal-

lows Ghoul and Flying Doltaur), whom Matare bore in the Calvary Cavern were born a foursome, not either a twosome or threesome;
- the Byronic Nucleus and the hence Apocalyptic Nucleus cathonitized each other the next day, the 6th of Tantalar, an event that brought to an end the war of the Apocalyptics and also resulted in what was left of D-Brig's expulsion from Temporis by Lakshmi Arthadot;
- when Sedon, Great Gods and/or Master Devas possess sentient beings for procreative purposes, their resultant offspring are often long-lived and, once in a while, unnaturally gifted mortals known as deviants;
- it seems likely that many of the Outer Earth's so-called supranormals or supras also had devic half-parents; this is especially true of supras born as a result of the Simultaneous Summonings of 59/1920;

• **Significant Lazaremists**

» **Harmony**, called Datong Harmonia by bygone Illuminaries of Weir;
- the Unity of Balance as well as Panharmonium (her pet project, a planetary panacea for beneficial devils and their worshipful multitudes alike; as per "The 1000 Days of Disbelief" {DAZE}, actually existed from roughly 5000 to 5500 Year of the Dome);
- reputedly, by a matter of a few seconds, the first Master Deva ever born; beauty incarnate as well as loveliness personified;
- her power focus or Tvasitar talisman is a golden torc, the so-called Necklace of, as you might expect, Harmony; from it she conjures her golden, chain-mail gowns and the broken chains often manifested manacled to her wrists; from them she sometimes shoots… what else? Chain lightning;
- also associated with auroras such as the Northern Lights;
- folklore has it that Harmony is incomparable because she is mostly Gypsium and, therefore, not humanized by demons; probably isn't true, however;
- those who beheld her thought they were seeing their ideal female;

» **Freespirit Nihila**, from WAR-POX, GAMBIT and HELMOON, claims she was once Harmony (from FEEL THEO and DAZE);
- she also told Kronokronos Akbar and Wilderwitch in the Faerie Garden of Temporis, on the 6th of Tantalar, that she believed the Witch was her incarnation;

• **The Thanatoids of Lathakra**

» **Methandra Thanatos**, a firstborn Mithradite also known, accurately, if perhaps somewhat disrespectfully, as Hot Stuff;
- a red-skinned, flame-haired giantess; almost always masked and thoroughly covered in fabrics invariably coloured different shades of red, pink or purple;
- power focus is a firebrand or matchstick (cane);
- the mother, while being subsumed by a bebrained, glassine daemon or demon pre-Genesea (the Great Flood of Genesis) of Klannit, the first azura;
- considered the devic patron of the Athenan War Witch sisterhood (to which Janna St Peche-Montressor, Fisherwoman, Superior Sarpedon and dangerous daughter Andaemyn, among others, belong in the mid-to-late 60th Century of the Dome);

- for thousands of years known as Mithras's Virgin; shunned the attentions of both her grandfather, Dark Sedon, and her father, Thrygragos Varuna Mithras, while in turn being ignored by true love and triplet-brother Tantal (King Cold);
- a self-proclaimed death goddess, that of heat and fire, who nonetheless became the conceptive and birthmother of the first members of a fourth generation of devakind (not to be confused with devazurkind) sometime after waking up from a thousand year sleep in 5908 Year of the Dome;
- her ten, fourth generational offspring from when she was possessing Miracle Memory and Tantal Heliosophos were Day and Night (Castella and Ereba), and the Four Elements (Antaeor-Earth, Acheron-Fire, Thalassa-Water and Aires-Air) and the Four Seasons (Veronas-Summer, Auraura-Winter, Constantin-Spring, and Orinth-Autumn);
- was pregnant with Sedunihas (who has yellow skin & only ages one year in five) and Motan (who was stillborn) when hit by Sedona's Spell of Disproportionment on Antheal 14, 5933, on the slopes of Sedon's Peak;

» **Tantal Thanatos**, firstborn Mithradite commonly known as King Cold;
- a gigantic, blue-skinned, icicle-bearded, archetypal-Viking whose power focus or Tvasitar talisman is a labrys (a double-headed war axe);
- pre-Dome father, while being subsumed by a bebrained daemon or demon pre-Genesea (the Great Flood of Genesis) of Klannit, the world's first azura;
- besides his thought-father, Thrygragos Varuna Mithras, probably the most prolific male Master Deva in terms of having azura offspring;
- self-proclaimed death god, that of cold and ice, who nonetheless became the conceptive and birthfather of the first members of a fourth generation of devakind (not to be confused with devazurkind) sometime after waking up from a thousand year sleep in 5908 Year of the Dome;
- his ten, fourth generational offspring from when he was possessing Heliosophos and Methandra Miracle Memory were Day and Night (Castella and Ereba), the Four Elements (Antaeor-Earth, Acheron-Fire, Thalassa-Water and Aires-Air) and the Four Seasons (Veronas-Summer, Auraura-Winter, Constantin-Spring, and Orinth-Autumn);
- hit by Smoky Sedona Spellbinder's Spell of Disproportionment on Antheal 14, 5933, while coming down from Sedon's Peak with sister-wife and ten fourth generation children;
- also the father of yellow-skinned Sedunihas the Artist who came along in 5955 and only ages one year in five;

» **Klannit Thanatos**, the world's first azura; presumably the entire cosmos's first azura as well;
- Thanatoid parents were subsumed by demons, one of whom was a glassine Klannit, when she was conceived pre-Dome;
- aspires to becoming a Master Deva in her own right but can't dominate sentient beings unless they're either simpletons or else dead;
- nevertheless has a near-devic affinity for mirrors; so much so she can both far-see and communicate either verbally or mentally through them;

- when they were both strictly spirit beings she and Anvil the Artificer, the Lazaremist master craftsman named Tvasitar Smithmonger, were lovers; he has been striving for nearly four thousand years to craft her a functional shell such that they can be lovers again;
- claims to have been to the Outer Earth a number of times during the so-called Suprawar, aka Secret Wars of the Supranormals (which lasted from early 1938 until late 1955);
- claims further to have brought her affinity for mirrors to a couple of those selfsame supras; says her supra codename was the Mirror Mentalist even though her simpleton shells sometimes had different codenames;
- appeared a number of times throughout **the Phantacea Mythos**, most notably in GAMBIT, wherein she occupied Nanny Klanny, the brain-damaged Sraddhite who looked after Thartarre Holgatson once his parents disappeared in the 5940s;
- it was her affinity for mirrors that allowed her locate her decathonitized, fourth generational siblings on the Outer Earth's moon during HELMOON;

» **Aires** and **Thalassa D'Angelo**, Air and Sea, D-Brig's Elemental Twins codenamed Airealist and Sea Goddess, Summoning Children adopted by Gloriel's parents Raphael and (Sainted) Sophia nee St Synne in April 1933 but now believed to be fourth generational Thanatoids;

» **Sedunihas**, evidently the last non-cathonitized, or otherwise unaccounted for, devic offspring of Tantal and Methandra Thanatos;

- one definite brother (Antaeor, Demon Land) appeared in WAR-POX, which came out in 2009; another brother and two sisters seem somehow connected to Airealist (Aires-Air), Sea Goddess (Thalassa-Water) and Radiant 'Rainbow' Rider (Castella-Day), three members of the Damnation Brigade who also appeared in WAR-POX;
- his ice-statues of elder siblings Ereba-Night, Castella-Day, Acheron-Fire, Auraura-Winter, Constantin-Spring and Orinth-Autumn allowed Klannit to find them on the Outer Earth's moon during HELMOON;
- a yellow-skinned, age-retarded artist who specializes in producing exceedingly lifelike statuary;
- for reasons not as yet provided in tremendous detail, was not given birth until 5955;
- the highborn Byronic, Smoky Sedona's Spell of Disproportionment rendered Methandra six inches tall in 5933; she thereupon transferred the twin foetuses to Klannit, who was by then in a homunculus crafted for her by Tvasitar Smithmonger around the same time; the foetuses were transferred back to her once the spell reversed and Methandra reverted to her giantess size, whereupon Tantal became six inches tall;
- the spell reversed again before she could give birth; this happened a few times until Sedunihas was born 5955 YD;
- like all ten of his 4th generational brothers and sisters, born a twin, not a triplet; also unlike Master Devas, all twelve were born with possibly daemonic bodies; there is, however, thus far no indication he's a metamorph like they were;

- as yet inexplicably, his twin brother, named Motan, was born (and remains) altogether dead;
- also for reasons not yet detailed, Sedunihas only ages one year in five; consequently appears to be only five years old in Tantalar 5980;
- a bust he was preparing of his grandfather, Thrygragos Varuna Mithras, was destroyed during the course of Gambit by the never-remember Smiling Fiend (Smiler, Bad Rhad, Rhadamanthys in the ***PHANTACEA*** comic books, Sodom to Pyrame's Gomorrah, also Ahriman, who could never have existed since no one remembers him);
- seems to have a 'thing' for Athena 'Tina' Zeross, age 6 in 5980, which may or may not come into play again during mini-novel;

• **Significant other Mithradites**

» **King Harvest**, Underlord Yama Nergal, a fifth-born, so-called Earthling;
- when the Lathakran Empire conquered the Penile Peninsula (better known as Iraxas, Sedon's Mutton Chop on a map of the Hidden Headworld), he helped cathonitize Vanthysces Vastness (Scarecrow), the Byronics' Reaper;
- he thereafter fused the latter's power focus, a scythe, with his own, a miner's pickaxe; hence King Harvest, the Mithradites' Grim Reaper or Harvester;
- for millennia alternated, on a lunar basis, impregnating duties of much younger sister Fecundity (Nergal Vetala) with brood-older brother Gravedigger (Zuvem Nergalis);
- unchallenged devic ruler of the radioactive Ghostlands since circa 4825 YD;
- Death's Angels, whose touch can kill but, being predominantly animated by Nergalazurs, bodily dissolve in rain or running water, are his to command;
- more so than the first-born Thanatoids of Lathakra or the eighth-born Primary Apocalyptics' Mother Murder (the Medusa, Mater Matare, who wasn't born until, at the earliest, Mithras's Twelfth), he's considered the devils' primary Death God;
- in Sedon's Sweat Glands (the Flood and Lake Lands on a map of Sedon's Head), during the first week of Tantalar 5980, suffered a severe setback to his efforts to march his Inglorious Dead from the Ghostlands to Hadd; thus failing to bring much needed reinforcements to Janna Fangfingers in Hadd;
- forced to retreat to his usual domicile Pettivisaya (Wailing Souls), which was Dark Sedon and Pyrame Silverstar's power base prior to events described in 2010's "The Death's Head Hellion" (HELLION); as such, and for most of the Hidden Headworld's history, Pettivisaya was known as Grand Elysium;

• **Moderately Significant Byronics**

» **APM All-Eyes**, as she is most commonly known, is the lone daughter born in Bodiless Byron's third brood;
- as such, a member of his secondary Nucleus (along with her triplet brothers, Damon Goldenrod and Nevair Neverknight);
- a love goddess, Byron's Venus, bygone Illuminaries of Weir named her Aphropsyche Morningstar, hence APM;
- likes to appear as if composed entirely of eyes, hence All-Eyes;
- her witch-followers, who aren't just confined to the Byronics' territory of Aka Godbad at the time of the mini-novel, are known as love-loving Afrites;

- as per HELMOON, an aspect of APM survived the attack on Godbad by an outraged All of Incain; it, a dinky, winged eyeball akin to Gloriel's little angels, did so inside of Janna St Peche-Montressor (q.v.), a love-loving Afrite as well as an Athenan War Witch, who was APM's most frequent host-shell in 5980;

» **Rufous Rudra Silvercloud**, Bodiless Byron's only firstborn son, his Beast Master, also his Storm Lord;

- as per HELLION, a onetime friend and ally of the Thanatoids of Lathakra who, along with sister-wife Umashakti, led Byronic forces during the First War between the Living and the Dead;
- involved in the Byronic ploy at the beginning of Tantalar 5980 that saw Apple Isle's devic Dand Plathon (the Bull of Mithras, a third-born Mithradite), the Devil Child Tralalorn (from Mithras's Ninth), the Ghostlands' King Harvest (a fifth-born), the Flood Lands' Klizarod Rex (from Mithras's Seventh) and, among others, the Lakelands' colourful Emperor Chameleon (also a seventh-born) humiliated and nearly ill-starred;
- as of the 6th of Tantalar, along with Uma, the eldest surviving Byronic on the Hidden Headworld;
- after events detailed in HELMOON one of the last three highborn Byronics;

» **Umashakti Silvercloud**, Unmoving Byron's only remaining firstborn daughter;

- a Moon Goddess, she waxes and wanes with its phases; consequently sometimes called Lunar Uma;
- her attribute is gravity; hence why devils usually address her as just that, Gravity;
- as per HELLION, a onetime friend and ally of the Thanatoids of Lathakra who, along with brother-husband Rudra, led Byronic forces during the First War between the Living and the Dead;
- in the absence of Devil Wind (Vayu Maelstrom, one of Byron's Primary Nucleoids) freed from All of Incain at the beginning of Tantalar 5980;
- immediately thereafter became involved in the Byronic ploy that saw Apple Isle's Devil Child Tralalorn, the Ghostlands' King Harvest, and, among others, the Flood Lands' Klizarod Rex humiliated and nearly ill-starred (cathonitized);
- like Methandra Thanatos and Freespirit Nihila barely survived GAMBIT;
- as of the 6th of Tantalar, along with triplet-husband Rufous Rudra, the eldest surviving Byronic on the Hidden Headworld;

» **Deneb Makara**, one of Great Byron's Winder Zodiacals, Capricorn the Goatfish;

- the recurring deviant, Pusan Wanderlust, who always comes back in one of her daughters or granddaughters, claims Makara was her devic half-mother;
- others argue that Goatfish committed devic suicide by cutting out her third eye during the time of the Goddess Culture on the Outer Earth ca 2000 to 2500 YD (2000 to 1500 BC) and that therefore Pusan is what's become of her (in much the same way Rumour of Lazareme became Jordan 'Q for Quill' Tethys);

- Makara's Tvasitar talisman or power focus is a pedum, which is akin to a bishop's crosier or a fairy godmother's shepherd's crook; it comes back to Pusan whenever and wherever she reincarnates;

» **Malar Tzigame**, Byron's Butterfly;

- odds on favourite to be the devic half-mother of Akbar and Meroudys Artha while being possessed by the Temporis Faerie Queen known as Cabala (Dand Tariqartha would have be occupying Faerie King Archon);
- in early Tantalar 5980 among those involved in the Byronic ploy in the borderlands between the Flood and Lakelands (Sedon's Sweat Glands) that almost led to the cathonitization of the Ghostlands' King Harvest and also saw the Devil Child Tralalorn devolve the Lake Lands' Emperor Chameleon;

» **Pyçonja Volant**, another of Great Byron's Winter Zodiacals, Pisces the Fish;

- odds on favourite to have been Fisherwoman's devic half-mother because when the newborn Fish (Scylla Nereid, Lady Achigan now, but once the marital Queen of Godbad) was found by Aortic Merthetis, Volant's Tvasitar talisman or power focus, a Fisher's Gaffe, was found beside her;
- prior to and during Fish's Godbadian Queenship, its air force was known as the Royal Byronic Volant in her honour;
- if she was Fish's devic half-mother then she must have been humanizing Miracle Memory, the Female Entity, when Fish was conceived in 5917/18;

• **More Lazaremists**

» **Irisiel Mercherm**, Lazareme's preferred Heliodromus or sun-runner;

- called Speedy by devils for reasons irrefutable; as such the only Master Deva who can get into and out of the Weirdom of Cabalarkon unimpeded, let alone captured in a Trinondev's eyeorb or prison pod;
- in common with other, usually fairly low-born sun-runners like her brother in Lazareme, Djinn-Ghoster, and Djinn Domitian (Mithras's Leontocephalic Trumpeter), both from FEEL THEO, she seems able to enter Cathonia, the domain of Dark Star Sedon;

» **Krepusyl Evenstar**, Lazareme's second-born Venus,

- once Mariamne Dawnstar, she of Daybreak; 800-years currently the Devic Dand of Crepuscule, Sedon's Outer Nose, the Land of Twilight;
- triplet sister of Flowery Anthea (Lazareme's Spring) and Titanic Métis (Metisophia, Wisdom of Lazareme), both of whom are mentioned in the mini-novel;
- presumed to be Wilderwitch's half-mother from when she was humanizing Miracle Memory in the mid-Twenties;
- also presumed to be Tsishah Twilight's devic half-mother from when she was possessing Morgianna born Nauroz, but by then Somata (a hybrid Utopian who later became Superior Sarpedon on the Outer Earth and the Inner Earth Hellions' Morrigan), in the early Thirties;
- also known as the Grey Lady and Miss Mist, the inspiration behind the Witch's bedtime tale of Miss Murk (also Murk Mist), Mad for Mud Magpies (Mudpies);

» **Amal-Althea Brand**, Lazareme's long missing, goatish Female Healer; previously seen in FEEL THEO;

- Mel-Illuminatus appears to have her power focus, a caduceus, which Mel pretends is actually akin to the gargoyles Utopian Trinondevs manifest off their eye-staves in the Weirdom of Cabalarkon;
- Mel claims she acquired it from the Olympian Tantalus in the Forties on the Outer Earth, which is possible, but there's plenty of speculation that while, as a pureblood Utopian she can't be possessed, as a Summoning Child she may have been born with Althea Brand inside her the same as Barsine Mandam was born with Nergal Vetala inside her;

» **Unholy Abaddon** (the Unity of Chaos), Thunder and Lightning **Lord Yajur** (the Unity of Order), **Tvasitar Smithmonger**, the devic Prometheus (Anvil Artificer, the Master Craftsman), **Mandorla Auricaura** (Bright Enlightenment of Lazareme, another possible devic half-mother of Fisherwoman because Fish's bellybutton bauble is Mandorla's power focus, a Vesica Piscis) and Battle Babe (the Morrigu **Badhbh**) – whose loyal forces are in the process of taking over Hadd's western neighbour New Valhalla (the Bloodlands, Sedon's Inner Earth), home of the Sangazur Glorious Dead, many of whose devic mother she is by Mars Bellona, the Apocalyptic of War – are among the other Lazaremists who are either mentioned or appear, howsoever briefly, in the mini-novel;

- **More Byronics**

» **Chimaera Glimmenmare** (Byron's Stallion), along with triplet siblings, (Smoky) **Sedona Spellbinder** and **Devil Wind** (the Whirling Deva, aka Vayu Maelstrom), are Byron's Primary Nucleoids; **Draconic Yati,** Byron's Dragon (beware his burps), was last seen in HELMOON devouring Sharkczar;

- **More Mithradites**

» **Phantast** Thanatos, the third of the firstborn Thanatoid Death Gods; called Dream or Dreamweaver by devils;
- cathonitized circa 4000 YD (Year 0 AD) for masterminding the Crimson Conspiracy on the Outer Earth along with **Strife** (Mithras's Ewe for Aries, aka Kore-Eris, Discord, Kanin Marut, Fitna Marutia, among many other names);
- decathonitized on the 30th of Maruta 5980, so presumably possessing a cosmicompanion in an as yet unidentified cosmicar somewhere beyond Cathonia;
- may already be influencing events on the Hidden Headworld; certainly both Wilderwitch and Saladin Devason are experiencing very disturbing dreams during the course of the mini-novel;

» **Sinistral Sloth**, **Domdaniel-Pride** and most of the other former or eventual Prime Sinistrals of Satanwyck and their Grand Vizier, Chancellor Ibal, are mentioned, usually by name, during the course of the mini-novel;

» **Pyrame Silverstar**, the Pauper Priestess, the fabulously female (adult) Perpetual Presence; formerly (sometimes) called Providence, among many another name or title;
- decathonitized on the 30th of Maruta 5980, was possessing Cosmicaptain Nehrini Purandar in the cosmicar that crash-landed in Satanwyck (Sedon's Temple, Hell on Earth, then currently the domain of Sinistral Sloth);

- unless programmed otherwise, All of Incain obeys her; hence why she can often be found occupying the She-Sphinx on the Prison Beach of Incain, at the bottom of the Cattail Peninsula (Sedon's Ponytail on a map of the Hidden Headworld), about as far south as one can go on the Head without having to swim or ride in a boat;
- had no need of a devic power and daemonic body in 2000 YD (because she was already a solid entity, having been fused with her daemon while imprisoned pre-Dome in one of the Sphinxes and becoming Sed-mom shortly after her release ca 0 YD) when Anvil the Artificer first discovered how to render Master Deva individually solid and powerful entities;
- due to her lack of a power focus, for centuries after Anvil began making them Pyrame relied on her relationship with the recurring Attis to get hold of always mutable power foci anyone can use (he would give the foci of vanquished foes to her as tokens of his affection);
- as per FEEL THEO she had to give them up on Thrygragon (Mithramas Day 4376 YD); thereafter relied on Sedon, All or a variety of psychopomp demons to get about beneath the Dome;
- for reasons not fully explained in the mini-novel, she was cathonitized in 5950; that suggests she somehow lost her formerly (and perhaps still, at least partially) bebrained, daemonic body, disputably that of Primeval Lilith, the Demon Queen of the Night, much like she did in 4824 YD when, as per HELLION, they were jointly occupying Morgan Abyss, the Melusine Master of Weir;
- devic half-mother of Saladin born Nauroz Devason, the Master of the Weirdom of Cabalarkon since 5950; (half-father: the Moloch Sedon — it may therefore be that Saladin is the last Sed-son or sedon, small case, left alive beneath the Cathonic Dome);
- some believe she was the devic half-mother of Meroudys and Akbar Artha near the beginning of the Cathonic Dome's 59th Century (it's now late in the Dome's 60th Century), though that was more likely Byron's Butterfly;

» **Tralalorn** (White Dwarf, the child devil who along with Pyrame Silverstar and the Moloch counts herself one of the Hidden Headworld's three Perpetual Presences), her brood sister Cathune '**Apocalyptic of Drought**' Bubastis, Diluvia '**Flood**' Ran, Mars '**War**' Bellona, Mater 'Mother Murder' or '**Mundane Death**' Matare and their fourth generational 'Quadrang' daughter, **Flying Doltaur**, are also mentioned in flashback during the mini-novel;

========

## 4. Demons, Faeries, Deviants and Mandroid Monstrosities

- **Demons**

Soulless, often nearly brainless, chthonic creatures also known as eldritch earthborn and Indescribables. (Similarly spelled **daemons** {meaning 'spirit' or 'deity'} are generally less antagonistic to humans.) The Mantel replicates of Temporis are related to demons, as are the capricious, but much more intelligent faeries of Crepuscule, the Land of

Twilight (Sedon's Outer Nose), and those of Subcranial Temporis (notably Archon and Cabala, their king and queen).

To this day (5980), certain highly skilled witches and rogue Utopian biomages can manufacture demons by using tellurian raw material found in the Hell-Well of the World, which underlies most of the Upper Head. (Some of these rogue Utopians, usually hailing from the former Weirdom of Samarand, once Sedon's Tongue Stud, nowadays dwell on Shenon, Witch Isle, where they are protected by the Panharmonium-supporting Aortics Amphitrite of Lemuria and Tsishah Twilight.)

Although mostly confined to Satanwyck and the Forbidden Forest of Kala Tal (whence Hadd's Indescribables), they can be found throughout the Hidden Headworld. Much feared, omnivorous walking appetites, contrary to many traditions they are notoriously flammable. As the Morrigan, Morgianna born Nauroz (Morg, Superior Sarpedon) was able to compel them to do as she desired.

Demons come in all shapes and sizes, with a wide of variety of so-called magical or supernatural abilities. Morrigan Morg wore a teleportive demon she brought back from Satanwyck prior to the final battle for by then Diminished Dustmound. Psychopomps are likewise empowered and therefore may be at least part demon.

» **Primeval Lilith**

- the Demon Queen of the Night, sometimes called Lethal Lily;
- ageless, apparently both immortal and unkillable, partial mother of the Sedsons (sedons, small case) on both sides of the Dome;
- arguably the source of Pyrame's Earth-long hold over the Moloch Sedon;
- apparently Machine-Memory got hold of her during the events of 5950 (the Challenge of Weir, also the Siege of Cabalarkon) but expelled her on the Moon (thirty years and ninety odd lifetimes later) while thinking she was Erebe Thanatos (Dame Darkness) from a future lifetime;

» **Daemonicus**, the long time, pre-Flood King of Demons (Dark Sedon is the current King of Demons; has been for well over six thousand years);

- evidently as ageless and immortal as his forever mate Lilith;
- seems to be just a wearable body these days, with no mind left;
- when last seen, during NUKE, Solomon 'Boom-Boom' Mandam was wearing him;
- people who wear Daemonicus, such as Judge Warlock in the '40s and '50s, tend to speak ***like this***;

» **Faceless Strife**

- probably not a demon; more likely what's left of Marut Kanin (Fitna Marutia, Kore-Discord), a second-born Apple Goddess, known in legend (as well as, most notably, FEEL THEO) as Mithras's Ewe for Aries, meaning she was with him from roughly 2000 to 4000 Years of the Dome;
- Balkis (Faerie Flight) Mandam, Solomon's twin sister, was occupied by Faceless Strife throughout much of NUKE;

- witches regard Strife as a sentient virus; as per WAR-POX, she's why Wilderwitch refused to carry anyone through the Weird in the aftermath of Damnation Isle on the 30th of November 1980;
- Harmony thought she'd disposed of her, Strife, ca 4000 YD in the Brainrock cauldron of Sedon's Peak;
- as per HELMOON, Miracle Maenad reckons she disposed of her inside Sainted Sophia (born St Synne, Cybele's presumed sister, D-Brig's Gloriel D'Angelo Dark's Mama Sofa) at least temporarily on the 9th of December 1980;

» **Shahiyeda**, the first child born of Solace born Sunrise (Sorciere); father: D-Brig's John (Blind) Sundown;

- born in 5934 on the Hidden Continent, Blind Sundown may not know of her existence (let alone of her 'survival') until 5980, if then;
- an apparent Outer Earth supranormal turned into a demon at some point; all indications are that, even as a demon, she retains some of her brain and her main supra talent, an ability to bite back vampirism;
- Tsishah Twilight currently wears said Shah-Demon; seems to have since events that took place in 5960 of the Dome;

- **Deviants**

When Great Gods and/or Master Devas possess sentient beings for procreative purposes, their resultant offspring are often long-lived and occasionally unnaturally gifted mortals known as deviants.

» **Fisherwoman** (Fish), amphibious Piscine born sometime in 5918;

- as a newborn, found in the Belly of the Beast (Island Leviathan) by Aortic Merthetis who gave her the name Scylla Nereid;
- tends to fishify, a form of not always rhyming or alliterative fay-saying that often makes her difficult to understand;
- something of a breeder, first child (Wave or Winifred) born in 5934 and raised by Godbadian Royal Family (the House of the Crimson Gold) because they believe her father was Achigan Auranja, a Summoning Child;
- Achigan, 5980-nowadays the sitting Duke of Achigon (sic), Sedon's Lower Lip-tip, in the north-westernmost corner of the subcontinent of Aka Godbad, was therefore only 13 when Fish conceived Wave-Winifred, but already the nominal King of Godbad;
- because of their child, Fish married King Achigan prior to Master Kyprian, the then Master of Weir and Whole Earth's Anthean Superior, taking over her training when she was sixteen;
- eventually learns that her parents were Ulysses Heliopolis and Miracle Maenad, who was seemingly possessing three Master Devas simultaneously (Pyçonja Volant, Diluvia Ran and Mandorla Auricaura);
- if so, then this explains the three devic power foci Merthetis found beside her in the Belly of the Beast: a fisher's gaffe (Byron's Pisces), a gillnet (Mithras's Apocalyptic of Flood) and her bellybutton bauble (a Vesica Piscis formerly belonging to Lazareme's Bright Light Enlightenment);
- in 5950 became Master Kyprian's champion such that she could compete in that year's Challenge of Weir on her behalf; resigned her role when Kyprian died under the usual mysterious circumstances;

- despite their former enmity, seemingly became 'involved' with Saladin Devason in 5960; may have had a son as a result, someone she called, typically fishily, 'Sal-man' (as in salmon);
- in 5980 known as Lady Achigan since she and her husband, Godbad's reigning King and marital Queen, were deposed during the Godbadian Civil War in the vicinity of twenty years earlier;
- briefly fused with Freespirit Nihila during GAMBIT;
- has a self-made daemonic psychopomp (spirit carrier) she calls Ronnie Ray-Bum, after the incoming POTUS; others call it Eagle Ray Revenant;

» **Saladin** born Nauroz called Devason;

- Master of the Weirdom of Cabalarkon as of 5950 YD, when he beat Golgotha Nauroz (a clone), Demios Sarpedon (disqualified for being a year too young) and Fisherwoman (Scylla Nereid) in that year's Challenge of Weir;
- as per GAMBIT, humiliated on not-yet-diminished Dustmound in Hadd on the 7th of Tantalar by niece Andaemyn ('Without Demon) Sarpedon; rescued by Jordan 'Q for Quill' Tethys (the Legendarian, conceivably once Rumour of Lazareme);
- first depicted in 1980's **Phantacea Six**; mother Pandora 'Hush' Mannering and father Augustus Nauroz (as the devil-transformed faerie tricksters, Young Life & Young Death) appeared in Sister-Grandmother, a short story published in 4EVER40;
- has an abiding hatred of witches;
- presumed devic half-mother: Pyrame Silverstar; presumed devic half-father: none other than the Moloch Sedon himself;
- (arguably) the last Sed-son or sedon, small case, alive beneath the Cathonic Dome (equally arguably, Sedon St Synne is the last living sedon beyond it);

» **Morgianna 'Morg' Sarpedon** (born Nauroz become Somata, an Inner Earth Summoning Child, Saladin Devason's year-younger sister;

- apparently killed in Hadd by John Sundown during the final battle between the Living and the Dead on by then Drenched Dustmound; when last seen in HELMOON was somehow forming a cocoon around her evident corpse;
- probable devic half-mother: Pyrame Silverstar;
- mother Pandora 'Hush' Mannering and father Augustus Nauroz (as the devil-transformed faerie tricksters, Young Life & Young Death) appeared in Sister-Grandmother, a short story published in 4EVER40;
- husband: Demios; mother of Andaemyn by Demios; mother of Tsishah Twilight by the blue-skinned, faerie-human hybrid, Tom-Tiddly Tattletale (think Lazareme and the Male Entity) born Tammuz Rhymer of Dukkha;
- codenamed the White Witch on the Outer Earth; called Superior Sarpedon by Wilderwitch (who distrusts her intensely) during WAR-POX;
- the Hecate-Hellion's Morrigan, disgraced Anthean Superior on Outer Earth, became an Ant Nightingale then the Athenan War Witches' acting Mother Superior after daughter Tsishah left Shenon on the Spring Equinox of 5980;

» **Pusan Wanderlust**, the trail-blazing Traveller;

- the fauna or female satyr who runs the DDD (the Dinq, Doinq, Danq Cavern Tavern) on the far, north-eastern slopes of the Diluvia Mountain Range;

- a recurring deviant who's been coming back as one of her daughters or granddaughters since the time of the Outer Earth's Goddess Culture ca 2000 to 1500 BC (2000 to 2500 YD);
- some claim the long missing Byronic Goatfish (Deneb Makara, a Winter Zodiacal) was her devic half-mother;
- others argue that Goatfish committed devic suicide by cutting out her third eye and that therefore Pusan is what's become of her since;
- Makara's Tvasitar talisman or power focus is a pedum, which is akin to a bishop's crosier or a fairy godmother's shepherd's crook; it comes back to Pusan whenever and wherever she reincarnates;
- nevertheless, many – including Pusan herself – hold that her devic half-mom was Amal-Althea, the notoriously randy Lazaremist healer associated with Mel-Illuminatus;
- in this scenario the earliest recurring deviant Taurus Chrysaor Attis (last seen in FEEL THEO) was her father and that he gave her Makara's power focus as a birthday gift;
- a long time associate of Tsishah Twilight and her mother, Superior Sarpedon;
- as such, heavily involved in the witches' Panharmonium project that resulted, on the Outer Earth, in Kamikaze Kaligula and the apparent destruction of the Cosmic Express on the 30th of November 1980 (story mostly told in NUKE);

» **Lakshmi of Lemuria**, called Arthadot due to the fact she's Dand Tariqartha's half-daughter;

- born on the 5th of Tantalar, Year of the Dome 5962, in Goddess Culture Temporis, wherein her crabby mother, long time Aortic Amphitrite (Lady Lemurian), was masquerading as her namesake, the demigod Amphitrite, and Dand Tariqartha was playing at being trident-wielding Poseidon;
- was scheduled to be married to her quarter cousin, eventual Senator Sophiscient, Akbarartha's son by the Lady Takeda Mikoto, on the 6th;
- once the Awesome Akbar (OMP, Old Man Power, an Outer Earth supra), still thinking himself Obadiah Melvin Power, a high level Outer Earth Xuthrodite, showed up on her 18th birthday, she peremptorily dumped his son and, on Tariqartha's insistence, became engaged to marry him instead;
- when their half-father self-cathonitized on the 6th, Lakshmi gained his mutable power focus (Power Sceptre, similar in appearance to Akbar's Homeworld Sceptre) and expelled what was left of the Damnation Brigade, including betrothed Akbarartha, its by then rightful Kronokronos Supreme, from Temporis;
- secretly in love with someone other than Sophiscient or Akbar;
- because of Tariqartha's genetic strength looks more human than Lemurian, though still has gills behind her ears and slightly scaly skin;
- wears a shape-shifting guard body and carries Tariqartha's Power Sceptre while acting as Temporis's Kronokronos Supreme;

» **Eden Nightingale**, believed dead since 5955;

- Fish and the Witch's sister in the Dual Entities, born in 5909; as such, one of the Trigon Triplets, who were believed to be incarnations of the three Great Goddesses (Trigregos Demeter, Sapiendev and Devaura);
- mother, by her then husband Loxus Abraham Ryne (the Great Man, the Outer Earth Xuthrodites' now 80-year old patriarch), of Aranyani Nightingale (who was born on the same day as Gloriella D'Angelo, Good Friday, April 14, 1933) and her older brothers, the twins David (D-Brig's Cyborg Cerebrus) and Saul (Magnifico, the Magnificent Psycho), who were born four years earlier, in 1929;

» **Tsishah Twilight**, born Rudar 5934 (September 1934);

- devic half-mother: Krepusyl Evenstar, presumed therefore to be Wilderwitch's quarter-sister;
- mother: Morgianna then Somata, eventually Sarpedon; father: Tammuz Rhymer of Dukkha, by then a blue-skinned faerie type known as Tom-Tiddly Tattletale;
- mother of a number of children by Jester Jaguar (Mani-Balam, probably Solace Sunrise's twin brother by Shaman Manitoulin and Lamia Louise St Synne, which technically should make him Miracle Maenad's half-brother);
- in Tantalar 5980 the still acting, non-Lemurian Aortic or Quarter Queen of Shenon (Witch Isle); due to (finally) retire come the Spring Equinox, which in many parts of the Hidden Headworld is celebrated as its New Years Day;

» **Jesus 'Jesse' Mandam**, the King Conqueror, the Conquering Christ, but probably not the otherwise never identified ('Bolder-Brain') Conqueror;

- believed to be, by a matter of seconds, the first Summoning Child born on either side of the Cathonic Dome (just after midnight Christmas Day 1920 on the Outer Earth, Mithramas on the Hidden Continent of Sedon's Head;
- son of Magister Joseph 'Old Joe' Mandam and Mary Magdalene born Ryne; brought up as the twin brother of Barsine (Vetala) eventually Holgat-wife even though didn't look like her;
- early on (in the late 1930s) declared himself the Christ-like Saviour of Supranormalkind;
- known as Wiccan Warlock on the Inner Earth; as such, incorrectly assumed to be the son of Judge Warlock (Sedon St Synne) who wore the Daemonicus shell while on the Hidden Headworld);
- a great friend of Saladin Devason during the late Thirties and throughout the Forties; evidently stole all his advanced technology from the Weirdom of Cabalarkon during this time;
- unstated in Nuke, but strongly suggested in both Helmoon and DecDam, much of the tech used by New Century Enterprises, to build the Cosmic Express, and by WORLD, to counter it with Kamikaze Kaligula, Crystallion, Hell's Horsemen and their Nuclear Dragons, was derived from Jesse's notes, as kept in the Soviet Supracity throughout the Fifties, Sixties and Seventies;
- killed when Blind Sundown and Raven's Head dropped a prototype Soviet Hydrogen Bomb atop him on Salvation Island on his 33rd birthday in 1953;

» **Legendarian** (Jordan 'Q for Quill' Tethys, devic half-father: Rumour of Lazareme, devic half-mother: Metisophia, Wisdom of Lazareme), **Miracle Maenad** (Cybele St Synne, born 5909, a Trigon Triplet, grandmother of Solomon and Balkis Mandam) and **Human Memory** (Mnemosyne D'Angelo Heliopolis, the third Trigon Triplet, might be Ventricular Telepassa of Godbad's mother) are among the deviants mentioned in the mini-novel;

- **Probable Deviants**

  » **The Molech Xibalba**, a Black King or Vampire Maker born as a result of the Simultaneous Summonings of 59/1920;
  - a long-thought dead Irache shaman believed thoroughly sliced and diced (killed both decisively and irretrievably) by Second Fangs (Janna Fangfingers) sometime prior to 5980 YD;
  - possibly has a twin brother or sister who became an Outer Earth supranormal during its Secret War or Wars thereof;
  - as per the "Janna Fangfingers" (FANGERS) mini-novel, in the subcontinent of Aka Godbad (starting in the province of New Iraxas, Godbad's huge but thoroughly polluted oil field) went by the name Reilly Haddeus, an Irache rabble-rouser, before true identity revealed;

  » **Night Owl**, otherwise unnamed (Lamechlan?), presumed Inner Earth Irache who became a vampire during the Simultaneous Summonings of 59/1920;
  - most likely Xibalba's father;
  - somehow associated with Metisophia (Titanic Metis, Wisdom of Lazareme, devic half-mother of the Legendarian);
  - as such, becomes an owl rather than a bat when he transforms into anything non-human other than smoke;

- **Mandroids**

  » **All** the (self-proclaimed) Invincible She-Sphinx of Incain; as per FEEL THEO, once Ginny the Gynosphinx;
  - based on Weir's original Mother Machine and made, long pre-Dome, by Machine-Memory to capture daemons, can also eat and therefore imprison Master Devas;
  - Mandroid Mother Machine as well as occasional monster maker;
  - more often than not appears as a huge and winged griffin type; a therefore perhaps surprisingly mobile psychopomp;
  - as such, can travel at will through the Weird (between-space, the dark-grey universal substance of Samsara, mundane reality), though always leaves a root of herself behind on the Prison Beach of Incain;
  - used by devils, especially Unmoving Byron and the Unities of Lazareme, as both a temporary holding cell or a long-term prison for their transgressing fellows;
  - in addition to highborn devils, though not to the Moloch Sedon, whom she's designed to eat, All tends to be responsive to Pyrame Silverstar (q.v.);
  - All, whose human head resembles the Female Entity (think Harmony), tongue-tugs Pyrame and non-devils she favours (notably Chrysaor Attis, from FEEL THEO, and the Legendarian) through the Dome to her otherwise

moribund male equivalent out there, the Egyptian Sphinx, whose head resembles the Male Entity (think Lazareme);
- although possessed of a modicum of sentience, if not much in the way of actual intelligence, still a machine; as per HELLION, can be turned off and on as well as reprogrammed;

» **Demogorgon**, the much-feared conglomerate devil, a version of whom may have appeared in FEEL THEO speaking ***like this***;
- comes out of All, Incain's (self-proclaimed) Invincible Mandroid Monster Maker (q.v.);
- composed of the multitude of Master Devas still imprisoned within All either FANGERS-recently or over the course of her millennia-long existence.

========

## 5. Mortal Descendants of Original Extraterrestrials

- **Utopians of Weir on Earth**

» **Utopians** living in the Weirdom of Cabalarkon are brought up to hate the Moloch Sedon and his devic progeny;
- oddly, as if to prove their non-Earth heritage, pureblood U-men are always black whereas pureblood U-women are invariably white;
- pure U-bloods can't be possessed;
- the be-all and end-all of most completely cognizant U-bloods, pure or hybrid, stuck on the Whole Earth (either beneath the Cathonic Dome or, due only in part to an absence of functional spacecraft, beyond it) remains the destruction of their ancient enemies;

» **Illuminaries** of Weir, Utopian polymaths, supposedly learned in a wide variety of not-necessarily-related matters;
- the highest educated class in Cabalarkon, Illuminaries could also be found in former or decrepit Weirdoms like Godbad City, Samarand (Sedon's Tongue Stud), the Gleaming City of Manoa (Hadd's Necropolis, Fangfingers' Capital), and the five hundred years ruined Kanin City, in the vast Plains of Marutia near the Gregarian Fields (Sedon's Mole);
- often act as advisors to the reigning Master, many of whom were elevated from their ranks (Quoits Tethys, Melina born Tethys Somata and Kyprian Somata were once High Illuminaries of Weir); seldom not pure U-bloods;
- Melina nee Sarpedon Zeross, an Inner Earth Summoning Child codenamed Illuminatus in the Thirties, Forties and Fifties, became the High Illuminary of Cabalarkon during the reign of by-then brother-in-law Saladin Devason (which began in 5950);

» **Imbeciles** of Weir, also the idiots of Weir; inbred and therefore very much low functioning Utopians; almost always purebloods, hence the inbreeding;

» **Trinondevs** of Weir, Weir's Warrior Elite, nowadays mostly clones but formerly almost always purebloods who managed to overcome inbreeding in order to function as soldiers;
- their main weapons operate by willpower channelled though extraterrestrial devices such as Mother Machines and eye-staves;

- eyeorbs placed atop eye-staves double as prison pods in that they can suck devic and azura spirit being out of the shells they're occupying and into them, thus incarcerating them;
- eyeorbs supposedly work on demons, too, though being so flammable they're easier to kill;
- once an eyeorb is full it ceases to function as anything except a prison pod; if it's not replaced, the eye-stave becomes useless;
- eye-staves, like all their other anti-devil weaponry, never functioned in the Weirdom of Kanin City during the reigns of Zalman then Melina, Sraddha or Janna Somata;
- since Saladin Devason began his reign as Master in the Weirdom of Cabal–arkon in 5950, its Trinondevs are exclusively male;

» **Utopian Development Teams**, surrogate parents charged with raising non-born clones as well as difficult, natural born children like the Master's felt-entitled kids and those born of Outer Earth 'imports';

» **Cabalarkon**, Cabby the Daddy, the Undying Utopian; a biogeneticist when he lived and worked on, or travelled off of, the First Weirworld ca 200,000 light years earlier;

- when he was a wholly alive and ambulatory Utopian Scientocrat, the Dual Entities used his right eye to jumpstart the process that resulted in the Moloch Sedon, hence Cabby the Daddy;
- currently subsists in a tub of life-preserving, but animation-suspending, Cathonic Fluid beneath the Citadel of the Thinkers in Cabalarkon City; as such is probably the oldest, continuously alive mortal in the entire cosmos;
- it, like the rest of the territory composing the Weirdom of Cabalarkon (Sedon's Devic Eye-Land on a map of the Hidden Continent of Sedon's Head), is named after him;

» **Melina born Sarpedon** become Zeross, twin sister of Demios; may have been named after the Trigregos Titaness of the Dome's 55th Century (Melina born Tethys become Somata from "Contagion Collectors" {Contagion});

- a Utopian pureblood, an Inner Earth Summoning Child like twin brother Demios and Morgianna by then Somata, who first came to the Outer Earth in 1938 and attended the first Amsterdam Academy of Man until it closed with the outbreak of war;
- there, on the Outer Earth during its Secret War (or Wars) in the Thirties, Forties and Fifties, codenamed Illuminatus;
- became the High Illuminary of Weir (Cabalarkon) during the reign of (deeply disapproving) brother-in-law Saladin (born Nauroz but called Devason), which began in 5950; Sal, who hates Demios, seems to have been enamoured of her, but she rejected him for reasons as yet only implied;
- the mother by much younger Aristotle (Ringleader) Zeross (born in 1943) of three daughters: Persephone, Helen and Athena, all of whom appear in Gambit, Helmoon and DecDam);
- directly descended from the Sarpedon underclass who, as revealed in Hellion, are inclined to worship Thrygragos Lazareme since they see him as the Male Entity;

» **Demios Sarpedon**, twin brother of Melina become Zeross;
- pure U-Blood Summoning Child who first came to the Outer Earth in 1938, along with twin sister Melina; there served under the clone Golgotha Nauroz as a bodyguard for eventual wife Morgianna;
- there also, during its Suprawar (or Wars) in the Thirties, Forties and Fifties, codenamed Blackguard then the Ace of Spades;
- pure U-Blood Summoning Child who first came to the Outer Earth in 1938, with twin sister Melina serving under the clone Golgotha Nauroz as a bodyguard for eventual wife Morgianna;
- there, during its Suprawar (or Wars) in the Thirties, Forties and Fifties, codenamed Blackguard then the Ace of Spades;
- exiled, along with wife Morgianna, from the Weirdom of Cabalarkon once Saladin (born Nauroz but called Devason) won the Challenge of Weir in 5950 and became its Master;
- considered Saladin Devason's chief rival for what passes as Cabalarkon's throne and the Weirdom's Mastery;
- reputedly possesses the oldest eye-stave in the world (Morgan Abyss, the Death's Head Hellion, had it in HELLION);
- directly descended from the Sarpedon underclass who, as revealed in HELLION, are inclined to worship Thrygragos Lazareme since they see him as the Male Entity;

» **Capputis**, teenage, apparent clone with an overlarge head (hydrocephalic), scaly skin and gills behind his ears
- claims to have been bred amphibious deliberately so as to become Weir's ambassador to the Hidden Headworld's mostly Akadan-based, undersea realms, who tend to be anti-Godbadian;

========

## 6. Norman & Norma Notables

- **Inner Earthlings**

» **Alpha Centauri**, called the Fatman for reasons immediately apparent to anyone who sees him;
- founder, in 5945, and to-this-day head of Centauri Enterprises, the de facto corporate government of supposedly democratic Godbad;
- CE, as it's often called, is why the subcontinent and territories neighbouring it in Goatwood, the Gulf of Aka and Sedon's Underlip, as well as Krachla, at the tip of the Penile Peninsula, and on the coast of the Inner Ocean of Akadan of the near-western Cattail Peninsula, is best known as the Corporate State of Greater Godbad;
- an obese Outer Earthling born **Alfredo Sentalli,** he's so grotesquely fat he's confined to an automated wheelchair for most of his waking hours;
- reputedly the only way he survived being so massively overweight for so long is because he was often the very willing shell of none other than Thrygragos Byron himself— proof, as he, despite his Roman Catholic background and persistent faith, very much begrudgingly acknowledges, that devic possession can be beneficial;

- since Bodiless Byron is now a (very bright) star in the night's sky above the Hidden Headworld this is no longer possible;

» **Janna St Peche-Montressor**, wife of Yataghan raised Montressor, daughter-in-law of Alpha Centauri, evidently the most common host of APM All-Eyes in 5980 YD;

- a Lovely Lady Afrite as well as an Athenan War Witch;
- effectively the Fatman's nursemaid as well as his chief bodyguard in Aka Godbad City, where – until All of Incain destroyed his living quarters – he lived in the same Outer-Earth-modern building that houses the ancillary headquarters of Centauri Enterprises.

» **Achigan Auranja**, hereditary head of the Royal (Bandradin) House of the Crimson Orange;

- former King of Greater Godbad; deposed during the Godbadian Civil War of the Fifties by (at first) anti-devil, Republican forces supplied with Utopian weaponry by a then-nascent Centauri Enterprises;
- an orange-skinned, orange-textured Bandradin, Fisherwoman's estranged husband;
- in 5980, lives in exile on Godbad's far, north-westernmost shore: namely, the lip-tip-principality of Achigon (with an 'o', not an 'a', though probably named after a member of his royal family);
- Byronics invited his royal forbearers to Godbad proper, from their ancestral homeland in the Cattail highlands, at an unspecified time in the past (probably some time in the previous century);
- apparently has had considerable dealings with faerie tricksters from Twilight (Sedon's Outer Nose on a map of the Hidden Headworld);

» **Gomez Niarchos**, Godbad's dead, but Sangazur-animated ambassador to the Bloodlands (New, Valhalla, Sedon's Inner Nose);

- a friend of the Legendarian, albeit from earlier incarnations, Gomez is charged with negotiating the neutrality of Bloodlanders (Valhallans, the Glorious Dead of FEEL THEO), all of whom are dead and, after the elimination of both Guardian Angel Tyrtod and an imbecilic Apocalyptic of War, leaderless;

» Among the Hidden Headworld's other notable, presumed mortals mentioned in the mini-novel include **Holgat Sraddha Anvilson** and **Barsine born Mandam Holgat-wife** (both of whom were Summoning Children) as well as their son, **Thartarre Sraddha Holgatson**, the current High Priest of the Brown-Robed Sraddhites, Godbadian General **Quentin Anvil**, Senator **Sophiscient Akbarson**, **Telepassa of Godbad** & her four daughters (**Ino**, **Agave** + **Autonoe**, who are triplets, and the youngest **Semele**);

» Among generally non-Head, presumed mortals mentioned in the mini-novel include **Angelo** & **Aristotle 'Harry' Zeross** (father and son Ringleaders), Harry's mother **Megaera** (Hellion Grudge, the second Olympian), Harry's brother **Demonites** (the third Olympian) and sister **Oriani** become Ryne, Alpha Centauri's son **Yataghan** (Sentalli) Montressor, Eden become Ryne's daughter **Aranyani Nightingale** and Wilderwitch' daughter **Fey Woman.**

********

www.ingramcontent.com/pod-product-compliance
Ingram Content Group UK Ltd.
Pitfield, Milton Keynes, MK11 3LW, UK
UKHW041829200726
13854UKWH00002BA/907